GOTHIC HEROINES ON SCREEN

Gothic Heroines on Screen explores the translation of the literary Gothic heroine on screen, the potential consequences of these adaptations, and contemporary interpretations of the form.

Each chapter illuminates the significance of this moving image mediation, relating its screen topics to their various historical, social, and geographical moments of production, while maintaining a focus on the key figure of the investigating woman. Many chapters – perhaps inescapably – delve into the point of adaptation: the Bluebeard story and du Maurier's *Rebecca* as two key examples. Moving beyond the Old Dark House that frequently forms both the Gothic heroine's backdrop and her area of investigation, some chapters examine alternative locations and their impact on the Gothic heroine, some leave behind the marital thriller to explore what happens when the Gothic meets other genres, such as comedy, while others travel away from the usual Anglo-American contexts to European ones.

Throughout the collection, the Gothic heroine's representation is explored within the medium, which brings together image, movement, and sound, and this technological fact takes on varied significance. What does remain constant, however, is the emphasis on the longevity, significance, and distinctiveness of the Gothic heroine in screen culture.

Tamar Jeffers McDonald is Reader in Film at the University of Kent and co-organiser of the Gothic Feminism research group. She has published on issues of film genre, film costume, stardom, performance, and movie magazines.

Frances A. Kamm is an early career researcher and Associate Lecturer at the University of Kent, and co-organiser of the Gothic Feminism research project. She was awarded her PhD in Film Studies with the thesis entitled 'The Technological Uncanny and the Representation of the Body in Early and Digital Cinema'.

GOTHIC HEROINES ON SCREEN

Representation, Interpretation, and Feminist Enquiry

*Edited by Tamar Jeffers McDonald
and Frances A. Kamm*

Routledge
Taylor & Francis Group

LONDON AND NEW YORK

First published 2019
by Routledge
2 Park Square, Milton Park, Abingdon, Oxon OX14 4RN

and by Routledge
52 Vanderbilt Avenue, New York, NY 10017

Routledge is an imprint of the Taylor & Francis Group, an informa business

British Library Cataloguing-in-Publication Data
A catalogue record for this book is available from the British Library

Library of Congress Cataloging-in-Publication Data
A catalog record has been requested for this book

ISBN: 978-1-138-71099-3 (hbk)
ISBN: 978-1-138-71100-6 (pbk)
ISBN: 978-1-315-20054-5 (ebk)

Typeset in Bembo
by Swales & Willis Ltd, Exeter, Devon, UK

CONTENTS

CONTRIBUTORS

Guy Barefoot is Associate Professor of Film Studies and member of the Centre for American Studies at the University of Leicester. His publications include *Hollywood's Gaslight Melodramas: From Victorian London to 1940s Hollywood* (Continuum, 2001, reissued Bloomsbury, 2016), *The Lost Jungle: Cliffhanger Action and Hollywood Serials of the 1930s and 1940s* (University of Exeter Press, 2017), and *Trash Cinema* (Columbia University Press, 2017).

Gisèle M. Baxter is a sessional lecturer in the Department of English Language and Literatures at the University of British Columbia. Gisèle's teaching and research interests include 19th- to 21st-century literary and cultural studies, Gothic studies (especially Victorian monstrosities and the supernatural, and representations of gender in Gothic film), dystopian and post-apocalyptic narratives, children's literature and the contemporary *Bildungsroman*, and British and Irish Modernism. She is co-editor, with Brett Grubisic and Tara Lee, of *Blast, Corrupt, Dismantle, Erase: Contemporary North American Dystopian Literature* (Wilfrid Laurier University Press, 2014).

Lee Broughton is a freelance writer, critic, film programmer, and lecturer in Film and Cultural Studies. He is the author of *The Euro-Western: Reframing Gender, Race and the 'Other' in Film* (I.B. Tauris, 2016), a monograph in which he employs the Gothic as an optic that provides new and culturally specific readings of a cycle of idiosyncratic and generically unstable British westerns. He is also the editor of *Critical Perspectives on the Western: From* A Fistful of Dollars *to* Django Unchained (Rowman & Littlefield, 2016) and *Reframing Cult Westerns: From* The Magnificent Seven *to* The Hateful Eight (Bloomsbury Academic, forthcoming).

Katerina Flint-Nicol is an assistant lecturer and early career researcher at the University of Kent. She has recently been awarded her PhD in Film Studies with the thesis entitled 'Men, Manors, Monsters: The Hoodie Horror and the Cinema of Alterity' (2018). She has previously published on the Gothic world of the singer PJ Harvey, and is currently working on publications on the relationship between horror and realism in contemporary British cinema.

Lawrence Jackson is a Senior Lecturer at the University of Kent, where he is studying part-time for his PhD in Film Studies on landscape in contemporary British cinema, provisionally titled 'The Pestilence in the Ditch: Eerie, Pastoral, Heritage and Epic Landscapes in Contemporary British Cinema'. His research interests include genre storytelling, landscape, British cinema, and hauntology.

Tamar Jeffers McDonald is Reader in Film at the University of Kent. She read English at Somerville College, Oxford, before studying for her PhD in Film at the University of Warwick. The author of several books on film genres, costume, performance, and stardom, she returns to the study of movie magazines, begun for her 2013 publication *Doris Day Confidential: Hollywood, Sex and Stardom* (I.B. Tauris), for her current monograph *Stars and Hypes: Hollywood Movie Magazines and the Rise of Celebrity Culture* (Routledge, forthcoming). The co-organiser of the Gothic Feminism research group, she is currently also working on a project about portraits in the Gothic.

Frances A. Kamm is an early career researcher and associate lecturer at the University of Kent, and co-organiser of the Gothic Feminism research project. She was awarded her PhD in Film Studies with the thesis entitled 'The Technological Uncanny and the Representation of the Body in Early and Digital Cinema'. She is working on several publications on technology, the Gothic, and visual effects, and is the book reviews editor for *Film Studies* (Manchester University Press).

Lies Lanckman recently finished a PhD in Film Studies at the University of Kent, where she currently works as an associate lecturer. She is the co-founder of NoRMMA, the Network of Research: Movies, Magazines, Audiences, and is currently co-editing an edited collection on methodologies for the study of movie magazines. Though she primarily researches Hollywood history of the 1920s to 1940s, her focus on the gendered aspects of film history has fostered an enduring interest in Gothic cinema and the roles of women therein.

Sarah McClellan gained a PhD in English Literature from the University of Glasgow, where she taught as an associate lecturer. Her research interests concern women and comedy, especially feminist exploration of the abject and parody as forms of subversion in television comedy. She has also published on identity, mythology, and the supernatural in black British women's writing. Her thesis explored how postcolonial writing utilises the Gothic as a way of understanding otherness.

Christina G. Petersen serves as Christian Nielsen Associate Professor of Film Studies at Eckerd College. She has published on serial star Pearl White and avant-garde film, the African-American race film industry, the history of the youth film as a modernist genre, and the phenomenon of youth spectatorship in the United States. She recently completed a monograph, *The Freshman: Comedy and Masculinity in 1920s Film and Youth Culture* (Routledge, 2019).

Paula Quigley is Assistant Professor of Film Studies at the School of Creative Arts, Trinity College Dublin. She has published on a range of topics in film studies, including the work of Sergei Eisenstein and André Bazin, the impact of psychoanalysis on film theory, and studies of the short film. In addition, she has published on issues of genre and gender, with a focus on iterations of the 'woman's film' in diverse cinematic and cultural contexts.

Johanna M. Wagner is an associate professor of English at Østfold University College in Norway. Specific areas of research are the representation of women in film and literature, the Gothic, gender and queer theories, theories of mimesis, affect, and narrative, and American and British literature. Dr Wagner is currently working on a book manuscript focusing on women protagonists in modernist film and literature.

A. Dana Weber is an assistant professor of German in the Department of Modern Languages and Linguistics at Florida State University. Her monograph *Blood Brothers and Peace Pipes: Performing the Wild West in German Festivals* is forthcoming at the University of Wisconsin Press. Dana is also the editor of *Performativity – Life, Stage Screen. Reflections on a Transdisciplinary Concept* (LIT Verlag, 2018). Dana's interdisciplinary research is informed by culture, folklore, performance, literature, and film studies.

ACKNOWLEDGEMENTS

The editors and Lee Broughton would like to thank I.B. Tauris and note that parts of Chapter 9 have previously appeared in Lee Broughton, *The Euro-Western: Reframing Gender, Race and the 'Other' in Film* (I.B. Tauris, 2016). Similarly, an earlier version of Paula Quigley's work in Chapter 14 appeared as 'When Good Mothers Go Bad: Genre and Gender in *The Babadook*' in the *Irish Journal of Gothic and Horror Studies* 15, 2016.

INTRODUCTION

Frances A. Kamm and Tamar Jeffers McDonald

Since its literary beginnings, the Gothic has featured distinctive female characters who engage with, and are often central to, the uncanny narratives characteristic of the genre. The eponymous 'Gothic heroine' conjures up images of the imperilled young and inexperienced woman, cautiously exploring the old dark house where she is physically confined by force – imprisoned by the tale's tyrant – or metaphorically trapped by societal expectations of marriage and domesticity. The Gothic heroine is habitually motivated by an investigative spirit and usually explores her surroundings in a quest to uncover a sinister secret that will, for example, reveal her love interest's past or provide explanation for her supposedly supernatural encounters.

This heroine is no stranger to those of us who have long enjoyed joining her on the mystery quest within the 18th-century works by Ann Radcliffe, or in the navigation of her strained marriage – along with a domineering maid, and an overbearing, deceased wife – in Daphne du Maurier's *Rebecca* (1938). We saw the Gothic's female protagonist pick up her candelabra again in a series of books released by Ace Books during the 1960s and 1970s, the covers of which showcased the genre's iconic tropes: the heroine, wearing a flowing nightgown, flees the domestic space – sometimes a mansion, often a castle, and always at night.

The literary Gothic heroine is thus well established, known, and loved, but what of her translation onto the screen? How and when has the Gothic heroine been depicted by the filmic medium, and what are the consequences of such an adaptation? These questions formed the basis for a conference hosted in May 2016 at the University of Kent entitled 'Gothic Feminism: The Representation of the Gothic Heroine in Cinema'. The conference brought together researchers from several countries, working within diverse disciplines and from a variety of theoretical approaches, but the modest event illuminated an element that is the central focus of this book: the longevity, significance, and distinctiveness of the Gothic heroine in screen culture.

The timing of the conference proved serendipitous: only a few months prior had come the release of Guillermo del Toro's *Crimson Peak* (2015), a film that self-consciously evoked the imagery of, and overtly contextualised itself within, the traditions of the Gothic and the Gothic heroine noted above. The film, as Tamar Jeffers McDonald notes, recycles 'as many of the traditional elements of the Gothic as it can':[1] the heroine, the house, and the husband are all present in a film that emphasises the mystery, terror, and suspicion that emerge when these three key ingredients interact within the world of the Gothic. Indeed, the distinctly *Gothic* nature of this story is stressed by del Toro himself, as he describes his film as a 'modern Gothic romance', an assertion he repeated several times during the film's promotional period where, in particular, the director was keen to correct critics and confirm *Crimson Peak* is not a horror film.[2]

Crimson Peak pays tribute to the Gothic heroine's literary beginnings: beyond its adherence to the genre's conventions, the film is most explicit in this reverence by characterising Edith as a writer cut from the same cloth as Radcliffe, Austen, and Shelley, the latter two of whom are mentioned in dialogue during an early sequence that depicts Edith's struggles with the prejudices held against female authors. The link between the Gothic and literature is solidified in the transition the film makes from the scene depicting Edith's traumatic encounter with her dead mother as a child and adult Edith navigating her way – literally and figuratively – within New York society some 14 years later. As the film uses an iris fade to black on child Edith's gaslight lamp, the image fades back in on a close-up shot of a cloth-bound book bearing the name 'Crimson Peak'. The camera moves in closer to these words, before the book opens and lands on a page featuring a drawing of the crowded city of Buffalo. The line drawing dissolves and becomes a graphic match for the establishing shot for the above scene, which introduces adult Edith. And – should the connection between the film's events and Edith's writer ambitions not make this frame narrative overt enough – during the film's end credits, this same book now closes and beneath the title on its cover are the words 'Edith M. Cushing'.

The whole film thus becomes an act of book-to-screen adaptation, with the former's presence within these key moments reframing the narrative's events as an act of translation, rather than an original creation or conceit. Given the Gothic's literary roots, this is a particularly appropriate approach, and the Gothic on screen, more generally, can be historicised by tracing the link between literature and film adaptation: indeed, the film widely considered to have started the cycle of Hollywood Gothic films made in the 1940s was Alfred Hitchcock's *Rebecca* (1940), a relatively faithful adaptation of the du Maurier text.

Yet there is something specifically *filmic* about *Crimson Peak*'s telling of its story and the representation of Edith as its Gothic heroine. Tellingly, del Toro situates *Crimson Peak* within a history and context that is also specifically cinematic: he talks about the production design in films such as *Rebecca*, *Jane Eyre* (1944) and *Great Expectations* (1946), and the influence of his other Gothic-looking films *The Devil's Backbone* (2001) and *Pan's Labyrinth* (2006). His Gothic ambitions are inextricably linked to the specificity of the filmic medium: 'I wanted to make this opulent sort of operatic movie because gothic romance is about excess, albeit a very controlled sense of excess – in the acting, in the *mise en scène*' (quoted in Diesto-Dópido, 2015: 25).

Even *Crimson Peak*'s overt evocative of the theme of literary adaptation functions to emphasise the importance of the fact that this story is told as a film. It is significant, for example, that the introduction to the book occurs after the film's opening shot of a bloodied and tearful Edith – in a scene that, chronologically speaking, takes place near the end – and after child Edith's ghostly encounter, described above, which would have happened before. Once the book is shown, the film then shifts to 'present-day' Edith, but, of course, the revelation of the author's name on the cover at the end of the film alerts us to the fact that the book would have been created after all of the events it is framed within during its first on-screen depiction: indeed, the book's final close-up reveals its cover to be slightly worn and stained. It has seen the passage of time.

The theme of literary adaptation thus becomes complexly mapped onto the film's plot trajectory and its visual presentation of events. Knowledge of the book's existence within the diegesis raises the question of not *who* is narrating the story – Edith's authorship over the text is confirmed by the end – but from *when*. One could argue that this enigma is resolved by the revelation of Edith's name on the cover, although this fact is only disclosed after the film's conclusion and within the film's end credits, in a space that exists outside of the main diegesis of the narrative. Rather, the first appearance of the book appears as something of an anomaly, albeit a functional one. On the one hand, the book serves as a temporal ellipsis, segueing from child Edith to adult Edith, but, on the other, its existence raises more questions than it answers: the book helps to convey narrative exposition economically – in fact, its presence implies responsibility for the images portrayed – while paradoxically breaking this very cohesion of the story world by also evidently being spatially and temporally disruptive.

The book reinforces similar questions that are present in Edith's voice-over. Edith's authorship is reinforced by a unification of her image and voice in the film's opening shot, although when her voice-over returns at the film's conclusion, the relationship between picture and sound has now shifted: as Edith concludes her musing about the existence of ghosts, the camera tracks back towards Allerdale Hall, exploring the now abandoned space before finding Lucille's spectre. The images are both motivated by Edith's words – of what keeps the dead in a place – and seemingly independent, depicting the supernatural aftermath of Lucille's demise in a manner Edith could not have *personally* witnessed. The tension in this hierarchy of knowledge between Edith and the film's presentation of events is an ongoing negotiation, most overtly raised by the portrayal of scenes (such as her father's murder) without Edith's physical presence.

These inconsistencies raise concepts not unique to cinema. Complex chronologies, the ellipsis of time, and the questionable reliability of a narrator are familiar storytelling conventions, but it is significant that *Crimson Peak* raises such issues in a manner that is inextricably linked to the film medium's mediation of the narrative. Image, sound, and plot development are brought into constant tension within individual scenes and across the whole film, oscillating from coherence to contradiction. The effect is appropriately Gothic: this presentation of the plot evokes an unsettling and eerie mood, which in turn reinforces the significance of Edith, the Gothic heroine at the centre of this story. *Crimson Peak*'s Gothic tone is thus created by the language of the moving image.

This filmic depiction of Gothic stories is at the heart of this collection. Each chapter, in its own way, illuminates the significance of this moving image mediation. Sometimes such an exploration starts – perhaps inevitably – from the point of adaptation: the Bluebeard story is a major influence in many of the films explored, some of which are based upon other literary works. However, the Gothic heroine's representation is explored within a medium that brings together image, movement, and sound, and this technological fact takes on varied significance within the following pages. It could be that the history of film genre becomes the backdrop through which the conventions of the Gothic are both informed and shaped, as in Lee Broughton's chapter, or, as in A. Dana Weber's chapter, film as an industry and cultural product illuminates the Gothic elements within individual texts. Alternatively, the movement of the Gothic from page to screen becomes filmic on more than one level: in an example from Tamar Jeffers McDonald's chapter, *Before I Go to Sleep* (2014) is the adaptation of a novel, but this translation to a film is explicitly emphasised within the diegesis: Christine's journal-keeping in the original book becomes, in the film, the heroine's video diary made using a digital camera.

However, linking the following chapters through their emphasis on the Gothic in film or screen culture is not to suggest that this collection is reliant upon a single, theoretical basis, including that concerning the conceptualisation of film and its ontology. The focus upon the heroine on screen as a facet of film history deserving of scholarly research does not imply a teleological argument concerning the Gothic's movement from literature to screen in the examples explored, nor does there exist a value judgement in observing the differences between these media. Indeed, the reader will quickly infer how the authors of this collection are both researchers and personal fans of the Gothic in all its forms.

Several of the chapters share critical approaches to the Gothic heroine or are informed by similar research on the Gothic and on film. The literary tradition of the Female Gothic, perhaps unavoidably, features predominantly. The influence of Ellen Moers' work is both implicitly and directly addressed within the collection, thereby contributing to the continuous re-evaluation of her work in appraising the relationship between the Gothic and women.[3] In addition to scholarship focusing on the literary tradition of the Gothic, the work of Mary Ann Doane, Maria Tatar, Diane Waldman, and Helen Hanson on Gothic film also appear frequently. Despite these similarities, however, there is no single dominant theoretical discourse between the chapters: where one emphasises the Freudian implications of a film, as Lawrence Jackson's chapter does, another will adopt a historical and production-oriented approach, as with Guy Barefoot's work.

The theoretical diversity of the chapters helps to emphasise how, even in a collection that brings a different and new emphasis in its study of the Gothic heroine, the Gothic genre itself refuses to be contained within a single approach or encapsulated by a definitive definition. As Paula Quigley aptly notes in her chapter within this book, the 'Gothic is best understood as an extensive category that traverses temporal and geographical conditions; its elasticity offers opportunities for reflecting and/or resisting "women's lot" across a diverse range of media and sociocultural contexts'. This 'elasticity' of approaches, topics, and discourses within the collection means that the book's application itself offers a myriad of opportunities: the Gothic student may find herself drawn to the familiar genre conventions discussed within, while the film researcher and cultural historian will be attracted to the chapters' emphasis on specific case studies. All other fans of the Gothic heroine and exploring scary houses at night are strongly welcomed.

Other unifying aspects that link the chapters in this collection, apart from the central premise of the Gothic heroine on screen, include the emphasis on close textual analysis and feminism. The first illuminates again the interest shared by all the authors in considering how the moving image and sound of the screen intersect with the depiction of Gothic's female protagonist. In doing so, the latter element of feminism and the question of representation is explicitly evoked. All the films selected for study in this collection are the result of interdisciplinary research that leads back to the question of female representation and gender discourses, topics that are intimately linked to the development of the Gothic as a genre, and its portrayal of women.

Many of the works featured in this book are international co-productions, although the majority concentrate on the Anglo-American sphere, with cisgendered female protagonists existing within stories focusing on heteronormative relationships. This trend echoes the Gothic's continued preoccupation with conservative notions of womanhood and marriage, as featured in the Radcliffean model and reinforced within 1940s Hollywood. Queer readings of these texts are certainly possible, as is evidence of the Gothic influence in films that fall outside of essentialist gender definitions or the white 'norm': *Beloved* (1998), *Gothika* (2003), and *The Duke of Burgundy* (2014) are examples of texts that take the Gothic armature, *mise en scène*, or tropes in order to redeploy them in different contexts. However, a reinforcement of heteronormativity continues to plague the Gothic films within this collection, and this has two major significances for the volume. First, the Gothic's equation of marriage with patriarchy forms a key theme throughout the film examples explored, despite their diversity. In fact, even when marriage or the relationship between a woman and a man is absent (as in Frances A. Kamm and Lies Lanckman's chapters), the heroines can still be seen to be subject to specifically male power and control. Second, the gendered norms presented in these films say much about the male and white privilege that continues to dominate the film industry, an obscene fact that has received much (overdue) attention recently. Hollywood promises to change, and the Gothic would provide an appropriate forum through which to observe such increased diversity: indeed, just as Ellen

Moers observed the attraction of the Gothic form to women writers, the genre has perhaps already proved similarly fascinating to female film-makers – approximately one-third of the films or television shows discussed in this collection were directed by women, which, considering the above context, is a fact of no small significance.

As with the scheduling of the conference that inspired this collection, the timing of this book also proves poignant. On a personal level, we, the editors, have seen the popularity of the topic of the Gothic heroine on screen increase within our teaching: the module 'The Gothic in Film', taught at the University of Kent, looks specifically at the historical lineage of the Gothic heroine beginning in 1940s Hollywood up to the present day. In our experience, the students enjoy exploring a topic that, at first, appeals for its historical resonance but then quickly becomes relevant in the contemporary world: topics such as feminism, violence against women, and sociopolitical inequalities are themes that are inextricably linked to the exploration and interpretation of the films screened. The growing popularity of the topic within our student community contributed to the decision to form the Gothic Feminism research group, which hosted the conference mentioned above.[4] This book is both a culmination of the research we have personally conducted, disseminated, and taught, and an engagement between a wider group of scholars who are making important, original, and urgent contributions in their own research on the Gothic heroine. It is especially significant that this theme has provided a platform for women scholars, and we are very proud that the majority of the chapters within this book are written by female researchers.

In light of the continued inequalities experienced by women all over the world, it is perhaps unsurprising that the relevance of the Gothic has not diminished, and in fact maintains a contemporary significance in the way artists remain evidently drawn to the genre. *Crimson Peak* is an example of this; you will find many more examples – from the past and present – within these pages. How one interprets the heroine in these films remains an urgent process in all of the case studies presented: Does this imperilled woman overcome terror and oppression of the plot by, for example, maintaining narrative agency and an overwhelming visual power? Or is the on-screen heroine ultimately trapped within the *mise en scène* and the conservative conclusion of the story? A. Dana Weber writes in her chapter that the Gothic derived from the Bluebeard tale is 'a meditation about oppression and tyranny, and the risks of confronting them with curiosity and courage'. These notions of 'tyranny' and 'courage' have additional resonance for the Hollywood film industry at the moment, with female (and male) artists exposing contemporary and historic abuses of power against women, as encapsulated by the Time's Up and #MeToo campaigns. It is against this backdrop of debates around gender inequalities, feminism, and political conservatism that the Gothic continually reinvigorates its cultural currency. This book hopes to capture an essence of such a context within screen culture.

The book is divided into four parts. The first, 'Bluebeard's ghost', concentrates on examples that are overtly influenced by this infamous fairy tale. Gisèle M. Baxter traces the significance of the story through several filmic examples before focusing on the short film *Little Lamb* (2014). Baxter notes how the dynamics of the tale – of which Perrault's version remains the most well known – is fundamentally altered in these films, particularly in respect to the Gothic heroine. Lawrence Jackson's chapter also focuses on the change motivated by adaptation, as he focuses on films that relocate the Gothic heroine from the rural into the urban. The setting becomes an integral part of interpretation for the heroines presented in *In the Cut* (2003) and *Red Road* (2006). Tamar Jeffers McDonald concludes this part with a focus on contemporary film, looking at three examples where the Bluebeard story has been reworked through the adoption of the tale's central motifs. This adaptation process points to the continued and contemporaneous currency of the Bluebeard story, as well as challenging the idea that the Female Gothic was isolated and limited to the 1940s Hollywood cycle of films.

The second part, 'Returning to Manderley', pays tribute to the huge influence of the film *Rebecca* in establishing the tradition of the Gothic heroine on screen. Christina Petersen's chapter opens the debate by exploring the technological achievements, in terms of miniatures, painted mattes, and back-projection that went into creating the film's version of the house. Her chapter thus exposes the importance that the purely *filmic* elements of the film had on inaugurating the Gothic, underlining this collection's commitment to exploring the genre via its moving images rather than literary antecedents.

The Gothic is regularly associated with the uncanny, and in the next chapter Guy Barefoot examines a little-known film that can be seen as *Rebecca*'s double even more than most, since it features so many of the same plot and visual elements, centring around the absent presence of a dead woman. *The Second Woman* (1950), however, interestingly gives up the power the Hitchcock film developed around the figure of the deceased 'first woman': unlike *Rebecca, The Second Woman* shows the object of everyone's obsessions alive, in a flashback. With a corporeal form, a physical body, and face to anchor her, Vivian, the later film's version of the Rebecca figure, proves easier to exorcise than Rebecca herself did.

Finally, Johanna M. Wagner explores the alternative fate that befalls the Gothic heroine when, instead of finding she 'either loves or hates the House, usually both' (Russ, 1973: 668), she forms her most important emotional bond with it, rather than its male owner, as is usual in the genre. Showing how Eleanor, the heroine of *The Haunting* (1963), differs from the nameless successor to Rebecca, Wagner details how she finds her rightful place in the ghost-ridden abode, Hill House, a locus that gives her both the sense of belonging and of heightened emotional experience for which she has been yearning. All three chapters thus return to Manderley for the start of their explorations, though they finish them in very different places.

The third part, 'The Gothic and Genre Forms', builds upon previous references to genre and adaptation explored thus far in the book but relocates this discussion within film genre specifically. Here, the Gothic heroine is transferred from her usual settings, and finds herself in the corridors of an Old Dark Spaceship or involved in gunplay in a town in the Old West. Furthermore, her vehicles shift in tone as well as locale and media, so that she ends up in – and complicates – televisual comedy or prestige programming. To begin this section, Frances A. Kamm reads action hero Ellen Ripley in *Aliens* as a Gothic heroine, and argues that it is the film's specific melding of science fiction/action characteristics with the tropes of Gothic that make it such a successful example of the latter genre. Next, Lee Broughton examines another generic hybrid, the Gothic western *A Town Called Bastard* (1971). Broughton shows that despite the stark binary oppositions that could be expected to exist between the western/Gothic – organised around such concepts as male/female, outdoors/indoors, and perhaps American/British – *Bastard* confounds expectations by blending them. That the film he explores is also a *British* western adds to both the confounding and hybridisation.

Merging the Gothic with comedy may seem even more antithetical to the genre and the seriousness of its usual core issues, centring around power, sex, and violence within marriage. Sarah McClellan's chapter, however, illustrates how humour can become another weapon in the arsenal that the Gothic heroine possesses with which to fight patriarchy in general, and overbearing husbands in particular, as she examines the mock-Gothic television series *Hunderby* (2012). Finally, still keeping with television, Katerina Flint-Nicol examines how use of familiar Gothic tropes is intended to lead the viewer astray in the 2015 adaptation of *And Then There Were None*. Its Christmas broadcast date and careful period costumes and setting might suggest that this is heritage TV, prestige programming with no complex agenda. But as Flint-Nicol details, the show exploits these assumptions, just as it does our expectations about the Gothic, where the heroine will work to uncover mysteries but not be the source of them herself. Taken together, these four chapters illustrate how lively and fruitful the Gothic is as a genre, ready to mingle productively with other classifications of films, to create surprising hybrid forms that yet underline the central and habitual topics of these screen texts: men, women, sex, and power.

The final part, 'National Cinema and the Gothic', seeks to expand the discussion of the on-screen Gothic heroine by looking beyond the Anglo-American sphere – an emphasis that inevitably dominates. Here, we have examples that are influenced by the 1940s Hollywood films in particular, but these tropes have been translated within different cultures and histories. A. Dana Weber begins by reading the Gothic into the context of Soviet-controlled East Germany, illuminating the representation of a heroine within a historically specific form of oppression. Lies Lanckman reads the relevance of the Female Gothic within an Austrian setting, and knowledge of this national specificity is both overt and implied within *Goodnight Mommy* (2014). Finally, Paula Quigley considers the Australian film *The Babadook* (2014) as a film that consciously reworks elements from the 'maternal horror film', the maternal melodrama, and the Female Gothic films from Hollywood in the 1940s. The film presents a challenge in appearing culturally and geographically specific (particularly regarding the appearance of the eponymous monster), but its incorporation of the Female Gothic mode on narrative and visual levels renders the film more extensive in theme and address.

Catherine Spooner notes how the 'Gothic has never been solely a literary phenomenon', appearing as a genre, mode of storytelling, or visual address in a wide variety of media outlets, including magic lantern shows, the theatre, comics, video games, and, of course, cinema (Spooner, 2007: 195). This book continues the recognition of this fact by illuminating the importance of the Gothic heroine within screen culture, in the first book-length study on the topic. In this collection, most examples are taken from commercial, feature-length films, but not all: there are also examples of the short film released on the festival circuit, television adaptations, and TV miniseries. In placing an emphasis upon the moving image, this book aims to illuminate the Gothic heroine within this type of media, and particularly emphasise the visual legacy of this archetypal character. Indeed, when Edith wanders around her haunted, bleeding house in *Crimson Peak*, her actions are inspired by her Radcliffean predecessors and yet her appearance is also peculiarly filmic in its referencing: her urgent searching within a threatening *mise en scène* dominated by chiaroscuro lighting and eerie noises on the soundtrack – which further allude to hidden secrets by evoking an off-screen space – are reminiscent of similar events depicted in *The Innocents* (1961). The white nightdress makes the link overt.[5]

In this way, this book pays tribute to the Gothic heroine but also to the pervasiveness of film imagery within popular culture and scholarly discourse alike. In addition to the narrative conventions shaping her characterisation, the Gothic heroine is a visual motif too; an image that, at least to a significant degree, has been shaped and popularised by her ventures on screen. The aesthetic, cultural, and historical importance of this figure is evaluated in this book in much the same way any study of film brings these elements into dialogue, as Richard Dyer notes:

> The aesthetic dimension of a film never exists apart from how it is conceptualised, how it is socially practised, how it is received; it never exists floating free of historical and cultural particularity. Equally, the cultural study of film must always understand that it is studying film, which has its own specificity, its own pleasures, its own way of doing things.
>
> *(Dyer, 1998: 9)*

The Gothic heroine on screen will, in the coming pages, navigate ideas about media, adaptation, representation, and interpretation in a manner reminiscent of how she explores the convoluted geography of the Gothic space. Along the way, we too hope to find many hidden rooms and unravel several secrets.

Notes

1 See Jeffers McDonald's chapter 'Blueprints from Bluebeard: Charting the Gothic in Contemporary Film'. The film is also referenced in Gisèle M. Baxter's chapter, 'Bluebeard's Women Fight Back: The Gothic Heroine in Contemporary Film and Heidi Lee Douglas' *Little Lamb* (2014)'.
2 The relationship between horror and the Gothic – and particularly *Crimson Peak's* relationship to these genres – were discussed at the second Gothic Feminism conference in 2017:

a paper given by Frances A. Kamm entitled 'The Presence of Absence: The Supernatural Gothic of *Crimson Peak*' and another presentation by Matt Denny, 'Don't Call It a Horror Film: The Uses of the Gothic in *Crimson Peak*', discussed this topic at length. Both papers will appear as articles in a forthcoming themed issue of a journal.

3 See Moers (1976), Smith and Wallace (2004), and Horner and Zlosnik (2016).

4 See the *Gothic Feminism* blog: https://gothicfeminism.com/.

5 See Kamm et al. (2016).

References

Diesto-Dópido, Mar (2015) 'Ghost Hunter'. *Sight & Sound*, November, 25(11): 22–26.

Dyer, Richard (1998) 'Introduction to Film Studies'. In John Hill and Pamela Church Gibson (eds), *The Oxford Guide to Film Studies*. Oxford: Oxford University Press, pp. 3–10.

Horner, Avril and Sue Zlosnik (eds) (2016) *Women and the Gothic: An Edinburgh Companion*. Edinburgh: Edinburgh University Press.

Kamm, Frances A. et al. (2016) *Passages of Gothic*. https://vimeo.com/170080190 [Accessed 28 January 2019]

Moers, Ellen (1976) *Literary Women: The Great Writers*. New York: Oxford University Press.

Russ, Joanna (1973) 'Someone's Trying to Kill Me and I Think It's My Husband: The Modern Gothic'. *Journal of Popular Culture*, 6(4): 666–691.

Smith, Andrew and Diane Wallace (eds) (2004) 'The Female Gothic: Then and Now'. Introduction to Special Issue of *Journal of Gothic Studies*, 6(1): 1–7.

Spooner, Catherine (2007) 'Gothic Media'. In Catherine Spooner and Emma McEvoy (eds), *The Routledge Companion to Gothic*. London: Routledge, pp. 195–197.

PART I

Bluebeard's ghost

1

BLUEBEARD'S WOMEN FIGHT BACK

The Gothic heroine in contemporary film and Heidi Lee Douglas' *Little Lamb* (2014)

Gisèle M. Baxter

I have long been fascinated by Bluebeard stories for two reasons: first, the story's variable reputation as a children's tale and its anomalies as a 'fairy tale'; and second, I have noticed an odd trend when teaching Perrault's iconic and literary 'Barbe Bleue', a reaction one could call the 'poor Bluebeard' response. This interpretation invariably includes sentiments such as: 'Poor Bluebeard! He only wanted to be loved! He could not help that he was ugly! His wife was just after his money! If only she'd just done as he asked!' I suspect (echoing Maria Tatar's [2004] reading) that this reaction is evoked by the non-descriptive, two-dimensionality of Perrault's story (a style characteristic of folk fairy tales): the wife is so functional as to be almost a non-entity. She fulfils her purpose, without action or agency, and is not rewarded at the end because she has defeated Bluebeard (her brothers accomplish that), but because of her legal position: she was his wife, and so she inherits all his money, so now she can reward her siblings and enter her second marriage with a dowry (significantly, the tale implies her first was brokered by her mother: marrying Bluebeard was marrying up). However, as described, she is almost devoid of interest except perhaps when she discovers Bluebeard's secret, as here she does acquire a sort of self-awareness: she realises she is in big trouble now. If she is the functional protagonist, the story seems more to be about Bluebeard: the interesting questions attach to him. And sometimes they allow readers to gloss over the gruesome contents of the mystery room and their implications.

This chapter offers a counter to this 'poor Bluebeard' response, and an exploration of the reasoning behind its evocation, by examining examples of the Bluebeard story in contemporary Gothic films that focus on the female protagonist. I will do so by first briefly commenting on the fairy tale's own unusual history and outlining, in particular, the challenges posed by identifying a Bluebeard text. The malleability of the story shall be further extrapolated through reference to a diverse selection of filmic adaptations depicting variations of the tale. Such analysis draws out how, in translating the fairy tale onto the cinema screen, these films shift the emphasis onto the transgressive wife or female protagonist, and in doing so ensure that the significant interpretations made possible by the text are now inextricably linked to her. Such possibilities raise a number of themes, including the relevance of *what* is included in the film's adaptation (for example, who is saved within the story and who performs such a rescue), *how* the story is visually depicted (such as the importance of setting and the camera's gaze), and *why* such aesthetic and narrative choices have been made. The latter is most important: I will argue that these examples lead to a reconsideration of the woman character in relation to Bluebeard and other male figures, ultimately raising the question of feminism. I bring these elements together by using Heidi Lee Douglas' 2014 director's cut of her short horror film *Little Lamb* as a central case study. I argue that, much like the other contemporary cinematic examples cited, this film's status as feminist depends a great deal on who is looking at what; in the way the characters' stories – and the events framing the portrayal of Bluebeard's 'wife', in particular – are visually framed and performed.

'Bluebeard' enjoyed a fairly long if problematic stretch as a children's story. The story presented the notion that a good scare can be pleasurable, although Perrault's version – perhaps the most well-known telling of the story – provided droll and somewhat ironic morals at the end of his tale. Perrault's Bluebeard was aimed at an audience of (primarily) marriageable young women at the French court in the late 17th century. By the 19th century, the fairy tale's legacy had solidified its appeal to adult and juvenile audiences, as the wife-murdering protagonist appeared a favourite topic for illustrators and popular drama as well as featuring in the children's anthology (Tatar, 2004: 11–15, 28–48; Zipes, 2006: 167–173).[1] The currency of Bluebeard as a children's tale often retold for adults is evidenced by its numerous adaptations and reincarnations within diverse media texts, although the shape of these re-presentations can differ. Not all stories of serial killers are Bluebeard stories. *Psycho* (1960) is not one, even though it is in a way about a series of young women failing a test they are unaware of. Nor are all locked-room mystery stories: *The Picture of Dorian Gray* (1890) is also not a Bluebeardian tale, though film versions play with Bluebeard tropes. *Jane Eyre* (1847) is closer in the way that it evokes the fairy tale's motifs. Arguably, the necessary components of 'true' Bluebeard stories are entrapment (with an unsettling, even uncanny aspect attached to the ensnarer), prohibition, a mystery that must be unlocked, and grave peril for the person who attempts to do so.[2] Use of the colour blue is actually optional.

Echoes of and motifs from 'Bluebeard' run throughout Jane Campion's 1993 film *The Piano*, but there is a pivotal scene where the story is performed as a combination of live action and shadow play by adult members of the community at a school pageant in mid-19th-century New Zealand.[3] The children who performed earlier are in the audience, shivering with excited terror beside their parents, and the sudden conclusion of the play, when the Maori in the audience invade the stage, opens up important questions about culture and storytelling, as well as engagement and detachment. An 1866 photograph by John Coates

Browne ('A Children's Play: Bluebeard's Wives') stages a scene from a children's play based on the Bluebeard story, and *The Piano*'s visualisation echoes this strongly, especially in the young wife's costume and the positioning of the dead wives seemingly suspended by their hair. However, *The Piano* engages as well with the Bluebeard story's much more significant legacy: as an adult story whose horror depends on secrets.

Little Lamb, despite its depiction of a master/servant relationship instead of a marriage, fits into a discussion about such adaptations, and more specifically as an example of modern films that revise the Bluebeard story in a broadly Victorian context, using the tropes of Gothic horror and/or Gothic romance. Both *The Piano* and Guillermo del Toro's *Crimson Peak* (2015) are also narratives where the prison-house of marriage and the cultural assumptions about women as the property of fathers then husbands allow for analyses of agency and restriction, as well as desire and sometimes transgressive sexualities. Indeed, Heidi Lee Douglas' use of archetype and history, with an awareness of real-life contemporary anecdotes (Douglas, 2015), echoes a point Tatar makes about the significance of the Bluebeard school play episode in *The Piano* and its effect on its audiences in terms of disruption in cinematic revision (while also raising the coloniser perspective in Tasmanian Gothic film noted by Jeni Thornley, whose work I will turn to later):

> The Bluebeard folktale, as enacted in the shadow pantomime, is so palpably real to the Maori tribesmen who witness it that they storm the stage to disrupt the performance, bent on rescuing the hapless wife from an ax-wielding tyrant. At first blush, this episode seems designed to highlight the naiveté of the natives, revealing that they are unable to distinguish representation from reality. Yet it also serves as an interesting parallel to the way in which Campion herself disrupts the folkloric tradition of Bluebeard narratives through her cinematic intervention. And as subsequent events make clear, the play staged in the film foreshadows in a strangely literal sense the violence that follows in the wake of its performance. It can be seen as the original of the counterfeit version played out in reality by Stewart, and it thereby carries an authenticity that makes it a natural target of disruption by the natives.
>
> *(Tatar, 2004: 124)*

However, this disruption can be complicated in such adult adaptations or appropriations of the tale. Consider the developed setting of *The Piano* or the potentially metafictional neo-Victorianism of *Crimson Peak*. Such films say much about how we reconstruct Victorian (and still construct) representations of gender, sexuality, class, and culture, but also about the enduring influence of popular romantic tropes in the insistence on a 'humanising' male figure who (even though he might not save the day) is there at the end to support the heroine. Both *The Piano* and *Crimson Peak* more or less uphold this tendency (even though arguably *The Piano*'s Ada chooses Baines as her 'savior', he seems to need Stewart's permission to take up this role). Len Wiseman's *Underworld* (2003) is a comparable Gothic film in this respect, albeit in a modern setting. Perhaps not strictly a Bluebeard story (even if its heroine does open doors forbidden to her), the film grants its protagonist Selene considerable agency, even to disrupting the structure of her vampire community and destroying her mentor, while her lover Michael plays the 'damsel in distress' role.[4]

Crimson Peak did not advertise itself as such, but it is a Bluebeard story (even to the colour blue unsettlingly echoed in the dark teal blue attire of the Sharpe siblings at home, which echoes the walls of Allerdale Hall's main rooms). However, in keeping with the above trend of contemporary cinematic adaptations offering reconfigurations of the original story's gender dynamics, *Crimson Peak* has Lucille as the principal Bluebeard figure: because Thomas redeems himself (and never seems nearly mysterious or ambiguous enough at any point), he and Alan McMichael function as the brothers who at least enable Edith's rescue, even if she is the one who dispatches Lucille at the end. It is tempting to view Edith as a New Woman riposte to the functional wife figure in Perrault's tale, with her apparently modern attitudes and practices: she learns to type to disguise her 'feminine' handwriting; she shuns the predatory marriage-market attitude and social world of Alan's sister; she is broad-minded about both technology and the supernatural; and in virtually all romantic scenes with Thomas, she takes the lead, and when they do have sex she is on top. Ironically, when Edith notices a volume of Arthur Conan Doyle in Alan's office, she asks if Alan fancies himself a detective, although, of course, it turns out both pursue detective type work; Edith's investigative instincts help her to discover the key, which she takes without any warning or prohibition, even after Lucille has told her she does not need her own copy of the house keys. Indeed, costume designer Kate Hawley refers to the embroidered gold dress Edith wears in some key scenes of exploration at the Hall as her 'Nancy Drew dress' (Hawley, 2016).

Yet if the ghosts are real, as Edith claims, and not just practical metaphors for the past, it becomes debatable to what extent Edith solves mysteries for herself, or the information is revealed because these spectres (sometimes literally) point her in the right direction. By the time Alan arrives with Mr Holly's documentary evidence, the pieces of the puzzle are pretty much in place. It is also possible that Lucille *allows* Edith to find the key to Enola's trunk, not least because the more Edith knows, the stronger the case Lucille can make to Thomas that the current Hall's mistress must go the way of his previous wives (indeed, this provides a more practical motive than ego – as in Perrault's tale – for keeping mementos of the crimes). Still, at the end, Edith is remarkably proactive: she has the ability to run and fight with anemia from poisoning and a broken ankle, in a sheer nightgown, in a blizzard; she impulsively repurposes household items, such as her pen, a kitchen knife, and a shovel, as deadly weapons; and she promises the wounded Alan (the men seem much less able to withstand injury in this last showdown than the women) that she will get help and return for him. Nevertheless, Alan is there for her, just as now-ghostly Thomas is there for her too, as if to lessen the risk of her becoming what she fights, or at least to make sure that Lucille is really dead and doomed to ghostly isolation.

This saving of the heroine from what she might become is more explicitly Michael's function in *Underworld*. Selene does emerge as the heroine: she rejects the role of consort and ultimately of 'daughter', humiliating the ambitious traitor, then destroying the deceptive father figure who executed his blood daughter. While Michael is consistently the 'damsel in distress' figure, midway through and at the end he 'humanises' Selene, takes the thorn from her paw, and enables her to admit to vulnerability in her residual grief over the long-ago loss of her family. In its contrasting approach to triumphant action heroines, Alex Garland's *Ex Machina* (2015) is much more obviously a Bluebeard story, while also strongly echoing the original-series *Star Trek* episode 'Requiem for Methusaleh' (1969). Reclusive tech genius Nathan's mystery closet is filled with the rejected prototypes of Ava, but Ava becomes the Bluebeard figure herself, a point reinforced by the song played over the end credits: post-punk women-led band Savages' 'Husbands'.[5] The choice suggests that if there is no proactive lover (nerdy Caleb does not measure up; at least *Underworld*'s Michael, thanks to Selene, can become a vampire/werewolf hybrid) to redeem or 'humanise' the female figure escaping her confines, this is what she will become.[6]

Ava and Selene are sexualised similarly: sleek modern figures with perfect bodies who are focal points of masculine desire, even though the men around them are invariably inferior and often physically weaker. This raises the (complicated) role of the gaze in film, as articulated by Robert Dale Parker's discussion of the enduring impact as well as the complexity of Laura Mulvey's 1975 essay 'Visual Pleasure and Narrative Cinema' and her subsequent work (Parker, 2015: 169–178). Parker's analysis evokes the questions: Who is looking at these women? How and why are they gendered and sexualised in the way that they are, and to what end? Does the nature of their sexualisation determine whether viewers read them as heroine, victim, or villain? Any answers to these questions would need to acknowledge the many variables at play in terms of production and reception, which again highlights the significance of Lucille as the true Bluebeard figure in *Crimson Peak*. This seems to cast her, as so many fairy tales might, as the pushy evil figure, the older woman, who has to learn her place as the spinster sister or be damned in Grand Guignol fashion for failing to do so. However, Lucille is also presented as sexually attractive and active, and it is the agency afforded by both her sexuality and villainy that defines her reconfigurement of the Bluebeard archetype. Indeed, such a characterisation can also be read through performance, and, in an interview with Sophie Heawood, Jessica Chastain revealed how her conceptualisation of Lucille translated onto the screen:

> 'Most people don't know this – Guill[ermo] doesn't even know this – but I played it that her fantasies are more about women than men'. Her character, Lucille, slowly poisons the women who marry her brother, and cares for them as they die, ostensibly so she can keep him to herself, and spend their money. Chastain describes the intimacy of that murderous act, 'of holding someone's hand as they die: it's a very sexual thing to do'.
>
> *(Heawood, 2016)*[7]

These examples therefore demonstrate how contemporary filmic rearticulations of Bluebeard can refocus attention towards the female figures, with complex results. *Little Lamb*, however, dismantles many more elements of the Bluebeard story in retelling it. Perrault's 'Bluebeard' lacks the affect or atmosphere, the motivation (indeed there is very little motivation), or the implication of the uncanny often associated with Gothic traditions, in what Donna Campbell (2014) describes as '[the e]lements . . . that challenge reality, including mysterious events that cause the protagonist to question the evidence of his or her senses and the presence of seemingly supernatural beings'. The closest the story gets to an implication of the uncanny is in the blue beard motif itself and the key with its irremovable bloodstain (which perhaps owes something to that other famous Gothic precursor, *Macbeth*), but these details are simply presented, not dwelt upon, in Perrault's story. And yet there is the *potential* for the uncanny and horror: it is there in the way the story narrates the unlocking of the secret room, briefly pausing over the clotted blood and the murdered wives. And in its retellings, that potential has taken many forms. Maria Tatar (2004), in examining the Bluebeard story's endurance, looks back to the stories of Eve and Pandora, and argues that readers 'obsessively return to [Bluebeard] to try to understand marital discord . . . [and to look at] how it reflects our anxieties as cultural symptoms . . . [and] shape[s] our fantasies and desires' (p. 173). Jack Zipes (2006), in *Why Fairy Tales Stick*, acknowledges but challenges this argument, claiming that the story is ultimately 'a tale about male power and calculation based on the instinctual drive for power that misfires' (p. 157).

In the production notes for *Little Lamb*, director Heidi Lee Douglas discusses her film-making background and her inspiration for the film, which introduces another way the Bluebeard story finds real-life applications:

> For ten years I lived near the original women's prison in Tasmania which was established during British occupation in 1829. The 13,000 convict women that were transported to Tasmania were forced into life in exile because of petty crimes, yet helped found the new nation of Australia. Now all that remains of the prison are the sandstone walls and empty courtyards, a silent reminder of the suffering the convict women endured. History has ignored these women, but their stories whispered to me, their ghosts asking to have their voices heard. . . . My background is in documentary filmmaking and I have witnessed many real life horrors, including war torn East Timor, the land rights struggles of Aboriginal Australians, and being personally targeted by logging giant Gunns Ltd in a five-year court battle for the right to free speech. *Little Lamb* draws on these experiences of struggling with oppression and channels these emotions into the story of a convict woman who wants to regain her self-determination. I also drew on the Bluebeard story as written by Clarissa Pinkola Estés about overcoming of predatory forces. Many women who worked on the film shared with me their own 'Bluebeard' stories – real life events that parallel this dark

fairytale, reinforcing to me the importance of sharing these old stories in new ways with modern audiences.

(Douglas, 2015)

Little Lamb (and throughout I am using its 2014 director's cut) begins with Mr Black, a settler, visiting the prison to secure a new servant. Agnes, an older inmate, tells Louisa, a young convict and a relatively new arrival, that he has done this regularly and that no one hears of the women again. However, Louisa says he does not look too bad, and pushes her way forward in the line, so that he chooses her (see Figure 1.1). She tries to escape into the bush en route to his farm but he warns her against the wild animals and wild men. Portents quickly arise: she spots the skeletal remains of a sheep, its head intact but rotting, pinned to a fence, and she spots a woman's discarded boot near the woodpile and thinks of Mary, a recent former servant Agnes mentioned. However, she also encounters a lamb and is immediately delighted and protective of the animal, even sleeping with it in her arms. Meanwhile, Mr Black lurks around, watching her through the window as she bathes, peering around her bedroom door as she sleeps, approaching her while undoing his belt as she kneads dough (only thwarted when she opts to stop kneading and reach for the rolling pin). Finally, in a sort of angry frustration, he announces he is going out hunting for the day and tells her to keep the doors locked. He also wants the lamb for his supper. Shortly after realising she cannot kill the lamb, Louisa sits down to cry and discovers blood: on her dress and on the lamb, although she did not hit it with the axe. It is coming through a broken wall in the barn, and, taking the lamb, a lantern, and a ring of keys, she searches the house. Wired to one big key is a tiny key that opens a storeroom, hidden behind bales of hay past a room full of hooks (one still has long blonde hair hanging from it, and the last inmate to disappear was golden-haired Mary), chains, and butcher tools.

FIGURE 1.1 Louisa (Georgia Lucy) meets Mr Black (James Grim) at the prison *Little Lamb* (Heidi Lee Douglas, 2014, Dark Lake Productions; photo: Eryca Green)

She finds this final, hidden room to be full of bloodstained boxes. She opens one, and finds mostly skeletal human remains and scraps of bloody clothing. At this point, Mr Black returns and pursues her in an increasingly frenzied bloodlust that moves from rage to horror and back to rage; she breaks the lantern over straw to set fire to the barn with him in it. Once outside, she grabs the axe to chop a hole in the wall, which permits the lamb to escape but also allows Mr Black to reach an arm through and grab her leg; after a short struggle, she chops his hand off. As the house burns, Louisa turns towards the wilderness, carrying the axe and the lamb.

How can a film attempting both painstaking realism and historical accuracy (in a departure from the film examples explored thus far), in which the female lead rescues herself, even be seen as a Bluebeard variant? To consider this requires a shift in focus from the (possibly more familiar and archetypal) Romantic and Victorian Gothic towards the regional Gothic, and to further contemporary understandings of the Female Gothic. In 'Australian Gothic', Ken Gelder (2007) points to late 19th-century Gothic romances that are best understood:

> first, through their creation of what Melissa Bellanta has called a 'fabulated' nation, full of wonders and strangeness, luxurious and Edenic, even utopian; and second, as a means of eliding (or at least, sublimating) both the depressed and dispossessed predicament of actual Aboriginal people by this time, and the harsh, austere realities of settler life in the bush.
>
> *(p. 116)*

However, drawing on Jim Davidson's work, he differentiates the Tasmanian variety from its Australian context, in 'accounting for the island's traumatic past as well as its often defiantly proclaimed sense of isolation and difference from mainland Australia' (p. 120), drawing a line from precursor texts to recent work such as Roger Scholes' 1987 film *The Tale of Ruby Rose* (Scholes co-produced *Little Lamb* with Douglas) and the developing body of Aboriginal Gothic fiction. Emily Bullock's (2011) 'Rumblings from Australia's Deep South: Tasmanian Gothic on Screen' points to the prevalence of horror in emerging Tasmanian cinema and to a landscape that creates a different sort of Gothic aspect from the enormous flatness and desert of the Australian outback, since these are:

> dark and wet landscapes, which register a paradoxical sense of beauty and menace. The dramatic inclines of Tasmania's topography, its volatile climate, together with the wild and dense temperate forest, which covers over a third of the state, form a forbidding *mise-en-scène* suggestive of a Gothic sublime.
>
> *(p. 73)*

Moreover, in a discussion of recent examples of this emergence (including *Little Lamb*), Bullock (2011) points to '[the Tasmanian Gothic] genre's concerns regarding an ominous, overwhelming environment and the haunting of a repressed past [that] run through many cinematic narratives about Australia's island state' (p. 91).

Jeni Thornley (2013) goes further in indicting the failure so far in this genre to let the repressed fully return:

> several recent fictional feature films produced about Tasmania by non-Indigenous film-makers, such as *Van Diemen's Land* (auf der Heide, 2009) and *The Hunter* (Nettheim, 2011) use the 'Tasmanian Gothic' trope (Davidson 1989; Bullock 2011), imagining an island with no Aboriginal people, past or present. Although it has been suggested that an evolving 'ecological gaze' intertwines with 'the Gothic' in recent Tasmanian films (Stadler 2012), in my view these works conjure up 'terra nullius' by ignoring Aboriginal presence. It seems to be a repeating tendency. . . . It is worth considering why fictional feature films about Tasmania stay locked in these tropes. Is it because few (if any) of them are developed with Tasmanian Aboriginal creative involvement?
>
> *(p. 129)*

This context provides the backdrop against which *Little Lamb* equally engages with the traditions of the Female Gothic, especially in its use of gaze. In 'Gothic Femininities', Alison Milbank (2007) points to the evolution of the Female Gothic in the early 21st century 'from straightforward feminist approaches as taking too essentialist an approach to the nature of gender, while psychoanalytic readings have given way to more historically contextualized approaches' (p. 156). She discusses the aspect of the 'explained supernatural' (p. 157) and the influence of Ann Radcliffe on writers who:

> continue the focus on female subjectivity through free indirect narration, which gives access to the heroine's thought processes and gives her perspective on events a privileged status in the narration . . . such novels contain an interest in the relation of the heroine to the natural world, as a series of vistas are presented to her sight . . . The heroine views these structures both from outside but also from within their labyrinthine complexities, and similarly the narration will move from viewing the heroine from the outside, as a figure in the landscape, and from within her mind.
>
> *(p. 157)*

This point is especially interesting in considering the use of landscape as a bridge between enclosed spaces in *Little Lamb*, and in the emphasis on a gaze that is *with* Louisa virtually throughout the film. In a round-table discussion of Australian women horror film-makers for *Senses of Cinema*, Heidi Lee Douglas (2016) takes up the uses of horror and subjectivity in the telling of women's stories:

> [in] horror writing I am drawn to writing about women evolving into leadership positions or empowering themselves through strong emotions like anger or grief . . . So my genre film writing has been very character driven,

focusing on women arming themselves to survive both emotionally and physically. I don't see stories like this onscreen enough, and so want to contribute to that.

Little Lamb's historical specificity (evident in its insistence throughout on period-accurate detail even to the staining on teeth, as well as the wear and tear on garments) *and* its Tasmanian setting are crucial to its creation of atmosphere, yet the film presents to the 21st-century viewer a Bluebeard story that is a contemporary, feminist Gothic tale. By eliminating the original tale's aristocratic elements, and indeed any specific reference to or signalling of the Bluebeard story, the implicit and gendered servitude of arranged marriage becomes actual servitude, a gendered power relationship. Stephen Frears' 1996 Victorian Gothic film adaptation of Valerie Martin's Jekyll and Hyde revision, *Mary Reilly*, is also a story of a master/servant relationship representing the eponymous servant's dealings with Dr Jekyll and Mr Hyde, but there is a romantic – or at least sexual/sexualised yearning – element in Mary's response; *Little Lamb* avoids this in Louisa. Whatever appeal Mr Black might have had at first glance swiftly disappears and even then seems mostly motivated by Louisa's desperate desire to escape the prison (already established in her night-time conversation with Agnes, which opens the film). The elements that do make *Mary Reilly* worth considering alongside *Little Lamb* are its emphasis on physical horror and Mary's perspective (especially her proactive agency in entering forbidden rooms, even though she does so when they have been left unlocked, and Mary only learns the secret when Jekyll/Hyde is ready to let her see it). However, Douglas' approach to carnage is arguably more horrifying in leaving vague exactly what Mr Black has done and why. Although the *mise en scène* provides chilling clues, the creation of visceral visual effects are predominantly achieved elsewhere: through location, including at and around the prison site in Tasmania; with the use of ambient light to render darkness (with almost no use of the blue electric light that often suggests night-time in films);[8] and in Douglas' drastic revision of the conclusion of Perrault's story. The use of landscape shots in natural light effectively bridges the two key sets, the prison and the farm, with the result that both become similar: houses of horror that can only be escaped with great difficulty and daring. It also suggests an unrevealed but hidden history to these places, upon which these forms of colonial intrusion have imposed themselves.

Little Lamb is a departure for Douglas in being a fiction film, a short film, and a horror film: working within those genres, frameworks, and conventions has necessitated the implying – rather than explicitly narrating – of the larger thematic and social concerns more characteristic of the director's documentary work. The structure and pacing of the film within its 22-minute runtime (expanded from a 10-minute first cut) create considerable tension and horror. This is especially apparent in the juxtaposed shots of Louisa discovering Mr Black's secret; of the sight of the male antagonist returning from his day's hunting bearing bloody carcasses; and in the 'gotcha!' shock moments when Mr Black grabs her leg through the hole in the burning wall, resulting in Louisa abruptly chopping off his hand (the impact of this final episode is set up by her earlier inability to kill the lamb, which places the axe in a convenient location for her eventual use of it). However, even within its length and genre parameters, the film also suggests depths in characterisation, not least through the use of the lamb. Louisa's bond with the lamb (a significant departure from any Bluebeard story and the element that gives the film its title) complicates her own motives, which move beyond a simple desire to escape and a desperate impulse towards survival, to include the protection of something she loves (see Figure 1.2). Significantly, this is not a family member or a romantic partner: in human terms, she is alone. There are also subtle ways in which the film establishes Louisa as perceptive and potentially proactive, as seen through her use of the rolling pin and the connection made between the discarded boot and Mary. Additionally, Louisa discovers Mr Black's murderous activities not through the use of an explicitly forbidden key, but of one that is logically chosen to open the door: she tries a couple of keys before realising one large key has a smaller one attached to it with wire. Louisa's discovery of the secret is presented as something that emboldens her in the sheer extent of its horror: unlike the wife in the traditional story who desperately tries to cover up her use of the key and entry into the forbidden room, Louisa deliberately sets fire to the barn once Mr Black is trapped in the chamber of horrors. Similarly, once she gets a firm grasp on the axe at the end, Louisa does not hesitate in chopping off his hand. She turns to the wilderness, alone except for the lamb, leaving Mr Black to a death she has enabled, to save herself and Lamby.

The defining element of this film is its rethinking of the Bluebeard characters. It is tempting when analysing contemporary folk fairy-tale revisions (Gothic and otherwise) to see the villain or antagonist as psychologically complex in motivation, possibly as understandable or even sympathetic: this is, after all, symptomatic of the 'poor Bluebeard' syndrome exhibited by my students, as mentioned at the beginning of this chapter. An integral part of how *Little Lamb* achieves its horror

FIGURE 1.2 Louisa (Georgia Lucy) with Lamby at Mr Black's farm
Little Lamb (Heidi Lee Douglas, 2014, Dark Lake Productions;
photo: Eryca Green)

is in how the film offers two closely linked levels on which to view Mr Black. On one, he is the familiar, possibly psychotic predatory villain, arguably with a note of frustrated anguish. On another, he is an archetypal predator in a very broad sense, a consumer of land and people, a more obviously dangerous version of Stewart in *The Piano*; it is significant that Mr Black's visit to the prison to procure a servant is treated as official routine, with the only anxiety evidenced among the women convicts, many of whom refuse to meet Mr Black's gaze as he inspects them. Indeed, as I suggested earlier, one question that remains open and is a significant part of *Little Lamb*'s horror is that of exactly what Mr Black does to the women. His actions around Louisa suggest a sexual lust, but the flayed sheep carcass and its similarity to the condition of the human remains Louisa finds in the one box she opens in the hidden room also suggest cannibalism.[9] Mr Black is a sort of reverse version of the othered exotic figure often found in Victorian cultural products, such as those especially popular 19th-century illustrations of Bluebeard (Tatar, 2004: 28–48) and the representation of the title character in *Dracula* (1897). Conversely, Mr Black is the fearsome foreigner come *from* the seat of empire to the renamed and occupied land, as shown within those landscape shots that bridge the prison and farm settings of *Little Lamb*. He is the werewolf of nightmares, the Big Bad Wolf: feral in his rage and unrelenting, but for all that not undefeatable.

And yet *Little Lamb* remains grounded in the open-endedness of its conclusion where, as is the case virtually throughout, the viewer's gaze is *with* Louisa. This differentiates her representation both from ultra-sexualisation through the heteronormative male-gaze conventions, and from contemporary genre tropes of the 'strong female characters', as seen in the earlier examples. Even in the moments when the gaze would seem to be Mr Black's – that of the predator observing Louisa – the shot quickly moves to a close-up of the protagonist's face or aligns with her: as seen when Louisa spots the shadow and hears breathing as she bathes and then quickly shudders and covers herself, or when the camera moves around the door frame and into the room where she sleeps and Lamby wakes her. The focus is on her reactions, reflective and emotional; even as she pushes her way between the boxes in the chamber of horrors to escape Mr Black, the emphasis is much more on her experience of terror than on his manifestation of threat: we experience this with her, not so much by looking at her, but *with* her. Louisa thus occupies the role not of fortunate victim, but of heroine: no woodsman required, even if no happily ever after is guaranteed or even implied.

Notes

1 The tension between Bluebeard's status as a children's story and its narrative content is further explained by Tatar (2004): "'Bluebeard' is one of those stories that did not travel well in the great eighteenth-century migration of fairy tales from the fireside and parlour to the nursery.... A tale that centers on marriage and focuses on the friction between one partner who has something to hide and another who wants to know too much, it did not prove attractive to adult sensibilities about what was appropriate reading for children' (p. 13).

2 Several of the papers at the 2016 Gothic Feminism conference at the University of Kent explored Bluebeard echoes in TV and film examples that made no specific reference to Perrault's story, including Katerina Flint-Nicol on the 2015 BBC adaptation of Agatha Christie's *And Then There Were None*, A. Dana Weber on Kurt Maetzig's 1965 East German film *The Rabbit Is Me*, and Frances A. Kamm on James Cameron's 1986 film *Aliens*. These papers have been published as chapters within this collection.

3 Tatar's extensive analysis of *The Piano*, both Jane Campion's film and Kate Pullinger's novelization written in collaboration with Campion, argues that it subverts several of Perrault's devices in making Ada 'the repository of a secret' who 'stirs our curiosity' while Stewart is a 'completely transparent character' (Tatar, 2004: 122–123).

4 I do realise that viewing/reading *Crimson Peak* as Edith's novel suggests more radical possibilities for analysis in respect to these gender dynamics, though applying that reading – given the design of the start and end credits – almost has to be done within awareness that the novel is a conceit of the film, of someone else's dream level, and this is a structural device applied as well in both del Toro's *Pan's Labyrinth* (2006) and *The Devil's Backbone* (2001).

5 'God I wanna get, get rid of it / Get rid of it / My house, my bed, my husbands . . . My room, my life / My husbands'.

6 This analysis alone does not do justice to the troubling complexities of *Ex Machina*'s conclusion.

7 Ironically, Tom Hiddleston's performance as Thomas Sharpe renders him so potentially sympathetic from the outset – a quality amplified by his considerable sexualisation via the perspectives of both Edith and Lucille – that Lucille's villain status is reinforced still further.

8 When I first saw production stills for Robert Eggers' *The Witch* (2015), I was struck by how much its visual style reminded me of *Little Lamb*, an impression reinforced when I saw the completed film. *The Witch* is also a film Douglas cites as among the 'modern horror' she loves: 'films that have an underlying line of enquiry but have a fantastical, suspenseful element' (Douglas, 2016).

9 This would not be without precedent in Tasmanian Gothic film: 'The release in late 2009 of Jonathan auf der Heide's debut feature film, *Van Diemen's Land* (2009), joins the current proliferation of films based on the notorious Tasmanian cannibal convict, Alexander Pearce. After the documentary *Exile In Hell* (Dowdall 2007), the horror-thriller *Dying Breed* (Dwyer 2008) and the docudrama *The Last Confession of Alexander Pearce* (Rowland 2008), which screened on the ABC on Anzac Day eve in 2009, *Van Diemen's Land* is the fourth to tell the gruesome tale of the convict who ate a total of six of his companions after fleeing twice from the remote west coast penal settlement at Macquarie Harbour in 1822. Together, these films suggest a renewed cinematic attention to Tasmania, its dark and troubling past as a brutal penal colony, and its dramatic and unforgiving natural settings' (Bullock, 2011: 71–72).

References

Browne, John C. (1866) 'A Children's Play: Bluebeard's Wives'. Printed *c*.1975, modern gelatin silver print from the original collodion negative, George Eastman House Museum of Photography and Film, Rochester, New York.

Bullock, Emily (2011) 'Rumblings from Australia's Deep South: Tasmanian Gothic On Screen'. *Studies in Australasian Cinema*, 5(1): 71–80. www.tandfonline.com/doi/abs/10.1386/sac.5.1.71_1?journalCode=rsau20 [Accessed 2 April 2018]

Campbell, Donna (2014) 'Gothic, Novel, and Romance: Brief Definitions'. *Literary Movements*, Washington State University, 3 July. http://public.wsu.edu/~campbelld/amlit/novel.htm [Accessed 2 April 2018]

Douglas, Heidi Lee (2015) 'Director's Q&A'. *Little Lamb – Press Kit*. Dark Lake Productions.

Douglas, Heidi Lee (2016) 'Making Magic: An Australian Women Horror Filmmakers Roundtable'. *Senses of Cinema*, 81. http://sensesofcinema.com/2016/beyond-the-babadook/australian-women-horror-filmmakers-roundtable/ [Accessed 2 April 2018]

Gelder, Ken (2007) 'Australian Gothic'. In Catherine Spooner and Emma McEvoy (eds), *The Routledge Companion to Gothic*. London: Routledge, pp. 115–123.

Hawley, Kate (2016) 'Hand Tailored Gothic'. *Crimson Peak*. 2015. Blu-ray edition, Universal Studios.

Heawood, Sophie (2016) 'Jessica Chastain: "It's a Myth That Women Don't Get Along"'. *The Guardian*, 9 April. www.theguardian.com/film/2016/apr/09/jessica-chastain-myth-women-dont-get-along-jennifer-lawrence-fight [Accessed 3 April 2018]

Milbank, Alison (2007) 'Gothic Femininities'. In Catherine Spooner and Emma McEvoy (eds), *The Routledge Companion to Gothic*. London: Routledge, pp. 155–163.

Parker, Robert Dale (2015) 'Feminism and Visual Pleasure'. In Robert Dale Parker (ed.), *How to Interpret Literature: Critical Theory for Literary and Cultural Studies* (3rd edn). Oxford: Oxford University Press, pp. 169–178.

Perrault, Charles (1901) 'Blue Beard'. In Charles Welsh (ed.), *The Tales of Mother Goose as First Collected by Charles Perrault in 1696*. Lexington, MA: D.C. Heath. www.gutenberg.org/files/17208/17208-h/17208-h.htm#BLUE_BEARD [Accessed 3 April 2018]

Savages (2013) 'Husbands'. *Silence Yourself*. Matador Records and Pop Noire.

Tatar, Maria (2004) *Secrets beyond the Door: The Story of Bluebeard and His Wives*. Princeton, NJ: Princeton University Press.

Thornley, Jeni (2013) '"Islands of Possibility": Film-Making, Cultural Practice, Political Action and the Decolonization of Tasmanian History'. *Studies in Australasian Cinema*, 7(2–3): 123–136. http://dx.doi.org/10.1386/sac.7.2-3.123_1 [Accessed 3 April 2018]

Zipes, Jack (2006) *Why Fairy Tales Stick: The Evolution and Relevance of a Genre*. London: Routledge.

2

BLUEBEARD IN THE CITIES

The use of an urban setting in two 21st-century films

Lawrence Jackson

Introduction

In *Secrets beyond the Door*, Maria Tatar (2004) explores 'how the Bluebeard plot competes with the Cinderella story as our culture's paradigm for romantic excitement and how it provides opportunities for reflecting on the play between intimacy and distance, disclosure and repression' (p. 8). This chapter will look at how the Bluebeard fairy tale is updated by two distinctive films of the first decade of this century, Jane Campion's *In the Cut* (2003) and Andrea Arnold's *Red Road* (2006). In doing so, I will explore how the Bluebeard story is altered by the decision to transpose it to an urban setting, and how Tatar's binary oppositions of intimacy/ distance and disclosure/repression are tested by the relocation of Bluebeard to the city. An overview of significant historical adaptations of the story, and a consideration of the relevance of location in three particular examples of the tale, will establish the link between the Bluebeard narrative and the role of landscape therein, after which I will examine the importance of a specifically urban setting to both films' successful drawing out of Bluebeard's themes. I conclude with a reflection on the centrality in the films of the play between psychology and place.

In the Cut and *Red Road* share several similarities: both are written and directed by women, both feature female protagonists who actively court danger, both include frank depictions of sex, both pair the heroine with an 'homme fatal', and both take as their backdrop an urban environment – New York and Glasgow, respectively – that is presented as a literal and moral wasteland. In their handling of the latter two aspects – the figure of the male antagonist and the setting – the films make an intriguing use of tropes from the fairy tale and update these within contemporaneous stories. *In the Cut*, adapted from Susanna Moore's novel by Campion and Moore, focuses on an academic in the pre-Giuliani sin city of 1980s Manhattan who, in her Faustian arrogance, carries out increasingly risky research that takes her into the underbelly of the city's nightlife. This in turn leads her to enter into an affair with a police detective investigating a series of grisly murders, and places her on a collision course with a predator. *Red Road*, Arnold's debut feature film, focuses on a lonely woman in contemporary Glasgow who uses her job in surveillance to obsessively follow, via CCTV, the behaviour of one man in particular. As she goes to the pub where he drinks and becomes intimate with him, we realise that a darker motive lies behind her actions.

In their indebtedness to, and subversion of, the Bluebeard fairy tale, both films remain faithful to the original's thematic darkness and at the same time demonstrate that the narrative's modern urban context gives it present-day relevance. These are screen works by and about accomplished, self-aware, modern women, yet the fears they explore return us to the primal stories of childhood. Why should Campion and Arnold choose to put this old wine into new bottles? One answer might be that the sex and violence inherent in the mythic elements of the story present material at once challenging and attractive to film-makers, who can invoke Bluebeard as a means of amplifying dread and catharsis in the viewer. This study argues, however, that what is key to the film-makers' aesthetic achievement in revisiting the fairy tale is the relocation of the scenario from an isolated rural location to the crowded modern city, showing that the source story's tension not only survives, but thrives on being transported to an urban setting.

Bluebeard

In *From the Beast to the Blonde*, Marina Warner (1993) attributes the allure of the Bluebeard story to its combination of the core elements of sexual fascination and generic thriller:

> Bluebeard is a bogey who fascinates: his very name stirs associations with sex, virility, male readiness and desire. His bloody chamber, which his latest wife opens with the key he has forbidden her to use, reveals the dead bodies of her many predecessors, and warns her of her impending doom: the fairytale written by Charles Perrault in 1697 thrills like a Hitchcock film before its time, it foreshadows thriving twentieth-century fantasies about serial killers and Jack the Rippers.
>
> *(p. 241)*

The Hitchcockian analogy is developed further by Maria Tatar (2009):

> When Alfred Hitchcock made *Notorious* in 1946, he may not have had the Bluebeard story in mind, but he managed to take up its terms in ways that are oddly prophetic about the direction it was to take in the latter part of the twentieth century . . . Alicia becomes an investigator with complete confidence in her powers, a 'notorious' woman who knows how to outwit, out-strategize and out-manoeuvre her love-smitten husband.
>
> *(p. 19)*

Both Warner and Tatar read the fairy tale as a parable of the fate awaiting a curious heroine, and Warner (1993) concludes:

> *Bluebeard* is a version of the Fall in which Eve is allowed to get away with it, in which no one for once heaps the blame on Pandora . . . Eve [is] the woman who disobeys and, through curiosity, endangers her life. After Perrault, the story often comes with a subtitle, 'The Effect of Female Curiosity', – or, in case we should miss the point – 'The Fatal Effects of Curiosity', to bring it in line with cautionary tales about women's innate wickedness.
>
> *(p. 244)*

Thus, the attraction held by the Bluebeard fairy tale for its many adapters grows out of the aesthetic and moral tension created by, on the one hand, its capacity to thrill and, on the other, its ability to raise philosophical questions about the nature of obedience. This tension confers upon it the status of a kind of cautionary thriller and is a significant factor in the story's survival and regeneration in many forms. A brief overview of some of these adaptations reveals that, despite the inevitable difference in stylistic approaches over the centuries, the story's core elements remain relatively unchanged.

Published in 1697, Charles Perrault's 'La Barbe Bleue' tells the story of a mysterious nobleman in the habit of murdering his wives, and the attempts of one wife to avoid the fate of her predecessors. With the aid of her sister and brothers, the new wife is successful in this endeavour and Bluebeard is killed. The narrative contains elements that subsequent retellings repeat and embroider upon: the forbidden chamber, the discovery of the corpses of Bluebeard's murdered wives hanging within it, and the key from which the blood – evidence of the wife's transgression – cannot be washed away. Perrault's version has left its imprimatur upon later literary, musical, and cinematic versions, including Richard Barham's collection *The Ingoldsby Legends* (1840) where, in the jaunty doggerel of 'Bloudie Jacke of Shrewsberrie, the Shropshire Bluebeard', the story is recast as Victorian English folk horror; Bela Bartok's one-act opera *Duke Bluebeard's Castle* (1911), which maps the heroine's loss of innocence and descent into hell through a series of colour-coded rooms; Robert Nye's novel *The Life and Death of My Lord Gilles de Rais* (1990), a semi-documentary eyewitness account of the crimes of one of Joan of Arc's most trusted companions at arms, the Breton nobleman hanged in 1440 for alleged crimes of Satanism and the murder of hundreds of children, and said to be the original model for Bluebeard; and the title story in Angela Carter's collection *The Bloody Chamber*, revisionist in that it subverts, deepens, and stretches the roles of heroine and male antagonist, and feminist in that it is told unwaveringly from a self-aware, female point of view and depicts sex, graphically, from the woman's perspective. Well into the new century, films such as Catherine Breillat's *Bluebeard* (2010), Heidi Lee Douglas' *Little Lamb* (2012), and Alex Garland's *Ex Machina* (2015) have reimagined the myth to show its potency is undimmed.[1]

These adaptations develop the aforementioned tension at the heart of the Bluebeard story by integrating their treatment of its central relationship, between heroine and male antagonist, with the role of landscape to accentuate questions of violence, trauma, and gender representation. For example, 'Bloudie Jacke of Shrewsberrie, the Shropshire Bluebeard', 'The Bloody Chamber', and *Little Lamb* all share a rural setting and, at one level, can be interpreted as examinations of the urban sophisticate's fear of the countryside. Barham's collection of myths, legends, and ghost stories from the early Victorian era comprises cautionary tales suffused with gallows humour aimed at seen-but-not-heard children and their guardians. It predates the better-known and more sinister *Struwwelpeter* (1845) and also anticipates, in its counterpoint of violence and slapstick humour, later British traditions of music hall and pantomime. 'Bloudie Jacke, the Shropshire Bluebeard' retells the fairy tale in a poem of 56 eight-line stanzas, in doggerel verse related by a knowing narrator and chronicling the secret marriage of a 'Maiden' to the eponymous villain, and their pursuit by the bride's indefatigable younger sister Mary-Anne:

> But the Maiden is gone by the glen,
> Bloudie Jacke!
> Mary-Anne she is gone by the lea;
> She o'ertakes not her sister,
> It's clear she has miss'd her,
> And cannot think where she can be!
> Dear me
> 'Ho! ho! – We shall see! we shall see!'
>
> Mary-Anne is gone over the lea,
> Bloudie Jacke!
> Mary-Anne she is come to the Tower!
> But it makes her heart quail,
> For it looks like a jail,
> A deal more than a fair Lady's bower,
> So sour
> Its ugly grey walls seem to lour.
> (Barham, 2009: 332)

What makes this strange quasi-ballad distinctive is how its tone, both lurid and disquieting, is combined with a vivid sense of place, in this case one that is remote and rural ('glen' and 'lea'). This dynamic is pushed further at the poem's climax when the villain receives his comeuppance at the hands of the vengeful community:

> They have pulled off your arms and your legs,
> Bloudie Jacke!
> As the naughty boys serve the blue flies;
> And they've torn from their sockets,

And put in their pockets
Your fingers and thumbs for a prize!
And your eyes
A Doctor has bottled – from Guy's.
Your trunk, thus dismember'd and torn,
Bloudie Jacke!
They hew, and they hack, and they chop;
And, to finish the whole,
They stick up a pole
In the place that's still called the Wylde Coppe,
And they pop
Your grim gory head on the top!
(Barham, 2009: 339–340)

Barham's version manifests little interest in human psychology, functioning chiefly as a gaudy postcard from the shires. Its cartoonish violence, however, is lent a genuinely unsettling quality by the precision of Barham's language in evoking the Shropshire landscape: the glen, the lea, and 'the place that's still called the Wylde Coppe' are real places, physically stained by Bloudie Jacke's legacy.

Angela Carter's title story from *The Bloody Chamber* locates the tale on the bleak Atlantic coast of France; its tone is simultaneously sexually explicit, linguistically descriptive, self-referentially playful and morally serious, and Carter effects an important shift in making its central relationship not that between bride and male antagonist, but between the first-person narrator heroine and her mother:

> My eagle-featured indomitable mother; what other student at the Conservatoire could boast that her mother had outfaced a junkful of Chinese pirates; nursed a village through a visitation of the plague, shot a man-eating tiger with her own hand and all before she was as old as I?
>
> (Carter, 1996: 111)

At the story's climax, the agent of Bluebeard's destruction is neither Perrault's siblings nor Barham's villagers, but the protagonist's parent:

> You never saw such a wild thing as my mother, her hat seized by the winds and blown out to sea so that her hair was her white mane, her black lisle legs exposed to the thigh, her skirts tucked round her waist, one hand on the reins of the rearing horse while the other clasped my father's service revolver and, behind her, the breakers of the savage, indifferent sea, like the witnesses of a furious justice.
>
> (p. 142)

In one image, Carter both reclaims the masculine heroic and aligns femininity with nature. Prominent in her version is the geographical remoteness from civilisation of Bluebeard's chateau. The narrative opens with the heroine travelling away from the great city of Paris and ends with her returning with her piano-tuner husband to run a music school on the outskirts. Carter contrasts the urban, representing freedom and family harmony, with what lies beyond in the rural, namely violence and captivity, and, a South London girl to the last, plumps conclusively for the former.

Heidi Lee Douglas' short film *Little Lamb* positions the Bluebeard story as a naturalistic Gothic thriller, set in 1829 in a women's prison in Van Diemen's Land, present-day Tasmania. It follows Louisa, a younger inmate who is selected by the mysterious Mr Black to follow in the footsteps of previous female prisoners and serve on his remote farm, where she discovers a hidden inner stable filled with the bloody corpses of her predecessors, and, in a climactic confrontation with Black, severs his hand, sets fire to the farm buildings that contain him, and escapes with the lamb he has symbolically ordered her to kill. The film's strengths lie in the bleak beauty of its landscape, its historically authentic depiction of women's captivity, and its storytelling panache. It is not, however, without a self-conscious striving for genre iconicity: for example, the final shot of the film depicts the victorious heroine, axe in hand, silhouetted against the flames that are consuming her antagonist. *Little Lamb* is an ethnographic take on Bluebeard where the deeper one ventures into the wilderness, the more unthinkable the atrocities. The rural represents captivity: literally in the case of the prison; figuratively in the case of Louisa's obligations to Black, which must be, and ultimately are, resisted with violence.

It can be seen that the recurrence in these adaptations of a rural setting as the dramatic arena results in the character of Bluebeard becoming an ogre of the bucolic and the countryside the epicentre of primitive violence. This contrasts with Campion's and Arnold's choice of an urban location for their retellings of the fairytale, an aesthetic decision that is reasoned because, as Warner (1993) notes, it opens up the antagonist's potentialities as urban predator in a line from Jack the Ripper to John Reginald Christie to the Son of Sam. To Campion's and Arnold's transgressing heroines, the overpopulated city represents adventure but also, ironically, far greater extremes of alienation and captivity than the countryside. *In the Cut*'s Frannie and *Red Road*'s Jackie are women alone, amateur sleuths whose obsessive investigations come at a price, disobedient Eves whose actions bring them into the orbit of *hommes fatals*: a New York homicide detective and a Glasgow ex-con, respectively. Stylistically, both films function as neo-noirs in that they fuse gritty contemporary urban locations with a swooning Gothic sensibility so that, on one level, the film-makers are creating fantasias of the offbeat, staging liaisons in sleazy bars with sexy bad boys, and on a more fundamental level the films update and subvert the Bluebeard story by transposing these narratives to the modern city. In so doing, they maintain the aforementioned tension at the heart of the fairy tale and remain faithful to its identity as cautionary thriller, a balance that enables them to ask contemporary questions regarding violence, trauma, and gender representation.

In the Cut

Set in New York City, *In the Cut* follows Frannie (Meg Ryan), a teacher of English literature who embarks on a passionate affair with Malloy (Mark Ruffalo), a detective on the trail of a serial killer. Campion escalates tension through a combination of childhood innocence with adult horror: marketed as an erotic thriller, the film might more aptly be described as a sensual fever-dream of big city existence on the cusp between loneliness and sexual desire. The opening establishes the interplay between setting and a sense of disquiet, ushered in by the atonality of Pink Martini's cover version of 'Que Sera Sera' under the credits, a melody that registers as a lullaby but whose minor key foreshadows that all will be far from well. The choice of music at the beginning is balanced by the later use of another popular song, 'Just My Imagination', in a scene of tenderness between Frannie and her sister Pauline that takes place immediately before the latter's violent death at the killer's hands. From the beginning, Campion gives her urban thriller a dimension of Romantic yearning tinged with fatalism: this lullaby will not lead to sweet dreams, and, if the lyrics are true that whatever will be will be, then both sisters should resign themselves to the ogre awaiting them. Campion retains the trope of the relationship of sisters from Perrault's and Barham's versions of Bluebeard – and its implied echoes of childhood closeness – but by making her sisters older, supposedly more worldly, and at large in the city, the director deepens our sense of their existential plight.

It is notable that Moore, in her source novel of *In the Cut*, employs a first-person narration for the heroine's voice, the same device Carter utilises in 'The Bloody Chamber'; in both cases, the technique offers both narrative immediacy and psychological richness, and doing so illuminates several of the fairy tale's motifs:

> Pauline has seven elaborate locks on her door. It takes her several minutes to open them. She handed me a glass of champagne as I came in, a reward for having to wait so long on the landing, listening to 'Windmills of Your Mind'. A favorite on the jukebox downstairs. After all, it was Happy Hour at the Pussy Cat. Or Unhappy Hour, as Pauline says. The early evening jukebox selections tended to the maudlin, which always surprises me, sentimentality being an emotion that for me usually attends later in the night.
>
> *(Moore, 1995/2003: 28)*

Here, the simplicity of the words 'seven', 'locks', and 'door' carries the primal charge of familiar fairy-tale tropes: seven being a number we associate with wives, sons, or dwarfs, while the notion of a locked door immediately recalls Bluebeard. Around these distant fairy-tale echoes, Moore sets up a tension between surface pleasure and an underlying sadness. The champagne, the jukebox, and Happy Hour suggest a fulfilment that is fleeting, whereas what we take away from the above passage is its subtext, captured in phrases such as Unhappy Hour, maudlin, sentimentality, and emotion; Frannie and Pauline, Moore implies, do not feel satisfaction, but its opposite. It is no coincidence that the song playing at the Pussy Cat, 'Windmills of Your Mind', is one of melancholy yearning. Added to this is the question of why Pauline needs so many locks on her door: literally and meta-phorically, because of the threat of the city. The use of the adjective 'elaborate' to describe the locks suggests that, from Frannie's point of view, Pauline is over-cautious, when in fact no amount of caution will be enough to save her from a horrific death. Beneath Frannie's closing phrase linking 'sentimentality' with 'later in the night', there is more than a yearning, rather an aching sadness. Even before the male antagonist has materialised, both sisters are afraid and hold on to each other for support, in a manner reminiscent of the sibling relationships depicted in Perrault and Barham. However, by recasting the sisters as mature, emancipated women exposed to an urban environment of vice and crime in the film, Moore and Campion heighten the women's vulnerability, rendering their predicament more, not less, troubling.

Moore's terse, staccato sentences are also redolent of male detective fiction, a genre to which Campion is faithful in creating her noir vision of New York City at night. Although the film of *In the Cut* is visually defined by its urban landscape of nocturnal neon-lit streets and bars, Campion increases the tension in the rela-tionship between sisters and location, reinforcing the above-mentioned tone of yearning, by using nature to suggest a lost Eden. For example, the opening scene introduces Pauline (Jennifer Jason Leigh) walking through petals in the garden of her apartment, like a contemporary Eve in Paradise, but this same location is where one of the serial killer's disarticulated victims will shortly be found; what was a place of refuge, security, and femininity in the heart of the metropolis transforms into a site of violation. Similarly, a later excursion by Frannie and Malloy into the woods outside the city manifests initially as a pastoral interlude as the couple kiss and make love, before the superficiality of the idyll is exposed: the scene's function within the story is for Malloy to find a suitably remote location where he can teach Frannie how to shoot his pistol in self-defence.

What further intensifies the supremely unsettling quality of Campion's film is how the heroine's present-day descent into an inferno of discovery and self-discovery in the city is punctuated by flashbacks to a childhood moment when, it is implied, she was abandoned by her father. In these sequences from Frannie's past, we see distant out-of-focus figures skating in a fairy-tale snowscape, before a hand-some, black-gloved figure, later revealed to be Frannie's father, pursues another woman. Campion chooses to have Frannie recall this nostalgic idyll imbued with the uncanny at a shocking moment in the present-day narrative framework: as she cradles her sister Pauline's head that has been decapitated by the killer. By conjoin-ing present and past traumas, emotional disarticulation with literal decapitation, Campion aligns absent father and pursued killer with each other, and thus makes both monstrous.

As commercial entertainment, *In the Cut* functions as a cocktail of police proce-dural, fairy tale, and Freudian psychology, and this triangulation liberates Campion to interrogate, even mock, masculinity. On a date with Malloy, Frannie is made to feel an outsider by his profane locker-room banter with his police partner Rodriguez; that Rodriguez will be revealed to be the killer, misogynistic to the point of nihilism, only makes the jokes darker. For Campion and Frannie, seen through female eyes, the male detectives' liking for mock-fighting or slapping a blaring red siren onto their car roof is simultaneously puerile and attractive. The film's use of phallic symbols to deconstruct the phallocentric spans the title of the book Frannie teaches her high school students, *To the Lighthouse*, the toy red lighthouse Rodriguez keeps on his police desk, and the real lighthouse he uses as a store for his human trophies. This deconstruction of maleness culminates in the metaphorical castration of Malloy, who Frannie handcuffs and abandons before she makes the, we assume, fatal decision to accept a lift in Rodriguez's car. Traditional gender roles are subverted in that the female victim will have to save herself, as she has rendered her male rescuer powerless.

It is at the climax of *In the Cut* that its delirious integration of the trappings of Gothic melodrama, urban noir, and the Bluebeard fairy tale becomes manifest, as a storm flickers over the night-time river and the killer drags the heroine to her doom in his tower. Moore's novel ends with the death of its narrator at the hands of its Bluebeard, whereas Campion's film has a different ending. An interview with Moore indicates the author's dissatisfaction with this: 'She finds an inauthenticity in happy endings . . . [the novel] ends in violent desolation – an ending travestied in the film' (Kellaway, 2003).

In fact, Campion collaborated on the screenplay with Moore, and while the film's climax does not adhere to the bleak ending of the original, it is far from being the travesty suggested. Rather, Campion the director skilfully translates to screen Moore's qualities of directness, compression, and melancholy, evident in the excerpts below from the novel's climax:

> He stopped the car in front of a small red lighthouse and turned off the lights. 'This is where I come to fish', he said. The lighthouse was like an illustration in a children's book.
>
> *(Moore, 1995/2003: 173)*

> 'You heard that joke about the Garden of Eden?' I could smell my blood. 'God was looking down, right? and he saw Eve go into the ocean for a swim and he yelled, oh no, how we going to get the stink out of the fish?'
>
> *(Moore, 1995/2003: 177–178)*

> For a moment, I felt the cool air from the river, smelling of fish. Smelling of Eve. It made me shudder. I was cold.
>
> *(Moore, 1995/2003: 180)*

The cool economy of Moore's language belies the passion and terror in its emotional charge. This quality is preserved by Campion in her attention to authentic location detail and use of elements such as weather, water, and lighting to create a compelling *mise en scène* that grounds the necessarily melodramatic content in everyday urban squalor. Despite the film's perceived lack of fidelity to the original denouement, ultimately Campion manages to pull off the impressive feat of both preserving the chilling tone of the novel and delivering a Hollywood happy ending, closing on an affirmative note where Meg Ryan does not die. It is distinctive that while the heroine of 'The Bloody Chamber' is rescued in the eleventh hour by her mother, Frannie not only rescues herself, but does so having first actively ensured her potential saviour's impotence, as if on an unconscious mission to demonstrate that she, and only she, will get herself out of this, and she doesn't need a shooting lesson to prove otherwise. For Campion, it is essential that her Eve can be disobedient, endanger her life, and survive.

Red Road

Set in contemporary Glasgow, *Red Road* follows another disobedient Eve, CCTV surveillance operator Jackie (Kate Dickie), whose obsessive interest in one subject, ex-con Clyde (Tony Curran), leads to a sexual encounter with him in his flat at the top of a high-rise on the deprived Red Road estate. Jonathan Murray (2016) describes Jackie as 'disembodied watcher rather than flesh-and-blood woman' (p. 208), and this is consistent with what appears to be her life at the edge of things. The plot will reveal the reasons for Jackie's inwardness and hesitancy, that in fact her motive in pursuing Clyde is to entrap and frame him for rape as an act of vengeance: he has been sent to jail for killing her husband and young daughter in a drunken hit-and-run accident. At the end, however, she relents, shows compassion, and begins to process her grief, and in so doing embarks on the road back to becoming, to use Murray's terminology, flesh and blood once more.

While in its modest budget, naturalistic acting, and use of real locations it superficially shares similarities with a more conventional example of British social realism, for example the contemporaneous *London to Brighton* (2006), *Red Road* is more accurately a personal odyssey of voyeurism and sexual obsession in the vein of *Vertigo* (1958) and *Blue Velvet* (1986). Jackie's loneliness is subtly presented through awkward moments of social interaction such as her refusal to dance at an old friend's wedding – as in Arnold's later *Fish Tank* (2009), dancing represents an act of self-actualisation – or her air of disconnectedness during perfunctory biweekly sex sessions in a car parked in the rough edgelands outside the city. Jackie seems most animated in the private act of watching the lives of others in the darkness of her CCTV control-room eyrie. As she sits in front of a wall of screens of ghostly images, able to zoom in or out at will, she resembles the wicked queen in Snow White, looking into not one but many magic mirrors, the first instance of the film's use of fairy-tale motifs. When Jackie zooms in to pixellated close-ups of Clyde and his friend Stevie (Martin Compston), there are echoes of Antonioni's *Blow-Up* (1966) in that we are witnessing an accidental sleuth piecing together a narrative based on visual evidence. But Arnold is manipulating the viewer: we believe Jackie to be an investigative heroine, about to transgress by leaving the safety of her throne room to physically engage with one of her subjects. The reason for Jackie's isolation is not yet known, but we believe her transgression to be fundamentally ethical, and that she is exploiting private information for personal reasons of curiosity and desire. Our empathy is earned by Arnold's skilful depiction of Jackie's loneliness and sexual need, but we do not know that her motive is revenge.

Arnold teases us not only in terms of plot, but also genre. *Red Road* is a hybrid of social realism, urban thriller, and Gothic melodrama to which elements familiar from the Bluebeard fairytale are discreetly and increasingly added. The isolated heroine as wronged woman entering upon a perilous situation with a patriarchal male antagonist recalls Victorian narratives such as Wilkie Collins' *The Woman in White* (1860) and Sheridan Le Fanu's *Uncle Silas* (1864), but then subverts them in that here Jackie is the oppressor and her prey gentler than she. Underpinning Arnold's aesthetic is a passionate Romanticism ascribed by Murray (2016) to 'the striking immediacy, flexibility and ubiquity of Arnold's preferred hand-held shooting style, a device so central that it might conceivably obscure the visual sophistication and ambition of her directorial practice' (p. 207).

This sophistication is on display in Arnold's careful counterpointing in *Red Road* of the urban with the rural, revealing an ambivalent attitude to nature. The majority of the story's action plays out on the streets and estates of inner-city Glasgow, liminal spaces within an intimidating, alienating urban environment, yet the narrative is consistently punctuated by suggestions of the rural beyond the city. Animal imagery recurs, from a bulldog to a budgie to a night fox, explicitly foreshadowing the red-haired anti-hero. When Clyde licks his plate in a café, the waitress' response is, 'Ah, ye're a fuckin' animal'. CCTV footage of Clyde dragging a log through the nocturnal streets shows him engaged in some criminal activity, we assume, but instead we will discover that he is scavenging raw material to work on as a sculptor. Nature also inflects *Red Road* in terms of its sound universe, from the fox's distant bark to the whistling wind heard at the top of the Red Road flats. This generic and imagistic hybridity creates a sense that we are in a liminal space, an interzone where, like Jackie, we are not at ease; for Arnold, the location of the city represents both freedom and captivity, humanity and alienation. It is a duality crystallised in the moment where Jackie feels the wind on her face through the open window many storeys above the ground: the city holds her captive, but she's there of her own free will. This synthesis of psychology and setting marks out *Red Road* as lying closer to poetic than social realism.

The tension arising from *Red Road*'s atmosphere of uneasy anticipation, of existing on a fault line between expectation and fear, is true to the roots of Bluebeard as cautionary thriller and is definitively explored in the climactic scene where Jackie waits alone in Clyde's room for him to return and have sex with her. She sees his phallic log sculpture with monstrous teeth carved into its tip, hears the sounds of the city nightscape floating in through the open window, all the while awaiting sex with a stranger who is the object of her hatred but also a source of her attraction. The curious, fascinated heroine alone in the forbidden but longed-for chamber carries echoes of Bluebeard but also of Jane in Rochester's study in another of the fairy tale's incarnations, *Jane Eyre* (1847). Arnold shows great command in the building of erotic tension, not only in the scene in Clyde's room, but in following elsewhere how Jackie greedily monitors Clyde's interactions with other women: it's evidence of her detective work, but, as with Scottie Ferguson in *Vertigo*, there is more to it than that. Murray (2016) connects Arnold's handling of subtext to her sensitivity to landscape: 'Like Arnold's feature work more generally, *Red Road* strikes a precise balance in its adjudication between different kinds of landscape, some private and psychological in nature, others public and physical' (pp. 196–197).

Thus, when Jackie approaches the Red Road flats, she is stepping into a public landscape; it is her own decision to leave her personal zone and inveigle her way into Clyde's circle, and Arnold shows Clyde's tower from an extremely low angle so the phallic and mythic resonances are unmistakable. As in 'Bloudie Jacke of Shrewsberrie, the Shropshire Bluebeard', the heroine is approaching the ogre's stronghold with trepidation and the camera's positioning links its physical oppressiveness with the strength of its male occupant. Other symbolic touches in *Red Road* include the redness of the flats' entrance signalling danger. Jackie enters Bluebeard's chamber to entrap him, but it matters morally that she arrives far from innocent; what she has been projecting onto him in the private and psychological space of her CCTV surveillance gallery amounts to covert erotic fantasies, and now she must enter the space, public and physical, of the object of her repressed desire. The escalating tension finally breaks as, having been driven by a motive of revenge, she now becomes the killer's lover, and, in a twist ending that differs from Bluebeard but nonetheless carries the morality of a fairytale, what transpires is the awakening of the heroine's conscience.

Conclusion

In their decision to locate Bluebeard in the cities, Campion's and Arnold's films offer sophisticated opportunities (as Tatar indicates) to reflect upon the play the fairy tale offers between intimacy and distance, and disclosure and repression. Furthermore, in transposing their narratives to urban settings, the film-makers demonstrate that they can preserve the tension inherent in the story and stir in contemporary questions regarding violence, trauma, and gender representation.

In concluding, I would like to offer some reflections on the heightened interplay in *In the Cut* and *Red Road* between place and psychology. A reading of Freud's essay 'The Uncanny', and in particular what he calls 'the unintentional return' (Freud, 1919/2003: 144), might offer a clue to Frannie's and Jackie's motivations in seeking danger in the city. Freud (1919/2003) describes an experience where he found himself walking in an unpleasant part of a small Italian town and hastily left, only to find himself returning again and again to the same street:

> I was now seized by a feeling that I can only describe as uncanny, and I was glad to find my way back to the piazza that I had recently left and refrain from any further voyages of discovery. Other situations that share this feature

of the unintentional return . . . may nevertheless produce the same feeling of helplessness, the same sense of the uncanny.

(p. 144)

This helplessness and sense of the uncanny is something that we identify as prominent in the voyages of discovery undertaken by the heroines of both films. Could a deeper reason for their wandering in urban areas where they are at risk be that it is an unintentional return? In the course of the narratives, both Frannie and Jackie confront their fears, but where do the roots of these fears lie? According to Freud (1919/2003), 'the frightening element is something that has been repressed and now returns' (p. 147). His more detailed articulation of this return is that 'this uncanny element is actually nothing new or strange, but something that was long familiar to the psyche and was estranged from it only through being repressed' (p. 148). Thus, Frannie and Jackie are mapping dangerous urban areas to discover something long familiar to their psyches: for the former, a father who abandoned her for another woman; for the latter, the husband and child who were taken from her. In both cases, place is of paramount importance, as the streets of the city represent the grid where the characters enact this unintentional return.

The continuing centrality of place to Campion and Arnold is evident in their more recent respective work, *Top of the Lake: China Girl* (2017) and *American Honey* (2016), where, instead of New York and Glasgow, the film-makers make imaginative use of Sydney and the American Midwest as connective tissue between character and theme. The visceral power of the Bluebeard fairy tale suits these film-makers' Romantic style and they adapt it compellingly, locating its tension in decadent cities possessed of an ancient, pre-urban wildness while remaining true to the original by making their adventuresses face antagonists with the heft of a timeless, patriarchal foe. Warner's association of Bluebeard with sex, virility, male readiness, and desire integrates with a sub-theme of both films: male pack behaviour seen through the prism of the female gaze. Cops or criminals, Malloy and Rodriguez, Clyde and Stevie, all are being watched, weighed, pitied, desired by the investigative heroines. Ironically, their territorial pack behaviour notwithstanding, the observed males lack power, and Rodriguez's disgust for womankind is borne of impotence. Contrary to Warner's (1993) contention that 'Bluebeard is a story . . . in which the mighty are cast down' (p. 244), Campion's and Arnold's men are not so much mighty as dispossessed.

The shifting, many-layered quality of the urban setting reflects the characters' psychological complexity. In updating Bluebeard, *In the Cut* and *Red Road* foreground a preoccupation with women's autonomy in modern urban society and reach the ambivalent conclusion that their heroines are less passive than their forebearers in Perrault's fairytale, but no less vulnerable. A key factor in this, handled with great subtlety by the film-makers, is the heroines' moral ambiguity. As Warner (1993) notes, 'As in the story of the Fall, the serpent may be at fault, but Eve is blameworthy too' (p. 246). Frannie and Jackie are depicted as manipulative, voyeuristic, angst-ridden, emotionally inarticulate urban individuals whose consciences are uneasy. By entering into sexual liaisons with Malloy and Clyde, they are both surrendering to passion and using them for their own ends. The films can ultimately be read as fantastically flexible female meditations on the exploitation of men, or even coded confessions of guilt for doing so. Finally, it is essential that Frannie and Jackie remain vulnerable as that is a prerogative of being human. That they emerge scarred but triumphant reflects the underlying optimism of the film-makers: for Campion and Arnold, the loss of innocence – as encapsulated by Eve's disobedience or the transgression of Bluebeard's wives – is not a burden, but a trophy.

Note

1 In addition to the analysis of *Little Lamb* provided in this chapter, the film is also discussed at length in Gisèle M. Baxter's chapter, while *Ex Machina* is discussed by Tamar Jeffers McDonald elsewhere in this collection.

References

Barham, Richard (2009) 'Bloudie Jacke of Shrewsberrie'. In *The Ingoldsby Legends*. The Ex-Classics Project, pp. 331–341. www.ex-classics.com [Accessed 3 April 2018]

Brontë, Charlotte (1847/2006) *Jane Eyre*. London: Penguin.

Carter, Angela (1996) 'The Bloody Chamber'. In *Burning Your Boats: Collected Short Stories*. London: Vintage, pp. 111–143.

Collins, Wilkie (1860/2008) *The Woman in White*. Oxford: Oxford University Press.

Freud, Sigmund (1919/2003) 'The Uncanny'. In *The Uncanny*. London: Penguin, pp. 121–162.

Hoffmann, Heinrich (1845/2000) *Struwwelpeter*. Mineola, NY: Dover.

Kellaway, Kate (2003) 'Write the Good Fight'. *The Observer*, 14 December. www.theguardian.com/books/2003/dec/14/fiction.features2 [Accessed 2 April 2018]

Le Fanu, Sheridan (1864/2000) *Uncle Silas*. London: Penguin.

Moore, Susanna (1995/2003) *In the Cut*. London: Penguin.

Murray, Jonathan (2016) 'Red Roads from Realism: Theorising Relationships between Technique and Theme in the Cinema of Andrea Arnold'. *Journal of British Cinema and Television*, 13(1): 195–213.

Nye, Robert (1990) *The Life and Death of My Lord Gilles de Rais*. London: Hamish Hamilton.

Perrault, Charles (1697/1989) *Histoires ou Contes du Temps passé/Stories, or Tales of Times Past*. Marc Soriano, ed. Paris: Flammarion, pp. 257–262.

Tatar, Maria (2004) *Secrets beyond the Door*. Princeton, NJ: Princeton University Press.

Tatar, Maria (2009) 'Bluebeard's Curse: Repetition and Improvisational Energy in the Bluebeard Tale'. In Griselda Pollock and Victoria Anderson (eds), *Bluebeard's Legacy*. London: I.B. Tauris, pp. 15–30.

Warner, Marina (1993) *From the Beast to the Blonde*. London: Vintage.

3

BLUEPRINTS FROM BLUEBEARD

Charting the Gothic in contemporary film

Tamar Jeffers McDonald

In the Bluebeard folk tale, after the hasty wedding that has joined the bride's fate to that of her azure-whiskered husband, there comes the moment when the newly married couple arrive at Bluebeard's mansion and he shows his new wife around the dwelling that is to be her home. While this scene has frequently caught the imagination of artists,[1] it can also regularly be found occurring in the cycle of films called 'the Female Gothic', woman-in-jeopardy pictures that are commonly believed to begin with 1940's *Rebecca*.

Although scholars have also claimed the Gothic ended with the 1940s, three much more recent films can be seen drawing on the scene above, and indeed on the Bluebeard story as a whole. In *Crimson Peak* (2015), a new bride is shown around the ancestral home of her husband; *Before I Go to Sleep* (2014) presents an amnesiac who has to be introduced, each and every new day, to her home and husband; and in *Ex Machina* (2015), a worker who has won a visit to the boss' mansion is shown around its imposing rooms by him. While these three moments come from films of very different genres – historical romance, thriller, and science fiction – each repeats the scene borrowed from the Bluebeard story, as well as from other, older films.

These recent films therefore problematise the assumption that the woman-in-jeopardy story finished with the coming of the 1950s. Far from belonging to such a fixed point in history, as some scholars, such as Mary Ann Doane,[2] insist, the Female Gothic is demonstrated by this chapter to be a pervasive mode that continues to surface in contemporary media texts. The moments referenced above indicate their films' allegiance to the Gothic; while each produces a different version of this scene, one which works within, and to further, its own narrative, each also rehearses the moment where Mrs Bluebeard is shown her new home, where her husband displays the building's features and luxuries, but forbids her that one locked room . . .

Each of the films grounds its narrative in a different historical moment; the first very much flaunts its Victorian trappings, the second unfolds its shocking story of amnesia and assault among the quotidian reality of contemporary suburbia, and the third adopts its futuristic *mise en scène*, including robots and artificial intelligence, from science fiction. However, as this chapter will explore, each also makes extensive use of a formalised Female Gothic template.

Scholars have provided several examples of the genre's routinised plot structure; Diane Waldman (1984), for example, contends that in the standard outline of such narratives, inevitably:

> A young inexperienced woman meets a handsome older man . . . After a whirlwind courtship . . . she marries him. After returning to the ancestral mansion of one of the pair, the heroine experiences a series of bizarre and uncanny incidents, open to ambiguous interpretation, revolving around the question of whether or not the Gothic male really loves her. She begins to suspect that he may be a murderer.
>
> *(pp. 29–30)*

Wartime Gothic films, including *Rebecca, Gaslight* (1944), *Dragonwyck* (1946), *Secret Beyond the Door* (1947), and others, clearly adhere to this structure, both with regard to story patterns and characters. For example, the narrative of the film *Rebecca* gives us a shy, unsophisticated, and nameless heroine who is drawn to mysterious, moody aristocrat, Maxim de Winter, and astonished but willing when he asks her to marry him. They return to his family's stately home, Manderley, and the bride has trouble adjusting to her new position as both Mrs de Winter and chatelaine. Her discomfort is worsened by the unfriendly behaviour of the housekeeper, Mrs Danvers, and especially by the all-pervasive memories of Maxim's not-long-dead first wife, Rebecca, which permeate the house and are especially manifest in her bedroom, which Danvers keeps unaltered as a shrine. When Rebecca's boat is found with her body on board, Maxim's erratic behaviour, Danvers' animosity, and the bride's bewilderment all grow to a climax.

Although this reductive synopsis does not do justice to the appeal of *Rebecca* or the sensitive performances, especially of Joan Fontaine as the bride and Judith Anderson as the terrifying housekeeper, it does make clear the text's adherence to what could be seen as the Gothic playbook. The hasty marriage, the opposition of poor, inexperienced virgin and wealthy man of the world as main characters, along with the mysterious events of the past affecting the heroine's present, are all from the standard template. There are additional elements worthy of note here too, however, and again these have been noted and taxonomised by earlier Gothic scholars, including Joanna Russ and Kay Mussell, who both note the frequent presence of the Other Woman.

Literary theorist Russ, looking at the publishing success of the popular paperback form of the Gothic in the 1960s and 1970s, maintains that the central couple are both echoed and contrasted with two other dominant characters, she by this

Other Woman and he by the Shadow Male. While Russ is examining Ace and Dell paperback Gothics, the films of the genre also clearly use these archetypes too. The Other Woman 'is at the same time the Heroine's double and her opposite – very often the Other Woman is [Bluebeard's] present wife or dead first wife' (Russ, 1973/1995: 668). Sexually experienced where the bride is innocent and virginal, the Other Woman is also frequently depicted as evil in these narratives, an association that has prompted some critics to call the genre conservative.[3] Rebecca herself clearly conforms to this character type.

Russ (1973/1995) also notes that the commonly found Shadow Male character is, unlike the Bluebeard figure, 'gentle, protective, responsible, quiet, humorous, tender and calm' (p. 669). Interestingly, in the pulp paperbacks, it is usually *he* rather than the brooding central male who turns out to be the actual villain; in the wartime Gothic films, however, this other man is the one who helps the heroine in her investigation, as played, for example, by Joseph Cotton in *Gaslight* (1944) and Robert Cummings in *Sleep, My Love* (1948). In the Gothic films, this man's symbolic purpose is to reassure viewers that it is the hero-villain who is *individually* at fault, rather than the whole institution of marriage, since he is there to form a heterosexual couple with the heroine at the narrative's conclusion. The perfunctory manner in which this character is often developed and this union achieved, however, tends to undermine any reassurance the plot could hope to derive from him.

While, as noted above, the typical template provides the main overarching plot and cast of characters for these and many other films, adherence to the woman-in-jeopardy Gothic also prompts the repeated usage of smaller elements of iconography. For example, inherited from the original 18th-century novels is the dominant presence of the Old Dark House. While this has been shared with horror cinema, where it has slightly mutated to become the Terrible Place (Clover, 1992: 30) employing varying locales, the woman-in-jeopardy Gothics maintain the accent on the family home. The key and the portrait are the other two main tropes that frequently recur and combine visual and narrative significance in the woman-in-jeopardy Gothic. Keys appear in the wartime films – for example, *The Spiral Staircase* (1946) and *Secret Beyond the Door* – and are the apt symbol for the active female investigator who operates in such texts, reading, thinking, detecting, and eventually solving the mystery. Similarly, the films employ the trope of the ancestral portrait; usually a large oil painting of a female ancestor belonging to the house, this forecasts what the heroine's future fate will be if she is unwary. Usually, in the 1940s films, the heroines, such as Paula in *Gaslight* and Miranda in *Dragonwyck*, for example, need to interpret the returned gaze of the woman in the portrait, in order to see that she represents what they may become if incautious – victims of male violence. Finally, emphasising the strand's interest in female subjectivity and the woman's point of view, the films, from *Rebecca* onwards, frequently feature a female voice-over.

Again taking *Rebecca* as the first and prime example of this strand of the Gothic, we find the film using many of these visual and auditory elements. Manderley, the great house, unsettles the bride with its immensity and privilege, the manipu-lated scale of the sets (as discussed by Christina Petersen elsewhere in this volume) underlining her feelings of inadequacy and lack of belonging. The portrait of Lady Caroline de Winter, Maxim's ancestor, provides a plot point for the acceleration of the bride's misery and her husband's mysterious behaviour. While *Rebecca* is the rare Gothic that does not make use of the key as a symbolic element, it does main-tain the female perspective – inspired by its source novel – as the film starts with the bride's voice-over telling the viewer, 'Last night I dreamt I went to Manderley again'. The voice-over does not persist throughout the entirety of the narrative, and indeed many Gothic heroines have their voices silenced during the course of their stories.[4]

With the main characters, plot points, and significant visual/auditory elements of the woman-in-jeopardy Gothic thus sketched, this chapter will now explore what each of the three more recent films under consideration makes of the Gothic template, as well as analysing their shared visual tropes.

Crimson Peak

Perusal of the narrative of *Crimson Peak* shows it overtly recycling as many of the traditional elements of the Gothic as it can. Our heroine Edith *is* young, lonely, soon orphaned; she engages in a whirlwind courtship with a mysterious, hand-some older man, marries him, and returns to his ancestral home, where ambiguous goings on, concerning him, her, and his sister Lucille, convince her there is an ominous secret about the place, and him. When she solves the mystery – he has been incestuously involved with Lucille – Edith *does* get to the bottom of the secret, which involves his previous serial marriages and the sister's mur-der of these other wives for money. And there is the other man in the form of her friend the doctor, who seems to hold out the promise of future couple for-mation at the film's close.

Crimson Peak can therefore be seen as very faithful to the narrative template, or more negatively as unimaginative in employing it so straightforwardly, con-forming with hardly any deviations to the Ur-text for the Gothic, the Bluebeard story. However, *Crimson Peak* does contribute one new story theme to the already heady brew of the genre: that of incest. This has the interesting effect of com-bining the 'Rebecca' and 'Mrs Danvers' figures in one character: sister Lucille is both the hyper-sexualised Other Woman of the husband's past, and the moody, forbidding servant who tends the family home.

The film adheres to further points in the tradition too, maintaining the tropes that operate at both visual and auditory levels. It foregrounds the named ancestral house,[5] even pointing out its own awareness of the significance of the domicile to the Gothic: in a rather overt self-referential turn, Thomas asks Edith as she first enters Allerdale Hall, 'What do you think? Does it look the part?' Like canoni-cal Gothics, *Crimson Peak* also has the female voice-over. Edith narrates her own story, and significantly, *unlike* many of the 1940s films, this endures throughout the entirety of the film, from her first line – 'Ghosts are real. This much I know'. – to the end, when, with the repetition of this line, she confirms we have been watching a lengthy flashback. Telling her own story gives the heroine a measure of control and agency, which is why it is troubling when the voice-over disappears. Though Edith seems in danger at points in the narrative, the recurrence of her voice-over reassures. The fact that she is a novelist also makes it fitting that her voice is narrating; after a prologue showing the child Edith encountering a ghost, the film begins with the image of a book – again self-referentially, it has *Crimson Peak* as its title – while the years that cover her growth to maturity are accomplished by the simple turning of its pages.

Crimson Peak also employs both the traditional key and the portrait; with the former, Edith first finds a locked trunk, and then discovers that the key she is sure will fit it hangs on Lucille's belt. When Edith appropriates the correct key, she finds the recording machine that gives her access to the voice of one of Thomas' previous wives, Enola, which helps her on her way to solving the film's mysteries. We can see that Enola is *literally* the key to unlock these; when she speaks to Edith via the recordings, she warns her successor, giving her vital information that helps her survive.

While in the 1940s Gothics, the portrait is of a beautiful woman whose fate forecasts the heroine's dangerous position, in *Crimson Peak* the painting is of the Sharpe siblings' mother, painted in her old age, and looking evil and foreboding ('She looks . . . quite . . .' 'Horrible? It's an excellent likeness'). Despite its visual difference from the usual painted portrait, however, its significance in the film, endowed through lighting, camera movement, and performance, is the same as usual with this Gothic trope: the painting acts as a warning, telling the audience, as well as Edith, that she, as the current Lady Sharpe, is in peril of repeating the fate of the previous one, of also being killed to cover up the incestuous and murderous schemes of Lucille and Thomas.[6]

With the key, portrait, dwelling, and female voice-over from an innocent young heroine, *Crimson Peak*'s conformity to the checklist of tropes is almost complete. It also complies with the emphasis on the Bluebeard husband too, despite introducing the character of Thomas' sister and having her share his guilty murderous past. While Lucille, as noted above, takes on aspects of both the Other Woman and the eerie Danvers-like housekeeper sometimes found in the genre, her guilt has to be established through actor Jessica Chastain's performance and through her lines in the script rather than through iconography. By contrast, *Crimson Peak* forecasts and underlines that Thomas is a husband in the lineage of Bluebeard visually. The scene where he shows Edith his workshop, where he designs machines and engines such as the one with which he is mining Crimson Peak's eponymous red clay, inevitably sets off echoes of Bluebeard guiding his new bride around their home, even if he does not forbid her access to the space. What does confirm his Bluebeard status, however, is the *mise en scène*, which is cluttered with bizarre objects, tiny 'little trinkets' that he used to carve to amuse his sister, a musical automaton magician, and three female heads, eerily smiling (see Figure 3.1).

FIGURE 3.1 The eerie smiling heads in Thomas's workshop evoke Bluebeard's brides *Crimson Peak* (Guillermo del Toro, 2015)

While these items add an uncanny element to the scene, it also seems important that Edith and Thomas exchange the first long-delayed passionate embrace of their marriage while surrounded by seemingly decapitated women. This underlines the dangerous nature of being involved with a Bluebeard husband, as is emphasised by the way the camera slides away from the couple hungrily kissing to the empty gaze of the heads, who can be seen to stand for Thomas' three earlier, murdered brides.

Crimson Peak assiduously makes use of the template and common elements of the Female Gothic, producing a text that taps into the Bluebeard story just as clearly as it recycles elements of the wartime genre. But the woman-in-jeopardy film does not have to repeat the historic setting of predecessors such as *Dragonwyck* even while it keeps so many of its shared tropes; Bluebeard can be found in a suburban house just as much as an ancestral mansion, as *Before I Go to Sleep* shows.

Before I Go to Sleep

The viewer has to look beyond the contemporary setting and *mise en scène* to see the Gothic in this film. Christine is a middle-aged suburban wife, living in a modern house with her schoolteacher husband, Ben. She herself is no innocent young girl, and theirs is no recent marriage, but a relationship of long standing. There is no ancestral mansion, no eerie housekeeper, no commanding portrait of a female ancestor.

Yet as the film unfolds, the narrative's debt to the woman-in-jeopardy story becomes very clear. A few years ago, Christine was attacked and very badly injured. While her body is now whole and well, her mind is not: she has not only lost all memory of the attack, but her short-term memory is damaged too. Every morning when she awakens, her mind has been wiped clean; her knowledge of her identity and the events that have occurred has been lost. Thus, every day she needs to be reacquainted with the facts of her life: her own identity, her husband, her home.

Luckily for her, her husband Ben is *so* patient and helpful. He has made a dossier of their life together to act as a primer for her, leaves her useful messages on a chalkboard, and has put annotated photographs in the bathroom, where she will see them first thing every day. Unluckily for her, 'Ben' is not actually her husband, but her former lover, Mike: he attacked her when she tried to end their relationship, then collected her from hospital when it became clear she had forgotten everything. The photos are fake, the memories of their wedding day, honeymoon, and holidays are all a lie. 'Ben' is Bluebeard: he shows Christine around her new home every day, because every day it is new.

The viewer coming to the film with expectations of watching a thriller may have suspicions of Ben from the start: after all, as countless detective stories – and, sadly, real life – have taught us, when a wife is threatened or hurt, 'it's usually the husband'. The spectator primed to expect a Gothic text, however, should be able not only to see the clear signs of Ben's guilt from the start, but also realise how the narrative fits with and builds on the woman-in-jeopardy pattern, comprehensively using its tropes while updating them to work in its contemporaneous setting.

While Christine's house, then, is not Old and Dark, but white-clad and modern, it is detached, set off at a distance from other houses among numerous trees that cluster like prison bars around it. Although at first glance designed in line with modern vernacular architecture, the house has an asymmetry to it – none of its angles seem to line up – which seems slightly menacing. It thus proves to be a fitting place for Christine, as Bluebeard's bride, to be incarcerated.

Before I Go to Sleep also reworks other standard Gothic tropes for its contemporary context, including the portrait and the key. Here, the lone oil painting of a relative is proliferated into more mundane-seeming photographs, but Christine still has to learn to read the message in these images, however, like her Gothic sisters before her. When a phone conversation with her old friend Claire leads her first to suspect that 'Ben' is not who she thinks, she finally sees the telltale lines and joins that indicate the photo 'memories' are actually Photoshopped mock-ups. Rather than looking at an ancestor, Christine is looking at her past self, a self who is as remote from her as an ancient relative, due to her almost total lack of memory.

The film exercises similar ingenuity when it updates the trope of the significant key to a modern-day milieu. First, the key is doubled, and then it proves to open mundane and contemporary locks: on a filing cabinet, on the suburban house's garden door. In keeping with the Gothic trope of the locked space representing an area of the mind, as with *Secret Beyond the Door*, however, the keys in *Before I Go to Sleep* also have metaphorical significance. This is made clear in the two scenes where Christine searches for and finds Ben's hidden keys. The first involves her looking for and then locating the filing cabinet key; the second iteration occurs once Christine has realised that 'Ben' is not Ben, but someone masquerading as her husband. She tries to leave the house but finds herself locked in; after searching, she locates the back-door key. But although the two moments initially seem analogous, the earlier forecasting the later, her Bluebeard has manipulated this scenario. The two spaces accessed by keys are *not* analogous: he intends to keep her locked out of one, the cabinet, but not the house: his plan is to lure her outside, where he can then drug her with chloroform and get her in his car.

Both keys, however, are significant as they have the potential to unlock not just spaces, but memories; while Ben wants Christine to remain locked out of the filing cabinet to keep her from seeing real photographs of Claire, and thus remembering her friend, he actually desires her to find the other key and leave the house so he can take her back to the hotel where he assaulted her previously. Her attacker wants Christine to be locked out of those memories that would link her to anyone other than him, in the same way she is locked into a life with him only, in their modern suburban home.

While the original novel of *Before I Go to Sleep* is an enjoyably twisty thriller, it does not have the same allegiance to the Gothic that the film manifests. Many details are added or changed to position the film within the lineage of *Rebecca* et al., from reproducing the main Gothic tropes to incorporating smaller details that can be seen as homages to other films. As noted above, the significant dwelling, bride and Bluebeard characters, and key and portrait tropes are all adapted to the narrative's contemporary context. The film also makes use of Russ' other two repeated archetypes, the Other Woman and the Shadow Male.

The former can be seen both as Claire, Christine's old friend who had a brief affair with the real Ben, and Christine herself. The Other Woman, as both Russ and Kay Mussell (1975) point out, is always connoted above all else as sexual;[7] in having an extramarital affair, the Christine of the past enacted this role and placed herself in jeopardy. The man Christine knows as Ben, who seems so patient and kindly in taking her through her traumatic story every day when she awakens again with no memory, is easily recognised as the Shadow Male. While seeming for much of the film to be in line with the more common film incarnation of this character, kindly, non-threatening Ben is actually much more the villainous version inherited by more recent Gothics from the popular paperbacks (Russ, 1973/1995: 669).

The film also has several moments when it playfully incorporates details from other Gothics, as with the *spiral staircase* prominent inside the house, as well as Ben's different accounts of the attack, with which he is clearly *gaslighting* Christine. There is even a wry smile to be derived in one scene from Ben cooking dinner while listening to the Supremes sing 'Set Me Free', since he is Christine's virtual jailor. However, it is one of the other major tropes, the female voice-over, that the film employs in the most innovative manner. Rather than have Christine narrate her story to us, her audience, which would either require some extensive use of flashbacks or be at odds with her medical condition – she cannot relate her story, as she does not remember it – the film uses as narratorial device the digital camera that her doctor gives her.

Whereas in the source novel Christine writes notes in a journal to try to counteract the effects of her anterograde amnesia, in the film she speaks directly to the digital camera: she can relay her discoveries, then leave herself a note to rewatch the videos after sleep has erased her first-hand memory of events. Christine thus becomes the narrator, but in the videos she is Past Christine telling Current Christine her interpretations. The camera diary-like entries, along with the manipulated photographs, provide concrete material evidence from one day that can carry on into another, unlike Christine's memory: together, they build up a picture that suggests Ben is lying. But trusting to external memory sources, since she has no internal ones, makes Christine even more vulnerable, as these memory-bearing media are vulnerable too. The warnings on the digital camera can be erased, photographs can first be faked and then removed. When Ben finds that Christine has been leaving herself messages, setting up her own account of events that run contrary to his, he deletes them all, just as he removes all the photographs that have told his version of their life together. The house, the camera, are now both blank, like Christine's mind. The Gothic has long associated the woman with her own dwelling place; here, *Before I Go to Sleep* adds to this association the equivalence of Christine with her recording device: since both are now blank, she can be seen *as* the camera. And this conceit proves to have a rewarding conclusion when Ben takes Christine back to the hotel where he assaulted her before and attacks her again: Christine hits out at him with the camera, using it to stun him so she can escape.

While it is possible to watch Christine's story unfold and enjoy it as a thriller, without appreciating its use of Gothic tropes, reading the film in this way does make it more enjoyable. Part of the pleasure to be had from any generic text is seeing how it employs the traditional elements of its genre; while *Crimson Peak*, as a pastiche of old Gothic, can engage directly with the portrait, the Old Dark ancestral House, the Bluebeard male, and a virginal bride who might seem particularly out of place if in a contemporary-set story, *Before I Go to Sleep* and, as I will now discuss, *Ex Machina* bring in the Gothic aspects and iconography they use in more roundabout ways.

Ex Machina

Unlike the other two films, *Ex Machina* eschews both historical and contemporary settings, choosing instead to position its story in a near-future moment. Similarly, unlike the other two, it overtly splits the role of Bluebeard's inexperienced victim between *two* characters. That this is not the only innovation it makes to the standard Female Gothic template becomes apparent by the film's conclusion.

In this retelling of the familiar tale, the shy innocent who comes to live in the huge mansion, there encountering secrets connected with the brooding master of the house, is a young man, Caleb, who works for Nathan, a reclusive technological genius. Caleb wins a competition to spend a week at Nathan's remote mansion/laboratory, and there is introduced to his boss' newest invention, Ava, a robot. In her, Nathan believes he has managed to create a sentient machine, a computer with a soul. Caleb's job will be to test her on this. Over the week, Caleb becomes disturbed by Nathan's arrogance and aggression to both him and especially Ava, falling in love with the beautiful and enigmatic female. She begs him to help her escape and he agrees, believing she reciprocates his feelings, but at the climax of the film all goes wrong for him: Ava kills Nathan, then coolly leaves Caleb and departs forever, leaving the young man fatally locked in the house with no hope of escape.

While the narrative aligns itself strongly with the futuristic through its paraphernalia – a Facebook-like all-pervasive tech company, artificial intelligence, and body parts interchangeable between robots – *Ex Machina* also interestingly incorporates elements of the traditional Gothic template into its sci-fi storyline. In fact, its success as a thriller, pitting itself against the wits of its viewers, is reliant on audience familiarity with Gothic tropes. With awareness of these, the viewer is directed to assume the young, inexperienced heroine's role is played by Ava, the mysterious, experienced, older, brooding man is clearly Nathan – he even has a huge beard, although the film baulks at dyeing it blue – and Caleb can be slotted into the role of the other man from the wartime films, the kindly gentlemanly sort who will help the heroine unravel the mystery.

However, only at the narrative's end do we see that it is actually *Caleb* who is the innocent. This alteration to the usual template tweaks and re-emphasises the importance of the triangular relationship at the heart of the story, with both Nathan, as expected, but also the 'woman', Ava, manipulating Caleb. While he takes on the usual *covert* quest of the heroine to uncover the central mystery – which might be summed up as 'What is going on in this house?' – his investigation is doubled by, folded back on, his *overt* quest to find out if, in Ava, machines have been endowed with consciousness. Unfortunately for him, Caleb does not spend sufficient time on this mystery, but much more willingly attempts to solve the enigma of the Bluebeard male that is the usual mission of the heroine.

Kyoko, the robot designed in the form of a sexualised Asian woman, can be cast as the Other Woman in comparison to the innocent-seeming Ava. The stereotype of the eroticised Asian woman is not new (Green, 2015), and one can imagine Nathan consciously planning Kyoto's looks both to suit his own desires – since, it is implied, he uses her for sex – and to construct a racist dichotomy that further confers purity on Ava. It should be noted that when the latter leaves the house and escapes to the city, she chooses to wear a white dress, which has obvious connotations of virginity.

While *Ex Machina* thus makes use of some of the narrative elements of the standard Gothic, it has no compunction in neglecting others. The film eschews the female voice-over; contrary to Russ' rules, the house has no name, and is hardly Old. Nevertheless, the film does maintain the focus on the importance of the dwelling. Caleb and the viewer with him are familiarised with the house in stages; it has the endless corridors, different levels, and forbidden spaces of the classic locus, containing spaces that dwarf Caleb and make him seem vulnerable in line with *Rebecca*'s Manderley and other Gothic mansions.

Even though the house is made predominantly of glass, and is thoroughly modernist in design, there is no transparency at the level of Nathan's motives, and he is ruthlessly traditional in his exploitation both of his female-appearing robots and the biological imperative that drives Caleb yearning for Ava: we learn that her appearance has been carefully devised in line with Caleb's pornography preferences.

As we saw with *Crimson Peak* and *Before I Go to Sleep*, modern Gothics are aware both that the Bluebeard folk tale is an important point of reference, and that the symbol of the key is one of the tale's most significant visual tropes. *Ex Machina* continues its commitment to a futuristic setting by making its keys electronic, and neatly brings in the portrait trope here too. When Caleb arrives at Nathan's house, he is photographed at the front door and his key is delivered as if from a photo booth, with his face printed on it. This use of the key motif seems at first *playfully* high-tech, but gradually is endowed with more ominous significance.

Ex Machina acknowledges Nathan's Bluebeard nature straight away with his appearance, and very soon on meeting Caleb, Nathan tells him there are some rooms in the house that are 'off limits'. Like the traditional figure, he also turns out to have a secret room stuffed with the bodies of his former 'wives'. Forbidden access to certain spaces within the house, yet trespassing in those spaces, means that Caleb, as well as Ava, is placed by the narrative in the position of *Mrs* Bluebeard.

Having doubled the heroine role, the film finally decides upon making Caleb the victim, when Ava destabilises the traditionally masculine power of the key, taking the dying Nathan's. This not only opens doors in the house, but also controls the computers and elevators. We have seen Nathan's card plugged in to his computer before, and at the end Ava appropriates this to make her escape. Whereas there had usually been a match between Caleb and the face on his key – his face – when he accesses rooms,[8] when Ava leaves the dwelling, abandoning Caleb to his fate, we see her use the key but Nathan's face with its prominent beard appear on the elevator display. The Gothic portrait motif is referenced, and here Ava has clearly learned the symbolism of the trope: rather than allowing herself to be paired with an earlier female victim, she readily aligns herself with the male villain. In this way, *Bluebeard* becomes a role, an identity, that can be adopted by Ava just as much as Nathan.

While, then, *Ex Machina* disregards some of the traditional elements of the Gothic genre, it skilfully co-opts others, merging them with its sci-fi *mise en scène* to create a futuristic telling of the Bluebeard tale, and intriguingly not deeming either the heroine or villain role as inevitably associated with specific genders.

Conclusion

This chapter has worked to illustrate the persistence and currency of Gothic tropes and aesthetic elements in films beyond those of the 1940s. The genre continues to influence both films made in blatant emulation of its older classics and those that co-opt some aspects of the traditional template but set them in contemporary or even future milieux.

While the beginning of this chapter drew analogies between three scenes from these films that evoked Bluebeard showing his new bride around his house, it seems significant that all three also stage a moment that openly conjures the central dramatic event of the story, the bride's discovery of the bloody chamber with its revelation of the fate of her predecessors.

Significantly, each of the films also uses this scene to further its creation of the particular aura of sexualised menace that so marks the products of the Gothic genre. *Crimson Peak*, as noted above, brings Thomas and Edith together for the first passionate kiss of their marriage in his workshop, juxtaposing them with eerie smiling carved heads to emphasise the fate of the previous women who have cared for Thomas, acting as yet another warning to Edith.

Before I Go to Sleep also locates its bloody chamber moment at the junction of sex and violence. After the attack, Christine was found outside a factory, and she revisits the scene with her doctor to see if the location produces any memories. Although all remains blank for her, the viewer can hardly fail to note the significant *mise en scène*. As Dr Nasch and Christine arrive to meet the factory caretaker, a lightning shot of the interior of the Portakabin where he works is shown, complete with a pin-up of a woman both topless and headless. The ominous tone this sets is continued when the factory's product – mannequins – are shown in successive shots (see Figure 3.2). When the trio walk through the factory, the camera records the numerous white plastic bodies, featureless apart from noticeable breasts on the female forms, hanging in rows, wrapped in clear plastic or, again, literally topless, cut off above the groin and legs, being moved by forklift. The staging ground for Christine's discovery after her attack has been carefully chosen; the factory is not in the book, and therefore its invention and its product are important. That it makes bodies – especially ones that are passive, naked, and sexualised – underlines the connection between sex and violence that drives both the Gothic as a genre and explains the attack on Christine, as the narrative goes on to relate.

The bloody chamber revelation scene is returned to again in *Ex Machina*, and again the moment juxtaposes the erotic and the violent. Caleb, looking for clues about Ava, steals Nathan's pass key and looks on his computer; he finds videos of

FIGURE 3.2 More brides: the motiveless shot of mannequins *Before I Go to Sleep* (Rowan Joffé, 2014)

other robots, Jasmine, Lily, and Jade, all being mistreated by their inventor. The viewer sees him enter a room where he finds Kyoko reclining naked opposite a wall of mirrored cupboards. Looking inside, Caleb finds the bodies of Nathan's former 'brides'; Lily is suspended on straps under her armpits as she has no legs or forearms. Nathan has confined his failures to these closets; that they are artificial women does not make their treatment seem any less heinous, or Lily's dismemberment any less shocking.

A wide shot of the room reveals that there are five previous 'wives' literally hanging in the closets in Nathan's room. One is headless, Lily's body finishes with her groin. All but one are naked, and all arranged in the coffin-like closets. With Kyoko as number six, Caleb takes on the role of the seventh bride, the one who, in the traditional story, manages to survive her marriage to Bluebeard. But *Ex Machina* has an eighth bride in Ava . . .

Very noticeably, the last two 'brides' behave very differently when they find their predecessors' bodies. Caleb opens the doors to all the cupboards widely, moving slowly, viewing with pity and horror, whereas Ava just looks into each closet individually, inquisitive but unmoved, almost as if she is browsing in a shop. This is indeed an apt simile, as she soon borrows from her predecessors, taking a forearm and some artificial skin from one robot, hair from another, and the outfit from a third. Her lack of emotion contrasts very strongly here with Caleb's reaction; where his adoption of the wider perspective literally placed him into the same frame as the other victims, Ava's composed study of individual brides denies the possibility of her joining them, and asserts her control over her own destiny.

The narrative template and classic tropes from the Bluebeard story undeniably affected the development of the wartime Female Gothic genre, but, as this chapter has demonstrated, their utility as storyline and symbols did not come to an end with the dawning of a new decade. Instead, the lure of the bloody chamber and its horrific secrets, simultaneously forbidden to the young bride and dangled before her as bait by Bluebeard, remain, with these character archetypes, key elements that can be used in narratives for the present and future.

Notes

1 See, for example, Gustave Doré (1867), Walter Crane (1875), and Arthur Rackham (1933).
2 Doane was one of the first feminist scholars to look at the Gothic, and she adroitly draws out many of the genre's significant points. However, she insists that the films are tied to a specific time frame, and a short one: 'The female gothic narrative is incarnated in cinematic texts in a relatively strictly delineated historical period – from *Rebecca* in 1940 to the late 1940s . . . Gothic narratives do not, however, die out at the end of their very short-lived cinematic career, but are displaced to another medium' (Doane, 1987: 124). While Doane rightly notes that the Gothic text enjoyed a resurgence in mass media popular culture in the 1960s and 1970s in the form of the bestselling paperback Gothic romance (the 'other medium'), I think it is wrong to assert the filmic form of the genre was tied so uniquely to wartime; arguably too, it neither was nor is solely a Hollywood genre, as other chapters in this collection will demonstrate.
3 See Russ (1973/1995), Kay J. Mussell (1975), and Janice Radway (1981).

4 Film noirs such as *Mildred Pierce* (1945) and *Raw Deal* (1948) share the troubling habit of losing the female voice-over with horrors such as *I Walked with a Zombie* (1943) and gothics such as *Rebecca*. See Karen Hollinger (1997).

5 According to Russ (1973/1995), 'To a large, lonely, usually brooding *House* (always named) comes a Heroine . . .' (p. 667).

6 See also my article on the use of the significant picture in the Gothic (Jeffers McDonald, forthcoming).

7 Russ (1973/1995) notes that this character 'is (or was) beautiful, worldly, glamorous, immoral, flirtatious, irresponsible, and openly sexual. She may even have been (especially if she is dead) adulterous, promiscuous, hard-hearted, immoral, criminal or even insane' (p. 668).

8 Caleb too steals Nathan's swipe card at one point, and the latter's face appears in the reader as he enters Nathan's bedroom. Since his motivation here is investigating Nathan's villainy, and especially his mistreatment of Ava, Caleb does not seem to be cast in a bad light by the film for this theft and trespass.

References

Clover, Carol J. (1992) *Men, Women and Chainsaws: Gender in the Modern Horror Film*. London: British Film Institute.

Crane, Walter (1875) *The Blue Beard Picture Book*. London: George Routledge & Sons.

Doane, Mary Ann (1987) *The Desire to Desire: The Woman's Film of the 1940s*. Basingstoke: Macmillan.

Doré, Gustave (1867) 'La *barbe-bleue*'. In *Les Contes de Perrault*. Paris: J. Hetzel.

Green, Amy (2015) '"I'll Give You Television, I'll Give You Eyes of Blue, I'll Give You a Man Who Wants to Rule the World": The Commodification of Women and the Desire for the West in Takashi Miike's *Imprint*'. *Horror Studies*, 6(1): 39–56.

Hollinger, Karen (1997) 'Film Noir, Voice Over, and the Femme Fatale'. In Alain Silver and James Ursini (eds), *Film Noir Reader*. New York: Limelight, pp. 243–260.

Jeffers McDonald, Tamar (forthcoming) 'Portrait of Mrs Bluebeard: The Ancestral Painting in the Woman-in-Jeopardy Gothic Film'.

Mussell, Kay J. (1975) 'Beautiful and Damned: The Sexual Woman in Gothic Fiction'. *Journal of Popular Culture*, 9(1): 84–89.

Rackham, Arthur (1933) 'Blue Beard'. In *The Arthur Rackham Fairy Book: A Book of Old Favourites With New Illustrations*. Philadelphia, PA: J.B. Lippincott.

Radway, Janice (1981) 'The Utopian Impulse in Popular Literature: Gothic Romances and "Feminist" Protest'. *American Quarterly*, 33(2): 140–162.

Russ, Joanna (1973/1995) '"Somebody's Trying to Kill Me – and I Think It's My Husband": The Modern Gothic'. Reprinted in *To Write Like A Woman: Essays in Feminism and Science Fiction*. Bloomington, IN: Indiana University Press, pp. 94–119.

Waldman, Diane (1984) '"At Last I Can Tell It to Someone!" Feminine Point of View and Subjectivity in the Gothic Romance Film of the 1940s'. *Cinema Journal*, 23(2): 29–40.

PART II
Returning to Manderley

4

IMPOSSIBLE SPACES

Gothic special effects and feminine subjectivity

Christina G. Petersen

Accounts of space in the Female Gothic or Gothic woman's film often emphasise the conflation between identity and architecture in which space serves as an extension of the Gothic heroine's paranoia. One of the most familiar visual tropes in the Female Gothic is a long shot of the protagonist dwarfed by a colossal space that engulfs and imprisons her, whether it be the desolate landscape of the castle, the mountainous ancestral manor, or the modern city with its 'dark, labyrinthine streets' (Botting, 1996: 2–3). Despite its spatial and temporal displacements and transformations, though, the Gothic woman's film has remained a thinly veiled modernist commentary on the time of its production, a return of the repressed made literal in the identification of these spaces with gone-but-not-forgotten women of the past haunting the present.

As Mary Ann Doane (1987) has argued, the Gothic woman's film is most often constructed around the trope of a 'woman investigating, penetrating the [Gothic] space alone', finally able to move past a barrier only to confront 'an aspect of herself' on the other side (pp. 135–137).

In this chapter, however, I will trace a different spatial trajectory in which the Female Gothic's use of special effects highlights the Gothic heroine's inability to move past such boundaries through the fantastic impossible spaces created by these films. In the famous opening point-of-view shot in *Rebecca* (1940), the camera holds on a long shot of an ornate, almost overgrown wrought iron gate as Joan Fontaine's nameless protagonist, 'I', intones, 'Last night I dreamt I went to Manderley again. It seemed to me I stood by the iron gate leading to the drive, and for a while I could not enter for the way was barred to me'. In this shot, both the image and sound tracks detail the classic Gothic dilemma in which, according to Eve Sedgwick (1980), a character is 'massively blocked off from something to which it ought normally to have access' (p. 12). Yet there is a shift in registers as 'I' (and the camera) overcomes her initial hesitation and begins to move, tracking slightly to the left and then in towards the gate, as 'I' continues, 'Then, like all dreamers, I was possessed of a sudden with supernatural powers and passed like a spirit through the barrier before me'. In this move, 'I', the camera, and the spectator enter the realm of the fantastic, according to Tzvetan Todorov's definition (Todorov, 1975: 33), and which Diane Waldman (1984) has discussed in relation to the Female Gothic, as a state of hesitation between 'natural and supernatural explanations' of narrative events (p. 31).

In supernatural fashion, yet explained as part of a dream, we apparate through the bars and float down the drive, while the house transitions from a full-size set to a detailed miniature of the Gothic mansion haunted by the memory of Fontaine's predecessor. In addition to visualising the Gothic trope of a character's obstruction from the source of her paranoia, this special effects shot provides the spectator with a commensurate experience of restriction from the image that further emphasises the film's grounding in fantasy. As Todorov (1975) argues, the fantastic is characterised by more than an uncanny event, but also by a reading position marked by distance from the supernatural events and spaces described (pp. 32, 38–39). Indeed, as we warily approach this space along with the camera, the spectator encounters the miniature as an impossible space that can never be entered.

Like other Gothic woman's films, *Rebecca* has been read by scholars such as Doane (1987) and Tania Modleski (1988) as mapping female subjectivity onto profilmic space, collapsing that of character and spectator, and drawing both into the illusory depths of the image. However, taking *Rebecca* and selected 1940s Gothic woman's films, including *Dragonwyck* (1946), *Gaslight* (1944), *The Spiral Staircase* (1946), and *Notorious* (1946), as my primary examples, this chapter will examine the modernist self-conscious, and at times self-reflexive, means by which these films refused depth in their presentation of fantastic impossible spaces by means of special effects. Through an examination of the production and formal construction of these films, I will explore how the use of special visual effects such as miniatures, painted mattes, rear projection, and deep focus cinematography emphasised Gothic heroines' and spectators' inability to move from the foreground to the background of the image. By containing both character and spectator in the claustrophobic flatness of on-screen space, these impossible spatial constructions, like other fantasy spaces, have the potential to make the spectator aware of the unreasonable nature of their situation both in these films and in feminised positions outside of the theatre. In this way, I offer a reading of Hollywood's production of gendered Gothic space through special effects as a correlate to the literary Gothic's trope of the portrait, as a style of subjective representation emphasising surface over depth with the opportunity for emergence. Unlike special effects in science fiction films, which Scott Bukatman (2003) has described as evoking boundlessness, infinity, and transcendence (p. 93), Gothic special effects create an experience of claustration and imprisonment with the possibility for distance and self-awareness.

As a popular cycle launched by the success of Hitchcock's adaptation of Daphne du Maurier's novel, the Gothic woman's film has garnered attention from scholars interested in how the use of space in these films has reinforced, but with possibilities for the disturbance of, the hegemony of the male gaze in classical Hollywood cinema. Doane, in particular, traces the means by which these films render uncanny the domestic space of the home while presenting self-reflexive images of female spectatorship as a means to point up yet ultimately punish the female gaze (Doane, 1987: 135). In Doane's formulation, the Female Gothic protagonist and the Female Gothic spectator are never allowed enough detachment from the image to occupy a position of power. Both within these films and in the theatre, 'what the female viewer lacks is the very distance or gap which separates, must separate the spectator from the image' (Doane, 1987: 153, 169). Modleski (1988) similarly argues for space in *Rebecca* as a means for the female spectator to 'experience a kind of annihilation of the self, of individual identity, through a merger with another woman' through the mediation of a male gaze (p. 49).

Indeed, a comparison between the opening of *Rebecca* and the end of the film would seem to reassert the male gaze as the only source of distance from the image. In contrast to the opening shot, in the film's final sequence, Maxim de Winter (Laurence Olivier) and his faithful retainer, Frank (Reginald Denny), return on the same road to Manderley to find the horizon awash in otherworldly light. Through a series of shot/reverse shots that employ rear projection, miniatures, and mattes, Maxim, Frank, and the spectator gaze in horror at the spectacle of Manderley on fire as Maxim begins searching for 'I' in the chaos (see Figure 4.1). The subsequent shot reveals a high-angle medium shot of a dog, Jasper, held on a leash by a woman only visible in a medium shot of her legs. The camera tracks to follow this duo, ultimately tilting up to examine the woman's body and reveal that it is indeed 'I', who is searching for Maxim as well. We briefly take on her point of view and then 'I' and Maxim are reunited in the foreground of the next shot with Manderley in flames in the background. As opposed to Maxim (and Frank), who are able to approach Manderley from a

FIGURE 4.1   A composite shot of Manderley on fire created through matting in the foreground, top half of the middle ground, and the fire in the background from separate shots
Rebecca (Alfred Hitchcock, 1940)

distance, moving inward into on-screen space, in every shot where 'I' appears, Manderley lurks in the background. Indeed, 'I' is only depicted moving laterally across the frame and only in a close-up during her very brief movement away from Manderley. The mansion, which represents Maxim's titular first wife, always remains just over 'I's shoulder even as she and Maxim passionately embrace, a constant visual reminder of a woman from whom 'I' cannot escape.

However, I would argue that the use of special effects, in particular the combination of the miniature, painted matte, and rear projection to represent Manderley as an unearthly incarnation of Maxim's previous wife, presents the space as not one of depth, but of flatness, which allows for the Female Gothic spectator to achieve a sense of distance from this fantastic space, even if 'I' cannot. While Hitchcock originally planned to shoot the exteriors for *Rebecca* in England, the war intervened, forcing the production to employ two miniatures to stand in for the imposing mansion seen in the opening shot, as well as a miniature of the road leading up the Manderley (Truffaut, 1983: 132; 'Fruition', 2001). In his interview with Hitchcock, François Truffaut observed that the shift reinforced the film's fantasy elements, as the 'use of miniatures resembling old woodcuts idealized the film and further strengthened the fairy-tale quality' (Truffaut, 1983: 132). According to Don Jahrous, head of the miniature department at RKO, the goals of miniatures were paradoxical in the same way that fantasy invites hesitation between the natural and the supernatural. In order to produce a miniature shot to 'perfection', it must aim to be 'completely realistic' and yet 'accomplish certain actions which would be impossible or impractical in actuality' (Jahrous, 1931: 9, 42). In miniature work, 'It is not a question of fooling the public, but one of giving them a better show for their money . . . which simplifies the difficult and makes the impossible possible' (Jahrous, 1931: 42). In this sense, the perfect miniature, such as those of Manderley, which helped to garner the film an Academy Award nomination for Best Special Effects, further encouraged the viewer's hesitation between the real and unreal elements of the text and an appreciation for the image as a representation rather than reproduction of space.

Increasing spectator distance from the image was a primary motivation for employing miniatures. As *Rebecca*'s production manager Raymond Klune reported in relation to the film's use of multiple models:

> you couldn't really get far enough away from [the larger of the two models] to get a full feeling of the scale of the estate itself . . . That's why we needed the smaller size miniature which enabled you to get way back.
>
> *('Fruition', 2001)*

Dev Jennings, who produced miniatures for Paramount during this period, also emphasised the importance of the perception of distance in the use of miniatures. According to Jennings (1934), the 'set-miniature' in particular, in which part of the set is constructed in full scale and part in miniature, created a shot of 'far greater depth than would be otherwise possible' (p. 104). Following *Rebecca*, miniatures in Gothic woman's films continued to underscore both the female protagonist and the female spectator's distance from these fantastic spaces despite any wishes to bridge that divide. Although Hitchcock's hand was forced by circumstance, Joseph Mankiewicz employed a similar miniature in *Dragonwyck* as a means to translate the Gothic trope of the imbrication of inside and outside into a visual experience of the foreboding house on the hill. Like 'I's hesitant approach towards Manderley, we first encounter Dragonwyck in a point-of-view shot that emphasises the initial distance between Gene Tierney's middle-class protagonist and the object of her bourgeois desire, the landed gentry estate.

As opposed to an objective, external space, Susan Stewart (1993) argues that the miniature as a cultural trope, much like the Gothic's mapping of subjectivity onto space, often represents the 'interior space and time of the bourgeois subject' (p. xii). The miniature, as a fantasy structure, transcends modern, shared notions of every-day temporality 'in such a way as to create an interior temporality of the subject' (p. 66). There is a 'theatricality' to the miniature in which it seems to openly present itself for the viewer's gaze, both speeding up and halting time (p. 54). And this is how Dragonwyck is first introduced as a distant spectacle for both Tierney's protagonist and the crowd of steamboat passengers who stop and gawk at the ancestral mansion from afar. The miniature in the Female Gothic thus epitomises the miniature's general function to reduce all senses 'to the visual, a sense which in its transcendence remains ironically and tragically remote' from its object (p. 67). When confronted with a miniature, we are prompted to view and openly marvel at it from a distance, 'with attention focused upon one scene and then another', as George Barnes' camera in the opening of *Rebecca* looks first in one window of Manderley and then the next (p. 63). Just as the use of miniatures was motivated by a wish to create a sense of literal distance for the Gothic woman's film spectator, the spectator's perception of these fantastic spaces as distant from her own situation allows for an opportunity to experience a potentially critical distance from these fairy-tale images of female desire for class rise through marriage.

Similar to the use of miniatures to represent impossible spaces, painted mattes emphasised depth as an illusion in the Gothic woman's film. For example, in the final sequence in *Rebecca*, the effect of Manderley on fire in the far background of the shot was created by photographing the foreground, middle ground, and backgrounds separately. The background fire footage, which peeks through the windows and towers over Manderley without interacting with it, was in fact the first footage shot for the film. On 10 December 1938, while Hitchcock was still working out a treatment for the film, Selznick International Pictures special effects department began production on *Rebecca* when shooting footage for the spectacular burning of Atlanta sequence in *Gone with the Wind* (1939) (Slifer, 1982: 126; Leff, 1987: 43). Working on both films as well as *Intermezzo* (1939) simultaneously, Selznick's special effects department shot background footage for the burnings of Tara and Manderley by torching old Pathé, DeMille, and RKO sets dating to the silent era (Slifer, 1982: 121, 126). Once principal pho-tography on *Rebecca* began, an extreme long shot of the exterior of Manderley was produced with the second storey, sides, and windows matted off to allow for the compositing of a second storey and the background fire footage. The final result is an arresting *trompe l'œil* that emphasises the unreality of the depth cued by the image in this sequence. In this fantasy world, the flames never seem to touch the building and yet destroy it at the same time.

In addition to the use of mattes to create the *trompe l'œil* of Manderley on fire at the end of the film, *Rebecca* and *Dragonwyck* used painted mattes to create the cavernous aristocratic spaces that dwarf their protagonists. These include the front hall of Manderley and that of Dragonwyck, producing fantastic film versions of the Gothic trope of live burial and claustration (Sedgwick, 1980: 9). In both cases, the painted matte transforms the space from its original scale – as large but not oversized – into a gigantic deep space by matting in a cavernous ceiling. In contrast to the miniature, which mirrors the interiority of the bourgeois individual, Stewart (1993) argues that the representation of the gigantic connotes the 'abstract authority of the state and the collective, public life' (p. xii). This is evident in how the vast space of the ancestral mansion achieved through matte paintings appears to enclose the protagonists of *Rebecca* and *Dragonwyck*, who are often depicted hesitating in the foregrounds of these spaces. As Sedgwick (1980) discusses, 'it is in the foreground, or in the difficulty of getting from the foreground to the background, that the compositions [of Gothic images] reveal themselves as prisons' (p. 25). She traces this trope to Giovanni Battista Piranesi's *Carceri d'Invenzione* (*Imaginary Prisons*) series of etchings as highly influential in the Gothic narrative's textual representation of impossible spaces that cannot be mapped onto architecture. Piranesi's 1761 work *The Pier with Chains* depicts a cavernous underground Roman pier marked by a proscenium arch in the foreground and a series of staircases, doorways, and windows interspersed with wooden struts and hanging chains in various states of decrepitude in the middle and background of the frame. Insignificant human figures alternately toil and rest in the space, frozen in time. Rather than a central human figure, a shaded gravestone with two embedded busts commands the centre of the frame. When viewed from a different distance or for a sustained amount of time, though, the gravestone also doubles as a recessed hallway leading into unseen depths. In *The Pier with Chains*, the illusory depth of the image contains the figures, and for Sedgwick (1980) it also cloisters the viewer on the 'hither side of the proscenium' (p. 26). I would argue that the Female Gothic's use of painted mattes to create similar impossible cavernous spaces confines the spectator, like *Pier in Chains*, to our own hither side of the proscenium, keeping us distinct from the screen just as the protagonists are kept separate from the background of the image. And in this, both are made aware of their disenfranchised positions.

In addition to special effects such as miniatures and painted mattes, deep focus cinematography further works to contain the Female Gothic protagonist and spectator to a single plane of the image. Much as in *Citizen Kane* (1941), deep focus in the Gothic woman's film extends the on-screen space for male characters who can move freely from the foreground to the background. However, for the female protagonist, deep focus cinematography exemplifies the Gothic trope of inability to move from the background to the foreground, but with some gestures towards reading these images self-reflexively. In *The Spiral Staircase*, depth of field is exploited to create a separation between the mute protagonist Helen (Dorothy McGuire) in the foreground and two brothers (and possible murderers of disabled women) in the background. As Albert (George Brent) warns his younger brother (Gordon Oliver) away from the family's ancestral home (and his secretary) in the far background, Helen enters the room from the right side of the frame and moves laterally across the middle ground and then into the foreground as she clears the dining table. Like the film's spectator, Helen looks through a Piranesian framing of the two men in conversation, complete with proscenium arch and a space cluttered with furniture, curtains, and a central object (a candelabra in this case) in the centre of the frame, that all compete with the human figures for our attention. When Helen makes too much noise clearing the plates, the two brothers suddenly stop and look at her and a crack of thunder underscores this Gothic moment in which we hesitate as to which of these brothers we should fear. However, just when the composition of the frame would seem to invite the spectator to mirror this male gaze at Helen, she glances fleetingly back at the camera. Here, Helen's look in the spectator's direction suggests an affinity with the film's spectator who is also separate from the illusory depth of the image identified with the male characters.

Gaslight similarly represents the burgeoning mental distress of its female heroine, Paula (Ingrid Bergman), through her confinement to the foreground in deep focus shots. For example, when her murderous husband (Charles Boyer) flirts with Angela Lansbury's working-class maid in the parlour of their London town house (another space haunted by a gone-but-not-forgotten woman), they are depicted interacting in medium long shots in the background of the image. By contrast, Paula is shown isolated from them in a medium shot in the foreground. Here, deep focus translates the growing gap between the newly married couple in spatial terms not unlike the newlywed montage in *Citizen Kane* where the table that separates husband and wife grows longer as they grow apart. However, in the Gothic woman's film, the female protagonist is contained in the foreground and kept separate from the narrative action as another indication of her imprisonment. Later in the film, as Paula begins to believe that she is losing her mind, due to the strange noises effected by her false husband, she bolts from her bedroom, tearing open the door, shouting for the maid, and running into the middle ground marked by a staircase bannister. Just as it would seem that she has reached the background of the image, though, the sequence cuts to a close-up of her face, once again flattening the image to one plane of focus, and then to a vertiginous deep focus shot of her leaning over the bannister looking downstairs at another woman, the maid, who is also entrapped by the image. Like every Gothic heroine, she has tried to escape her fears by moving from the foreground to the background of the image, only to find herself contained in a deep focus shot that reframes her in the foreground. Similar to *The Pier with Chains*, the spectator's sense of illusory depth is reinforced by the inclusion of a staircase in the centre of the frame that doubles as a source of immersion and emergence, a site of entry and a barrier to it that contains another image of femininity. In particular, the middle of the frame presents a *mise en abime* of a painting with a noticeable lack of depth of field that rhymes with the frame-within-the-frame created by the staircase. The suggestion, I would argue, is that spectators are invited to view Gothic deep focus as a faux depth, just like the painting enframed by the staircase banister (see Figure 4.2).

In this way, I am arguing for a modernist approach to the Gothic woman's film in which a critical self-reflexivity about the screen image *as an image* as a result of concerted production practices was a possible reading position available to the spectator. Perhaps the most compelling example of the treatment of Gothic space as self-reflexively impossible in this regard is rear projection. Much like other Hollywood films of this era, the Gothic woman's film employed rear projection ostensibly as a cost-saving device (Rogers, 2016: 71–72), sending the second unit out to shoot exterior footage and back-projecting the footage on the set as a means to create a composite of the location footage with studio footage of the lead actors. We find rear projection employed in all the films already discussed – *Dragonwyck, Gaslight, The Spiral Staircase*, and *Rebecca* – as well as throughout the cycle. In one sense, the use of rear projection in these films would seem to be oppositional to that of deep focus, mattes, and especially miniatures, as rear projection was rarely employed to depict the restrictive space of the uncanny house, but rather for outdoor scenes of relative freedom for the Gothic female protagonist. Yet from the perspective of the spectator, rear projection presents another *mise en abime* of a moving image within another moving image that offers a sense of the filmic space as one in which the foreground and background are separated by the mediation of a screen.

In her essay 'A Clumsy Sublime', Laura Mulvey (2007) discusses how the transitions between location and rear projection footage in all films 'inevitably emphasize the incompatibility between foreground and background, and therefore the artificiality and glaring implausibility of the rear-projection sequences' (p. 3).

FIGURE 4.2 Paula (Ingrid Bergman) finds herself confined to the foreground in this vertiginous, claustrophic *mise en abime* shot
Gaslight (George Cukor, 1944)

In *Gaslight*, for example, the shift from footage from a set of the Tower of London to rear projection footage is particularly glaring as it composites shots from the studio set rather than from an exterior location, likely due to issues in sound recording. For Mulvey, rear projection, like Sedgwick's notion of the Gothic, creates this sense of a 'paradoxical, impossible space, detached from either an approximation to reality or to the verisimilitude of fiction [which] allows the audience to see the dream space of the cinema' (Mulvey, 2007: 3). In Gothic rear projection, as with other Gothic special effects, this sense of spatial impossibility is linked to a sense of the woman's impossible, often nightmarish position in these narratives as caught between her love for a man she hardly knows and her fear that this man will kill her. In *Notorious*, for example, rear projection is continually employed during sequences that reinforce our sense of the female protagonist, Alicia (Ingrid Bergman), as trapped by patriarchal society and the state. Rear projection is employed repeatedly whenever the concerns of the US government, as represented by her love interest Devlin (Cary Grant), overpower Alicia's self-interest. For example, when Alicia and Devlin, who have subsequently fallen in love, discuss her charge by the government to seduce an old acquaintance, Alex (Claude Rains), in order to infiltrate the vestiges of a Nazi cell, she is shown in front of a rear-projected backdrop of the beaches of Rio de Janeiro. Then when Alicia and Devlin meet at the Rio racetrack and she reveals how she has prostituted herself for the American cause, their entire conversation takes place in front of a rear-projected backdrop of racetrack spectators, reinforcing the sense that they are alone amidst the crowd. Finally, after Alex discovers Alicia's deceit and begins secretly poisoning her, she and Devlin meet in a public park where the background is glaringly obvious as rear projection. When Devlin mistakenly reads Alicia's poor complexion as a sign that she has been drinking, the sequence cuts to medium close-ups of Alicia's face as she plays the part of an alcoholic for Devlin just as she has performed for Alex in order to gain access to his household. The blurry rear-projected background again creates the sense that Alicia is trapped both in the foreground of the image and by the image projected on her by these men. Like the miniature, there is a theatricality to rear projection that reinforces the spectator's sense of how shallow these male views of the female protagonist are. And, like the trope of the gigantic, rear projection reinforces a sense of the suppression of the individual by power of the state and other collective entities by surrounding the female protagonist on all sides.

In this way, the repeated use of a special effect such as rear projection becomes more than just a cost-saving device, but a motif that has the potential to comment on the unrealistic nature of filmic representations of gender as an intrinsic binary. This is perhaps most evident in Gothic woman's films' own fascination with scenes of projection, as in *Rebecca* and *The Spiral Staircase*. In the well-known home movie sequence from *Rebecca*, we watch as Fontaine's character literally makes herself into an image for her new husband both through copying a magazine image of femininity and as she is projected on the screen-within-the-screen produced by a travelling matte. The film's spectator watches the footage of Maxim and 'I's honeymoon along with the newlyweds until the film tears and the image disappears from the screen. As Doane (1987) discusses, this sequence highlights 'the position of female spectatorship as an impossible one' (p. 163). Yet the sequence film takes on a more ambiguous gender significance when we consider the motif of the image-within-an-image in relation to other, less overtly self-reflexive moments of projection in the film. For example, when we first meet Maxim, he is shown in a low-angle close-up looking outside the frame. Yet, unlike the point-of-view shot of the miniature in *Dragonwyck, Rebecca* refuses a simple eyeline match in favour of a cut to a composite of a medium shot of the back of Maxim's head superimposed over rear-projected footage of crashing waves. The rear projection in this shot creates a vertiginous effect on character and spectator, highlighting the distance between foreground and background while threatening to collapse the two.

It seems significant that rear projection is employed in this moment when the Female Gothic's male hero is arguably at his most disempowered. Alison McKee (2014) reads in *Rebecca*, particularly the home movie sequence, the possibility to question 'the certainty of the film's entire specular regime, male dominated or otherwise', in favour of a more 'fluid and androgynous' point of view that is 'both masculine and feminine and yet neither/nor' (p. 167). As she argues, the home movie sequence emphasises the projected image as an unstable source of gender identity through another 'impossible' shot (p. 166). After 'I' asks whether they are happy and Maxim states, 'Happiness is something I know nothing about', he turns the projector back on. The home movie ends with a track in towards the happy couple on the screen with both 'I' and Maxim framed on either side of the screen as spectators. The film thus conflates happiness with reaching the background of the image while Maxim paradoxically describes this shot as 'one where I left the camera running on the tripod'. McKee (2014) contends that the spatial irony of this shot – as one that seems to move inward into the image and yet is identified with fixity and stasis – undercuts 'any sense of closure at all, any sense of stability', and endeavours 'to underscore the fictionality of the depicted moment, as well as the foregoing sequence's neat construction of a binarily gendered point of view predicated on difference' (p. 167). In this sense, the depiction of projection as well as the use of rear projection highlights the impossibility of retaining strict boundaries between male and female points of view, as both 'I' and Maxim are depicted as occupying both the foreground and background of the frame simultaneously as subjects and objects of the camera's gaze.

In a similar fashion, *The Spiral Staircase* begins with a representation of projection that reframes the spectator's mode of viewing as we watch an early film along with the protagonist, Helen. The sequence begins with another proscenium arch, now a rectangular doorway obscured by a curtain through which two young boys and the hotel receptionist gaze. As the three male spectators peer through the curtain, the camera tilts upward to reveal a medium close-up of a sign above the entry that reads 'Motion Pictures: The Wonder of the Age' with a Renaissance-style painting hanging directly above. At first, it would seem that the shot suggests an opposition between the static versus the moving image. Yet if we view the succeeding shot — a cut to inside the makeshift theatre with a projector in the foreground, a screen-within-the-screen in the far background in the top third of the frame, and the audience in between — within the tropes of the Gothic, then I would argue that it functions as a precursor to the sequence of rear projection that carries Helen from the makeshift movie theatre to the Gothic mansion where the rest of the film takes place. While the opening painting employs elements of Renaissance perspective, its placement in the frame rhymes with the screen shown in the successive shot (as both are placed above symbols of 'motion pictures' — the projector and the words themselves), and suggests that both are a form of enframed but ultimately two-dimensional, fantastic representation.

It is difficult not to view these images of projection in relation to Sedgwick's discussion of the camera obscura as a symbol of the Gothic's trope of the imbrication of self and Other, inside and outside, that also marks the cinematic situation (Sedgwick, 1980: 44–45). However, as I have discussed, I am more interested to suggest that the use of rear projection along with miniatures, mattes, and deep focus cinematography are part of the 1940s Gothic woman's film's modernist stance. Diane Waldman has argued that the prevalence of the portrait in the cycle, including in *Gaslight, Dragonwyck*, and *Rebecca*, identifies the Gothic woman's film as on the side of illusionist rather than modernist art, particularly through its means of 'rendering space through perspective, and the suggestion of light and texture' (Waldman, 1981: 176). Yet the paintings in *Dragonwyck* and *Gaslight* present largely flat backgrounds while *Rebecca* borrows the trope of the portrait coming alive, as in Horace Walpole's *The Castle of Otranto*, emerging from its frame and approaching the viewer. And this emergence, as Tom Gunning (2007) has discussed in relation to Hitchcock's incorporation of paintings throughout his career, is indicative of the tension that invokes the spectator's awareness of the film image as a representation. Like the Gothic painting, which Helen Hanson (2007: 90) notes has the potential to threaten patriarchal authority, Gothic special effects suggest the uncanny influence of the ghostly image on the reality of the diegesis and call attention to the frame as a distinction between the real and the virtual, spectator and screen.

In conclusion, I would argue that it is this aspect of the Gothic that remains prevalent in contemporary uses of special effects in more recent films such as *Crimson Peak* (2015), *Shutter Island* (2010), and *Inception* (2010). In these later films, special effects are still the most frequent means to create warped, colossal spaces that dwarf their protagonists and make the spectator aware of these images as metaphors for contemporary gender politics. As A.O. Scott (2015) noted about *Crimson Peak*, the film worked 'hard to supply the kind of gothic, romantic, creepy-erotic mood that is not quite the staple of popular culture that it used to be' (p. C8), perhaps because its abject CGI ghosts were all too visible or because the fear of female subjectivity is now just as often aligned with male protagonists. In *Shutter Island*, the claustrophobic setting on an island-bound mental institution offered, as Scott (2010) had also earlier argued, the 'nightmare architecture of a Piranesi prison' (p. C1), similar to *Gaslight*'s *mise en abime* image and produced through the employment of miniatures much like *Rebecca* and *Dragonwyck*.

Yet in this film, a male, rather than female, protagonist, Teddy Daniels (Leonardo DiCaprio), realises that his own mind is the real prison in the wake of his wife's murder of their children. In *Inception*, the labyrinthine urban space created by special effects is revealed as the design of a young woman (Ellen Page) but peopled by the subconscious of the male protagonist (Leonardo DiCaprio again) haunted by his late wife. In both of these films, the aspect that these protagonists must confront is a woman from their past represented in impossible spatial terms through eye-popping special effects. In this way, just as Waldman (1984) notes that the Female Gothic's popularity in its original cycle was to offer a critique of contemporary gender relations, in these later films Gothic special effects now demonstrate that the one who cannot move freely from the foreground to the background is more often than not a male protagonist who is also forced to confront an aspect of himself marked as decidedly feminine. In the contemporary Gothic, then, we find a renewal of the post-Second World War shift towards affirmation of the feminine perspective found in the late 1940s Gothic woman's film, albeit now in a male body. According to Waldman (1984), this shift allowed for the acknowledgement for 'the potential of an alternative or oppositional discourse, perhaps made possible by the exigencies of war-time activities' that prompted women to enter the public sphere in greater numbers (p. 38). I would contend that the continued employment of special effects to depict a feminised point of view as constricted and claustrated but now identified with male protagonists reinforces the Female Gothic's challenge to traditional gender binaries by making the spectator more aware of strict distinctions between surface and depth, male and female, as impossible positions.

References

Botting, Fred (1996) *The Gothic.* New York: Routledge.

Bukatman, Scott (2003) *Matters of Gravity: Special Effects and Supermen in the 20th Century.* Durham, NC: Duke University Press.

Doane, Mary Ann (1987) *The Desire to Desire: The Woman's Film of the 1940s.* Bloomington, IN: Indiana University Press.

'Fruition' (2001) *Rebecca.* Disc 2. [DVD] Criterion Collection.

Gunning, Tom (2007) 'Hitchcock and the Picture in the Frame'. *New England Review,* 28(3): 14–31.

Hanson, Helen (2007) *Hollywood Heroines: Women in Film Noir and the Female Gothic Film.* London: I.B. Tauris.

Jahrous, Dev (1931) 'Making Miniatures'. *American Cinematographer,* November: 9–10, 42.

Jennings, J.D. (1934) 'Photographing Miniatures'. *American Cinematographer,* June. Reprinted in Linwood G. Dunn and George E. Turner (eds) (1983), *The ASC Treasury of Visual Effects.* Los Angeles, CA: American Society of Cinematographers, pp. 103–106.

Leff, Leonard (1987) *Hitchcock and Selznick: The Rich and Strange Collaboration of Alfred Hitchcock and David O. Selznick in Hollywood.* Berkeley, CA: University of California Press.

McKee, Alison (2014) *The Woman's Film of the 1940s: Gender, Narrative, and History.* New York: Routledge.

Modleski, Tania (1988) *The Women Who Knew Too Much: Hitchcock and Feminist Theory*. New York: Routledge.

Mulvey, Laura (2007) 'A Clumsy Sublime'. *Film Quarterly*, 60(3): 3.

Rogers, Ariel (2016) 'Classical Hollywood, 1928–1946: Special/Visual Effects'. In Charlie Keil and Kristen Whissel (eds), *Editing and Special/Visual Effects*. New Brunswick, NJ: Rutgers University Press, pp. 68–77.

Scott, A.O. (2010) 'All at Sea, Surrounded by Red Herrings'. *New York Times*, 18 February: C1.

Scott, A.O. (2015) '"Crimson Peak," a Guillermo del Toro Gothic Romance in High Bloody Style'. *New York Times*, 15 October: C8.

Sedgwick, Eve (1980) *The Coherence of Gothic Conventions*. New York: Methuen.

Slifer, Clarence W.D. (1982) 'Creating Visual Effects for *Gone with the Wind*'. *American Cinematographer*, August. Reprinted in Linwood G. Dunn and George E. Turner (eds) (1983) *The ASC Treasury of Visual Effects*. Los Angeles, CA: American Society of Cinematographers, pp. 121–135.

Stewart, Susan (1993) *On Longing: Narratives of the Miniature, the Gigantic, the Souvenir, the Collection*. Durham, NC: Duke University Press.

Todorov, Tzvetan (1975) *The Fantastic: A Structural Approach to a Literary Genre*, translated by Richard Howard. Ithaca, NY: Cornell University Press.

Truffaut, François, with Helen G. Scott (1983) *Hitchcock* (revised edition). New York: Simon & Schuster.

Waldman, Diane (1981) *Horror and Domesticity: The Modern Gothic Romance Film of the 1940s*. PhD, University of Wisconsin-Madison.

Waldman, Diane (1984) '"At Last I Can Tell It to Someone!" Feminine Point of View and Subjectivity in the Gothic Romance Film of the 1940s'. *Cinema Journal*, 23(2): 29–40.

5

THE CERTIFIED ACCOUNTANT GOTHIC HEROINE

Paranoia and *The Second Woman* (1950)

Guy Barefoot

'Last night I dreamt I went to Manderley again', says the nameless heroine at the start of Daphne du Maurier's *Rebecca* (1938/2003: 1) and the 1940 film version directed by Alfred Hitchcock. Her dream return to the house by the sea into which she moved following her marriage shapes the narrative of both novel and film. In turn, this narrative went on to influence other novels, and what Thomas Elsaesser (1987) has described as 'a whole string of movies often involving hypnosis and playing on the ambiguity and suspense of whether the wife is merely imagining it or whether her husband really does have murderous designs on her' (p. 58). Elsaesser's own brief comments have themselves been repeatedly returned to and modified in other accounts. Different names have been given to that 'string of movies'. Elsaesser (1987) referred to the genre as 'Freudian feminist melodrama' (p. 59). Most accounts identify the films as part of a Gothic, or more specifically Female Gothic, tradition. According to Elsaesser (1987), films such as *Suspicion* (1942), *Experiment Perilous* (1944), *Gaslight* (1944), *Undercurrent* (1936), *Secret Beyond the Door* (1947), and *Sleep My Love* (1948) 'tackled Freudian themes in a particularly "romantic" or "gothic" guise' (p. 58). Elaborating on this, Diane Waldman (1983) discussed the 'Gothic Romance film', while Helen Hanson (2007) has referred to the 'female gothic film cycle of the 1940s' (p. 1). More recently, the number of overlapping terms led Mark Jancovich (2013) to use the composite term 'Gothic (or paranoid) woman's film' (p. 20). The label 'paranoid' comes from Mary Ann Doane (1988), though she also linked what she called 'the paranoid woman's films' to:

> many of the elements of the Gothic novel in its numerous variations from Horace Walpole and Ann Radcliffe to Daphne du Maurier and beyond: the large and forbidding house, mansion or castle; a secret, often related to a

family history, which the heroine must work to disclose; storms incarnating physical torment; portraits; and locked doors.

(p. 124)

There has been some variation in the films discussed in different articles and books. Doane (1988), for instance, includes a number of films not mentioned by Elsaesser: *Jane Eyre* (1944), *Dragonwyck* (1946), *The Spiral Staircase* (1946), *The Two Mrs Carrolls* (1947), and *Caught* (1948) (p. 194). Hanson's (2007) longer list includes films such as *My Name Is Julia Ross* (1945), a B-film variant that retained the house on the Cornish coast but replaced the nameless heroine of *Rebecca* with a woman insisting on retaining her name as she discovers, as usual in the genre, that the man pretending to be her husband has murderous designs on her (p. 47). The over-riding pattern remains clear, however: a repeated return by a Gothic heroine to a Gothic house haunted by another woman.

My own return in this chapter examines another film: *The Second Woman*, directed in 1949 by James V. Kern for Cardinal Films and given a delayed release by United Artists in 1951 (see Brady, 1951). As I will indicate, in some respects, this film (also known as *Ellen*) diverges from the 1940s cycle and how it has been charac-terised. Its release falls just outside the 1940s but also outside the major Hollywood studios, pointing to a shift in American film production. Cardinal was a relatively short-lived company, run by Harry Popkin, who had previously run Million Dollar Productions, specialising in films for African-American audiences (see Cripps, 1977: 329). The best-known Cardinal film is probably *D.O.A* (1950), a film noir about a man investigating his own murder. It is as a film noir that *The Second Woman* has received some attention: Philippa Gates (2014) discusses the film and its heroine as an example of independence unpunished for the female investigator in classic film noir (pp. 28–29). As a film made at the very end of the 1940s, and from a slightly different production context, *The Second Woman* suggests how generic and industrial shifts led to changes in Hollywood's Gothic heroines. However, it is also of interest for the way in which it clearly and consciously draws on, while also revising, the conventions evident in *Rebecca* and the films that immediately fol-lowed that foundational text. It raises particular questions about the notion of the paranoid Gothic heroine. Paranoia is explicitly identified in *The Second Woman* but as a misdiagnosis, and one not linked to the heroine. In this, the film draws not just on *Rebecca*, but on *Gaslight*, and its narrative of manipulating events in an attempt to make a person appear to be deluded or paranoid, 'gaslighting'.

For Doane (1988), the paranoia in these films is revealed through 'the formu-laic repetition of a scenario in which the wife invariably fears that her husband is planning to kill her' (p. 123). The abbreviated courtship typical to the genre means that the heroine is inevitably, as Celia announces in her internal voice-over in *Secret Beyond the Door*, 'marrying a stranger'. In *Rebecca*, Maxim de Winter pro-poses to the naïve and nervous heroine just as Mrs Van Hopper, her employer, is about to take her off to New York. He takes her back to the family home, where she is intimidated both by the house and the housekeeper, and increasingly isolated from her husband. This continues up to the point when the dead body of Rebecca, Maxim's first wife, is recovered from the sea. In telling his second wife about the death of his first wife (an accident in the film, but a murder in the novel), Maxim also tells of Rebecca's adultery, revealing that far from still being in love with her, as his second wife had suspected, his first marriage had always been one of mutual antipathy. The pattern is similar (though not identical) to the one outlined by Joanna Russ (1973) in her discussion of 'Modern Gothic' paperback literature, often advertised as 'in the du Maurier tradition', and identified by ex-editor Terry Carr as appealing to women discovering that their husband is a stranger (pp. 666–667). Russ (1973) describes a repeated pattern in which a shy, orphaned heroine is both attracted and repelled by an older man, unsure 'whether he 1) loves her, 2) hates her, 3) is using her, or 4) is trying to kill her' (pp. 666–667). In these stories, as in *Rebecca*, the heroine is disturbed by the presence of another, apparently more beautiful woman, often the older man's now deceased first wife. Where that is the case, the heroine despairs at the possibility of living up to the widower's memories, until the secret is revealed about 'the Other Woman's ghastly (usually sexual) misbehaviour' or similar activities that identify her lover as victim rather than villain (Russ, 1973: 669).

Central to the setting of these developments, and to their Gothic identity, is a house, as brooding as the older man and also marked with the traces of the other (first) woman. Herein lies the uncanny nature of the Gothic romance film, as the *Heimlich*, the homely and familiar, is made *unheimlich*, strange and uncanny (see Freud, 1919/2003: 132). As Doane (1988) notes, the house is not a homogenous space (p. 134). In a number of these films, it draws on the Bluebeard story, containing a room to which the woman is denied access or warned against. This is highlighted most clearly in *Secret Beyond the Door* but evident in other films: the attic in *Gaslight* is blocked off so that the husband can search for the jewels belonging to the woman he murdered (his wife's aunt), while in *Rebecca* the heroine is warned against, but eventually goes to, the boathouse where Rebecca died.

Staircases, doors, and windows are also part of the Gothic architecture of spectacle and fear. It is on the staircase that the heroine is displayed for the male gaze, while staircases and doors function as a passage (or barrier) to the forbidden and the feared. For Doane (1988), images of women looking through a window or waiting at a window abound both here and in women's films as a whole, and the interface between two sexually differentiated spaces 'becomes a potential point of violence, intrusion, and aggression in the paranoid women's films' (p. 138). Doane goes on to note that the uncanny is brought into play when 'the outside threatens and invades the inside, the boundaries and identity of the house begin to be questioned' (p. 139). The house is uncanny for the woman, not the man, and for the traces of another woman that it bears (p. 140). One of the ways in which the traces of Rebecca are evident in both novel and film is through the portrait displayed above the grand staircase, which the heroine uses as a model for her appearance at the masquerade ball she persuades her husband to hold, thereby inadvertently modelling herself on her predecessor, who wore the same costume at an earlier party. Descending the staircase, 'she is unexpectedly confronted with the look of horror which greets her unintended mimesis of Rebecca . . . The female protagonist's phobia must, therefore, involve a fear of assuming the place of the preceding female (the mother)' (Doane, 1988: 143–144).

Doane's discussion of the woman's film of 1940s Hollywood was a response to questions raised by Laura Mulvey's (1975) 'Visual Pleasure and Narrative Cinema' and what possibilities it left for female spectatorship. Doane's (1988) conclusions were particularly negative in the case of 'the paranoid gothic films' where 'the attempt to attribute the epistemological gaze to the woman results in the greatest degree of violence' and where 'the cinematic apparatus itself is activated against the woman, its aggressivity an aggression of the look and the voice, directed against her' (p. 179). Thus, a scene in *Rebecca* in which the newly married couple watch a film of their honeymoon undercuts the image the heroine has constructed for herself (see Doane, 1988: 163–166). She has dressed up for the occasion, but this is undermined by Maxim's patronising response and the contrasting image of her projected in the film the couple are watching. Here, Maxim is in control of the gaze both in the room in Manderley, in that he controls the lighting and projection, and in the 'home movie', which shows him looking through binoculars. Interruptions to the screening reinforce the heroine's subservience, and at the end of the scene the gaze is directed against her, in a close-up of her distressed face, illuminated by the flickering light of the projector that Maxim has been operating. Again, in the boathouse scene, when Maxim speaks of Rebecca's death, his narrative is laced with 'quotes from Rebecca which parallel on the soundtrack the moving image, itself adhering to the traces of an absent Rebecca' (Doane, 1988: 174). The film thus moves from the heroine's opening voice-over, when the camera assumes her perspective, to a tracking shot that 'guarantees that the story of the woman literally culminates as the image of the man' accompanied by Maxim's vocal appropriation of Rebecca's 'I' (Doane, 1988: 174).

Others have given different readings of the latter scene in particular and the film in general. For Tania Modleski (1988), by not resorting to a flashback to show what happened on the night of Rebecca's death, the film stresses her absence as an active force: 'For those under the sway of Mulvey's analysis of narrative cinema, *Rebecca* may be seen as a spoof of the system, an elaborate sort of castration joke, with its flaunting of absence and lack' (p. 53). Reversing Doane's interpretation in a different way, Hanson (2007) refers to how 'the ventriloquism of Maxim by Rebecca's voice disturbs normative gendered subjectivity because it is a possession not just across the division separating male and female, but also across that separating living from dead' (p. 108). In a discussion of *Secret Beyond the Door*, Michael Walker (1990) argued that Doane committed a basic error in identifying a paranoid cycle of films in which the wife invariably fears that her husband is planning to kill her, pointing out that while this is true of *Suspicion* (as it is of the later Gothic novels discussed by Russ), in other films the wife's refusal to believe any such thing of her husband has a far greater narrative significance: 'the paranoia is located not in the heroine's responses but in the film's structure' (p. 17). At a more general level, John Fletcher (1988) objected that Doane's determinist approach precluded the possibility of critique or reflexivity (p. 9).

The absence of *The Second Woman* from these discussions can be attributed to its minor status, but also perhaps to the many ways it does not fit with the template other scholars have outlined; while in a number of ways it seems consciously to follow these, it also seems to reflect on an already mapped path even as it deviates from it. The film begins with the heroine's voice-over: 'Today I looked upon the cliff where Hilltop stood. I can still see its hanging roofs against the Cyprus trees. But Hilltop is no more'. Here, it clearly echoes *Rebecca* aurally through the voice-over of the heroine, Ellen (Betsy Drake), reflecting back on the now ruined house, while visually the spectator is also given the image of the house, and one that, like Manderley, is situated overlooking the sea. The opening of the film then repeats the familiar narrative of a heroine who meets and is attracted to a man with an uncertain past linked to another, now dead woman. Visiting her aunt Amelia (Florence Bates, playing a variation of the role she had played as Mrs Van Hopper in *Rebecca*) in California, Ellen meets Jeff (Robert Young), an architect whose fiancée died on the eve of their wedding. *The Second Woman* features not just a room, but a whole house, that is forbidden territory: the heroine's aunt is astonished when she hears that Ellen has visited Hilltop, ominously telling her that 'no one's been in Hilltop before . . . except Jeff'. That house then becomes one of the sites of a series of uncanny incidents, including a broken ornament (echoing the china cupid broken by the nervous heroine in *Rebecca*), missing architectural drawings, a painting that fades and then briefly disappears, deadly attacks on Jeff's horse, dog, and rose bushes, and the burning down of his house, as Manderley is burnt down at the end of *Rebecca*. In this way, the film draws overtly on *Rebecca*, but less obviously also makes use of *Gaslight*, the latter in its plot involving one character scheming to make another seem mad by (for instance) removing paintings from the wall.

One key difference between *The Second Woman* and these 1940s filmic predecessors is that Hilltop is a modernist house. Explicit links between Gothic fiction and the modern can be traced as far back as Horace Walpole's (1765/1968) second preface description of *The Castle of Otranto* as 'an attempt to blend two kinds of romance, the ancient and the modern' (p. 43). It is less often linked to modernist architecture, though the modernist building has been used in cinema to accentuate fear (see Heathcote, 2000). However, the modernism presented in *The Second Woman* is different from a film such as *The Black Cat* (1934), where the Bauhaus look is linked to European corruption, and the verdict of the clean-cut American on his architect – and murderer and Satanist – host is, 'If I wanted to build a nice, cosy, unpretentious insane asylum, he'd be the man for it'. In contrast, the California modernism of *The Second Woman* is treated sympathetically, as is the painting within the house, identified as 'by Del Lopez, the Mexican modernist'. As Waldman (1982) has pointed out, other examples of 1940s Hollywood Gothic, such as *Suspicion* and *The Two Mrs Carrolls*, viewed modern art with suspicion and hostility. In *Rebecca*, the response to the news that the heroine likes to sketch is,

'Not this modern stuff I hope'. *The Second Woman*, by contrast, gets as far as a brief defence of abstract art, while the hospital designs submitted by Jeff are praised for their 'good, clean, modern lines'.

There is another instance of this different approach in *The Second Woman* at the moment when Ellen first sees Hilltop. The first sight is emphasised within the film as usual, like the moment when the heroine first views Manderley in *Rebecca*. The response of the two women is different. Waldman's (1991) comment that the Gothic heroine 'may be awestruck and intimidated by her surroundings, unaccustomed to the trappings of luxury and responsibility her new circumstances imply' fits the 1940s films, along with her point that 'a crucial element of the modern Gothic is the heroine's ambivalence towards the house itself' (p. 61). In *The Second Woman*, Ellen is impressed but not intimidated, however. Unease is located elsewhere, in Aunt Amelia's astonishment when she hears that Ellen has been to Hilltop, and in Jeff's worried face, emphasised by the soundtrack and the camera's movement towards him after Ellen asks if he would mind if she took a closer look. Ellen herself walks boldly up and into the house (see Figure 5.1).

Designed by Boris Leven, who had trained as an architect at the University of Southern California, Hilltop has a modernist interior to match its exterior. It is an open space, with no clear division between exterior and interior, with sculptural tree trunks inside as well as out. The windows are not framed, but span the length of the wall and lie open. What we see is an undivided, horizontal L-shaped space. There are steps leading up to the house (which is itself a display, a model home rather than a lived-in space) but not the staircase found in *Rebecca, The Spiral Staircase*, or other examples of Hollywood Gothic. The only concealed space is revealed after the building has been destroyed by fire, when a panel falls down, revealing the sunlamp used to make the colours of the painting fade.

Similarly, *The Second Woman* retains some of the character ambivalence of *Rebecca* but in a different form. Jeff is a modernist architect, but the good, clean, modern lines of his plans contrast with his own 'Irish' superstition and belief in luck

FIGURE 5.1 The Old Dark House becomes the Light Bright Modernist House
The Second Woman (James V. Kern, 1950)

rather than design. When he first meets Ellen, he purports to read her fortune in the leaves of the tea she is drinking. Like his assumed Irish identity, this is an act – Ellen points out the teabag – but his explanation of uncanny events as bad luck initially serves to justify his lack of action in responding to them. In contrast, Ellen is identified with logic, reasoned assessment, and action, distinguishing her from Gothic superstition but also from the fatalism of film noir: she is the opposite of a femme fatale. This is evident not only through how she sees through Jeff's pretence of superstition and insists on looking for an explanation for the uncanny, but in her profession: she works for an insurance company as a certified accountant, more specifically as a risk-assessor. Yet Ellen is both a risk-assessor and a risk-taker. She encourages Jeff to drive fast to prove it was not his driving that led to the death of his fiancée Vivian (Shirley Ballard), and when he says to her, 'You'd better go now, you're not safe', her reply is, 'Suppose I don't want to be safe?'

There is a basic way in which this story lacks the paranoia of the repeated scenario in which the wife fears that her husband is planning to kill her. Ellen and Jeff are not married. This does not disconnect it from the films discussed by Doane, Waldman, and others: *The Spiral Staircase*, for instance, features a central character who dreams of a marriage ceremony but who is herself unmarried. *Jane Eyre*, the 1944 adaptation of the novel that can be seen as another key source of these films, features a heroine who only marries at the very end of narrative. But *The Second Woman* is distinctive in the way in which it is set on the borders of marriage. Jeff's fiancée died on the eve of their wedding, and the film ends with the prospect of his marriage to Ellen. A further couple, Keith and Dodo Ferris (John Sutton and Jean Rogers), are in the process of getting divorced. Like the heroine in *Rebecca*, Ellen misrecognises her partner's behaviour as a sign of lingering love for another woman, but the film avoids the 'I am marrying a stranger' anxieties that trouble films from *Secret Beyond the Door* to *When Strangers Marry* – cited by Hanson (2007: 64) as an example of the Female Gothic but different in its contemporary New York setting. *The Second Woman* also takes a different path in having its heroine confront and address the possibility of danger and madness. She is faced with the idea that Jeff is paranoiac in imagining himself the victim of a series of attacks, and that she is in danger from him. Her response is to assume her professional role of investigator.

The film explicitly addresses paranoia on four occasions. The first occurs in a conversation between the local doctor, Dr Hartley (Morris Carnovsky), and Ellen. Having asked whether her concern with risk percentages includes compiling figures on the likelihood of mental illness, the doctor asks, 'Do you know anything about paranoia?' which he goes on to define as 'delusions of persecution' that can lead to someone imagining that there is a conspiracy against him or her. On this occasion, the doctor is evasive: questioned by Ellen, he denies that he has a specific case in mind. That he does is confirmed the second time he brings up the subject. Visiting the police station as part of her investigation into the death of Jeff's fiancée, Ellen receives a call from the doctor, who explains that his office is just across the street, and asks her to call in. When she does, Dr Hartley tells her that Jeff is 'definitely paranoiac' and that she and her aunt, who are, in the doctor's words, 'two helpless women', are at risk from him. The point about paranoia, though also the doctor's obsession with it, is accentuated in the shot of the doctor speaking on the phone to Ellen, which begins with a close-up of a notebook, on which he is writing 'paranoia', again and again (see Figure 5.2).

The third direct reference follows back at Amelia's house, after Dr Hartley's warnings have been given seeming weight when an unidentified driver seems to try to run over Ellen. Interestingly, this incident is never properly explained; since this is the only occasion in which Ellen is placed in physical danger, it presumably serves as a shift towards the woman-in-jeopardy narrative. Speaking to Jeff when he returns to Amelia's house in a car similar to the one that almost killed her, Ellen, standing authoritatively above Jeff on the staircase, tells him that the doctor thinks he might be paranoiac. 'You don't think so, do you?' asks the perturbed Jeff, but he is relieved at her, 'No, I don't think so' answer. Thus, paranoia is introduced in an attempt to drive the couple apart, but this attempt has the opposite effect. The events that follow confirm Ellen's belief: there *is* a conspiracy against Jeff. In *Sleep My Love*, the villainous husband employs a phony, bespectacled psychiatrist as part of the plot to push his wife into insanity. The bespectacled Dr Hartley bears some resemblance to this character, but here, however, it is ultimately revealed that the doctor is not in on the plot, which is revealed to be a vendetta by Ben Sheppard (Henry O'Neill), Vivian's father, a man emotionally wounded when his wife left him and later mistakenly convinced that Jeff had been responsible for his daughter's death.

The fourth direct reference to paranoia comes in Jeff's climatic confrontation with Ben. The conversation's initial surface geniality shifts when Ben's proposal that the two of them go away on a trip is met by Jeff's suggestion that this might provide Ben with an opportunity for murder. Ben's 'You're crazy, Jeff, you're

FIGURE 5.2 The doctor's jottings reveal his somewhat overdetermined diagnosis of paranoia
The Second Woman (James V. Kern, 1950)

talking like a paranoiac' is followed by Jeff's, 'Where did you get that word, Ben? Did you read it in a book, complete with all the symptoms?' When Jeff goes on to elaborate further on Ben's plot, the latter tells him that he is beginning to think that the doctor is right – he does have delusions of persecution. Jeff is insistent on the correct vocabulary, answering, 'Paranoia, Ben, you learnt the word, use it'.

In the film's final scene, we find Ellen, Jeff, Amelia, and Dr Hartley together; the latter announces, 'Ben was the psychopath, of course, from the beginning. . . . Now he's had what the psychiatrists call a catharsis. He's brought his troubles out into the open . . . He'll be alright now, in time'. Thus, the paranoia-obsessed doctor, last seen doing his best to drive Ellen and Jeff apart, reassures the now happy couple that the psychopath who wanted to ruin and even murder Jeff, and perhaps Ellen, is on the road to recovery. This statement can only be understood in terms of Hollywood's need for closure and the film's specific emphasis on reason, restoration, openness, and cure. Gothic narratives are often anti-Gothic, pitting the rational against the irrational, light against dark. This is accentuated in *The Second Woman* through the film's particular emphasis on the modern (Hilltop), logic (risk assessment), catharsis, and medical science (the prospective hospital and prospective cure). Furthermore, the film's ideology of enlightenment stretches to the social structure. Ben is presented as a feudal figure, owning much of the local land, with, as Jeff puts it at the end, ranch-hands who think he is a king, and who do his bidding irrespective of legality. His hospitalisation can presumably provide the opportunity for a more democratic regime.

As with *Rebecca*, to some extent the ending of *The Second Woman* also shifts the blame back onto a female character, alongside her Lothario lover (Keith). As Gates (2014) noted, Ellen in *The Second Woman* is remarkable as an active heroine who remains unpunished (p. 28). Lacking the initial timidity of the second Mrs de Winter in *Rebecca* and the victimhood of Lina in *Suspicion*, she is more investigator than woman in jeopardy. But as the second woman, she is contrasted with the first. The death of Vivian in a car crash, occurring when she is escaping with the man with whom she had been having an affair, is ultimately explained by her own recklessness and unfaithfulness, or alternatively, in the words of her father, because of her own bad blood, inherited from her mother, who also deserted him. Vivian's visualised presence in the flashback, famously absent in *Rebecca*, means that she is not given the power possessed by the first Mrs de Winter as an unseen but seemingly omnipresent figure in the film that bears her name. Tamed by visual representation, Vivian's words are never heard.

The open-plan modernism of the house in *The Second Woman* also presents the film with a problem. As a Gothic romance, the film needs an uncanny house, but this is at odds with the way it presents Hilltop, as open, lacking enclosures, and also, in contrast to Manderley, with none of the signs of the other woman, except perhaps a painting that troubles the hero rather than the heroine. One solution to this was to make use of the film's second house. To give a longer version of Ellen's opening voice-over, the film begins:

Today I looked upon the cliff where Hilltop stood. I can still see its hanging roofs against the Cyprus trees. But Hilltop is no more. There is only a scar of jutting rock where once its windows glittered in the California sun. My aunt Amelia's house still stands next door. I was a welcome guest within its walls, but to me it will always be a house of fear.

The images that accompany the first part of this are of Hilltop, first as it was, then in its ruined state, but in both instances in daylight, in line with the reference to the California sun. Amelia's older and more obviously Gothic house is initially shown at night, and the reference to 'a house of fear' seems to identify it as the Old Dark House we expect in a Gothic narrative. One section of the film utilises the windows, stairs, doors, and rooms of Amelia's house as a Gothic space in a manner close to Doane's description. A night-time sequence begins with Ellen peering out of her bedroom window, attempting to work out what Jeff is doing outside, going downstairs and outside to investigate further, then returning to her room, followed by Jeff, his shadow cast ominously along the hall. He climbs the stairs, stands outside the door of Ellen's room, and takes out a gun. Ellen starts up as he enters her room, but only to greet him. He gives her the gun, telling her not to be afraid to use it if necessary. Here, the need to present Jeff as a potential threat, only to immediately neutralise that, utilises relatively traditional Gothic architecture.

The modernist house had potential as a house of fear, but this was exploited in the posters for the film rather than in *The Second Woman* itself. A *Film Bulletin* trade press advertisement (Anon., 1951a: 25) shows Jeff embracing Ellen, but behind them his modernist, clifftop house looms in front of a stormy sky, its windows lit in a manner that was to be used for the later Gothic paperbacks, next to one of the tree trunks, here made gnarled and sinister. Similar images were used in posters alongside the words, 'That night Ellen went to the strange dark house on the cliff', and, most strikingly, in Danish posters next to the title, *Frygtens Hus* ('The House of Fear') (see Cinemeterial, n.d.).

The movement between the light and dark Hilltop, and between Hilltop and Amelia's house as the house of fear, causes narrative problems. The burning of Manderley at the end of *Rebecca* is a sign of its importance: it is present from the very beginning of the film until the close, suggesting that the narrative can only end when the house has been destroyed. Hilltop is less central to *The Second Woman*, and is burnt down mid-film. But this is also one of the ways in which the film seems to be quite consciously playing with the conventions. It returns to the house by the sea, which in *Rebecca* is owned by the husband and haunted by his first wife, replacing the Old World Cornish mansion of the earlier film with California modernism. It also replaced the nameless, dreaming and childlike heroine of *Rebecca* with an accountant, whose name served as the title in some locations. It was recognised at the time as a variation on *Rebecca*. The *Los Angeles Times* review referred to the *Rebecca*-like mood, sustained with unexpected finesse by the director, James V. Kern (Scheuer, 1951). In *Time*, it was claimed that 'most of its twists come straight out of Alfred Hitchcock's *Rebecca* and *Spellbound*' (Anon., 1951b). It was in fact the later film that was particularly highlighted in publicity for the film. The tag line in the *Film Bulletin* advertisement was, 'Not since *Spellbound* . . . a picture like this'. The *Spellbound* connection may not have been only on account of suspense. It is the Hitchcock film with the most direct reference to psychoanalysis, made at a time when American media in general had latched on to the public's fascination with psychoanalysis and psychology in general (see, for instance, Walker, 1987: 201). The reference points in *The Second Woman* are psychiatric rather than psychoanalytical, but also belong to this media trend within post-war American culture. One of the film's complexities is the ambivalent role the psychiatric discourse plays. The ending emphasises support and cure to the extent that the man who has been orchestrating the plot against the hero is treated similarly to the hospital-designing hero. When Ben's insanity causes him to mistake Ellen for Vivian, the daughter who he now sees as having the same bad blood as her unfaithful mother, he fires his gun at her. Jeff is injured protecting Ellen, but in the final scene Dr Hartley announces that Jeff will be as good as new in a week. Similarly, the doctor asserts that formerly murderous Ben will 'be alright now. In time'.

Paranoia is clearly important to *The Second Woman*, but in a particular way. It is associated with the man rather than the woman. This Gothic heroine is presented as thoroughly level-headed, only moving away from the sensible in her calculated quest for excitement. The attempt to create paranoia becomes part of the conspiracy against Jeff, in line with the gaslighting narrative that became an element of Hollywood's Gothic romance films of the 1940s. However, in attributing the misdiagnosis of paranoia to a figure ultimately presented as reassuring, and insisting on the textbook origins of the concept, the film edges towards a critique of this particular medical discourse.

Does this mean that paranoia is located in the narrative itself? In *The Second Woman*, the heroine goes to a place in California that is essentially feudal, ruled by Ben Sheppard, an apparently genial patriarch who actually nurses an extraordinary animosity to his estranged wife and the man who he mistakenly holds responsible for his daughter's death. Ben conducts an elaborate vendetta against this one-time prospective son-in-law, a bitter crusade that includes sending servants to maim his horse, poison his dog and roses, steal into his house to break his ornaments, and place a sunlamp – presumably at regular intervals – in front of his prized painting so that its colours fade. He also has the house burnt down and appears to be responsible for an attempt on the heroine's life. Ben undermines the career of the architect he is apparently supporting by ensuring that his architectural drawings disappear. He also, with apparent ease, persuades the local doctor that his victim is paranoiac. When the truth about Ben's unfaithful daughter is revealed, the patriarch turns his mental animosity onto her, while his physical actions are directed against the innocent romantic couple. In the light of this, the doctor's closing comments that the man behind these elaborate machinations has now brought his problems out into the open can offer little more reassurance than the same doctor's earlier paranoia obsession.

This form of textual paranoia might be identified more generally in the Gothic romance films that Hollywood had made over the previous decade. *Gaslight* in particular has at its centre a woman who resists the idea that her husband is a criminal with malevolent intent towards her until she is forced to acknowledge this at the end of the film. Thus, the film depicts a world in which, to quote Doane (1988), 'the institution of marriage is haunted by murder' (p. 123), though here the murder of the heroine's aunt that takes place before the story begins is followed by a wider scheme of criminality and deception, and suspense is created through the heroine's denial of her own danger, as well as by greater focus on the architectural divisions of the Gothic house.

In *The Second Woman*, Old World malevolent design is offset by modern design and calculated risk assessment. This is in line with Gothic narratives, which repeatedly work through binary oppositions: old/new, dark/light, supernatural/natural. It is also in line with the way in which Hollywood replaces and reorganises the metaphoric furniture within its films. *The Second Woman* adjusts the generic formula in a knowing manner, contrasting the old house with one that is new. At least until the latter part of the film, it identifies resistance and inaction with the hero. It replaces the heroine who resists understanding the dangers that surround her, with one who is a risk-assessor, risk-taker, and explanation-seeker. These changes lead to tensions within the film, but they also indicate complications to the 'paranoid woman's film' label.

References

Anon. (1951a) 'Advertisement for *The Second Woman*'. *Film Bulletin*, 26 March: 25.

Anon. (1951b) 'Cinema: The New Pictures'. *Time*, 19 February. *The Second Woman* clipping file, BFI Reuben Library.

Brady, Thomas F. (1951) 'Popkin Plans Suit to Protect Movie'. *New York Times*, 17 January: 39.

Cinematerial (n.d.) *The Second Woman Danish Movie Poster*. www.cinematerial.com/movies/the-second-woman-i44013/p/nrewoes2 [Accessed 12 February 2019]

Cripps, Thomas (1977) *Slow Fade to Black: The Negro in American Film, 1900–1942*. Oxford: Oxford University Press.

Doane, Mary Ann (1988) *The Desire to Desire: The Woman's Film of the 1940s*. Basingstoke: Macmillan.

du Maurier, Daphne (1938/2003) *Rebecca*. London: Virago.

Elsaesser, Thomas (1987) 'Tales of Sound and Fury: Observations on the Family Melodrama'. In Christine Gledhill (ed.), *Home Is Where the Heart Is: Studies in Melodrama and the Woman's Film*. London: British Film Institute, pp. 43–69.

Fletcher, John (1988) 'Melodrama: An Introduction'. *Screen*, 29(3): 2–12.

Freud, Sigmund (1919/2003) 'The Uncanny'. In *The Uncanny*, translated by David McLintock. London: Penguin, pp. 121–162.

Gates, Philippa (2014) 'Independence Unpunished: The Female Detective in Classic Film Noir'. In Robert Miklitsch (ed.), *Kiss the Blood off My Hands: On Classic Film Noir*. Urbana, IL: University of Illinois Press, pp. 17–36.

Hanson, Helen (2007) *Hollywood Heroines: Women in Film Noir and the Female Gothic*. London: I.B. Tauris.

Heathcote, Edwin (2000) 'Modernism as Enemy: Film and the Portrayal of Modern Architecture'. *Architectural Design*, 70(1): 20–25.

Jancovich, Mark (2013) 'Bluebeard's Wives: Horror, Quality and the Gothic (or Paranoid) Woman's Film in the 1940s'. *Irish Journal of Gothic and Horror Stories*, 12: 20–43.

Modleski, Tania (1988) *The Women Who Knew Too Much: Hitchcock and Feminist Film Theory*. New York: Routledge.

Mulvey, Laura (1975) 'Visual Pleasure and Narrative Cinema'. *Screen*, 16(3): 6–18.

Russ, Joanna (1973) '"Somebody's Trying to Kill Me and I Think It's My Husband": The Modern Gothic'. *Journal of Popular Culture*, 6(4): 666–691.

Scheuer, Philip K. (1951) '*Second Woman* Absorbing Mystery'. *Los Angeles Times*, 3 May: A9.

Waldman, Diane (1982) 'The Childish, the Insane and the Ugly: The Representation of Modern Art in Popular Films and Fiction of the Forties'. *Wide Angle*, 5(2): 52–65.

Waldman, Diane (1983) '"At Last I Can Tell It to Someone!" Feminine Point of View and Subjectivity in the Gothic Romance Film of the 1940s'. *Cinema Journal*, 23(2): 29–39.

Waldman, Diane (1991) 'Architectural Metaphor in the Gothic Romance Film'. *Iris*, 12: 55–69.

Walker, Janet (1987) 'Hollywood, Freud and the Representation of Women: Regulation and Contradiction, 1945–early 60s'. In Christine Gledhill (ed.), *Home Is Where the Heart Is: Studies in Melodrama and the Woman's Film*. London: British Film Institute, pp. 197–214.

Walker, Michael (1990) '*Secret Beyond the Door* (1947)'. *Movie*, 34/35: 31–47.

Walpole, Horace (1765/1968) 'Preface to the Second Edition'. *The Castle of Otranto*. In *Three Gothic Novels*, ed. Peter Fairclough. Harmondsworth: Penguin, pp. 43–48.

6

'BUT IT'S HAPPENING TO YOU, ELEANOR'

The Haunting as a 'Buildingsroman'

Johanna M. Wagner

The female protagonist of Hitchcock's 1940 *Rebecca* set the standard for cinematic Gothic protagonists to come. As is well known, the nameless leading role holds characteristics and undergoes experiences that came to identify this cinematic protagonist against those of other genres. Diane Waldman's 1984 summary of the 1940s Gothic protagonist and her plot line (cited by Jeffers McDonald in this volume) succinctly illuminates the experiences of the second Mrs de Winter of *Rebecca*. This character, in film, however, did not stay stock long. The Gothic protagonist would soon complicate the 1940s formula while preserving some of its general resonance. One such protagonist who exemplifies this complication, who mingles with the echoes of the conventional yet forges a new path, is Eleanor Lance, the principal character of Robert Wise's 1963 *The Haunting*. This 1960s film creates a significant expansion in depth of character and development compared to the archetype that preceded her, while it also extends the usual periodicity of the genre.

By way of introduction, this chapter will briefly explore in what ways Eleanor Lance reminds us of an earlier protagonist, intersecting interestingly with the standard set by Hitchcock's archetypal nameless protagonist, while simultaneously moving away from, complicating, and deepening the tradition. After investigating her character type and personality, the chapter will explore the ways in which Eleanor's character develops much more strongly than her precursors. Her age and single status, as well as her ability to analyse her situation and speak out, illustrate her difference early on, but it is her desire for and need of some experience, and especially some 'place', that drives Eleanor's quest. The development of self, for Eleanor, seems to be only understood in conjunction with two things: having been a part of an experience, and having belonged somewhere through rightful permanent residence.

This chapter, then, suggests that *The Haunting* is a *Bildungsroman*, a story of development. But to go further, it is not simply a *Bildungsroman*, but also a

'*Buildingsroman*', a story of development in which a specific architectural design plays a primary role. It suggests that the homeless Eleanor Lance's principal emotional entanglement is not with any other character, but is an uncanny affiliation with the domicile in which she is situated. Wise's directorial decisions regarding the use of voice-over, sound, and point of view expressly present a protagonist whose internal and external discourse – with self and house – deepens her character and strengthens her own identity.

The mature naïf

With her worldly inexperience and naïvety, Eleanor Lance carries remnants of the conventional cinematic Gothic protagonist, but with her maturity in age she initiates a new kind of protagonist, a hybrid protagonist who is both vulnerable and resilient. Corresponding to the conventional protagonist, Eleanor is somewhat naïve, and infantilised by others (her sister, brother-in-law, her new friends at Hill House), but she is certainly not the typical youth; indeed, she is just four years shy of 36, the age Maxim de Winter deems unacceptable for the protagonist in *Rebecca*. She is a 'spinster' protagonist, or what Patricia White (1999) calls in her book *Uninvited* a 'maiden aunt' (p. 82). She is a single, mature woman who, from the beginning, carries herself in an adult manner. For example, unlike the conventional heroine exemplified by the nameless Mrs de Winter in *Rebecca* who physically shrinks in the car, mouth agape childishly, at her first sight of Manderley, Eleanor evinces a quizzical thoughtfulness rather than fear and intimidation when seeing her new residence. As the soundtrack by Humphrey Searle peals with a chillingly persistent staccato, the medium shot cuts to Eleanor in extreme close-up in the cab of her car; beneath a crashing, dissonant brass, she glimpses Hill House and slams on her brakes. The brass gives way to gentler though ominous woodwinds, eerily narrating a point-of-view shot that unhurriedly scans the height and length of the house under Eleanor's cool scrutiny. It is true that upon completion of her examination, an inner voice immediately warns her of the house's unspoken perils: 'Vile. Vile. Get away from here. Get away at once!' Nevertheless, she enters the space unreluctantly and of her own accord. Like her conventional counterparts, Eleanor has limited choices for physical shelter, but her more mature character exhibits an already expanding and deepening of the Gothic protagonist from the start. It is Eleanor who covertly takes the co-owned car from its garage. It is Eleanor who follows the directions from US 50 in Boston to Route 238. It is Eleanor who imagines, with hopeful anticipation, the possibilities Hill House may afford. Things are not simply done to Eleanor: she is an active protagonist, a doer in her own right.

Eleanor is also a more voluble protagonist than the conventional Gothic heroine. While the second Mrs de Winter seems almost incapable of speech at Manderley, especially in the presence of the menacing Mrs Danvers, Eleanor shouts at an unknown entity to 'Go away!' and 'You can't get in!' during the famous bedroom scene she shares with Theo. She yells, 'Stop it!' when she seems to overhear nefarious forces hurting a child, curses to hell an imagined Hugh Crain in the library, roars at Theo's subtle teasing: 'You're a monster, Theo! You're the monster of Hill House!' and at her treachery: 'How dare you! How dare you!'

Another important characteristic of Eleanor that sets her off from the convention is her unmarried status. She is *not* coming to the house as a bride or bride-to-be; neither is she actively looking for romance. The audience is given access to Eleanor's thoughts via voice-over during her drive to Hill House; the most significant subject she returns to is the idea of 'place': she is thrilled she is going 'someplace' where she is 'expected', that will give her 'shelter'; she fantasises about 'someday' having an 'apartment of [her] own', in a 'house'; any place seems to do; she might 'stop anywhere' and 'never leave again'.

Notably, this technique draws Eleanor's singularity even more to the fore, while paradoxically also multiplying it. This internal discourse, a constant throughout the film, allows the audience its first insight of her depth as a character, for Eleanor's deepest questions are discussed with *herself*. This technique has fed into the criticism that assumes Eleanor's mental instability. Most critics accept the fact that Eleanor's psychological state is, at best, precarious (see Schneider, 2002: 172; Keenan, 2007: 120, 126; Blake and Bailey, 2013: 31). I prefer a more open possibility. Like Patricia White (1999), who allows that Eleanor's mind 'may or may not be unhinged' (p. 78), I suggest Eleanor's precarity is not born of madness, but indicates a fragmented self, seeking to be united. Curiously, the voice-overs sometimes reveal two distinct voices with differing perspectives, but always with identical objectives: to *experience* and to *belong*. Both will be discussed in full presently.

To *Bildung* through the building

Bildung, in this chapter, will act as an overarching motivation of Eleanor's movements. Her objectives in the film are to experience and to have a place. These two ambitions fit well into the general aspects of the *Bildungsroman* tradition. While the *Bildungsroman* genre in literature comes out of a strict German tradition in which the protagonist was only young, male, and wealthy (McCarthy, 2008: 41), contemporary critical work in film and literature demonstrates the genre's propensity for expansion. As noted by Hardcastle et al. (2009) in *Coming of Age on Film*,

> Scholars of German literature such as [Jeffrey] Sammons and James Hardin . . . complain of the widespread misuse of the term by scholars who apply it to other national and literary contexts. Nevertheless, the word has come to be an accepted term to refer to the novel of formation.
>
> *(p. 11)*

According to Jeffrey L. Sammons, *Bildung* denotes 'the early bourgeois humanistic concept of the shaping of the individual self from its innate potentialities through acculturation and social experience to the threshold of maturity' (quoted in Hardcastle et al., 2009: 3). Margaret McCarthy (2008) agrees: in its most general form, *Bildung* is 'a process of cultivating inner talents and becoming integrated within a larger community' (p. 41).

In cinema, the coming of age film is the *Bildungsroman*'s parallel. Generally speaking, it is often seen as a film of adolescence or 'transition from childhood to adulthood' (Hardcastle et al., 2009: 1), but as with *Bildung*, at its most inclusive, 'coming of age designates the discovery implicit in any transformation' (Hardcastle et al., 2009: 1). With these more amenable genres, strict adherence to the original formula is no longer fixed. This inclusivity is how we can then discuss a protagonist such as Eleanor Lance – an adult, single woman who has already had adult experiences, albeit narrow and limited ones – in the vocabulary of the coming of age film or *Bildung*.

Gothic stories in themselves are often stories of interior development or transformation. As Carol M. Davison (2004), in her article 'Haunted House/Haunted Heroine', notes, the literary gothic protagonists' 'exploration' of their surroundings and 'confrontation with mysteries' tends to end in an 'ultimate unravelling [that] signifies a process of self-discovery' (p. 51). These narratives, she continues, 'conclude with a more mature, sensible heroine whose marital expectations have been rendered more realistic' (p. 51). Discounting the 'marital expectations' that are non-existent in *The Haunting*, one can certainly assume something has *happened* to the protagonist. What is more, one can assume that this happening has transformed her, matured her, in distinct ways. This chapter argues, however, that the impetus driving Eleanor's development in this *Bildung* is not 'society', but rather Hill House itself. In other words, this *Bildungsroman* is got to by way of an architectural structure. In substituting *Bildung* with *Building*, I highlight how Hill House, the edifice, primarily facilitates the transformation of Eleanor's character.

A fragmented subject: voice-over

To plot Eleanor's development and transformation, one must pay close attention to key technical features of the film. Voice-over in *The Haunting* is the single most important technical feature permitting the audience insight into Eleanor's character. Once Eleanor surreptitiously removes the car from its garage, beginning her literal and figurative journey – towards Hill House and personal development, respectively – we begin to glean her complexity. Taking the car in the first place is an uncharacteristic move, one that demonstrates a considerable sense of will. Eleanor suggests this herself in voice-over: 'They would never have suspected it of me. I would never have expected it of myself. I'm a new person'. Within four minutes of the suggestion that she is 'new', her voice-over fragments into two, and this bivocal voice-over – an internal *dialogue* rather than monologue – then endures persistently throughout the film.

Its earliest appearance is in Eleanor's first visual appraisal of the house, exhibiting literally two minds about the building and her relation to it. The first voice is a defensive one, cautious and protective of Eleanor. It finds the house alarming, as noted earlier: 'Get away from here. Get away at once . . . Anyone has the right to run away'. But the second voice, a startling second-person point of view, is a reflective one that tends to scrutinise the assumptions of the first: 'But you *are* running away Eleanor. And there's nowhere else to go'. This voice, which I will refer to as Eleanor's minor voice, the other being her major voice, addresses Eleanor by name and refers to her as 'you', definitively separating the two voices.

Like notes in a musical scale, these two voices, major and minor, have diverse reactions to the action of the plot, and seem at times divergent as well in tone and timbre. When Eleanor's major voice is startled by her own mirror image, her minor voice tells her to 'Pull yourself together!' and later when her major voice stifles a whimper because she feels small, insignificant in the house, her minor voice tells her, 'Now Eleanor Lance you just stop it!' When Eleanor explains to herself her rationale for locking her bedroom door, her minor voice asks, 'Against what, Eleanor? Against what?' In music, major and minor keys can work complementarily, but they can also be radically opposed to each other's objective. Eleanor's bivocal voice-overs seem to do much the same. They underscore each other at times, but can also undercut each other's perspective. However they work together, though, by merely being plural they expand and strengthen her inner struggles, deepening Eleanor's character. It is through Eleanor's bivocality that we understand her fragmented state at the start of her journey or *Bildung*, but she is intensely clear about how best to become whole. Indeed, it is through voice-over that we understand her two goals: to experience some*thing* and to belong some*place*.

Point-of-view fusion: anthropomorphism

Hill House's influence on Eleanor's development is directly related to the animation of the house and the subsequent bond established between it and the protagonist. In his early review of the film, Normand Lareau (1963–1964) suggests Hill House is a 'living, breathing monster' (p. 44). Echoing this sentiment, Pamela Keesey (2002) calls it a 'living, breathing entity', and Ashley Starling (2014) calls it a 'sentient' house (p. 68). Whatever it is, Hill House is fundamentally aware, and Wise informs us of this through his painstaking personification of the house as both anthropomorphic and possessing an uncanny affiliation with Eleanor. Because of its anthropomorphic qualities, the house's relationship to Eleanor becomes much more interpersonal than most characters' relationships with supposed inanimate objects. In fact, one might suggest there is a sense of objectophilia in the film, a sense of a real emotional attachment Eleanor develops toward the house, and vice versa. The dancing scenes in the atrium provide two examples of this, especially the latter in which Julie Harris' character so clearly dances for the pleasure of the house. We can assume the non-diegetic humming in both scenes belongs to the house, who uses it to accompany Eleanor's dance. Another example is the non-diegetic sigh and the invisible caress of the cheek the house gives Eleanor to express its interest in her. The writing on the wall is another example: while a crude, immature move to get attention, it is Hill House's attempt to show Eleanor her value to it. The psychogeographic experiences that will be explored later in this chapter are two more gifts Hill House gives to Eleanor. And finally, the loving and ecstatic countenance Eleanor expresses on the staircase while hugging the banister, and the affectionate touch of her hand and intimate placing of her face on the slate stone roof tiles, both near the end of the film, indicate a strong reliance on and affection between the two characters (see Figure 6.1).

Critics have noted this affection: Richard C. Keenan (2007) observes that Hill House has 'genuinely set its turret for Eleanor' (p. 121), Pamela Keesey (2002) suggests that the house is 'falling under Eleanor's spell', while Justin E. Busch (2010) goes so far as to suggest that at Hill House, Eleanor finds herself in a 'classic love triangle' with Theo as one angle and the other 'occupied by a supernatural force . . . just as obsessive in its attachment as a person might be' (p. 43). In other words, Eleanor experiences an actual entanglement of the heart *with* the house.

Parsing some of the cinematic techniques used to confirm these points can assist in the overarching argument about Eleanor's personal development. The corporeal realisation of Hill House seems to take a more robust role in its realisation of Eleanor. In a *Bildungsroman*, the protagonist finds interest in society, learns its ways and norms, and commits to perpetuating these norms via such things as manner, dress, and lifestyle. However, *The Haunting* narrates Eleanor's transformation away from human society towards a communion with a different kind of body. The film's use of fluctuating point-of-view shots and the anthropomorphism of Hill House create a protagonist who is becoming *because* of the house, and finding her expanded character and wholeness through experiential fusion with it.

In 'Thrice-Told Tales' Steven J. Schneider (2002) observes that 'Wise bestows on Hill House a kind of proto-consciousness' by 'alternating' shots between Eleanor and the house, 'thereby establishing a virtual dialogue between them' (p. 171). When Eleanor is introduced to the house, the reverse angle shot medley from her

FIGURE 6.1 Eleanor's affectionate touching of Hill House indicates her close relationship with it
The Haunting (Robert Wise, 1963)

eyes to the 'eyes' (windows) of the tower, as well as subjective shot cuts from her point of view to that of the house, work to illustrate Hill House and the protagonist as worthy associates. On the one hand, these shots exemplify a difference in levels of power: Eleanor is forced, after all, to look up at the house while the house looks down at her. The slanted, high-angle point-of-view shots from the house allow us to join it in observing Eleanor's car creep into the frame, again implying a size discrepancy. In spite of these dichotomies, however, the shots also place the two characters on an equal plane of significance through editing. The cutting back and forth provides nearly equal time to each as they measure up the other. Eleanor's voice-over stating unironically, 'It's staring at me', in a delayed match cut between her eyes in extreme close-up and a close-up of the two arched windows of the tower, assists in demonstrating their equivalence, while foreshadowing their importance to each other early on.

During the initial haunting scene in the bedroom, the subjective shots shift between Eleanor and Theo and the house, so much so that it disorients distinct point of view, exhibiting the next stage of the fusion between protagonist and house. Hill House's distinct point of view is introduced over halfway into the scene. As Theo screams, 'It's against the top of the door!' the objective camera cuts to the point of view of the house. The energy behind the sound peers into the room from the textured transom window above the door. The women – in distortion from the 30 mm lens Wise so famously utilised to great effect in the film – are miniaturised and frozen left-centre of the screen in a high-angle shot. Again, the point of view cuts back to the women, as Eleanor witnesses the turning of the doorknob, and again a fast cut to the house as the high-angle point-of-view window shot is repeated. And finally, there is a brisk back and forth of objective and subjective shots. It is especially during this fluctuation where the house's point of view and its subject coincide to produce an uncanny merger. The soundtrack stills, leaving only a muffled brushing against the door, breathing, shuffling, and movement outside. The camera, remarkably, is on the *inside* of the door with Eleanor and Theo; therefore, the audience assumes their point of view. However, tilting, in sync with sound, produces the effect that the point of view is that of the house, attempting to gain entry. Inside and outside merge perplexingly.[1]

The intermingling of shifting point-of-view shots and sound give the audience a forecast of what Eleanor will more fully realise later, as her subjective interpretation of her life and her own experiences become more and more reliant on that of the house. Later in the film, we see this line of subjectivity blurred further, as Eleanor alone is offered explicit experiences from the house's private memory.

Point-of-view fusion: gifts of experience

Eleanor's backbend on the balcony mirrors her stunning horizontal acrobatics in the library. Both scenes entail the progress of Eleanor's fusion with the house. The events double each other, while also doubling previous deaths at the house, one named by Markway early on – the companion from the staircase railing – and one not mentioned, but which Eleanor alone seems to know. This layering of place with time, present with present and present with past, respectively, is what Deleuze claims is a 'special propert[y] in Gothic cinema, one predominantly inclined toward psychogeography or "place-memory"' (quoted in Powell, 2009: 91). In other words, these scenes exemplify Eleanor's privileged situation with the house, her positioning both physically and mentally in correlation to the structure.

In the balcony scene, her desire to look up at the window where a nameless woman met her fate retains Eleanor's gaze. Although her major voice has just claimed the tower 'vile' and 'hideous', and she has turned her back on it, she cannot help but gradually return her gaze as her minor voice intriguingly asks, 'I wonder what it would be like looking down from there? That's where she did it. From that window'. Immediately following her full explanation of the woman's experience, the steep, low-angle point-of-view shot from Eleanor to the tower shifts to a steep, high-angle point-of-view shot from the tower down to the miniscule Eleanor, centre frame. The movement from major to minor voice, as well as the developing relationship with Hill House, is specifically accentuated by the soundtrack. Behind her major voice, which tends towards defensiveness, are dissonant woodwinds with complementary strings, but the shift to the minor voice, the one that is reflective about Eleanor's situations, drops the woodwinds, keeping only two gentle, dissonant violins with an accompanying unobtrusive and mild xylophonic ring. The movement from many instruments to two – woodwinds to strings – denotes Eleanor's duality as well as the twofold subject relationship between Eleanor and the house. The ring doubles that of an earlier one, recalling the initial introduction between Eleanor and Hill House. During the introduction, however, the ring was solitary, persistent, frantic, but this ring differs in tone and timbre. It is a mild, unobtrusive sound at a regular cadence, paralleling Eleanor's narrative of the unknown woman: as she describes the woman 'Climbing out through the bars. Hanging on for an instant. Hanging on . . .' the violins reproduce the words, ascending in tone while the complementary ring also rises in pitch, acoustically visualising the woman's climb, and ending with a light, tremulous ring dangling in the air, 'hanging on'.

This auditory/visual twinning continues with the steep tracking shot descending from the tower to Eleanor on the balcony below, bending her backward, perpendicular to the wall. Although what happened to the woman 'hanging on' to the window is not explicitly stated, the frenzied tracking shot aurally and visually tells the end of the story, while Eleanor experiences the heady drop. Importantly, the house's point of view and Eleanor's are muddled here, insomuch that Eleanor undergoes the tower's experiential narration of a past event. Hill House does not tell or show Eleanor the event; it bequests her the literal physical experience.

Although there are many interpretations of this scene, I suggest the house gifts Eleanor the experience of the unnamed woman she so curiously questions. It seems the scene certainly 'illustrates the visual dynamic the film establishes between Eleanor and Hill House', as Shari Hodges Holt (2016: 162) notes, but I would go further and suggest the visual evokes the emotional entanglement and progressive fusion of the two as well.

The later staircase scene in the library doubles this gifting of experience to Eleanor by the house. Similar to her escape from her human family – the mother she had nursed for 11 years and her tyrannical sister – she is now a fugitive, running towards Hill House and away from the society of people gathered there. Her developing norms will not coincide with those of the people, but those of the house. Her *Bildung* is now associated with the house and her desire to find her place in it.

Discovering herself in the library, Eleanor's interest is immediately drawn towards the staircase. The helical tracking point-of-view shot preceding her subsequent ascent is an extravagant 18-second climb, uncut, which Norman Lareau (1963–1964) suggests is meant 'to approximate the feeling that Eleanor is being intrigued by it, that its spirit is calling her' (p. 45).

The promised experience repeats that of the companion who had hung herself from the landing at the top. Contrary to the earlier observation of the staircase by Theo, Luke, and Markway, which is an objective tilt shot from the outside, Eleanor's preview is a subjective tracking shot from *within* the staircase; what is more, it doubles the companion's trip up the staircase and reverses the camera trip down after her demise. Wise acknowledged the bravura nature of this piece of filming:

> The one shot we did on [the film] that fascinates people the most is when the camera is at the bottom and goes up. We designed the banister of the stairway to be so wide and thick that it would fit a small rig with wheels on it – a little, light dolly that would hold a hand-held camera. We had our camera on that and we had a control wire underneath, all the way down. We simply took the camera up to the top on this rig, started it, rolled it down, and then reversed the film. It was all done on that balustrade.
>
> *(quoted in Passafiume, n.d.)*

Wise's technique here in shooting the rapid descent down the staircase after the companion's death is the same technique he used for Eleanor's preview ascent: he took the same shot and 'reversed the film'. This repetition and replication indicates how closely Eleanor's point of view has merged with the house.

To the audience, these 18 seconds evoke a mounting foreboding dread, and even terror. The camera makes its way up the staircase accompanied by a timpani footstep on the soundtrack, while faint woodwinds and strings gain in number and volume with each step, ending in a terrific dissonance. Yet replicating her measured response at her initial meeting with Hill House, Eleanor's first sight of the staircase is again one of interest and cool examination: a barely furrowed brow softens and opens up an inquisitive face. In the aftermath of the point-of-view shot, the audience may feel a heightened sense of anxiety and trepidation, but the preview for Eleanor again brings a fusion of point of view with the house.

With this fusion, Eleanor believes she has 'broken the spell of Hill House', as she chants, 'I'm home. I'm home. I'm home. I'm home'.

As with the tower before, Eleanor's curiosity is once again piqued. The bird's-eye shot catches the dissonance between the audience's experience of Eleanor's point of view and Eleanor's own experience: while we struggle with a dizzying dread, Eleanor glides in dance, circularly, towards the staircase, simulating the prior spherical preview and its own spiral design. Holding on to the rickety iron banister, Eleanor both carefully and ecstatically traverses the perilous library staircase until safely on the landing at the top. During her slow progress up the staircase, it quavers treacherously, and Eleanor responds with a long-suffering visage, one that implies an understanding of the house and patience with its eccentricities. Trembling with the staircase, her countenance turns into loving rapture. She smiles with interior knowledge of her relationship with the house.

Eleanor is eager for the experience promised by the preview of the staircase. As the soundtrack tonally follows Eleanor up the stairs, her response to Markway's yell, which both stops her and silences the soundtrack, is to choose the company of the house over that of the people: 'All that is gone and left behind'. She continues up, and when she is finally on the landing, Hill House offers her the remaining experience promised by the preview of the staircase. As Markway, who has followed her up, reaches out his hand for her, Eleanor is bowed backward again, perpendicularly, by Hill House, in a dangerously maintained horizontal posture accentuated by the increasing dissonance and force of the accompanying soundtrack. Rather than reach towards Markway for help, Eleanor clasps her hands over her mouth, seemingly to keep herself from crying out and arresting the re-creation of experience being conferred upon her (see Figure 6.2). Rather than retreat to safety, she deliberately twists her body sideways to look at the distant library floor below and obtain the full effect of the vertiginous experience.

In this scene, Hill House presents Eleanor with an iteration of the hanging experience of the companion. While the balcony scene furnishes her with the

FIGURE 6.2 The house helps Eleanor resist gravity
The Haunting (Robert Wise, 1963)

terrifying plummeting simulation from the tower window, the staircase scene allows Eleanor the same bird's-eye view of the companion, as well as a supernatural experience: defying gravity. Both are the kind of remarkable and significant experiences that Eleanor has yearned for from the start.

Point-of-view fusion: becoming whole

Her final journey down the drive is when Eleanor decisively realises her fusion with the house, and thus her unification of self; she comprehends that her desire for experience and place has been achieved. It is through voice-over, once again, that we learn this. As she smugly evades her three friends and guides the car down the driveway, her major and minor voices come to the fore in a clash of defiance, discord, and ultimate convergence. When Hill House takes over the steering wheel, Eleanor's minor voice whispers ecstatically, 'I knew it. I knew it. Hill House doesn't want me to go'. But as the ride becomes more reckless, she says audibly, 'Stop it, please! What are you doing! Let go! What are you doing?' It is unclear to whom she addresses this. Is it to herself or is it Hill House? Following this outburst, her major voice asks in terror, 'Why don't they stop me? Can't they see what is happening?' Her minor voice, however, calmly reflects on the situation and appealingly addresses Eleanor in the second person: 'But it's happening to *you*, Eleanor'. The voice then notably shifts from second to first person in the final voice-over: 'Yes. Something at last is really, really, really happening to me'. The shift from second to first person demonstrates a unification of Eleanor's voices, as well as implying integration with the 'you' (the house?) directing the car.

This final adverbial trio, 'really, really, really', neatly chimes with the two anticipatory calls in triplicate by Eleanor on her initial journey to Hill House. Her 'I hope, I hope, I hope . . .' in eagerness for experience, and her 'Someday. Someday. Someday . . .' in optimism for place are both radically fulfilled.

Help Eleanor come home

Shirley Jackson's character, Eleanor, is a curious Gothic protagonist and remains a most unique and complex character in Robert Wise's *The Haunting*. Although deceptively conventional and somewhat fragmented at first sight, her relationship with Hill House and her fusion with its point of view transform her into a more unified subject herself. Through Wise's complex camerawork, use of soundtrack, and voice-over, the film expresses a protagonist whose point of view and development of self is progressively influenced by that of the house.

As a story of *Bildung*, this film relies predominantly on the building to usher in the protagonist's transformation, rather than the conventional use of a human community. Eleanor is influenced by, and responds increasingly positively towards, the house, and it likewise responds to her and courts her affection. When the house seems to fall apart – 'The house is coming down around me. The house is destroying itself!' – so does Eleanor: 'I'm coming apart a little at a time . . . Now I know where I'm going. I'm disappearing inch-by-inch into this house'. With the previous fusion of perspectives between Eleanor and the house, and both house and character disintegrating, opening up simultaneously, the integration of these fragmentary parts into a new whole is made possible. And by the end of her final drive, then, Eleanor is fused with Hill House and Hill House with Eleanor.

Wise's technical decisions oblige us to perceive how integral Hill House's influence is on Eleanor's understanding of herself. That after all the experiences of Eleanor's journey, it is a human who evokes a terrifying scream out of Eleanor (twice) articulates how far away Eleanor has moved away from the community of people towards the community of the house.[2] Just as her name is scrawled on the wall without punctuation, offering murky denotation, there are various ways to understand Eleanor's place in the house. But two things are certain: fragmented Eleanor has become whole, and Hill House has become home.

Notes

1 An exceptionally detailed technical account of this scene is given by Elizabeth Mullen (2009) in her article 'Synæsthetic Specters: Haunting Hill House on the Silver Screen'.
2 It is interesting that Eleanor screams only twice in the film, and these are both because of a sudden appearance of a human body: once in the trapdoor of the tower, and once immediately prior to the crash of her car. She never screams at anything Hill House offers. She yells, at the force trying to enter the bedroom, at the thing hurting a child, but she never screams in fear. As noted earlier, she refuses to scream while suspended 40 feet above ground in the library. These incidents seem to indicate Eleanor's strong preference for and trust of Hill House over the people in it.

References

Blake, Marc and Sara Bailey (2013) *Writing the Horror Movie*. London: Bloomsbury.
Busch, Justin. E. (2010) *Self and Society in the Films of Robert Wise*. Jefferson, NC: McFarland & Company.
Davison, Carol M. (2004) 'Haunted House/Haunted Heroine: Female Gothic Closets in *The Yellow Wallpaper*'. *Women's Studies*, 33: 47–75.
Hardcastle, Anne, Roberta Morosini, and Kendall Tarte (eds) (2009) 'Introduction'. In *Coming of Age on Film: Stories of Transformation in World Cinema*. Newcastle: Cambridge Scholars Press, pp. 1–11.
Holt, Shari Hodges (2016) 'The Tower or the Nursery? Paternal and Maternal Revisions of Hill House on Film'. In Melanie R. Anderson and Lisa Kröger (eds), *Shirley Jackson, Influences and Confluences*. New York: Routledge, pp. 160–182.
Jackson, Shirley (1959) *The Haunting of Hill House*. New York: Penguin Books.
Keenan, Robert C. (2007) *The Films of Robert Wise*. Lanham, MD: Scarecrow Press.
Keesey, Pamela (2002) '*The Haunting* and the Power of Suggestion: Why Robert Wise's Masterpiece Continues to Deliver the Goods to Modern Audiences'. *Monsterzine*, 6(8). www.monsterzine.com/200201/haunting.php [Accessed 3 April 2018]
Lareau, Norman (1963–1964) '*The Haunting* by Robert Wise'. *Film Quarterly*, 17(2): 44–47.
McCarthy, Margaret (2008) 'Bildungsroman'. In David Herman, Manfred Jahn, and Marie-Laure Ryan (eds), *Routledge Encyclopedia of Narrative Theory*. New York: Routledge, pp. 41–42.

Mullen, Elizabeth (2009) 'Synæsthetic Specters: Haunting Hill House on the Silver Screen'. *Image & Narrative*, 10(1): 119–132. www.imageandnarrative.be/index.php/imagenarrative/article/view/204 [Accessed 3 April 2018]

Passafiume, Andrea (n.d.) *The Haunting (1963)*. TCMDb Archive Materials. Turner Classic Movies. www.tcm.com/tcmdb/title/1560/The-Haunting/articles.html [Accessed 3 April 2018]

Powell, Anna (2009) 'Duration and the Vampire: A Deleuzian Gothic'. *Gothic Studies*, 11(1): 86–98.

Schneider, Steven J. (2002) 'Thrice-Told Tales: *The Haunting* from Novel to Film . . . to Film'. *Journal of Popular Film and Television*, 30(3): 166–176.

Starling, Ashley (2014) 'Beware the House that Feels: The Impact of Sentient House Hauntings on Literary Families'. *Digital Literature Review*, 1: 68–76. http://bsuenglish.com/dlr/past/issue1_starling.pdf [Accessed 3 April 2018]

Waldman, Diane (1984) '"At Last I Can Tell It to Someone!" Feminine Point of View and Subjectivity in the Gothic Romance Film of the 1940s'. *Cinema Journal*, 23(2): 29–40.

White, Patricia (1999) *Uninvited: Classical Hollywood Cinema and Lesbian Representability*. Bloomington, IN: Indiana University Press.

PART III
The Gothic and genre forms

7

THE GOTHIC IN SPACE

Genre, motherhood, and *Aliens* (1986)

Frances A. Kamm

It is at around the halfway mark of teaching on the Gothic in Film module (described in the Introduction) that I introduce an unexpected – and perhaps strange – change for the students of the course: they watch a screening of James Cameron's 1986 film *Aliens*. The horror and action blockbuster is a marked departure from the uneasy tone of *Rebecca* (1940) or the uncanny occurrences in *What Lies Beneath* (2000), both of which also feature on the module. How does a film set in space, recounting a story about a marine corps engaged in a deadly battle against the so-called alien xenomorphs, relate to the domestic concerns of the female protagonists in these other films? The difference is one of distance, both literally and figuratively. *Aliens* sets its main narrative action on a distant planet, the remote location of which is further underlined by an emphasis on details such as hypersleep, spaceships, and the Company's colonial ambitions to 'Build Better Worlds'. In doing so, the film also raises themes such as the ethics of war, corporate greed, and the processes of racial othering. The quiet terror of *Rebecca* is evidently light years away from the 'sledgehammer action' (Greenberg, 1988: 166) of Cameron's space war. In short, there appears to be a barrier in terms of genre: narrative expectations, themes, and even tone present a challenge when conceptualising *Aliens* in terms of the Gothic.

It is the purpose of this chapter to do just that. I argue that *Aliens* is a Gothic film, and is in fact equally indebted to the conventions of the literary and filmic Female Gothic that are explored at length throughout this collection. This is not to deny the significance of 'action' and 'adventure' to the film's story, terms that IMDb uses to label *Aliens*; nor will this be an argument mitigating the relevance of science fiction, the genre classification given to the film on the AFI database. Indeed, quite the opposite is my aim: I will demonstrate that it is *Aliens'* adoption of key Gothic themes, characterisation, and visual address *within* its science fiction setting that, perhaps paradoxically, illuminates and emphasises the importance of the Gothic even further, particularly because the latter provides alternative readings of the film. To investigate the connection between these disparate lines of enquiry, the following chapter is divided into three sections. First, I will address the question of genre directly, revealing how, on closer inspection, the 'Gothic' nature of *Aliens* is readily apparent and sees the film tap into the longer tradition of Gothic science fiction hybrids. Next, I describe how a big challenge posed by the film is its depiction of Ripley as the central heroine. The controversy here concerns the predominant theme of motherhood, and in the final section I suggest that reading the film as a *Gothic* science fiction – specifically within the lineage of the Female Gothic tradition – allows the film to be analysed within a new light: *Aliens* is not necessarily a regressive response to the feminist potential of its predecessor, but rather a story actively engaging in the essentialising and radical potential of the Gothic form, which creates challenging but ultimately compelling representations of women.

'Generic monsters': Gothic and science fiction

Aliens is a sequel to the Ridley Scott film *Alien* (1979), the latter of which sees the majority of the crew of the *Nostromo* die at the hands of an alien being that has contaminated their ship after infecting Executive Officer Kane. Ripley, the commercial ship's Warrant Officer, is the only human survivor: after a final battle on board the escape shuttle, Ripley blasts the alien xenomorph into space and puts herself – and Jones the cat – into hypersleep. Cameron's sequel picks up where Scott's story ends as salvagers discover Ripley still in stasis, 57 years after the events of the first film. She is taken back to her employer, the Company (now given the name Weyland-Yutani), where her superiors do not believe her story about the alien creature she fought and killed. However, this changes when Ripley is asked to return to the alien planet where Kane first became infected – now called LV-426 – in order to advise the colonial marines who have been sent to investigate the disappearance of the colonists now living there. It is soon discovered that the xenomorph from the first film has returned in greater numbers, and the leader and mother of these aliens is revealed to be the Alien Queen: a larger, more ferocious creature who can seemingly procreate independently. In an echo of the film's predecessor, the marines fail to contain the alien attack, so Ripley once again becomes the saviour, fighting the Alien Queen directly and saving the life of an orphaned girl, Newt. Ripley and Newt – along with the last surviving marine, Hicks, and an android, Bishop – enter hypersleep to begin the journey home.

Aliens is not unique within the franchise for being categorised within genres other than the 'Gothic'. On the AFI database, *Alien* is labelled 'science fiction', correlating to the listings on IMDb and the BFI catalogue, both of which also add the descriptor 'horror'. *Alien 3* (1992) and *Alien Resurrection* (1997) – the final two films of the franchise – are both 'action, horror, science fiction' on IMDb, and 'horror, science fiction and fantasy' on the aggregate website Rotten Tomatoes. The latter describes *Alien* as 'drama, mystery and suspense, science fiction and fantasy', while *Aliens* is listed as 'science fiction and fantasy', but in conjunction with 'horror, action and adventure'. The differences speak to the 'contested arena' that is genre (Johnston, 2011: 12), although the fact 'the Gothic remains a notoriously difficult field to define' (Punter and Byron, 2004: xviii) compounds the issue, where there 'is not just one Gothic but Gothics' (Fleenor, 1983: 4). This may go some way to explain why the films of the *Alien* franchise have not been explicitly labelled as 'Gothic' on the databases cited, yet the ubiquitous presence of the 'science fiction' categorisation could also be a contributing factor. Itself a nebulous term, science fiction has been defined variously within strict limitations (Suvin, 1979), and as a film genre that recognises 'hybrid forms as a part of a spectrum' (Sobchack, 1988: 63).

However, broadly speaking, one could posit that the genre engages with themes such as 'the future, artificial creation, technological invention, extraterrestrial contact' – to name but a few – that link science fiction 'to change, mutation or evolution' (Johnston, 2011: 1–2). To combine these factors with the Gothic creates additional definitional challenges. As Sara Wasson and Emily Alder (2011) note, the notion of a Gothic science fiction creates a 'curiously contradictory hyphenation', particularly in respect to how the two genres 'seem mutually exclusive [in] their contrary relationships to time' (p. 3): if, as suggested above, science fiction is about 'the future', 'change', and 'evolution', this is opposed to the Gothic's emphasis on history and preoccupation with the past (Baldick, 1993). Where the Gothic looks back, to the past, to the what-has-been, science fiction is perceived as looking forward, to the future, to the what-may-yet-come-to-pass.

Yet the Gothic and science fiction can, and do, converge. Fred Botting (2008) notes that however 'strange' it may be for these seemingly oxymoronic genres – each a hybrid already – to mix, when they do the 'zones of intersection tend to be dark and disturbing, obscure regions, populated by terrors and horrors that knowledge has failed to penetrate or control' (p. 131). *Frankenstein* (1818) famously demonstrates this: if the Gothic is the 'unnatural, uncaring, and irresponsible parent of science-fiction', then Mary Shelley's 'hideous progeny' signifies the 'genesis of Gothic science-fiction' (Hughes, 2014: 1–2). Roger Luckhurst (2005) notes that the shared themes and tone of Gothic and science fiction reside in the 'sense of trauma induced in the subject by modernity [which] means that Gothic and SF writing are constantly in dialogue' (p. 5). The *Alien* films offer an important contribution to this conversation. Significantly, Luckhurst and Botting both use the franchise as a key example of one of these 'zones of intersection' between Gothic and science fiction. Luckhurst (2005) argues that *Alien* 'signalled a hybridization of science-fiction and Gothic forms' (p. 214), and elsewhere describes the film as a 'creaky Old Dark House in Space' (Luckhurst, 2014: 8). Botting (2008) goes further by contextualising the *Alien* franchise alongside the Female Gothic tradition, and specifically the 'flight of the heroine' trope Ellen Moers analysed in relation to Ann Radcliffe's work (p. 153).

With its 'roller-coaster ride of violence' (Ebert, 1986), one might assume that Cameron's *Aliens* mitigates this evocation of the Gothic, as Harvey Greenberg (1988) implies when he writes that *Aliens* bears 'little of the original's mystery, and less of its terror and beauty' (pp. 165–166). However, I argue that *Aliens* actually reinforces and extends the Gothic elements of the first film, representing thematically and stylistically the 'dialogue' between Gothic and science fiction, and particularly the relevance of the Female Gothic tradition. The film's opening sequence demonstrates this. After James Horner's tense score culminates in the film's title bleaching to a white screen, the first image shows Ripley's escape pod centre frame, a tiny shape within the vastness of space. A dissolve to the inside of the ship emphasises heavy shadow, as an inquisitive camera moves through the obscure space before finding Ripley's sleeping body within the hypersleep chamber. A cut to the inside of this structure identifies Ripley in a medium close-up. A series of shots show the on-board computer warn of a 'proximity alert', while outside Ripley's ship is engulfed within the shadow of a larger vessel. Back inside, a light pierces into the gloom through a small window, as a robotic arm cuts through the locked door. A scanning laser injects a blue haze into the space, illuminating the ethereal-looking smoke that emanates from the blowtorch's incision. The blue light passes over Ripley's face. Once the robot has retreated, three figures enter the room and a male voice confirms Ripley's 'bio read-outs' show her to be alive, as he laments, 'There goes our salvage, guys'. A close-up of Ripley's profile dissolves and becomes a graphic match for the shape of the Earth shown in the next shot.

Aliens infuses the science fiction motifs it establishes quickly here – space, interstellar travel, and advanced technologies – with a distinctly Gothic aesthetic. The remote wilderness one expects in a Gothic story becomes the ultimate vast landscape: outer space. Isolated and vulnerable within this geography, Ripley is shown not within the conventional 'Old Dark House' (Russ, 1973/1995), but on a spaceship, and similar vehicles and locations elsewhere in the narrative – the space station in the next scene or the colony on LV-426 – replace the ancestral mansion as the site where terror confuses and complicates the distinction between the public and the private, wider political issues, and domestic concerns. If the first film's opening sequence only obliquely references the abject horrors to come – the camera's revelation of the sleeping crew in *Alien* is 'marked by a fresh, antiseptic atmosphere' (Creed, 1993: 18) that works in opposition to the later 'abjected maternal body' of the alien craft (Constable, 1999: 182) – then *Aliens* alerts the viewer to danger straight away. The creeping score on the soundtrack and the slow, deliberate camera movements immediately evoke an uneasy tone, a mood compounded by the heavy use of shadow. The darkness and vastness of space is visually translated into the interior of the ship, rendering the place 'anisotropic', just like the Gothic castle, which is 'literally or metaphorically, *larger inside than outside*' (Aguirre, 2008: 6, original emphasis). Where *Alien* emphasised light and clarity, *Aliens* dwells in the darkness and unknown, even evoking the uncanny: the escape pod appears at the end of the first film, but is now rendered *unheimlich* with its unfamiliar and unknowable geography.

Importantly, these Gothic associations are motivated by – and inextricably linked to – the film's introduction of Ripley. The sight of Ripley sleeping convolutes the space further: the technical equipment that is glimpsed is now uneasily juxtaposed with the intimacy of sleep. The camera's exploring gaze becomes intrusive, and the close-up of Ripley's unconscious face emphasises further her vulnerability to the threat of invasion or attack. The sudden appearance of the robot arm and the salvagers confirm this defencelessness, and Ripley's status as the Gothic heroine or woman in peril is underlined as she is seemingly in danger from a threat that is technological *and* male. The immediate jeopardy may be misdirection – a nod, perhaps, to the Radcliffean 'bait-and-switch' (Kawin, 2012: 112)[1] – but the camera's discovery of Ripley playfully reimagines another important influence to the Female Gothic tradition: the Bluebeard fairy tale. Just like this seminal text, *Aliens* emphasises the idea of hidden, locked spaces that contain secrets of violence and death. The escape pod represents these horrors by referencing back to the first film, and, in *Aliens* as in Bluebeard, this chamber is revealed to contain the body of a woman. Ripley is not, of course, a corpse, but her physical confinement in stasis and sleep mimics the appearance of one. The scene emblematically represents the merging of Gothic and science fiction – Ripley's sleep sees the 'what-has-been' merge with the 'what-may-yet-come-to-pass' on narrative and generic levels – while also prophetically predicting the climax of this story with the Alien Queen: another scene that reworks the Bluebeard scenario of concealment and revelation in relation to threat. Thus, whereas *Alien*'s opening (and, one could argue, the narrative as a whole) offers a particular 'representation of the human' in general (Constable, 1999: 184), *Aliens* establishes immediately that this Gothic science fiction story, along with its uneasy tone and threats of danger, is specifically *female*-focused and -oriented.

Heroine, mother, bitch

The centrality of Ripley to *Aliens* is a fundamental part of how the film evokes the Female Gothic, but this factor also illuminates the reason why the film is heavily criticised within scholarly discourse. The next scene in the film's opening illuminates the point. After the dissolve to the planet, the camera reveals an orbiting space station and cuts to an interior room, where a nurse tends to Ripley in a hospital bed as she stirs. Ripley learns she has been there 'a couple of days' before a man dressed in a suit enters holding Jones the cat. A dialogue exchange between Ripley and the man reveals the latter to be Company employee Carter Burke and Ripley has been floating in space for 57 years. As the shock of this news sinks in, the camera frames Ripley's profile in a close-up, a composition that echoes the shots of her sleeping in the previous scene. The sound of Ripley's heartbeat dominates the soundtrack and an edit sees Jones hiss in Ripley's direction. A series of edits show Ripley – in slow motion – writhe in pain, knocking the glass of water Burke offers to the floor, and struggling against the hospital staff who attempt to restrain her. She begs through gritted teeth, 'Kill me!' before she is framed in a medium shot raising her shirt to expose her abdomen. A reverse shot sees the doctor react in horror and then the film,

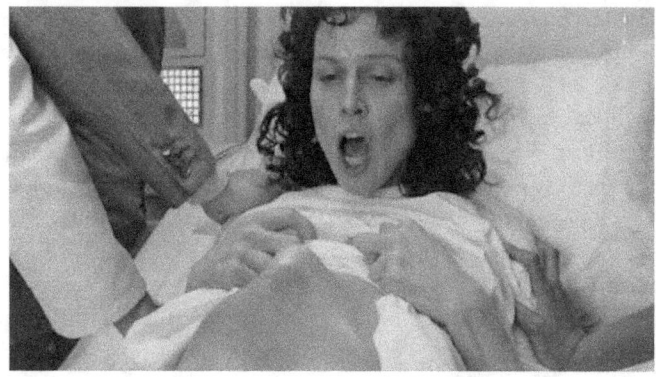

FIGURE 7.1 Ripley's nightmare
Aliens (James Cameron, 1986)

cutting back to its original position to explain this terrified response, reveals a gruesome growth unnaturally push its way up from beneath Ripley's skin. She screams as the creature's head is about to pierce her flesh. An edit then suddenly shows Ripley in the same room jolting awake, grabbing her chest: the sequence was a nightmare (see Figure 7.1).

Aliens reaffirms again how the future-oriented world of science fiction is integrated here with the past-obsessed mode of the Gothic: Ripley exists in a diegesis that is defined by an emphasis on developed technologies, but the action of the scene is reliant on past events, in what is, narratively speaking, old history. The knowledge of this is, of course, reliant on the viewer's engagement on an extra-textual level, as *Aliens* self-consciously acknowledges its status as a sequel and deliberately provokes the memory of Kane's violent death in *Alien* with the infamous 'chestburster'. And yet there is a significant difference. Whereas Kane's death can be read as the patriarchal reaffirmation of the monstrous-feminine because the horror of this event is predicated on when a 'man's body becomes grotesque because it is capable of being penetrated' (Creed, 1993: 19), *Aliens* removes this subversive subtext by re-presenting the threat of a chestburster – of birth – upon a *woman*'s body. The fact the event is only a dream does not lessen the film's preoccupation with redefining birth and motherhood in terms of the female sex: Ximena Gallardo-C. and C. Jason Smith (2004) note that this association is re-emphasised again when the marines find a – specifically female – colonist cocooned on the infected planet, and this woman, in an echo to Ripley's nightmare, begs to be killed. The writers argue:

> That we never see a male 'give birth' in this film refocuses the horror from the feminization of males and the desexing of the human body to the more traditional image of a female body being subjected to a violent birth.
>
> *(p. 93)*

There are other 'traditional' images or ideas about the female body that are emphasised in *Aliens*. Ripley's nightmare could be read as 'the fear of biological motherhood' (Gallardo-C. and Smith, 2004: 75), a notion that is thematically linked to the sequel's revelation that Ripley had a daughter who died during her time away.[2] Ripley's new-found status as a mother is re-emphasised through Newt, the orphaned girl Ripley rescues, and who at the end calls her 'mommy'. Motherhood finds a third, albeit monstrous outlet: the xenomorph creature itself. The alien chestburster has already been aligned with the female body, but the significance for Ripley runs deeper. Her nightmares are clearly a 'classic symptom of post-traumatic stress disorder' (Greenberg, 1988: 167), not only for the death of the *Nostromo* crew, but also for her own 'rape': betrayed by her employer, Ripley is a 'woman raped by the system' (Gallardo-C. and Smith, 2004: 84). Ripley's abuse by the Company continues unhindered in *Aliens* – she is sanctioned for her actions in the first film and then convinced to return to the place of her trauma – and the physical threat is intensified: Burke's plan to implant the alien into Ripley and Newt demonstrates how her 'dreams are lies that include truth' (Kaveney, 2005: 156). And Ripley is not the only mother, of course: the Alien Queen offers an alternative form of hero-ism and maternal instinct, one that tellingly results in the monster being labelled with the gendered insult 'bitch'.

For some scholars, *Aliens'* forefronting of Ripley as heroine, mother, and bitch (killer) is problematic, and thus the film encounters negative criticism, particularly in comparison to the first film. These comments are pervasive in film scholarship, so it is worth quoting a small selection at length:

> [While] Ellen Ripley is the undisputed hero of James Cameron's *Aliens*, the film also essentializes Ripley in ways that reinforce the fundamental, natural, and intrinsic connection between being female and having a lower social status than males, as well as the fact that being female means being, always already, a mother.
>
> *(Wood, 2010: 34)*

> [*Aliens*] effectively draws the New Woman back into the fold of the patriar-chal structure where she will protect traditional WASP morality, the nuclear family, John Wayne masculinity, and, perhaps most importantly, the sacred cow of motherhood.
>
> *(Gallardo-C. and Smith, 2004: 66–67)*

> *Aliens* reintroduces the issue of sexual difference, but not in order to offer a newer, more modern configuration of that difference. Rather, by focusing on Ripley alone, the question of the couple is supplanted by the problem of the woman as mother. What we finally get is a conservative moral lesson about maternity futuristic or otherwise: mothers will be mothers, and they will always be women.
>
> *(Penley, 1990: 124–125)*

For these writers, the problem is Ripley's motherhood. As argued above, to be a mother is to be female, and Ripley's previous lack of conventional 'womanhood' – or indeed of any gendering characteristics aside from her appearance – is perceived to be the strength of *Alien*'s version of a Gothic science fiction world. If the franchise as a whole moves towards a 'post-modern, post-feminist, post-human' form of identity (Botting, 2008: 180), then *Alien* lays the firm foundation. The crew of the *Nostromo* are not divided along gendered lines, overtly sexualised, or romantically involved. Indeed, one could argue that the film is concerned less with gender dynamics and more with other philosophical questions such as how changing technologies alter the 'conception and representation of the lived world' (Sobchack, 2007: 220). Within this line of reasoning, *Aliens* removes the possibility for this post-feminist, egalitarian humanist future, and this interpretation finds further poignancy when one historically situates the film. Released in 1986, *Aliens* was produced and released during the Reagan Administration, a period defined by the rise of the New Right, prompting 'an era of radical change, as "marketization" transformed economic, social, civic and private life' (Luckhurst, 2005: 196). Specifically, Reagan's presidency oversaw increased tensions during the Cold War, promoted pro-life rhetoric, stigmatised 'abnormal' sexuality against the backdrop of the AIDS epidemic, and launched the 'War on Drugs' campaign. The feminist movement was landed a particular blow when the Equal Rights Amendment officially failed to gain ratification to become law in 1982.

Susan Jeffords (1994) argues that this context is culturally represented on screen in the 'hard body' films of Arnold Schwarzenegger, Sylvester Stallone, and Chuck Norris. These men, whose films are often within the action genre, 'stand as the emblem of the Reagan philosophies, politics, and economies' (p. 25). These hard bodies are defined, in part, in opposition to the 'soft body' that embodies 'sexually transmitted disease, immorality, illegal chemicals, "laziness", and endangered foetuses' (p. 24); this body 'invariably belonged to a female and/or a person of color' (p. 25). The Ripley of *Aliens*, then, seems to be at odds with the context of her own making. The film – which, as has been noted, is often also categorised within the action genre – features a central female protagonist who motivates plot development and is framed as a fighter; on arrival to LV-426, Ripley is quickly shown to be more competent in battle than the marines' Lieutenant Gorman. However, Ripley's motherhood sets her apart, and thus sees the female character's strength restricted within a patriarchal sphere whereby the heroine is defined by her biological functions:

> [Unlike] Colonel Braddock and Rambo, Ripley is a woman, and women, especially in the Reagan years, just did not pick up guns, grenades, and missile launchers and start blowing things to hell. Not without a real reason . . . the most obvious and enduring reason for women to spring into action is the unchecked threat to children, husband, and family when all male authority has failed.
>
> *(Gallardo-C. and Smith, 2004: 73–74)*

This is an interpretation that requires nuancing. While this historical contextualisation remains an important and convincing claim, one must be careful not to overstate the perceived feminist/post-feminist/female-oriented nature of the original film – upon which much of the criticism of *Aliens* relies. The role of Ripley was not necessarily written as female, or marked as the obvious survivor (Kaveney, 2005: 131). The *Nostromo* crew wear similar attire that emphasises how the differences between the characters are not drawn along gender lines, but this representation is undermined by the end: Ripley strips to her underwear and, with the camera in a low-angled shot looking up towards her crotch, the sexual nature of this gaze is emphasised. Indeed, Barbara Creed's classic reading of *Alien* is based upon the notion of sexual difference that the film supposedly denies: specifically, the film promotes the 'monstrous-feminine' where the horror is reliant on the female and 'is almost always in relation to her mothering and reproductive functions' (Creed, 1993: 7). The difference between *Alien* and *Aliens*, then, is not a removal of gender in the first and a reinsertion of stereotypical femininity in the latter. Rather, following Creed, *Aliens* makes overt what *Alien* represented through allusion, allegory, and inference. The implicit 'archaic mother' – never seen in *Alien* – becomes explicit and embodied in the mothers of *Aliens*. For a tradition that concerns itself with the depiction of women within patriarchal contexts, the Female Gothic thus provides a particularly apt framework through which to analyse these representations, expanding *Aliens*' interpretative possibilities.

'Who's laying the eggs?' Gothic science fiction meets motherhood

In many ways, the criticisms levelled towards *Aliens* are emblematic of those that haunt the Female Gothic. As detailed in the introduction to this collection, the Female Gothic 'bears a political charge' (Hanson, 2007: 63), which complicates how one interprets such female-oriented stories. Female Gothic narratives typically '[straddle] contradiction and challenge, persecution and pleasure' (Botting, 2008: 153), meaning that whether the genre or mode 'should be seen as radical or conservative has been an issue of particular concern' (Punter and Byron, 2004: 280). Even the term 'Female Gothic' is gender-essentialising in a manner analogous to Ripley's reimagining as a specifically *female* fighter,[3] which, as already seen, 'means being, always already, a mother' (Wood, 2010: 34). The Bluebeard and the Female Gothic traditions usually centre upon marriage, and while these stories may come 'close to voicing a critique' of gender inequalities (Waldman, 1984, 34–35), the conventional conclusion to such narratives makes such a reading difficult:

> All of these patterns in the gothic formula suggest the pervasiveness of the need to believe in the traditional feminine roles rather than unconventional ones. The formula 'proves' that if women fulfil traditional roles, the family can be a viable institution.
>
> *(Mussell, 1975: 88–89)*

Aliens does not feature a heroine imperilled by her husband, but the narrative does still 'stage a double movement between agency and victimization' (Tatar, 2004: 107) in its depiction of Ripley, framing her against a patriarchal backdrop[4] that overtly thematises the 'traditional feminine roles' Mussell highlights here. These 'roles' converge around the maternal: the anxiety and suspicion emerging from the mysterious male figure is transplanted onto the question of the woman-as-mother. As noted, it could be argued that this theme was, in contrary to some critics' objections, already present in *Alien*, but the franchise's genre hybridity – particularly in the case of *Aliens* – emphasises its relevance further. Science fiction has a strong precedent for displacing the 'anxiety concerning the technological' onto 'the figure of the woman or the idea of the feminine . . . [what] is at stake in these representations [is] *reproduction*' (Doane, 2007: 182, original emphasis). Elsewhere in film history, there is also the tradition of the maternal melodrama, which is a contemporary to the 1940s Hollywood Gothics (Williams, 1987; Kaplan, 1992), and the 'maternal horror film' in horror cinema (Arnold, 2013). The Gothic too is 'haunted' by motherhood:[5] Claire Kahane (1985) argues that the Radcliffean heroine is motivated to embark on her investigations by the absent or dead mother, a figure who thus becomes both an inspiration and a fear. Indeed, Gothic and science fiction can be said to emerge together because of the maternal: Ellen Moers (1976) argues that *Frankenstein* (1818) – a seminal science fiction text – is a core example of the Female Gothic because it is a 'birth myth', exploring Shelley's own 'early and chaotic experience' of motherhood (p. 92).[6]

The problems some writers identify in *Aliens* are thus at the heart of what emphasises the film's Gothic credentials, as well as horror, melodrama, and science fiction allegiances. The ambiguity of the Female Gothic form, in particular, helps to illuminate the contrasting interpretations that are made possible by the film's emphasis on motherhood, and how, importantly, such readings can be and are held in tension. The scene where Ripley discovers the Alien Queen exemplifies these points. After Ripley makes the decision to return to the complex in order to rescue Newt, a series of close-ups details the modifications the heroine makes to the marine pulse rifle; the film emphasises the film's science fiction and action conventions by upping the weaponised ante. Yet, as before, such details are diffused through the Gothic: heavy shadows and smoke obscure much of the frame, and flashes of light from the destabilising colony offer brief illuminating shots in a manner comparable to the blue laser that scans the sleeping Ripley in the opening scene. Indeed, this climactic sequence echoes the opening in that another female character is about to be saved, and this rescue will also require entry into an unknown chamber. Ripley's descent in the lift to this dangerous place is emphasised, its lower location reinforcing the idea that terror lurks in the liminal spaces of corridors, basements, and netherworlds. Significantly, the camera's exploration of this space is motivated by Ripley's movements and her perception is emphasised: a close-up on the heroine's face with her eyes shut, bracing herself for what threat may attack, is detailed before the elevator door opens (and a similar reaction shot is shown again when Ripley despairs after failing to find Newt via the tracking device).

As Ripley first emerges from the elevator, a point-of-view shot provides the establishing shot of the now infested complex. Ripley's search through the area showcases an uncanny geography: the industrial grating that dominates this space – an area already doubled through its function for both professional and domestic purposes – is rendered *unheimlich* with the unfamiliar organic tissue that now clings to the metal fixtures. In a science fiction-inspired reimagining of the archetypal Gothic heroine investigating the labyrinth space of a dark house or castle, illuminating the gloom with a candelabra, Ripley manoeuvres through the convoluted corridors and stairwells, blasting her flamethrower for light. As she turns one corner, the glare from the flames highlights the fleshiness of the aliens' cocoons on the walls, the veined, muscular, and almost translucent texture appearing like skin. The transformed *mise en scène* forecasts the grotesque and abject sights to come. In a break from the viewer's alignment with Ripley, the first of these sights appears as Newt is shown restrained by a thick mucus-like substance, with a nearby pulsating egg slowing revealing the long fingers of an approaching 'facehugger'. This is the moment when Ripley finally rescues Newt after hearing the girl's screams, but the imagery also acts as a reminder of the conundrum implicit in *Alien* but outwardly spoken in *Aliens*: 'Who's laying the eggs?'

The answer arrives soon afterwards. As Ripley flees with Newt in her arms, her sudden halt is captured in a close-up on her face before a wider shot reveals her to be standing among rows of eggs. The soundtrack is no longer dominated by the computerised audio warnings of the complex's imminent explosion, and instead, through Ripley's laboured breath, an unidentified slimy noise is heard. In another break from the viewer's shared hierarchy of knowledge with the heroine, Ripley sees the source of these sounds just before a reverse shot reveals the horror for the spectator: a phallic appendage contracts and secretes an egg, its retracting skin leaving a trail of slime. While intercutting with shots of Ripley's and Newt's unnerved expressions, the seemingly subjective camera tilts and pans to follow the gruesome sac and 'oviposter', before finding a fanged, monstrous face at its end. The camera repositions to frame Ripley and Newt from behind, standing in front of the incredible creature: the Alien Queen's huge, backlit form dominates the space, her arachnid limbs unable to be contained within the frame of a single, static shot. *Aliens* transforms the inference of the archaic mother's presence into the spectacle of her confirmed existence: the slow camera pan, motivated by Ripley's gaze, reveals the monstrous-feminine in all its repulsive, abject glory. In this way, the Alien Queen is not just repulsive because she is a monster, but because she is a *mother* (see Figure 7.2).

The scene is a 'transgressive improvisation' of the Bluebeard story (Tatar, 2009). Like the 17th-century fairy tale, this concealed room contains a deadly secret and the bodies of victims are on display in this space; indeed, they are literally part of the walls. However, the hidden chamber reveals not the grisly result of male violence, but the gruesome sight of female procreation. This Bluebeardian chamber is thus one of death but also now of birth. The danger of marriage has been transformed and replaced with the violence of motherhood. If one were to read the scene in

FIGURE 7.2 Ripley – with the viewer – sees the Alien Queen
Aliens (James Cameron, 1986)

psychoanalytical terms, the horror is generated here by a re-enactment of the primal scene, which, as Creed (1993) contends, leads to the necessary abjection of the mother. The staining of the key with blood in Bluebeard can also be interpreted in this way, except the sexual awakening or knowledge gained in the film is an alien one. Alternatively, in the film's historical contexts, the Alien Queen represents 'a contemporary crisis in the realm of reproduction' (Doane, 2007: 185), and thus the societal oppression of this aberrant 'soft body' (Jeffords, 1994). In both cases, the secret beyond the Bluebeardian door is another affirmation of the patriarchal requirement to control the maternal because the (abject) mother always needs to be defiantly rejected: in the case of *Aliens*, this motherhood is violently ejected into outer space. In this way, the Alien Queen functions to maintain 'a hegemonic version of the maternal that offers only compliance or abjection' (Carpenter, 2016: 46).

However, there are two mothers in this scene: the Alien Queen and Ripley, and both present opportunities to upset the above binary. By exorcising the monstrous-feminine onto the figure of the Alien Queen, the film thereby contains the source of the abject present everywhere in the first film. This means that Ripley is the Gothic heroine with whom the audience are aligned *and* she is *not* abject: motherhood may appear in another form and for a different purpose. In Ripley's case, she uses her identification as a mother to defy this othering of female reproduction and the patriarchal systems that would enforce such 'compliance': at this point in the narrative, all symbols of male control (such as the Company and the marines) have been removed or incapacitated. Significantly, Ripley's motherhood is also not a biological imperative here, but a choice that motivates her engagement with the space and becomes the basis through which she regains the humans' control. One could go further and suggest that the Alien Queen represents a brutal, primitive force that is opposed to – and eventually defeated by – the civilised and technologically advanced. It is important that Ripley's mother status sits firmly with the latter. In this way, Ripley may begin to reappropriate the definitions of motherhood away from the abject – a concept whose meaning is, after all, reliant on its relation to the male – in order to portray new variations from a distinctly feminine perspective.

Alternatively, it is important to remember that this scene presents not just one female agent of action, but two: the other being the Alien Queen herself. The Queen's perception of events is equally emphasised during the mothers' confrontation. After the maternal xenomorph's introduction, which is framed by Ripley's and Newt's reactions, the two humans are depicted from the front in a medium to long shot, the camera's positioning approximately aligning to their distance from the creature. Although not strictly a point-of-view shot, this re-presentation of the lair's geography implies the scene's perspective now resides with the Alien Queen. The events that follow reinforce the shift in agency. In order to escape the Queen's Bluebeardian chamber, Ripley threatens the alien's eggs and the monstrous mother acquiesces to her demands by silently calling back the xenomorph minions lurking in the shadows. Despite the unspoken agreement for safe passage, Ripley then launches an attack on the Queen's offspring, the gratuitous spectacle of which is celebrated by the film's rapidly edited shots of burning and exploding eggs. It is a troubling moment. One could argue that this celebration of violence dramatises the expulsion of the abject, thereby reinforcing – and even endorsing – the patriarchal demand for such a process. Equally, Ripley's aggression inspires a momentary sympathy for the Alien Queen. The shifting of the camera axis encourages on both formal and narrative levels a change in perspective: the Queen's feminine experience is now the one tested for validation (Waldman, 1984) and the alien mother is not found wanting; in fact, the aggressiveness of Ripley's assault throws into relief the fluidity of Gothic boundaries. Constance Constable (1999), using terminology reminiscent of Botting's description of Gothic science fiction 'intersections', argues that Ripley's eventual defeat of the Queen/Other does not remove the number of 'resemblances' between them: this 'intersection means that the structures of horror are continually placed in jeopardy' (p. 189). *Aliens*' Bluebeardian encounter necessitates a re-evaluation of who is the physically and morally monstrous. In this case, the abject is very much in the eye of the beholder.

Not just 'another bug hunt'

In defending the film's emphasis on motherhood against criticism, Roz Kaveney (2005) argues that the theme gives Ripley 'motivation that has shadows and ambiguities to it' (p. 152). The choice of language here is suitably Gothic. *Aliens* shrouds the technology of science fiction, and the violence of the war and action film, in a Gothic gloom, presenting visually the uncanny terrors that psychologically haunt Ripley as the Gothic heroine. The film's generic blending is inextricably linked to its representation of female experience: indeed, as the opening and climactic scenes demonstrate, the film's *mise en scène*, narrative action, and plot development are consistently reframed through feminine perceptions, themes, and concerns. How one interprets this story – and ultimately the re-presented Ellen Ripley – is, as Kaveney hints, ambiguous. The Female Gothic could be said to consistently have the 'woman who has passed beyond the door . . . now permanently encased behind it' (Tatar, 2004: 107), and yet the genre's emphasis on patriarchal oppression, gender inequality, and violence against women may be read in more radical terms. In Ripley, there is the '*potential* for subversion by calling attention to existing gender roles' (Schubart, 2007: 183, original emphasis), although, as the confrontation with the Alien Queen demonstrates, the parameters of these 'existing gender roles' should not be taken for granted. Indeed, Elizabeth Hills (1999) argues that Ripley is a 'transgressive, transformative and controversial' figure who needs to be appreciated beyond the 'habitual readings or conventional theoretical modes which claim to know in advance what female bodies are capable of doing or what can be said about them' (pp. 39–40). It is apt that *Aliens* presents such potential through Gothic science-fiction, reworking the Bluebeard scene specifically, the latter of which itself holds in tension conservative reinscriptions of gender stereotypes with progressive or alternative interpretative possibilities. Reading *Aliens* via the Female Gothic thus allegorically becomes another candelabra (or flamethrower) in the darkness, illuminating new ways to navigate the complex geography of Gothic science fiction, motherhood, and female representation – as well as hunting bugs.

Notes

1 The term refers to Ann Radcliffe's adherence to the 'supernatural explained' conclusion of her narratives, whereby seemingly ghostly occurrences or threats are given a rational explanation. I explore this trend – and how it changes in cinematic adaptations – in a forthcoming chapter on *What Lies Beneath* (2000).
2 This information is revealed in a scene from the extended cut of the film and is not present in the theatrical version. The additional scenes – which also include Newt with her biological family – reinforce the theme of motherhood, however Gallardo-C. and Smith (2004) argue that 'Cameron's intent to make Ripley a mother and the maternal themes remain in the film regardless of the cuts' (p. 66).
3 The point is underlined again by the fact Ripley is known only her surname in *Alien*. In *Aliens*, Cameron removes the androgyny of her name by reinventing the heroine as Ellen Ripley.
4 The patriarchy of the film is embodied by the male characterisation of the Company (notably, the executives during Ripley's interrogation all wear suits and ties, regardless of gender), which is further incorporated and refined by the Burke figure, who becomes the Gothic's male threat. The marines are also characterised by stereotypically male traits and bravado, which – despite the gender parity – are the reasons Greenberg (1988) believes the attempt to read the film as feminist is greatly 'naïve' (p. 170).
5 I borrow the phrase from Paula Quigley's chapter in this collection analysing *The Babadook* (2014).
6 I explore this relationship between motherhood and the Female Gothic film further in a forthcoming chapter comparing *Under the Shadow* (2016) and *The Babadook* (2014).

References

Aguirre, Manuel (2008) 'Geometries of Terror: Numinous Spaces in Gothic, Horror and Science Fiction'. *Gothic Studies*, 10(2): 1–17.
Arnold, Sarah (2013) *Maternal Horror Film: Melodrama and Motherhood*. Hampshire: Palgrave Macmillan.

Baldick, Chris (1993) *The Oxford Book of Gothic Tales*. Oxford: Oxford University Press.

Botting, Fred (2008) *Gothic Romanced: Consumption, Gender and Technology in Contemporary Fictions*. London: Routledge.

Carpenter, Ginette (2016) 'Mothers and Others'. In Avril Horner and Sue Zlosnik (eds), *Women and the Gothic: An Edinburgh Companion*. Edinburgh: Edinburgh University Press, pp. 46–59.

Constable, Catherine (1999) 'Becoming the Monster's Mother: Morphologies of Identity in the *Alien* Series'. In Annette Kuhn (ed.), *Alien Zone II: The Spaces of Science Fiction Cinema*. London: Verso, pp. 173–203.

Creed, Barbara (1993) *The Monstrous-Feminine: Film, Feminism, Psychoanalysis*. London: Routledge.

Doane, Mary Ann (2007) 'Technophilia: Technology, Representation and the Feminine'. In Sean Redmond (ed.), *Liquid Metal: The Science Fiction Film Reader*. New York: Columbia University Press, pp. 182–191.

Ebert, Roger (1986) *Aliens*. www.rogerebert.com/reviews/aliens-1986 [Accessed 2 April 2016]

Fleenor, Juliann E. (ed.) (1983) *The Female Gothic*. Montreal: Eden Press.

Gallardo-C., Ximena and C. Jason Smith (eds) (2004) *Alien Woman: The Making of Lt. Ellen Ripley*. New York: Continuum.

Greenberg, Harvey R. (1988) 'FEMBO: "Aliens" Intentions'. *Journal of Popular Film & Television*, 15(4): 164–171.

Hanson, Helen (2007) *Hollywood Heroines: Women in Film Noir and the Female Gothic Film*. London: I.B. Tauris.

Hills, Elizabeth (1999) 'From Figurative Males to Action Heroines'. *Screen*, 40(1): 38–50.

Hughes, William (2014) 'The Gothic'. In Rob Latham (ed.), *The Oxford Handbook of Science Fiction*. Oxford: Oxford University Press. DOI:10.1093/oxfordhb/9780199 838844.013.0036

Jeffords, Susan (1994) *Hard Bodies: Hollywood Masculinity in the Reagan Era*. New Brunswick, NJ: Rutgers University Press.

Johnston, Keith M. (2011) *Science Fiction Film: A Critical Introduction*. London: Bloomsbury.

Kahane, Claire (1985) 'The Gothic Mirror'. In Shirley Nelson Garner, Claire Kahane, and Madelon Sprengnether (eds), *The (M)other Tongue: Essays in Feminist Psychoanalytical Interpretation*. Ithaca, NY: Cornell University Press, pp. 334–351.

Kaplan, E. Ann (1992) *Motherhood and Representation: The Mother in Popular Culture and Melodrama: Feminism, Psychoanalysis and the Material American Melodrama*. London: Routledge.

Kaveney, Roz (2005) *From Alien to The Matrix: Reading Science Fiction Film*. London: I.B. Tauris.

Kawin, Bruce F. (2012) *Horror and the Horror Film*. London: Anthem Press.

Luckhurst, Roger (2005) *Science Fiction*. Cambridge: Polity Press.

Luckhurst, Roger (2014) *Alien*. London: Palgrave Macmillan.

Moers, Ellen (1976) *Literary Women: The Great Writers*. New York: Oxford University Press.

Mussell, Kay J. (1975) 'Beautiful and Damned: The Sexual Woman in Gothic Fiction'. *Journal of Popular Culture*, 9(1): 84–89.

Penley, Constance (1990) 'Time Travel, Primal Scene and the Critical Dystopia'. In Annette Kuhn (ed.), *Alien Zone: Cultural Theory and Contemporary Science Fiction Cinema*. London: Verso, pp. 116–127.

Punter, David and Glennis Byron (2004) *The Gothic*. Oxford: Blackwell.

Russ, Joanna (1973/1995) '"Somebody's Trying to Kill Me – and I Think It's My Husband": The Modern Gothic'. Reprinted in *To Write Like A Woman: Essays in Feminism and Science Fiction*. Bloomington, IN: Indiana University Press, pp. 94–119.

Schubart, Rikke (2007) *Super Bitches and Action Babes: The Female Hero in Popular Cinema, 1970–2006*. Jefferson, NC: McFarland.

Sobchack, Vivian (1988) *Screening Space: The American Science Fiction Film*. New York: Ungar.

Sobchack, Vivian (2007) 'Postfuturism'. In Sean Redmond (ed.), *Liquid Metal: The Science Fiction Film Reader*. New York: Wallflower Press/Columbia University Press, pp. 220–227.

Suvin, Darko (1979) *Metamorphoses of Science Fiction: On the Poetics and History of a Literary Genre*. New Haven, CT: Yale University Press.

Tatar, Maria (2004) *Secrets Beyond the Door: The Story of Bluebeard and His Wives*. Princeton, NJ: Princeton University Press.

Tatar, Maria (2009) 'Bluebeard's Curse: Repetition and Improvisational Energy in the Bluebeard Tale'. In Griselda Pollock and Victoria Anderson (eds), *Bluebeard's Legacy: Death and Secrets from Bartók to Hitchcock*. London: I.B. Tauris, pp. 15–29.

Waldman, Diana (1984) '"At Last I Can Tell It to Someone!" Feminine Point of View and Subjectivity in the Gothic Romance Film of the 1940s'. *Cinema Journal*, 23(2): 29–40.

Wasson, Sara and Emily Alder (2011) *Gothic Science Fiction: 1980–2010*. Liverpool: Liverpool University Press.

Williams, Linda (1987) '"Something Else Besides a Mother": *Stella Dallas* and the Maternal Melodrama'. In Christine Gledhill (ed.), *Home Is Where the Heart Is: Studies in Melodrama and the Woman's Film*. London: BFI Publishing, pp. 299–325.

Wood, Peter (2010) 'Redressing Ripley: Disturbing the Female Hero'. In Elizabeth Graham (ed.), *Meanings of Ripley: The Alien Quadrilogy and Gender*. Newcastle upon Tyne: Cambridge Scholars.

8

THE GOTHIC HEROINE OUT WEST

A Town Called Bastard (1971)

Lee Broughton

Introduction

'Gothic' and 'feminine' are terms that we might not immediately tend to associate with the western genre for obvious reasons. In terms of its gendered aspects, Jackie Byars (1991) indicates that the western has traditionally functioned as a 'masculine' genre (p. 9), and this is underscored by Jane Tompkins' (1992) assertion that 'in Westerns (which are generally written by men), the main character is always a full-grown adult male, and almost all of the other characters are men' (p. 38). Ultimately, Frederick Woods (1959) concludes that 'the West is a man's world' where women 'remain onlookers to the main action' (p. 30). By contrast, many of the writers of British Gothic literature were women, and Alison Milbank (2007) notes that distinctly 'feminine qualities were emphasized' in their female character-led stories (p. 155). This led to a gendered subgenre of storytelling that Ellen Moers (1976) subsequently dubbed the 'Female Gothic'.

Further distinctions are evident if the western and the Female Gothic's spatial aspects are scrutinised. John H. Lenihan (1980) observes that the western tends to promote the 'lyricism of the great outdoors' (p. 166), while Tompkins (1992) notes that when the western's action is not set outdoors, it is set 'in public spaces – the saloon, the sheriff's office, the barber shop, the livery stable' (p. 38). This would seemingly position the western firmly at odds with the Female Gothic, which, as Lyn Pykett (1989) points out, is concerned primarily with 'confinement within the domestic space' (p. 78). That is not to say that westerns that have been described as being either 'Gothic' *or* 'feminine' do not exist; they do, but they are scarce when considered in terms of the western's voluminous catalogue. And it goes without saying that singular westerns that can be described as being both Gothic *and* feminine are even fewer in number. Indeed, I have argued elsewhere that the inclusion of both Gothic and feminine elements in westerns is a phenomenon that is most readily and consistently found in a strand of idiosyncratic British westerns that were produced between 1939 and 1973 (Broughton, 2016). This chapter will offer a close reading of one of these British westerns, Robert Parrish's *A Town Called Bastard* (UK/Spain, 1971), in order to argue that the film is wholly notable for the way in which it presents the adventures of a Gothic heroine out West.

Gothic and feminine westerns

Fred Botting (1996) notes that it is virtually 'impossible to define a fixed set of conventions' for the Gothic (p. 15), and the same holds true for the Gothic western. Suffice to say that we know one when we see one. Much like the Gothic literature that inspired it, the Gothic western exists in two distinct forms: those that feature genuinely supernatural or monstrous elements and those that do not. In terms of the former, Cynthia J. Miller and A. Bowdoin Van Riper (2016) observe that the 'supernatural first began to menace the West onscreen in the late 1950s' when Edward Dein's *Curse of the Undead* (USA, 1959) was released (p. 32). *Curse of the Undead* is a truly original and authentically Gothic western that cleverly transposes many of the tropes associated with vampire films to an Old West setting. Here, a black-clad gun for hire, Drake Robey (Michael Pate), turns out to be a vampire who has designs on his pretty new employer, Dolores Carter (Kathleen Crowley), until the local preacher, Dan Young (Eric Fleming), vanquishes him with a bullet that has a crucifix fashioned from holy wood embedded in its tip.

Although *Curse of the Undead*'s striking content clearly pointed towards a bold new direction for both the western and the horror film, other American directors were slow to respond to Dein's innovative approach. William Beaudine eventually directed a drive-in double bill that featured *Billy the Kid versus Dracula* (USA, 1966) and *Jesse James Meets Frankenstein's Daughter* (USA, 1966). However, Beaudine's films were campier in nature when compared to *Curse of the Undead*. That being said, both films do sport some recognisably Gothic features, albeit in a quite rudimentary way at times. The body of westerns that feature genuinely supernatural or monstrous elements has grown substantially in the years following Dein's and Beaudine's initial efforts, but the bulk of these films are perhaps best described as being horror westerns rather than Gothic westerns.

In terms of Gothic westerns that do not feature genuinely supernatural or monstrous elements, Italian-made spaghetti westerns tend to lead the way. Evert Jan van Leeuwen (2008) and Marcus Stiglegger (2012) have both reported small clusters of Italian westerns that they describe as being Gothic westerns. These clusters feature the following films: *Django* (Italy/Spain, 1966), *Django Kill/Se sei vivo spara* (Italy/Spain, 1967), *Vengeance/Joko invoca Dio . . . e muori* (Italy/West Germany, 1968), *Django the Bastard/Django il bastardo* (Italy, 1969), *And God Said to Cain . . ./E Dio disse a Caino . . .* (Italy/West Germany, 1970), *Keoma* (Italy, 1976), and *A Man Called Blade/Mannaja* (Italy, 1977). While the Gothic aspects of these westerns are quite varied and appear inconsistently from film to film, they do remain quite compelling signifiers. Key examples include seemingly resurrected gunslingers, archly diabolical and/or grotesque villains, fog-laden landscapes, funereal imagery, fiendishly designed and executed torture sequences, baroque *mises en scène*, labyrinthine cave formations, and emphatically imperilled female characters. Echoes of some of these Gothic signifiers would subsequently appear in Clint Eastwood's American westerns *High Plains Drifter* (USA, 1973) and *Pale Rider* (USA, 1985).

Classical American westerns that might be described as feminine texts are also rare, but they are better documented since their content has inspired numerous articles that have sought to study the actions of the films' striking female characters in order to better understand the gender dynamics and representational rules of the western genre. In these American westerns – typical examples include *Destry Rides Again* (1939), *Duel in the Sun* (1946), *Calamity Jane* (1953), *Johnny Guitar* (1954), and *Forty Guns* (1957) – the lead character is a strong, active, and independent woman who is able to carry out traditionally masculine activities such as shooting guns, riding horses, and running businesses such as saloons or cattle ranches. However, as writers such as Rebecca Bell-Metereau (1993) and Pam Cook (2005) have noted, these unruly women are usually 'tamed' by their film's end. Tough female gunslinger types will invariably fall in love and start dressing in a more feminine way before giving up their guns in order to become the domesticated weaker partner in a normative heterosexual relationship, while successful businesswomen types will invariably lose their businesses, their power, and their authority before finding themselves needing to be rescued by a man. Those strong women who fail to be tamed in these ways will be harshly punished at a narrative level, usually by death.

These narrative patterns can be likened to those that are found in the strands of Gothic literature that feature the Gothic heroine and the feminine monster. David Punter and Glennis Byron (2004) note that although Female Gothic texts allow their heroines to pursue adventures in which their experiences 'become the focus of attention', these stories also foreground happy endings in which traditional gender boundaries are restored when the heroine 'is reintegrated into a community and acquires a new identity and a new life through marriage' (p. 279). Similarly, Peter Hutchings (1993) observes that when a Gothic story features a female monster who enjoys narrative focus and agency, traditional gender boundaries are necessarily restored by the death of the monster (p. 163). However, the strong and active females that appear in Gothic-tinged British westerns are wholly notable because they defy the gendered rules of both the western and the Gothic tradition and they survive without being tamed or punished at their film's end.

The Gothic, the Female Gothic, and British westerns

Having first been established as a literary form in the late 18th century, the Gothic became popularly associated with the horror stories written by authors from the British Isles during the late 19th century. Indeed, writers such as Bram Stoker, Sheridan Le Fanu, and Robert Louis Stevenson led the way in this regard. These Gothic horror stories, which, unlike most of their 18th-century predecessors, were primarily written by men, featured threats that were determinedly monstrous or supernatural in nature, and can, for the most part, be categorised as 'masculine' texts. By contrast, E.J. Clery (1995) indicates that the stories found within the Female Gothic subgenre (which were primarily written by women) provided uncanny chills by employing the 'supernatural explained' device (p. 106). Introduced by Ann Radcliffe in *A Sicilian Romance* (1790), Clery (1995) observes that the device can be identified when 'apparently supernatural occurrences are spine-chillingly evoked only to be explained away in the end as the product of natural causes' (p. 106).

Interestingly, the 'supernatural explained' device would also prove to be a trope that was used extensively by British film-makers. Hutchings (1993) indicates that strict censorship guidelines resulted in the production of British horror films being actively discouraged until the late 1950s when Hammer Films began specialising in Gothic horror productions (p. 24). However, David Pirie (1973) observes that prior to Hammer's timely emergence, British film-makers had endeavoured to defy the censor by including supernatural-seeming scenarios and Gothic-inspired imagery within a multitude of what were essentially non-horror films (p. 25). Walter Forde's *The Ghost Train* (UK, 1941) is a good example of this approach since it features the depiction of apparently supernatural activity that is eventually revealed to be diversionary fake phenomena staged by enemies of the state in order to cover their nefarious activities. British cinema audiences thus became accustomed to finding allusions to the supernatural, the uncanny, and the Gothic within films from a variety of non-horror genres. Hence, the seemingly incongruous inclusion of such allusions in British westerns can in fact be understood to be in keeping with local film-making practices and audience expectations.

Similarly, the literary works of female writers such as Ann Radcliffe, Eliza Parsons, and the Brontë sisters had ensured that sections of the British public had become accustomed to narratives that depicted the adventures of uncharacteristically bold and active female characters, and this approach became relatively commonplace in subsequent British media texts: Agatha Christie's *Miss Marple* books and the films that they inspired, the music-hall films of Gracie Fields, the films of the British New Wave such as *A Taste of Honey* (UK, 1961), the television series *The Avengers* (UK, 1961–1969), and so on. Thus, the seemingly incongruous appearance of strong and active women in British westerns can be understood to be in keeping with the representation of women in a wide variety of other British media texts. Interestingly, Punter and Byron (2004) have observed that the Gothic is 'a genre that re-emerges with particular force during times of cultural crisis and which serves to negotiate the anxieties of the age by working through them in a displaced form' (p. 39), and a similar function might be attributed to British westerns too.

The British westerns that feature strong women and Gothic-inflected scenarios were produced during periods when the British nation was judged to have been suffering from acute crises of masculinity. As I have noted elsewhere:

these crises of masculinity are generally accepted to have been prompted by Britain's appeasement of Nazi Germany (1930s), loss of Empire territories and the Suez Crisis (late 1950s), the rise of the consumer society (1960s) and the emergence of second-wave feminism (early 1970s).

(Broughton, 2014: 138)

Indicative perhaps of the severity of the crises of masculinity that the British nation suffered during these periods, the British westerns in question did not actually function to allay societal concerns in this regard. Indeed, by replacing narratives in which men tame or punish unruly females with narratives in which strong women defy and best wholly inadequate men without suffering any kind of punishment at all, these British films ultimately served to confirm societal concerns about the emasculation of the nation state. Certainly, when *A Town Called Bastard* was produced in 1971, gender and sexual equality were the subject of much public debate. Fiona A. Montgomery (2006) notes that pressure from the women's liberation movement and efforts by British political parties to attract female voters resulted in 'much legislation' relating to 'women's issues' being introduced during 'the late 1960s and early 1970s' (p. 164) – for example, the Matrimonial Property Act (1970) and the Equal Pay Act (1970). It is thus possible to detect scenarios that chime with public debates relating to feminism and sexual equality within a diverse body of contemporaneous British films, including such horror flicks as *Dr Jekyll & Sister Hyde* (UK, 1971), comedies such as *On the Buses* (UK, 1971), and westerns such as *A Town Called Bastard*.

A Town Called Bastard

The British production company Benmar was responsible for producing four westerns during the early 1970s. Seeking to emulate the success of the numerous spaghetti westerns that had been shot on location in Spain, the company built a western town set close to Madrid. The incongruous look of this set – perhaps best described as being a walled medieval monstrosity that would have been better suited for the production of period horror films – would bring a Gothic ambience to most of the company's westerns, but none more so than *A Town Called Bastard*, whose narrative unfolds almost exclusively within the set's walls. Indeed, Botting's (1996) observation that 'medieval edifices – abbeys, churches and graveyards –' presented in 'generally ruinous states' are key Gothic locations (p. 2) would readily apply to the town's crumbling walls, its dilapidated stone buildings, and its prominently featured church and graveyard. Similarly, when discussing the locations found within Gothic novels, David Stevens (2000) notes that 'in some instances, the setting itself appears to be the main character and gives the novel a title: *Wuthering Heights*, for example, in which characters and setting seem fused together' (p. 55). This is also true of *A Town Called Bastard*, where the eponymous setting is home to a disparate community of miscreants who appear to have been brought together and trapped by fate.

Set in 1905, the film's narrative is driven by an American woman, Alvira (Stella Stevens), who journeys to the Mexican town of Bastard with a hired gun called Spectre (Dudley Sutton) in tow. Seeking revenge for her husband's death, Alvira offers a reward of $20,000 to any citizen of the town who is willing to name his killer. Key Gothic-tinged characters that Alvira encounters in Bastard include an aristocratic Federale Colonel (Martin Landau), the Priest (Robert Shaw), the town's bandit mayor Don Carlos (Telly Savalas), and his villainous deputy La Bomba (Al Lettieri). Needless to say, violence and mayhem soon erupt when the town's unscrupulous inhabitants set about trying to claim the reward money falsely. Interestingly, when Alvira and Spectre are first introduced, they appear to be travelling in a liminal space outside of time. On-screen text indicates that the film's brief prologue, which introduces the characters that viewers will come to know as the Colonel and the Priest, is set in 1895. It is revealed here that the pair were once revolutionary brothers in arms, and the duo are seen leading an insurgent attack on Bastard and carrying out a massacre inside its church. At the height of the massacre, the Priest kills his namesake and damages an ornamental cherub in the process.

The action immediately cuts to a shot of an ornate horse-drawn hearse being driven through barren countryside. When the hearse stops, its black-clad and sallow-looking driver, Spectre, dismounts and climbs inside to check the body of an apparently dead woman, Alvira, who is laid out in an open coffin. However, when Spectre assertively commands, 'Wake up, we're almost there', Alvira opens her eyes and smiles at him. When Spectre subsequently commands, 'Whatever happens, you do what I tell you', Alvira nods in subservient agreement before closing her eyes again. The symbolism present in this exchange – only the commanding male character has an audible voice – serves to highlight unequal gender relations, and the same can be said of the sequence's cinematography. Shot from above, Alvira appears to be in a submissive position while Spectre, who is shot from below, appears to be in a position of power. When Spectre and Alvira's journey recommences, the camera tilts upwards to reveal the malevolent silhouette of Bastard at the top of a far distant hill. The action then cuts to Bastard, where a group of Mexicans are returning to the town with two American prisoners, at which point on-screen text reveals that the film's time frame has jumped ten years to 1905. The editing and on-screen text thus make it difficult to judge with certainty which time period (1895 or 1905) Spectre and Alvira are travelling in initially. If read in an abstract and symbolic way, the wholly cadaverous-looking Spectre (whose name alone brings its own supernatural connotations) could be the angel of death incarnate who has chosen to resurrect the coffin-bound Alvira and transport her through time and space in order to grant her vengeance from beyond the grave (see Figure 8.1).

This image of Alvira as a supernatural vengeance-seeker might serve to position her as a monstrous female, and there are other instances in the film where such a reading of the character is encouraged. During Alvira's first conversation with the Priest, he nervously states that she has been appearing in a recurring nightmare that has plagued him of late: 'You have a knife. You come into my room.

FIGURE 8.1   Shots of Alvira (Stella Stevens) asleep in a coffin draw upon imagery
more normally associated with Gothic vampire films
A Town Called Bastard (Robert Parrish, Irving Lerner, 1971)

Put the knife in my back'. The Priest's nightmare is duly represented on screen,
and a supernatural version of Alvira is seen to slowly and menacingly advance
towards the camera. Dressed in a black billowing shroud, her skin possesses a
cadaverous pallor and her hair is unkempt. Coded as a vengeance-seeking rev-
enant, the supernatural Alvira raises a dagger above her head before bringing it
downwards in a stabbing motion. Alvira is understandably perplexed by the Priest's
revelation since the pair have never met before, and this scene serves to give the
film a determinedly supernatural aspect by suggesting that the Priest possesses
the power of premonition.

In contrast to her monstrous representations, the plain but smart appearance of
Alvira's turn-of-the-century dress and her black-cowled robe gives her the look of
a typical Gothic heroine, and many of her actions and experiences can be linked to
those of Gothic heroines too. Punter and Byron (2004) observe that the Gothic 'has
always been concerned' with 'issues of secrecy' (p. 70), and this notion is reflected
in Alvira's search for her husband's killer. It is obvious that the Priest is being secre-
tive from the outset, and he is eventually revealed to be withholding information
concerning the death of Alvira's husband. The mystery concerning Alvira's husband's demise revolves around the secret identity of a revolutionary figurehead who
was known only as 'Aguila', and in order to solve the mystery Alvira has to become
an investigative Gothic heroine. However, as Punter and Byron (2004) note, the
Gothic heroine will typically also find herself 'trapped and pursued' within a 'labyrinthine space' where threats 'to her virtue or to her life' will be made (p. 279), and
Alvira does endure such experiences.

Don Carlos threatens Alvira's virtue on her first day in town when he instructs
La Bomba to 'Take the señora to the hotel and see that *we* [reflective pause], see that
she gets a nice clean room'. However, in keeping with the general sense of respect
that *A Town Called Bastard*'s narrative affords to its lead female character, this threat

of rape is never acted upon nor raised again. Being the only Anglo female in a town populated by mostly Mexican men means that Alvira is exoticised to some extent, but she is rarely objectified, and her modesty is always spared. The length of her robe and her period dress means that her legs and her body are never displayed, and Alvira is never presented or framed as an erotic spectacle; similarly, a romantic subplot of any kind is out of the question because she is still mourning for her late husband. Indeed, this contextual detail stops the fact that she is single at the film's end from being read as a narrative punishment. It might be that Alvira's apparent wealth and Anglo status prompts the citizens of Bastard to grant her a sense of privilege, but the fact remains that Alvira is treated as an equal by the film's male characters, and she remains free to engage with people at any level of the town's society and free to traverse any and all of its public spaces. This represents something of a departure in terms of both the western and the Female Gothic genres.

Interestingly, the spatial aspects of both the western and the Female Gothic genres are cleverly employed during the staging of Alvira's generic entrapment scenarios. In the first instance, Alvira is entrapped within a western/public space – the town itself – when Don Carlos' men close and lock Bastard's gates in order to prevent her from escaping. Furthermore, the town itself comes to function as a Gothic labyrinthine space of sorts. Its main locations are shot from angles that invariably promote a sense of spatial disorientation, and it is often impossible to determine what lies beyond the Gothic pillars and ornamental archways that crowd the backgrounds of many of the film's exterior shots. For example, the town's graveyard is featured prominently, but how the film's characters actually make their way from the church to the graveyard remains unclear, and although the town is a public space it is allotted the functions of a private-domestic Gothic house on occasions. In the same way that the interiors of large Gothic houses and their baroque decorative features are sometimes symbolically employed to dwarf or overwhelm female protagonists, here director Robert Parrish presents long shots in which Bastard's imposing ramparts and parapets dwarf and threaten to overwhelm Alvira (see Figure 8.2).

Similarly, a sense of the concealed space that is accessed by a secret panel, which is often associated with private-domestic Gothic houses, is evoked in a public space in *A Town Called Bastard*. When one of Don Carlos' assassins attempts to creep up on Alvira as she meditates at the side of her husband's grave at dusk, he crawls beneath the hearse that is parked behind her. Quite unexpectedly, the underside of the hearse is seen to slide back, and Spectre, who is secreted within the base of the vehicle, covertly lowers his hands and garrotes the man. The failure of his assassins soon prompts Don Carlos to launch a more concerted and public attack on Alvira and Spectre. As a consequence of this, Alvira becomes entrapped in a Gothic private-domestic space when she is forced to take refuge in the Priest's quarters in the church's tower, to which Don Carlos' men then lay siege. This private-domestic space is also the site of an investigation that is undertaken by another female character: unbeknown to Alvira, the Priest's concerned partner – a strangely silent Mexican girl – searches for and finds evidence that

FIGURE 8.2 The western town set specially built for the film features decidedly
Gothic architecture
A Town Called Bastard (Robert Parrish, Irving Lerner, 1971)

reveals the Priest once knew Alvira's husband. In keeping with the workings
of the 'supernatural explained' device, it is here that an aspect of the Priest's
apparently eerie foresight is revealed to have an everyday explanation: the
Priest possesses Alvira's husband's saddlebag and it contains photographs of her,
which explains why her likeness in his nightmares was so accurate. These old
photographs – which are also enigmatically flashed on screen when the Priest
and Alvira first meet – feature a young Alvira, as opposed to another similar-
looking woman, but they similarly possess a symbolic function akin to that of
the old portraits found in the Female Gothic films that Helen Hanson (2007: 92)
has discussed: just like those portraits, these photographs indicate that the past is
about to intrude on the present and the repressed is about to return.

Don Carlos' actions continue to threaten Alvira's life until he is deposed and
executed by the duplicitous La Bomba. La Bomba himself is deposed and a new
patriarchal reign of terror is imposed on the town when the Colonel and his men
arrive and begin their own search for 'Aguila'. Clive Bloom (2007) suggests that
much of the gothic 'can be boiled down to relentless persecutions and agonizing
efforts to escape' (p. 234). The balance of power within Bastard shifts continually,
and this results in all of the film's major antagonists becoming the victims of vicious
persecutions that, despite their best efforts, they are unable to escape. Indeed, the
Priest's wry observation that 'every other stranger who's come to this town's ended
up in the cemetery' further encourages an abstract reading of the film, in which
Alvira and Spectre might be supernatural entities who have come to transport the
Priest from a place of purgatory.

Rachel Hutchinson (2007) asserts that the Mexican border towns that appear in
westerns are essentially liminal spaces, before arguing that by being 'beyond definition, the liminal space is open to any possibilities we can project upon it' (p. 183).
The town of Bastard is such a liminal space, and it possesses a strangely timeless and
limbo-like aura. The two Americans who are taken to the town explain that they

are in the area because they are 'lost'. When Alvira asks Don Carlos to reveal how her husband died, he answers, 'I don't remember, señora. I don't even remember him'. She is clearly perplexed by this response, and she counters that 'it was not so long ago'. Carol Zaleski (2008) observes that purgatory is 'the condition, process, or place of purification or temporary punishment in which, according to medieval Christian and Roman Catholic belief, the souls of those who die in a state of grace are made ready for heaven'.

With this idea of punishment in mind, it is interesting to note that Punter and Byron (2004) observe that 'the male gothic generally has a tragic plot, with the protagonist punished for his breaking of . . . taboos' (pp. 278–279). Here, the Priest is undoubtedly being punished primarily for the taboo murder of his namesake ten years earlier. Furthermore, a flashback reveals that the Priest is still troubled by another memory from his days as an insurgent: his decision to let an untrustworthy foot soldier live led to a betrayal that cost the revolutionary leader 'Aguila', and most of his men, their lives. The Priest has spent his recent years atoning for his sins by offering religious counsel to Bastard's wayward inhabitants and by repairing the damage that he caused to the church when he led his revolutionary assault on the town. However, the repair and rehanging of the ornamental cherub that the Priest damaged as he killed his namesake seemingly symbolises that the Priest's period of atonement is coming to its end. Zaleski (2008) notes that an individual 'may undergo correction, balance [their] life's accounts, satisfy old debts, cleanse accumulated defilements, and heal troubled memories' during their time spent in purgatory: the Priest would indeed appear to be working through such a process.

Milbank (2007) observes that 'Gothic heroines always cause the downfall of the patriarchal figures or institutions that seek to entrap them' (p. 155). Furthermore, Milbank (2007) asserts that the gothic heroine's 'resistance to patriarchal control' makes her 'a proto-feminist' (p. 155). Both observations could be readily applied to Alvira's dealings with – and attitudes towards – the film's male characters. For example, while Spectre is commanding and dominant at the start of the film, and clearly able to talk, once he is inside Bastard's walls he becomes a brooding 'deaf mute'. By contrast, the previously silent and subservient Alvira is seen to become a particularly vocal, active, and commanding woman. There is no explanation for these personality changes within the film's narrative, but their presence prompts the viewer to contrast the content of later scenes with that in which the two characters were first introduced. Ultimately, this contrast symbolically signals that unequal gender relations can be successfully disrupted.

In most shots where the pair are shown walking around Bastard, Spectre is seen respectfully following on a few paces behind Alvira who always leads the way. Removing Spectre's voice and positioning him behind Alvira in key shots is – in terms of the filmic representation of gendered relations – an inversion of usual cinematic norms. Thus, at a symbolic level, Spectre has been emasculated and Alvira has been empowered. Alvira remains a strong, active, and determined character who will avenge her husband's death without considering the cost to others. Certainly, her attitude and actions provoke the events that result in the deaths of the Colonel, Don Carlos, La Bomba, and the Priest. Seemingly reflecting the crisis of masculinity prompted by public debates regarding feminism and calls for sexual equality, these filmic events permit parallels to be drawn between these male characters' deaths and Hutchings' (1993) observation that the narratives of Hammer's early 1970s Gothic horror films dealt with 'the wider rejection and casting out' of male authority figures (p. 159).

Furthermore, Hutchings (1993) notes that in contemporaneous Hammer films such as Roy Ward Baker's *The Vampire Lovers* (UK, 1970) there are sequences where shots of a male character looking at a female character are followed by shots of the male character in a state of powerlessness or inadequacy (p. 163). The same configuration of shots is seen throughout *A Town Called Bastard* but is perhaps best realised when the Priest and Alvira hold their final conversation. Here, in what is essentially another inversion of popular cinema's usual approach to the representation of gendered relations, Alvira interrogates the Priest who subsequently makes a confession to her. The Priest reveals that her husband was 'Aguila', and, upon receiving catastrophic injuries in an ambush, he begged the Priest to kill him as an act of mercy that would also perpetuate the spirit of their revolution. Again, in keeping with the workings of the 'supernatural explained' device, this confession reveals that a second aspect of the Priest's apparently supernatural foresight had an everyday explanation: it was his own feelings of guilt that prompted the nightmares in which he was stalked by the avenging spirit of Alvira. When Alvira argues that her husband could instead have been returned to her for long-term care, the Priest replies that that was not what he wanted, which implies that 'Aguila' preferred death to living in an emasculated state where he would be reliant upon a woman for his basic needs. The Priest throws himself at Alvira's mercy and pleads his case, but to no avail: the vengeful widow is seen to satisfy her need to have her husband's killer executed by Spectre despite the fact that the content of his confession effectively served to legitimise his actions.

If *A Town Called Bastard* was a purely Gothic tale, Alvira's lack of mercy might position her as a feminine monster that must be destroyed in order to restore traditional gender boundaries. However, in terms of the film's status as a Gothic western, her physical appearance serves to distance her from accusations of monstrous activity. Alvira's clothing and her general demeanour suggest that she is a cultured and educated lady from the East of America, a popular western character type that Jenni Calder (1974) describes as 'the decorative heroine, who is associated with civilisation, domesticity, the schoolhouse and the church' (p. 170). Furthermore, the symbolic rules of the western that Calder (1974) details would suggest that Alvira's fair complexion and blonde hair are signs that she is 'decent', 'respectable', and law-abiding (p. 171). Alvira is thus afforded the moral high ground, and the narrative rules of the western demand that she must survive the film on the 'winning side'. But Alvira also remains an atypical female western character because her parallel function as an investigative Gothic heroine allows her to defy the gender-related prescriptions – such as inactivity and an over-reliance on men – that are usually attached to the western's decorative heroine stereotype.

Equally, Alvira is stronger and more focused than most Gothic heroines because she also functions as a 'woman out West', and the inherent sense of 'frontier spirit' that is an attribute of this character type grants her the ability to keep her nerve, avoiding the kind of hysterical breakdowns that often plague the Gothic's female characters. Indeed, Alvira endures strained relations with threatening, evasive, and duplicitous males who hold commanding positions of public office – the mayor Don Carlos, the Priest, and the Colonel – but she never succumbs to paranoia or self-doubt. Similarly, she witnesses several horrific occurrences during her stay in Bastard – the most notable being the hanging of a brother and sister who were tortured into giving false murder confessions, the shooting of the siblings' mother as she protested their innocence, and the death throes of both Don Carlos and the Priest – without flinching. Ultimately, Alvira is a Gothic western heroine who is able to challenge and defeat patriarchal order without being tamed or punished in any way at a narrative level. Indeed, Alvira leaves Bastard with the Priest's body – a body that is representative of patriarchal order – confined within the coffin that she herself occupied at the film's start. This striking symbolic turnabout can surely be taken as evidence that supports Hanson's (2007) observation that the Female Gothic invariably 'bears a political charge' (p. 63).

Conclusion

By offering a close reading of *A Town Called Bastard*, I have argued that the film is a western that pointedly incorporates several notable aspects of the Female Gothic genre. I have also shown that the film's representations of gender and space serve to transgress the norms that are typically associated with both genres. This sense of transgression is best represented by the film's lead female character, a vengeance-seeker called Alvira who comfortably embodies the contradictory aspects of the Gothic's monstrous female and investigative heroine types *and* the western's civilised Eastern lady and tough 'woman out West' types. Ultimately, I have suggested that this merging of character types allows Alvira to break the gender-related rules of both genres. Indeed, Alvira's strong, active, and determined character allows her to successfully complete her quest for vengeance against a symbol of patriarchal authority without suffering any form of narrative punishment. As such, I conclude that the striking content of this British Gothic western chimes with that of other British films from the early 1970s that have been judged to reflect a national crisis of masculinity prompted by public debates relating to the emergence of second-wave feminism and attendant calls for sexual equality.

References

Bell-Metereau, Rebecca (1993) *Hollywood Androgyny* (second edition). New York: Columbia University Press.

Bloom, Clive (2007) *Gothic Horror: A Guide for Students and Readers* (second edition). Basingstoke: Palgrave Macmillan.

Botting, Fred (1996) *The Gothic*. London: Routledge.

Broughton, Lee (2014) 'Upsetting the Genre's Gender Stereotypes: *Ramsbottom Rides Again* (1956) and the British Out West'. In Cynthia J. Miller and A. Bowdoin Van Riper (eds), *International Westerns: Re-Locating the Frontier*. Lanham, MD: Scarecrow Press:, pp. 121–141.

Broughton, Lee (2016) *The Euro-Western: Reframing Gender, Race and the 'Other' in Film*. London: I.B. Tauris.

Byars, Jackie (1991) *All That Hollywood Allows: Re-Reading Gender in 1950s Melodrama*. London: Routledge.

Calder, Jenni (1974) *There Must Be a Lone Ranger*. London: Hamish Hamilton.

Clery, E.J. (1995) *The Rise of Supernatural Fiction, 1762–1800*. Cambridge: Cambridge University Press.

Cook, Pam (2005) *Screening the Past: Memory and Nostalgia in Cinema*. Abingdon: Routledge.

Hanson, Helen (2007) *Hollywood Heroines: Women in Film Noir and the Female Gothic Film*. London: I.B. Tauris.

Hutchings, Peter (1993) *Hammer and Beyond: The British Horror Film*. Manchester: Manchester University Press.

Hutchinson, Rachel (2007) 'A Fistful of *Yojimbo*: Appropriation and Dialogue in Japanese Cinema'. In Paul Cooke (ed.), *World Cinema's 'Dialogues' with Hollywood*. Basingstoke: Palgrave Macmillan, pp. 172–187.

Lenihan, John H. (1980) *Showdown: Confronting Modern America in the Western Film*. Urbana, IL: University of Illinois Press.

Milbank, Alison (2007) 'Gothic Feminities'. In Catherine Spooner and Emma McEvoy (eds), *The Routledge Companion to Gothic*. London: Routledge, pp. 155–163.

Miller, Cynthia J. and A. Bowdoin Van Riper (2016) 'The Fantastic Frontier: Sixguns and Spectacle in the Hybrid Western'. In Lee Broughton (ed.), *Critical Perspectives on the Western: From* A Fistful of Dollars *to* Django Unchained. Lanham, MD: Rowman & Littlefield, pp. 27–40.

Moers, Ellen (1976) *Literary Women*. Garden City, NY: Doubleday.

Montgomery, Fiona A. (2006) *Women's Rights: Struggles and Feminism in Britain c. 1770–1970*. Manchester: Manchester University Press.

Pirie, David (1973) *A Heritage of Horror: The English Gothic Cinema 1946–1972*. London: Gordon Fraser.

Punter, David and Glennis Byron (2004) *The Gothic*. Oxford: Blackwell.

Pykett, Lyn (1989) *Emily Brontë*. Savage, MD: Barnes & Noble Books.

Stevens, David (2000) *The Gothic Tradition*. Cambridge: Cambridge University Press.

Stiglegger, Marcus (2012) 'Sons of Cain: Traditions of Gothic Horror in Antonio Margheriti's Spaghetti Westerns'. In Ivo Ritzer and Peter W. Schulze (eds), *Genre Hybridisation: Global Cinematic Flows*. Marburg: Schüren, pp. 72–80.

Tompkins, Jane (1992) *West of Everything: The Inner Life of Westerns*. New York: Oxford University Press.

van Leeuwen, Evert Jan (2008) 'Gothic Eurowesterns: A Grotesque Perspective on a Hollywood Myth'. *Bright Lights Film Journal*, 30 April. http://brightlightsfilm.com/gothic-eurowesterns-a-grotesque-perspective-on-a-hollywood-myth/#.WKsh6xRw7Hg [Accessed 3 April 2018]

Woods, Frederick (1959) 'Hot Guns and Cold Women'. *Films and Filming*, March: 11–30.

Zaleski, Carol (2008) 'Purgatory'. *Encyclopaedia Britannica Online*. www.britannica.com/EBchecked/topic/483923/purgatory [Accessed 3 April 2018]

9

LAUGHING AT PERIODS

Gothic parody in Julia Davis' *Hunderby*

Sarah McClellan

The narrow corridors of the gloomy mansion are darkly candlelit, its inhabitants are all seemingly sleeping. All except the young wife, newly married, lost in its halls, her white nightgown softly billowing and buttoned up tightly to her neck. But here comes the housekeeper, gliding with a tray bearing a silver-cloched dish that she leaves on the floor outside a door, from behind which human moans are heard. The heroine dips into an empty room to avoid being seen: Arabelle's room. The housekeeper has already told us that 'The first Mistress Suffolk-Finches' room was the most beautiful in the house . . . A sunset gold that seemed to glow as she did'. Our heroine now turns slowly around in awe of this room, while a faint music box tune plays briefly, inviting the audience to see her as the mechanical doll, reflected in a three-way mirror, fixed to the spot. The music ceases abruptly as the housekeeper appears silently and still in the back of the shot. She says, 'You've been wanting to see Mistress Arabelle's room for a while now, ma'am . . . You need only have asked . . . We keep everything exactly as was'.

If this begins to appear familiar, then it is no surprise. Aside from the reference to *Jane Eyre* and Grace Poole's nightly visits to the attic in the early part of the scene, the parallel moment in Hitchcock's *Rebecca* (1940) is mined not only for plot, but for mood, props, shots, and even for dialogue. These two texts are the parents of a cross-breed genre, the modern Gothic (Russ, 1973: 666), which in turn Julia Davis plunders for her 2012 BAFTA-winning television series *Hunderby*. In *Rebecca*, the young new wife stumbles upon the bedroom of the dead first wife, a room that is not used anymore: 'The most beautiful room in the house'. Here too, the housekeeper appears behind the heroine, silently, still, backlit behind gauzy curtains with no directional clue of how she arrived there, saying:

You've always wanted to see this room haven't you, Madam? Why didn't you ask me to show it to you? I was ready to show it to you every day. Everything has been kept as Mrs de Winter liked it. Nothing has been altered.

Mrs Danvers' line, 'I fancy I hear her' becomes, in *Hunderby*, 'I fancy I can smell her'. In both, wardrobes are opened, clothes lifelessly hang in rows, conjuring the bodies that once filled them. Mrs de Winter's underwear, 'made especially for her by the nuns in the convent of St Clare', becomes 'Her honeymoon underments [*sic*]. This housed her breasts. Her nipple dents – still there'. Both housekeepers paw and sniff at the intimate clothing of their deceased mistresses; both whip back the bed sheets, literally and metaphorically; both implant a ghostly notion in the minds of their vulnerable new mistresses. Mrs Danvers' lines in the film run thus:

> Do you think that the dead come back and watch the living? Sometimes I wonder if she doesn't come back here to Manderley and watch you and Mr de Winter together . . . a quick, light step. I can almost hear it now.

In Davis' hands, these are echoed: 'I sometimes wonder if the dead come back to watch the living. If she watches you and Master Edmund. I fancy I saw her . . . just then . . . in . . . here!' In this Gothic parody, Hitchcock's tense, psychological, woman-in-jeopardy thriller is also mined for filthy laughs. Davis' housekeeper, Dorothy, proceeds to sniff the bed sheets of the late Mistress Suffolk-Finch, extravagantly, insisting that she 'can still smell the whiff of her end place'.

Comedy writing by women is undergoing a renaissance and finding some very dark places to go to in exploring current anxieties around representations of the female body and lived experience on screen. Television writers such as Davis and Barunka O'Shaughnessy, but also Jo Brand, Vicky Pepperdine, Joanna Scanlan, and Phoebe Waller-Bridge, are subverting and parodying the tropes of canonical Gothic literature, the woman-in-jeopardy film, and the modern Gothic 'romance' novel. These earlier texts, written (though not produced/directed/published) by women for women uphold the patriarchal status quo, which states that 'The Love Story . . . for women [is] the only adventure possible' (Russ, 1973: 686). Gothic parody, however, seeks not to supply escapism from and vindication of 'Occupation: Housewife' (p. 686) provided by the original texts and by their small screen derivations, but to rehabilitate and normalise what has, in these texts, been hidden, made unnatural, and horrifying about women. As evidenced by this generation of comics, laughter is an effective antidote to the fear, victimhood, grim silence, and stoicism of the small screen Gothic heroine who, more often than not, is the body found in a lane or dragged from a lake, a pliant and either devoted or suspicious secretary, a good wife, a mad wife, mad would-be wife, or an evil wife/stepmother. At best, she is a 'Lady Detective' doing her best to survive in a man's world (by running rings around him).

It was less than ten years ago that Christopher Hitchens (2007), in an article for *Vanity Fair*, asked, 'Why are women . . . not funny?' He suggested that 'for some reason, women do not find their own physical decay and absurdity to be so riot-ously amusing [as men do theirs]', but really this is because he does not want us to laugh at our bodies. His article states that it 'is childish' to laugh at 'gross stuff', and that is the preserve of men; he needs women to be grown-ups. He concludes that:

> For women, reproduction is, if not the only thing, certainly the main thing. Apart from giving them a very different attitude to filth and embarrassment, it also imbues them with the kind of seriousness and solemnity at which men can only goggle.

Hitchens' article became the last word in the fatuous 'women are not funny' debate, not least because, as the stupidly funny Bridget Christie (2015) noted, he is 'conveniently dead' (p. 64). This supposedly 'unfunny woman' whose 'physical decay' is publicly masked or hidden, whose 'absurd body' is publicly censured and sanitised, whose sole purpose is to be impregnated and bear children with 'serious-ness and solemnity', is easily recognisable in the self-contained Gothic heroines of the past. However, Julia Davis' Gothic parody takes its cue from Bakhtin's work on the carnivalesque, which suggests that by embracing the 'bodily lower stratum', we can challenge the status quo. In fact, that perfectly self-contained woman – something akin to an automaton – corresponds with the 'smooth, transcendent, monumental, static, self-sufficient, closed and symmetrical body of the new bodily canons', which, according to Mikhail Bakhtin (1984), 'was the body identified with official culture and later also with the rationalism, individualism and the nor-malizing aspirations of the bourgeoisie' (Viljoen, 2014: 103). This image of the female body as self-contained and distanced from itself by the enduring presence of the male gaze can be countered by *laughing at and with* the absurd and decay-ing female body that Hitchens' woman finds unamusing and embarrassing. In so doing, the female body can be rehabilitated and reclaimed, so that representations of women in 'official culture' are not restricted to the airbrushed, epilated, and per-fectly manicured. This chapter will examine presentations of the 'grotesque female body' in series one of Davis' *Hunderby* and argue that, far from being the source of the 'strange, the scary, the terrible, the alienating and the inhuman' (Viljoen, 2014: 103), it is more normal, familiar, life-giving, and preserving than the perfectly self-contained woman predominant on both the big and small screen, and therefore worthy of celebration, not shame. Furthermore, as Glen Cavaliero (1999) suggests, 'Even when the parody is largely celebratory . . . it is also purposeful, its target the tyranny of the monolith, its aim to be liberating and remedial' (p. 60) The 'mono-lith' that Davis successfully challenges in *Hunderby* is the binary representation of women on the Gothic screen and in the dominant culture as either a serious, self-contained heroine or grotesque, unboundaried monster. In her comic realisations of Helene, Dorothy, Arabelle, and Hester, each of which contains elements of the heroic *and* monstrous, Davis liberates the female body on screen and remedies hitherto reductive and censored representations of women. The remedy comes with the notion that 'humour encourages sympathy rather than condemnation'

(Horner and Zlosnik, 2000: 5); in this instance, it is a sympathy with and for the realities of the female body and female experience.

Hunderby is set in a fictional English village in the 1830s. It opens as a young woman is washed ashore after her ship is wrecked. This deliverance from the waves serves as a rebirth for the heroine, Helene, who the audience later finds has escaped from the rapacious clutches of her hunchbacked husband, John Whiffin. She is pulled, unconscious, from the sea by an unlikely midwife, 'the noble Blackamoor, Geoff'. In true romantic form, Helene, our heroine with a dark secret, is fought over by the passionate, sensitive, but married Dr Foggerty – the Shadow Male, according to Joanna Russ' taxonomy of Gothic tropes (Russ, 1973: 669) – on the one hand, and widower, local pastor, and Master of Hunderby, Edmund – the Super Male – on the other. She must navigate both the practicalities of being female and friendless in a strange land and the insistent pull of her own desires with only female cunning and her naïve wit to help her (see Figure 9.1).

On the surface, this is a crudely drawn farce that parodies the various Gothic sensibilities of the English pastoral, Victorian melodrama, and the Gothic romance novel to evoke a squeamish and childish pleasure in its audience. Yet Gothic parody is an ideal position from which to explore contemporary anxieties. For Avril Horner and Sue Zlosnik, in 19th-century Gothic parodies such as Eaton Stannard Barrett's *The Heroine*, the anxiety concerned 'women and property'; for a 21st-century woman writer, this might conceivably mean the properties of her own body. As Horner and Zlosnik (2000) note:

> Parodic texts tend to have been read as limited in their significance, their very provenance in another work constraining the critic's engagement with wider issues; they are therefore frequently dismissed as low comedy at best or parasitic or reactionary at worst.
>
> *(p. 1)*

FIGURE 9.1 'The noble Blackamoor, Geoff' rescues Helene from the sea
Hunderby (Julia Davis, 2012)

Yet they go on to argue that the accomplished parodic text does not merely react to another text or genre (although that may be its starting point); rather, it forms part of a sophisticated cultural dialogue in which humour and wit assert themselves (p. 1). With *Hunderby*, Davis recognises the comic richness of the Gothic and its potential for exploring, and ultimately exposing through parody, the myth of the virtuous, self-contained woman versus the wicked, monstrous one.

Horner and Zlosnik use Jean Paul Richter's concept of the 'inverse sublime' as explored in his 1804 *Vorschule der Aesthetik* (*School for Aesthetics*) to 'attempt to define the complex cultural role played by parody' (Horner and Zlosnik, 2000: 5). They suggest that:

> For Richter, whereas the sublime evokes terror, awe and fear, the 'inverse sublime' invites an ironic detachment from the world. This results from the juxtaposition of the details of a finite world against the idea of the infinite: we thus become aware of the world's folly and detached from 'both great and small, because before infinity everything is equal and nothing'.
>
> *(p. 5)*

Parody allows us to view the world at a remove; thus, in laughing at characters in *Hunderby*, they assert, we are not laughing at individuals, but at humanity – at our own absurdities and follies. In being able to achieve an ironic detachment from the world and ourselves in it, we are better able to expose, examine, and potentially *address* contemporary anxieties about the realities of female bodies and female sexuality, which, as Cavaliero (1999) suggests, is ultimately restorative.

Ironic detachment is not only achieved through parody, however. Davis' humour plays in the space between '*being* and *having* a body . . . that is the human being can subjectively distance itself from its body, and assume some sort of critical position with respect to itself'. Critchley (2002) goes on to argue that:

> the comedy of the body is most obviously and crudely exemplified in scatological humour, where the distinction between the metaphysical and the physical is explored in the gap between *our souls* and *arseholes*, where we are asked to look at the world with the 'nether eye'.
>
> *(pp. 45–46, original emphasis)*

He cites the 'anal wit' of Chaucer and Rabelais as examples of how we reconcile our material body with our fears and desires. Charlotte Runcie (2015), however, has argued that *Hunderby*'s script merely 'cloak[s] a variety of dirty jokes in flowery circumlocution', and further that 'the script [i]s hung *entirely* on this premise of filthy goings-on in a decadent period setting' (added emphasis). Horner and Zlosnik (2005) also note that some hybrid, Gothic comic texts may 'appear on first reading as merely diverting or frivolous. Yet in their own way they, too, explore the fragmented condition of the modern subject' (p. 3). The 'dirty jokes' involving the 'bodily lower stratum' of excrement, vomit, ejaculate, menstrual blood, but also breast milk and bleeding wounds, growths and lesions, are themselves a critique of the status quo and the perfectly self-contained heroine of an outdated Gothic imagination. In the male-dominated field of comedy, such tendentious jokes may be simply hostile, but in giving *Hunderby* a 'decadent period setting' and employing parody, Davis removes the aggression, if not the obscenity, through which a sense of pleasure is derived, and offers sympathy instead. Further than simply parodying the moral codes and social niceties of the 19th- and early 20th-century Gothic novel, then, the 'nether eye' that Davis employs, that which produces what might be deemed obscene or other, serves to reconcile the audience with their messy, stubborn, often frightening, material bodies through laughter.

In the opening episode of *Hunderby*, Edmund contrives to save Helene's 'wretched soul' and arse(hole) on the beach, and, upon being resuscitated, she vomits seawater on to his face. In this reversal of a pornographic trope, Davis emasculates the Super Male, Edmund, and exposes, on the small screen, in the domestic sphere, the humiliation and aggression in the act of a man ejaculating on a woman's face. To a 19th-century audience, perhaps vomiting on the face of a clergyman would be no less shocking than the pornographic alternative might be to a 21st-century one. Yet here the audience sympathises with the aggressor, Helene, over the victim, Edmund, not out of a sense of misanthropy exactly, but because we relate to her loss of bodily control. Helene enters into an engagement with Edmund that she hopes will lead to 'a benign marriage'. However, during his proposal, Edmund, almost simultaneously, questions her virginity and requests that she cover up a lesion on her face for their wedding day. Helene therefore moves away from the self-containment of a traditional Gothic heroine and comes to embody that which is grotesque; her vomit and her lesion exceed the boundaries of her body. She is 'spoiled' in the rational eyes of the official culture both by her lack of sexual purity and by the physical manifestation of her moral deformity. However, the 'nether eye' sees only her desire for a kind man who will accept her imperfections and desire her in spite of her abject state.

In *Powers of Horror*, Julia Kristeva (1982) identifies the fear inherent in the abject, suggesting 'It is . . . not lack of cleanliness or health that causes abjection but what disturbs identity, system, order. What does not respect borders, positions, rules' (p. 13). Therefore, we can see that Edmund is unnerved by Helene's facial growth on one level because it may signify physical impurities or disease; it casts doubt on the material quality of his prospective bride, challenging official societal conventions of beauty, which has the potential to threaten his status and pride. It also raises questions about the integrity or properties of her body and its ability to bear children (a defining factor in his need to marry, as the audience later finds). However, the growth, in not respecting the physical and self-contained boundaries of the body, inspires a deeper revulsion and fear because, ultimately, it reminds Edmund of his own fragility and mortality.

Indeed, the juxtaposition of life and death in *Hunderby* is explicit in the opening scene of episode one when Helene asks Edmund where the congregation are, as they arrive at the church to be married. 'They prefer to go to the hanging', he replies. The camera cuts away to the villagers enjoying the carnival atmosphere of the marriage feast with a hanging corpse, strung from the gallows, dominating the foreground. Aside from the allusions to the opening scenes of both David Lean's 1946 film of *Great Expectations* and Michael Reeves' 1968 film *Witchfinder General*, which bodes ill for the newlyweds, Davis' employment of this Gothic trope also serves to confront the fragility of life and the historical dangers of transgressing from societal norms or laws, particularly for women. Furthermore, the incongruity of the gallows placed in close proximity to the chaotic wedding party – the spasmodically dancing Edmund satirising all those careful recreations of period balls where husbands are got in Jane Austen adaptations – can remind the audience of high maternal and infant mortality rates in the 19th century. As Zlosnik and Horner (2000) note in relation to Gothic parody in literature, 'the post-feminist reader may still laugh . . . but it is with the knowledge that beneath the farce and grotesquery lie . . . poignant truths about the social and economic status of early nineteenth-century women' (p. 2); marriage really could kill you.

Death's place in carnival is inextricably linked to the female, and Felicity Collins (2002) asserts that:

> Bakhtin's . . . image of the earth as both womb and grave is central to feminist reappraisals of the grotesque female body as a source of *comic* rather than melodramatic attitudes to sexuality, death and the material life of the body.
>
> *(added emphasis)*

If we can read humiliation as a kind of 'little death', Edmund's inability to consummate the marriage on their wedding night, or indeed thereafter, also enacts a kind of sexual death (and death of his ancestral line) in being unable to satisfy or impregnate his wife. His prior warning to Helene that 'there may be a sharp, searing pain throughout' is punctured by her observation, frequently repeated thereafter, 'Edmund, 'tis not in!' Davis makes it clear in the repetition of the phrase over the course of the series that this equals *his* failure rather than her shame. Thus, the female body is rehabilitated, since, instead of passively accepting sexual violence in marriage, something sanctioned by law in the United Kingdom until 1991, Davis renders Edmund impotent. In fact, it is no surprise that Edmund's repeated humiliations throughout *Hunderby*, and the close conjunctions between life and death, culminate in the final episode of the series. In an actual near-death experience, he is crushed and paralysed by the bloated, obese body of his first wife, Arabelle, who is not after all deceased, as she falls from the attic of the bell tower through a weak ceiling and into the room where Helene is about to give birth. As discussed at the opening of this chapter, Arabelle's memory has been preserved and idealised by the housekeeper, Dorothy, in the manner of Mrs Danvers, in order to erode Helene's own position and identity. The image of the perfectly self-contained Gothic heroine described by Dorothy is subverted when Arabelle, barren, locked in the attic for three years, and reported dead, finally does expire, on top of her husband. She has been fed to excess – we are told 'she's eaten nothing but eggs' – by the devoted but malevolent Dorothy to the point where the attic can contain her no more. As in *Jane Eyre*, the Super Male is finally fully emasculated by his hidden wife who has transgressed societal norms and been banished for it. This familiar trope in Gothic literature of the female failure to procreate or obey accepted rules determining appropriate female sexual behaviour, embodied by Bertha Mason, is given in *Hunderby* a corresponding male 'failure'. Thus, Davis goes some way towards redressing the balance and rehabilitating the barren 'mad woman in the attic' by killing off her over-inflated, ill-used image. This shorthand for the 'grotesque female body' defined by lack is surely now laid to rest.

In *Hunderby*, Davis parades a carnival of monstrous women, made so by this inability of their bodies to respect the status quo – from the leprous heroine, Helene, to Edmund's aged mother with her 'silent bowel', and the morbidly obese, Arabelle, no distortion of the socially acceptable, contained female body is left unrepresented. Horner and Zlosnik (2005) note with interest the rise in popularity of the Gothic novel with the 'roughly contemporary . . . birth of melodrama [and] rise of the circus . . . as popular entertainment' (p. 6). It is as if these distinct genres converged in some way to serve a similar need to confront fears and anxieties in 19th-century society. Chief among these monstrous women in *Hunderby*, however, is Dorothy, played by Davis herself. Her cruelty and willingness to abase herself, as she considers the world only and entirely through the 'nether eye', challenges what it is to be a woman in the 'official culture' of both the 19th and 21st centuries. In literature and on screen, the spinster, whose virginity was once prized, is now often pitied, as she is left childless, is undesired, or presumed to have 'unnatural desires'. Davis rehabilitates this monster too. Like Mrs Danvers, Dorothy is devoted to the 'memory' of the supposedly deceased Arabelle, preserving the monogrammed nightgown that she wore 'the night [Edmund] burst her', and insisting Helene wear it on her own wedding night. Elsewhere, she serves Arabelle's favourite meal, 'Thrush buns in a dark gravy . . . Mistress Arabelle liked her gravy very thick'. However, Dorothy's tormenting of Helene is not out of loyalty to or a barely suppressed desire for Arabelle, as it is in *Rebecca*, but is more likely located in her own desire to secure absolute control of Hunderby, that 19th-century anxiety about women and property resurfacing as a larger 21st-century anxiety about identity and equality. Furthermore, in Dorothy, Davis presents the audience with a woman who is bold and unapologetic in authoring her own adventure. She seeks a way out of servitude in the manner of Jane Eyre, but without sleeping with the enemy, the censorious, post-Enlightenment Super Male embodied by Edmund. What Dorothy achieves, in the end, is the liberation of a divorce without the preceding bad marriage.

Dorothy's monstrosity, then, arises not out of her lack – of a husband or heir or of a desire for either – but out of her cruelty and willingness to transgress social boundaries, in order to self-promote and achieve, as Mistress of Hunderby, an elevated position in a society that disempowers women through inheritance law and strict moral codes. In episode one, she blinds herself with Edmund's infantilising night-time drink of 'bubbly milk', a concoction that, the audience later finds, is in fact her own breast milk. 'I've always oozed a snowy broth', she says, imbuing the breast milk with paradoxical virginity or purity via 'snowy', but contradicting this with 'oozed', which suggests something infectious or diseased. Davis satirises the 21st-century fetishisation of motherhood; the fact that Dorothy, a supposed virgin, produces breast milk renders the ability to breastfeed mundane rather than a source of anxiety in contemporary debate around 'the mother'. That the milk is potentially poisonous – perhaps another attempt on Dorothy's part to kill Edmund off and secure Hunderby for herself – subverts the synonymy of mother and nurturer. Blindness, however, is a common enough trope in Gothic literature where it implies impotence in its male sufferers, from Rapunzel's prince to Rochester. Dorothy's 'blindness' is phoney and further advantages her over Helene, whom she blames for the 'accident'. Dorothy takes to wearing an eye patch, an homage by Julia Davis 'to Bette Davis in *The Anniversary*'. (Gilbert, 2015) Davis, as Mrs Taggart, in the 1968 Hammer film, is a powerful widow who emasculates her three sons as a way of exerting control; in the same way, Dorothy controls Edmund through bubbly milk, ultimately thwarting his attempts to produce an heir who will inherit Hunderby.

In an interview with Gerard Gilbert (2015) for the *Independent*, Davis says that her 'small-screen monsters are a reaction to her being self-censoring in real life'. Here, her comedy confounds Hitchens' argument that society expects women to be more civilised, and therefore more self-censoring and less funny, than men. Dorothy's dialogue is littered with the uncensored, the base, and the scatological, which is the flip side of tendentious comedy. Davis' delight in the language of abasement, as well as visual representations of the grotesque body both female and male, are the main sources of humour as well as horror here, roundly disproving Hitchens' theory. Echoing Mrs Fairfax as she leads a naïve Jane Eyre around Thornfield for the first time, Dorothy explains to the newly married Helene:

'We never go in here, madam. It leads to the bell tower and the stairs are quite rotten, so 'tis kept locked at all times', which is, again, followed by loud, very human groaning.

'What's that?' asks Helene, as Jane had done before her. Dorothy replies:

''Tis likely owls, madam, they do defecate through their mouths'.

In fact, the audience knows that the bell tower houses the grotesque Arabelle. Davis keeps the image of the once self-contained, now turned mad, heroine firmly associated with excrement, and under lock and key until she is ready to dispatch her at the climax of the series.

In her ministrations to Edmund's mother, Matilde, Davis' use of language elevates the elderly woman's bowel movements, or lack thereof, to mythical status; indeed, among Dorothy's first words in the series are 'her bowel has still not spoken'. Helene's menstrual bleeding is described in similarly religious terms – in this case, as evidence of her inability to conceive. Dorothy presents her bloodstained undergarments to Edmund at the breakfast table, saying:

'Satan's jam hath once again burst her bristled bun'.

'Why does it weep, month upon month, its vicious red tears?' he replies, incredulously.

The violence of the language is disguised, not in 'flowery circumlocution', as Runcie would have it, but in rich and alliterative prose, which itself provokes a pleasure and sensuality in the hearing and repeating. Thus, the audience finds itself laughing at periods – actual red bloodstained underwear as opposed to the innocuous and medicalised blue liquid of sanitary towel advertisements – and in doing so feels sympathy, not derision or hostility, towards the menstruating heroine.

In fact, as Horner and Zlosnik (2005) assert, this hybridity of the comic and the Gothic has always existed within the genre. They suggest that:

> it is, perhaps, best to think of Gothic writing as a spectrum that, at one end, produces horror-writing containing moments of comic hysteria or relief and, at the other, works in which there are clear signals that nothing is to be taken seriously.
>
> *(p. 4)*

They insist that the comic Gothic turn 'functions within Gothic as a critique of modernity' (p. 4), and argue that even the original Gothic novel, *The Castle of Otranto* (1764), 'offers readers several moments of farcical humour'. In this, the servant girl, Bianca's, concern for her possessions, as she flees 'a supernaturally giant hand' in the castle strikes them as 'an incongruous note of practicality and materialism' (p. 5) They suggest:

> Bianca's immediate concern about what she owns (not much, presumably) and what she should or should not strive for in a rapidly changing social world ('Would I had been content to wed Francesco!') comically relativizes the large themes of inheritance, primogeniture, property, marriages of convenience and aristocratic lineage that inform the main plot.
>
> *(p. 5)*

In *Hunderby*, the presence of 'Satan's Jam' at the breakfast table alongside actual jam comically reflects, and thus normalises and creates critical distance from which to examine, anxieties around female reproduction in our society. Horner and Zlosnik (2005) further employ Walpole's own preface to *Otranto* to support the notion that comic parody and farce have always been agents provocateurs within the Gothic. Walpole suggested his work was 'in the spirit of Shakespeare [a] mingling of the tragic and the comic within the same text'. Horner and Zlosnik (2005) suggest that this 'retrival of the bard's agenda had much to do with the construction of an English national identity that separated itself off from European culture, including Voltaire's judgement that to mix buffoonery and solemnity was "intolerable"' (p. 5). I imagine that Voltaire and Christopher Hitchens may have become friends. The 'camp' exclamatory dialogue with which Horner and Zlosnik credit Walpole is the stuff of Davis' writing on *Hunderby*: 'Edmund, 'tis not in!'

Davis' confrontation of the abject female, her engagement with the post-reproductive female body as well as the horrors of childbirth, the willingness to say what has previously been unsayable and show what has been unshowable on the small screen, leads to glorious triumph in *Hunderby* and presents the realities of the material female body in contemporary culture in a way that has not been achieved before. Helene, finally pregnant, is induced at six months in order to give birth within a year of the death of Edmund's mother and so fulfil the terms of her will. Dorothy and her sidekick, Biddy Ritherfoot, administer a noxious brew through an 'anus funnel' to 'encourage the womb to splay'. Davis does not shy away from the indignities of childbirth with processes still recognisable in even modern obstetrics. 'My girls always seem to split belly to back when they force them out early', says the unsavoury Biddy, adding, 'probably best off cutting her first'. Dorothy gives birth a magical realist spin when explaining to Edmund, 'Sometimes when a womb tears it does not stop at the belly but splits right up to the face until she breaks in two like a ladybird', parodying historical male ignorance of the process. The horror is compounded when Helene is strapped down 'to prevent her from punching babby in the face' when she first sees him. The glow of maternity so often present on the small screen in the past, or else circumvented altogether, is well and truly diminished here. However, Davis does not opt for gore either; it is merely implicit in the verbal violence of the exchanges between Dorothy and Biddy, which renders it far more shocking for a contemporary audience fatigued by or increasingly inured to body horror.

In the closing frames of the series, while Dr Foggerty and Helene cradle their newborn son nestled in the bucolic grounds of Hunderby, Dorothy observes the pastoral scene from an upper window. Silhouetted against the light, unshackled from her stiff, black, housekeeper's gown, wearing a white cotton chemise, her hair tumbling down her back, she smokes a clay pipe in quiet contemplation. The camera pans round and we see a young Fijian man, reclining naked on her bed smiling coquettishly at her. The final shot is of Dorothy at the window, her young lover nuzzling her neck, and as she lifts her gaze she stares straight into the camera at the viewer. She takes another drag on the pipe, and shoots the audience a knowing look. Davis has pulled a trick: the monster is revealed as the heroine. Both Dorothy and Helene have got what they want: Helene her passionate beau who accepts her because and in spite of her imperfect body, Dorothy her sexual autonomy and undisputed dominion over Hunderby and its master. The harmony that is restored at the end of *Hunderby*, tenuous though it may be since Edmund and Hester both loom on the horizon, is achieved *in spite of* the monstrous nature of all its characters. Davis offers us a return to the status quo after the carnival. However, though Helene is redeemed as a wife and mother, it is as a sexually awakened woman and good-enough parent; she all but drops the baby in order to receive a passionate kiss from Dr Foggerty, who turns out not to be a murderer (Russ, 1973: 669). Thus, something has shifted in the retelling. If we look closely enough, we see that, in the true spirit of farce, Helene is not really his wife, but is instead still married to his father and he to his sister. In breaking the fourth wall in the final sequence, the audience is invited to identify with the monstrous Dorothy, perhaps in recognition of the abject within ourselves (see Figure 9.2).

FIGURE 9.2   Dorothy, played by Julia Davis herself, regards the viewer at the series' end *Hunderby* (Julia Davis, 2012)

The rehabilitation and restoration of the female body can be achieved by embracing the grotesque, as Davis shows in *Hunderby*. In offering up the abject female body on screen as a critique of what has been done to them, put in them, or pulled out of them in the Gothic literature and cinema of the past, Davis succeeds in forcing us to gaze unflinchingly onto that which has previously been rejected as unwomanly, and by laughing at it, not taking it seriously, engaging in widespread buffoonery, asks us to consider larger themes about women's ownership of their own bodies and their representation in society. Though in her Reith Lectures, *Managing Monsters*, Marina Warner (1994) cautions against the liberating possibilities of representing women as monstrous, saying, 'ironies, subversion, inversion, pastiche, masquerade, appropriation – these postmodern strategies all buckle in the last resort under the weight of culpability the myth has entrenched' (p. 11). I would argue that we need to redefine what *is* monstrous in relation to the way that women's bodies are represented in the official culture. For it is not their abjection or grotesquery; far scarier is the airbrushed, epilated, and perfectly manicured automaton we have come to accept as 'womanly'.

References

Bakhtin, Mikhail M. (1984) *Rabelais and His World*, translated by H. Iswolsky. Bloomington, IN: Indiana University Press.

Cavaliero, Glen (1999) *The Alchemy of Laughter: Comedy in English Fiction*. Basingstoke: Macmillan.

Christie, Bridget (2015) *A Book for Her*. London: Arrow Books.

Collins, Felicity (2002) 'Brazen Brides, Grotesque Daughters, Treacherous Mothers: Women's Funny Business in Australian Cinema from *Sweetie* to *Holy Smoke*'. In Lisa French (ed.), *Womenvision: Women and the Moving Image in Australia*. St Kilda: Damned Publishing:, pp. 162–192. Reprinted in *Senses of Cinema*. http://sensesofcinema.com/2002/feature-articles/women_funny_oz/ [Accessed 19 November 2018]

Critchley, Simon (2002) *On Humour*. London: Routledge.

Gilbert, Gerard (2015) 'Hunderby Creator on Giving Her Darkest Comic Impulses Free Rein in the Bafta-Winning Sitcom'. *The Independent on Sunday*, 6 December. www. independent.co.uk/arts-entertainment/tv/features/julia-davis-interview-hunderby-creator-on-giving-her-darkest-comic-impulses-free-reign-in-the-bafta-a6762481.html [Accessed 22 May 2016]

Hitchens, Christopher (2007) 'Why Women Aren't Funny'. *Vanity Fair*, January. www. vanityfair.com/culture/2007/01/hitchens200701 [Accessed 22 May 2016]

Horner, Avril and Sue Zlosnik (2000) 'Dead Funny: Eaton Stannard Barrett's The Heroine as Comic Gothic'. *Cardiff Corvey: Reading the Romantic Text*, 5. www.romtext.org.uk/articles/cc05_n02/ [Accessed 11 September 2016]

Horner, Avril and Sue Zlosnik (2005) *Gothic and the Comic Turn*. Basingstoke: Palgrave Macmillan.

Kristeva, Julia (1982) *Powers of Horror: An Essay on Abjection*, translated by Leon S. Roudiez. New York: Columbia University Press.

Runcie, Charlotte (2015) 'Cartoonishly Grotesque'. *The Telegraph*, 10 December. www. telegraph.co.uk/culture/tvandradio/tv-and-radio-reviews/12044376/Hunderby-review-cartoonishly-grotesque.html [Accessed 22 May 2016]

Russ, Joanna (1973) '"Somebody's Trying to Kill Me and I Think It's My Husband": The Modern Gothic'. *Journal of Popular Culture*, 6(4): 666–691.

Viljoen, Louise (2014) '"I Have a Body, Therefore I Am": Grotesque, Monstrous and Abject Bodies in Antjie Krog's Poetry'. In Judith Lütge Coullie and Andries Visagie (eds), *Antjie Krog: An Ethics of Body and Otherness*. Durban: UKZN Press, pp. 98–132.

Warner, Marina (1994) *Managing Monsters: Six Myths of Our Time*. London: Vintage.

10

'THERE'S A SECRET BEHIND THE DOOR. AND THAT SECRET IS ME'

The Gothic reimagining of Agatha Christie's *And Then There Were None*

Katerina Flint-Nicol

In a pivotal sequence from the final episode of the BBC's Christmas adaptation of Agatha Christie's crime thriller *And Then There Were None* (2015), the focal character of Vera Claythorne, holding a lamp, ascends the stairs of the doom-laden weekend retreat of Soldier Island (see Figure 10.1). As an image, it is iconographic and speaks of a heritage of both televisual and cinematic Female Gothic narratives, a visual departure from the usual television renditions of Christie's novels. The depiction of an inquisitive female heroine navigating the contours of her home to investigate the secrets housed within the architecture is a recurring image in female-centric films, as exemplified by *Secret Beyond the Door* (1947), *The Innocents* (1961), *The Others* (2001), *The Duke of Burgundy* (2014), and *Crimson Peak* (2015). The repeated use of such a specific sequence of female representation conveys a persistence not only in female visual narratives, but also of the Gothic as an aesthetic in illuminating the female experience. While this adaptation of *And Then There Were None* draws upon such a Gothic tradition, there are critical distinctions that need to be drawn. First, while the character of Vera Claythorne is centralised and presented as a focal figure for the audience throughout the serialisation, she is one character in what is essentially an ensemble crime drama. Acknowledging this does not disavow Vera's depiction or negate reading her within the parameters of the Female Gothic, but rather warns against situating the adaptation as a whole *solely* within the Female Gothic mode. The narrative does not exclusively belong to Vera. Vera may be described in places as paranoid or as repressing her sexuality, but the drama is broader than offering a critique on gender relations and anxieties over domesticity, as scholars Tania Modleski (1984) and Diane Waldman (1984) consider the Female Gothic cycle of the 1940s to do. Second, to return to the visual treatment of Vera climbing the stairs, while the image may belong to the Gothic tradition, Vera's motivation and agency depart from that of her predecessors, creating a frisson between the visualisation and the narrative trajectory of Vera.

Miss Giddens in *The Innocents*, Grace in *The Others*, and Edith from *Crimson Peak* are exploratory figures who seek to resolve the disturbances in their home: the Gothic woman desires to know the secret behind the door. In comparison, Vera in ascending the stairs strives not to uncover, but rather endeavours to escape her fate, suppress her past, and deny her character. The disturbances in the home on Soldier Island, her secret, her past, are waiting for Vera, and the audience, as she reaches the landing. For in *And Then There Were None*, Vera *is* the final secret behind the metaphorical door. The Bluebeard story that provides the narrative structure for tales of the Female Gothic disrupts Vera as the 'woman in peril'. The rendering of both Vera and the domestic setting in this sequence is symptomatic of the adaptation in that both are treated with a Gothic sensibility that centralises ambiguity, suspense, and the uncanny in the adaptation process, engaging the audience in a crime mystery that oscillates between rationality and the fantastic. It is the Gothicisation of the crime thriller that is the focus of this chapter.

As the title conveys, the attention here is to illuminate the BBC's serialisation as a Gothic reimagining of the Agatha Christie novel, and will draw upon scholarship on the Gothic and the Female Gothic. With a concentration on close textual analysis of the domestic setting of the house on Soldier Island and the characterisation of Vera, this chapter's concern arises from the structural proximity of both the crime drama and ghost story, and will illuminate how the adaptation seeks to shift and return an Agatha Christie novel to the *psychology* of crime, untethering the emphasis away from the resolution of a traditional televisual whodunit. Furthermore, the chapter seeks to explore how the BBC production draws upon the Gothic as a mode to render the time period of the novel's setting. Indeed, this adaptation draws upon, and manipulates, conventions, concerns, and iconography of staple British TV fare, both crime and heritage dramas, the Female Gothic drama, and the Christmas horror tradition, that had been revived by the BBC in recent years.

FIGURE 10.1 Vera (Maeve Dermody) seems to be the classic Gothic heroine as she explores the house with a lamp
And Then There Were None (Craig Viveiros, 2015)

As an example of textual and formal borrowing, this version of *And Then There Were None* disrupts, recontextualises, and transforms prior discursive structures and fragments of 'what has already been said', resulting in the novel animated here as a Gothic whodunit.

'What HAS the BBC done to Agatha Christie?'

Screening over three consecutive nights during the Christmas period of 2015, the BBC's adaptation of Christie's *And Then There Were None* was the jewel in the crown of the broadcaster's festive fare and prominently programmed, with the first instalment airing on Boxing Day evening. The viewing figures repaid the BBC's confidence in the production. Averaging just under 5.5 million viewers over the three episodes, the serialisation helped the BBC dominate the television ratings over the Christmas period (Jackson, 2015). The casting of acting stalwarts such as Miranda Richardson, Sam Neill, and Charles Dance established the production as a period and costume piece and suggests a move of gravitas towards a serious drama, which the marketing and trailers capitalised on. The book is consistently held as the bestselling crime novel of all time, and triumphed as Christie's most popular novel in a 2015 public vote launched by the author's estate to mark Christie's 125th birthday (Flood, 2015). The thriller's plot sees ten strangers invited to holiday on a remote island just off the Devon coast by a mysterious host, U.N. Owen. Cut off by the sea, the guests are confronted with prior murderous acts they have each committed and each are adroitly killed off one by one, in line with the poem 'Ten Little Soldier Boys'. The first murder is the young, reckless socialite Tony Marston, killed by a dose of cyanide: 'Ten little soldier boys went out to dine. One choked his little self, then there were Nine'.

Cultural and television commentators were divided on the Christmas adaptation, with critical analysis riven in relation to what constituted the appropriate form of an Agatha Christie novel on screen. Chris Hastings of *The Daily Mail* bemoaned that 'Christmas viewers will be stunned by controversial new adaptation featuring drugs, gruesome violence and the F-word' (Hastings, 2015). Hastings' reverence of Christie adaptations appears to decouple violence and horror from the very act that underpins Christie's thrillers – murder. The implication here is that watching Christie on the small screen, especially during the festive season, should be a reassuring and homely experience, despite the subject matter, with murders taking place off screen so the audience can engage solely with the resolution of a mystery. As the crime writer Sophia Hannah (2015) comments, 'some people still see Christie as a writer of cosies – fun puzzles that are all surface and plot, with little depth or substance to them'. To substantiate the newspaper's claim, a scholar of Christie's work, Dr Curran, provided further unfavourable commentary by challenging the authenticity of the adaptation because of the sex, drugs and violence, deeming the serialisation as 'not Agatha Christie' (Hastings, 2015). So enraged was *The Daily Mail* that this version would not be 'tweed' enough for a Christie outing that the paper protested by demanding 'What HAS the BBC done to Agatha Christie?'

(Hastings, 2015). The concern that the adaptation would not be 'Christie' enough revolves around what constitutes faithfulness and authenticity to the novel and the on-screen genre.

Key to illuminating the Gothicisation of *And Then There Were None* are the comments made by the screenwriter Sarah Phelps on her approach to adapting the crime thriller to the small screen. Phelps explained her bewilderment over how staple British TV crime dramas, such as *Marple, Poirot*, and *Midsummer Murders*, were unconcerned with the taking of a life, but rather focused on the unravelling of plots and murder by 'letter openers to the eye' (Conlan, 2015). In *And Then There Were None*, Phelps found not only a brutality and philosophical enquiry in what it means to take a life, but also an unrelenting and remorseless narrative that offered no redemption for its characters. As Phelps summarises the characters, plot, and fate in the novel, 'You're not going anywhere, you're pinned, you're fixed, it doesn't blink, look at you squirm' (Conlan, 2015). What Phelps did see was potential for a reimagination of the staple TV crime drama that went beyond using death as a plot device; what underpinned the novel for Phelps was a forensic examination of guilt, of transgression and culpability. In adapting the novel for the small screen, Phelps subtly balanced the scales to focus on the psychology of the characters, rather than a creaky plot trajectory investigating the killer's identity, by mining, exhuming, and returning individual characters' histories and secrets to haunt their present. Phelps was also aware of the timing of the novel, written in 1939 with Britain on the brink of declaring war. Phelps understands how the characters are products of the First World War, of what she perceives as 'madness . . . the loss of status – the posturings of Empire are over and they are the last gasp of it' (Conlon, 2015). The characters, as representations of British class and social types, suggest a cultural and social context, but the adaptation's focus on the characters' simmering psychopathy, misogyny, domestic violence, homophobia, racism, and classism subverts the usual 'cosiness' of television crime thrillers and projects a rejection of nostalgia for the time. The Gothic as a mode that reveals irrationality, the immoral, and the unstable (Botting, 1996: 1–2) is a fitting sensibility here to prune away any of the nostalgia usually associated with period dramas, and to return murder and immorality to individual responsibility rather than the organisation of narrative logic of television crime drama. In reimagining the novel within the mode of the Gothic, the adaptation endeavours to capture both the decline of Britain's colonial power and the impending war with the refocus of responsibility with murder. The inevitability of death in *And Then There Were None* is entwined with culpability. As David Punter (1980/1996) writes of Gothic fiction, 'the reason why it is so difficult to draw a line between gothic fiction and historical fiction is that Gothic itself seems to have been a mode of history, a way of perceiving an obscure past and interpreting it' (p. 52).

And Then There Were None is subjected to a process of Gothicisation that draws out and visualises the morality, evil, and psychopathy that, for Phelps, underpins the novel. For what better sensibility, mode, and discourse to reconfigure such a hybridity and richness in form, while distorting the distinction between what is real and what is phantasmic, than the Gothic, a disparate and multi-voiced mode that transforms the familiar into the strange? As Helen Hanson (2007) notes, the Gothic is a fecund and fluid aesthetic with a propensity to 'renew and assert its relevance', evoking cultural and social anxieties through its focus on the past, on secrets, and revelatory events (pp. 33–35). The process of Gothicisation applied to the adaptation renders it an uncanny yet self-aware form, one that is known to the spectator, but yet strange and unfamiliar, and as a form the spectator must engage with and work through.

While this Gothic adaptation invigorates the British television crime drama, scholarship has previously perceived the proximity between the detective and the ghost story. Tzvetan Todorov (1975) observes how both genres necessitate the reader/spectator to deliberate over possible solutions that operate upon a binary axis of rationality/irrationality and probable/improbable (p. 49). Todorov observes how the organising principles of both coalesce in the structures of Christie's *And Then There Were None*, likening it to a sealed-room story (p. 50). The narrative poses solutions that are too improbable for a rational reading (no one else other than the party is on the island, and the information provided does not implicate anyone *in* the party), and so directs the audience to hypothesise on a supernatural intervention as the probable and rational explanation (pp. 49–50). Helen Hanson (2007) broadens this discussion by perceiving the similarities between Female Gothic narratives and detective narratives in that both operate on the employment of suspense, investigation, and suspicion that drive and maintain an intertwined relationship between ambiguity and knowledge, both for the characters and for the spectator (pp. 47–49). The reimagining of *And There Were None* as a Gothic whodunit is situated within hybrid mechanisms that centralise the uncanny, as an aesthetic strategy within the murder mystery plot, while inviting the textually informed viewer not only to react to the effects of the uncanny, but to also play the role of investigator, an armchair detective. It is not enough for the audience to watch passively as the female protagonist weaves her way through to the conclusion. The audience members are invited to engage actively, as there are clues to see and collect, and mysteries to uncover and solve.

Crisis of vision and temporality: Soldier Island as haunted house

As mentioned earlier, the textual analysis of this chapter focuses on Vera and the domestic setting. In Bluebeard Gothic and Female Gothic narratives, the house and home are posited as sites of violence and domestic anxieties. Constructed within the iconography of the Gothic tradition and exploiting the recognisable aesthetic and obligations of the Old Dark House, the house on Soldier Island is presented as a murder house and one that houses secrets. Temporality is central to the house's animation, through its *mise en scène* via visitations of temporal ruptures and through the house's function within the narrative structure and pace of the adaptation. As a Gothic whodunit, the serialisation traces over the Gothic treatment of the house with 'sleight of hand' trickery of a whodunit by inserting visual clues for the viewer.

Visually, specifically in the initial stages of the narrative, the adaptation's strategy is to suggest the house is home to supernatural intervention, a motif that acknowledges Todorov's observation of the novel's inclination towards the uncanny. An early shot of the interior establishes the ambiguous status of the house. An image of the butler, Rogers, standing in the hallway waiting for the arrival of the party is rendered from a low angle, with the camera placed on the floor and lingering longer than is usually required for such an establishing shot. The camera placement and length of time suggests a presence, something phantasmal and uncanny, waiting for the guests, prompting an initial analysis of the home as a haunted house and the adaptation as a Gothic venture. It is a visual strategy of the programme in animating a sense of dread, hesitation, and suspense for the audience. Exterior shots of the house and island corroborate the haunted house motif. Subverting the long vistas of televisual and cinematic heritage homes, the adaptation instead aligns itself with the anti-nostalgic structures of the Gothic and Female Gothic (Wheatley, 2006: 99), as these exterior shots of the house and island punctuate the narrative throughout all three episodes. As the plot gathers pace and the rate of murders quickens, so the visual animation of the house corresponds accordingly. The vista is increasingly wrapped in darkness and progressively stormy weather, cementing Soldier Island within the Gothic lineage of the 'dark and terrible house' where the domestic setting is saturated with a lurking malevolence and housing a secret. Visually, the house is presented as a haunted presence. But the placing of these shots has further temporal significance as they aid in structuring the pace of the serialisation format as well as organising the temporality of the narrative. Time is fundamental to *And Then There Were None*. As the screenwriter Sarah Phelps (Conlan, 2015) and crime writer Sophie Hannah (2015) observe, inevitability is central to the fate of the characters and to the narrative structure and strategy. This inevitability and a temporal countdown are imbued into the *mise en scène* and narrative structure. The poem 'Ten Little Soldiers' hangs on the walls of the house, and with each murder there is one fewer corresponding statue on the dining-room table, removed by an invisible hand. The house establishes the temporal inevitability of the characters' fate, an inevitability that is strengthened for the audience with the persistent return to long shots of the house and island. Wheatley (2006) perceives the domestic space of the Female Gothic to be configured as a place of anxiety, entrapment, and prison, a place engulfed by family secrets (pp. 104–105), but a space the protagonist works through to achieve a cathartic resolution (pp. 90–122). However, the house in *And Then There Were None* denies the characters this opportunity. The closure dismisses a supernatural explanation in favour of a more improbable but human intervention, denying the early representation of the house as haunted. Within the logic of the narrative, then, the presence as referred to earlier cannot be otherworldly, but rather is found within the more rational logic of the universe. The aesthetics of the house are the visualisations of what waits for the guests – justice (in the form of accountability) and murder. The house is reconfigured as an implement of judgement, justice, and execution. The constant return to images of the home and island serve as a marker of temporal inevitability, a visual rhythm of fatalism for the party that cues spectator expectations with regard to the narrative's rejection of redemption. As Phelps herself said of the narrative, no grey-haired lady in tweed or fastidious Belgian detective will solve the mystery and catch the culprit (Conlan, 2015). There is no redemption, no escape, only the inevitability of death as punishment.

The house is not the only tool to be in service to the momentum of justice within the narrative, however; the adaptation also concerns itself with temporal ruptures, animated as a crisis of the subjective for the characters. The Gothic is interested not only in secrets, but with a troubled past returning (Curtis, 2008: 16), with disruptive events of the irrational. The Gothic home, as a site of past violations and transgressions, offers up its history to pass judgement on the present, with ghosts piercing temporality, seeking vengeance and justice for past wrongs (Curtis, 2008: 10).

Barry Curtis (2008) summarises haunted house narratives as revolving around all that 'go wrong' with houses (p. 16), with conflicts and confrontations arising between space, its troubled past, and present inhabitants. Often there has been a family tragedy in the history of the house and a mystery that requires resolving. Ghosts, by piercing temporality, seek vengeance by demanding justice for past wrongs. Often the investigator is female (p. 15), especially in Gothic tales, and a crisis in objectivity is experienced by the present occupants (p. 24). The protagonist explores the sinister labyrinths in order to uncover what the house seeks to conceal. The house itself is a porous structure, a 'dark place' (p. 10) often found at the edges of towns, isolated and inscribed with tension and malevolence where 'objects refuse to stay stored' (p. 11). Haunted house narratives, then, are concerned with crisis and instability, temporal frissons and confrontations, a restless past and indeterminate futures, and a righting of injustice.

As already established, the plot resolution determines that the house on Soldier Island is not haunted, but in the initial action the adaptation visualises apparitions. The house, as a Gothic structure, functions as a portal for manifestations that punctuate temporality that are presented as exhibitions of an internal crisis of each character. But deviating from Barry Curtis' (2008) thoughts of the Gothic house, these spectres are not bound to the architecture of the house, but rather are mobile apparitions tethered to the individual characters. Dr Armstrong sees his blood-soaked patient who died on the operating table because he operated when in an inebriated state. Vera envisions the mother of Cyril, the boy Vera purposefully drowned, standing in the doorway to the library. Objects too function as gateways for the return of an individual's past. General MacArthur's hat in his bedroom is transformed into a soldier's helmet, reawakening his memory of murdering his wife's lover. The phantoms are mechanisms that objectify subjective states of feelings and serve to function on three levels. First, as a crisis of vision of the characters, the phantoms adhere to the Gothicisation inherent in the adaptation. Second, the spectres provide characterisation, by presenting opportunities for the various wrongdoers to display guilt, shame, or regret for their past actions, positioning the characters as victims and inviting a more empathetic reading from the audience. Lastly, the visions verify the accusations levelled at each guest via the recorded message of judgement played during their first dinner, as actualities, privileging the spectator with knowledge of the events.

As the adaptation fluctuates between the structures of the gothic and the murder mystery, the final area of the house I wish to discuss veers towards the problem-solving of the obligations of the crime thriller. Mary Ann Doane's (1987) analysis of the 1940s Female Gothic films asserts the home as a domestic space that is 'yoked to dread, and to a crisis of vision' and conceals violence in 'places which elude the eye' (p. 134). Approaching *And Then There Were None* as a Gothic whodunit, the serialisation can be appreciated for how its presentation of the problem-solving aspect of the production develops what is 'unseen' via a Gothic misdirection. The promise of violence is hidden in plain sight for characters and audience alike. By drawing upon conventions of a whodunit, 'sleight of hand' trickery is employed to dupe spectators, while inviting them to play at sleuthing. The future instruments of murder are placed strategically with the frame, rather than clues to the criminal's identity. The liver that Justice Wargrave will utilise in faking his own murder receives an extended shot of its own, as do the axes that will be used to kill the butler, Rogers. A more oblique shot of the polar bear rug that will be implemented in killing Inspector Blore is rendered from a low angle, with the polar bear strategically placed in the foreground, drawing the attention of the audience to its presence (see Figure 10.2). These visual clues are images that serve to create suspense and provide the spectator with knowledge the characters do not possess. To use Elizabeth Cowie's (1997) analysis of suspense narratives, the characters' restricted knowledge positions them as victims of the narrative, reinforcing what is suggested through the visualisations of the characters' fractured psyche (pp. 52–53). This also corresponds with Fred Botting's (1996) assessment of the Gothic where 'ambivalence and uncertainty obscure single meaning' (p. 3), resulting in characters subjugated to the sovereignty of the narrative. What is sleight of hand for the spectator is, however, a failure of vision

FIGURE 10.2 Clues hide in plain sight: the polar bear rug hides a murder weapon
And Then There Were None (Craig Viveiros, 2015)

on the part of the characters. Hanging on the wall in every room is the framed poem 'Ten Little Soldiers', functioning as the weekend itinerary of murders. Thus, all characters are provided with the knowledge of their fate, and Rogers, Vera, and General MacArthur are explicitly shown reading the framed poem. Vera is the first character to observe the decreasing number of the corresponding figurines, and the General the first to forecast the guests' inevitable fate, describing the party as 'rats in a barrel'. Yet, as communicated by the party's general denial at the charges levelled on the recorded message, there is an initial failure to read the clues, to recognise they have been judged and sentenced to death. The Gothicisation of the house and all its objects renders it an uncanny structure that toys with the expectations of a weekend party, a party that initially does not see or comprehend manipulations of conventions, allowing for its duplicitous nature to exist in plain sight.

'I have an instinct about you. I think you're pretending' (Philip Lombard to Vera)

Lombard's comment to Vera is a warning for the spectator, introducing doubt as to her character and constructing Vera within a projection of vacillation, a trope of the Female Gothic narrative where the female character oscillates between victim and heroine (Hanson, 2007: 60). Vera exists within the narrative strategy of suspense and hesitation found in both the crime thriller and the Gothic. Indeed, the character of Vera draws upon the conventions and iconography of the Gothic female persona and the thematic concern of veiling and revealing, through the employment of costume, that traverses both the whodunit and the Gothic, giving rise to the stratagem of ambiguity associated with both genres. Vera is duplicitous and is herself the Gothic mystery needing to be solved. Animated as a Gothicised body, Vera fulfils the generic obligations of the Female Gothic by performing the role of paranoid female and the woman in peril. As the narrative progresses, and she is consumed by her past that punctures temporality and space, her body is exposed as a site of anxiety until her past eventually claims her. Vera's death allows the production one last 'twist' in the narrative in creating a scene of suspense and implicating the spectator in a final act of judgement on Vera.

As the focal character in both novel and adaptation, Vera is central to the serialisation, which fosters an empathetic relationship between the character and audience through the use of the flashback, suggesting Vera is a victim. In seeming to be privileged with access to Vera's past through the device of the flashback, the audience too is invited to perform the role of investigator by piecing together the fragments of the flashbacks into a coherent narrative of Vera. The spectator is invited to deconstruct the fragmentation of the Gothic in order to solve the mystery of the crime. Vera's flashbacks also function as another source of suspense and unease by drawing upon the convention of the Gothic of a mystery within a mystery and offering an alternative to the whodunit convention of the revelation of the killer's identity as the story's resolution. The strategy of the flashback further aligns Vera within the Female Gothic narrative in centralising the point of view of the female protagonist. Helen Wheatley (2006) observes how the Female Gothic directs a shared subjective position between heroine and spectator that implies both optical and aural points of view, subjective camerawork, and narrative point of view (p. 111). Part of what determines this marked subjectivity of Vera is the use of flashbacks, inviting the audience to identify her as a sympathetic character. Lastly, in a final play with generic conventions, Vera's flashbacks provide the ultimate revelation that not only confirms that the audience was duped by Vera, but also disrupts Vera as Gothic heroine by positing Vera as Bluebeard. Taking Maria Tatar's application of Bluebeard to Tom Ripley in *The Talented Mr Ripley* as a cue, we can interpret the flashbacks as articulating the duplicitous nature of Bluebeard's offer of a key to his wife. Here, the flashback is a temporal and visual space 'harboring the forbidden chamber storing Bluebeard's secrets and inspiring the wife to uncover those secrets, the dwelling becomes the site of mystery and morbid fascination' (Tatar, 2006: 50–52).

The *mise en scène* of the flashbacks, in terms of colour and Vera's costume, establish a temporal distance between the Vera of the present narrative and the Vera of the past, constructing an initial arcadia of romance, agency, and future for Vera. Initial flashbacks situate Vera with her charge, Cyril, in an idyllic setting that seeks to challenge the charge of Vera as murderer by introducing doubt on the judgement by presenting Vera as a caring nanny to Cyril. This preliminary ambiguity of Vera's character proposes a possibility the adaptation will reconfigure the ending in Vera's favour, further aligning Vera with the identity of Gothic heroine. The organising structure of this Christmas serialisation assembles the pace of the flashback to disclose Vera's own story in counterpart with the narrative in the present. The revelatory backstory runs through all three episodes, effecting a further avenue of suspense that runs parallel to the identity of the murderer in the present. The dramatisation of Vera's past engages the viewer with a dual function of empathetic reading of Vera's character and solving the puzzle. The recurring image of Vera dressed in a red swimming costume floating in the sea punctuates the narrative and broadens the hesitation that surrounds Vera's character. The image is presented in a dissonance of meaning, its significance initially decoupled from the rest of Vera's story, providing a clue, but one that requires further context to solve. Romance, a distinctive characteristic of the Female Gothic narrative, is introduced in the flashback when Vera begins a relationship with Hugo, Cyril's uncle. As Hugo's backstory of losing an inheritance to Cyril is revealed, empathy for Vera is challenged and finally rejected when Vera's intentional drowning of Cyril is revealed. The significance of the image of a floating Vera is shown to be the visualisation of Vera as murderer and culpable. Initial punctuations of Vera suggest she is drowning as a result of trying to save Cyril. As the mystery of Cyril's death is resolved, the image communicates this is a pretence, and that Vera calculates the time it takes for Cyril to drown and then rolls over in the water pretending to be drowning herself. The hesitation over Vera's culpability is resolved.

The costume significance of the red bathing suit adheres to the Gothic's concern with both temporality and identity, and illuminates Vera as a Gothicised body. Catherine Spooner (2004) argues garments that clothe the Gothic body articulate that body in terms of Gothic concerns (p. 3), while Anne Hollander (1993) asserts that Gothic clothing functions as an aesthetic and mechanism of containment (p. xiii). As her past engulfs her and this crisis of self escalates, Vera's surface is also disrupted and disturbed, as symbolised by an increasingly dishevelled appearance. The shedding of the respectable clothing of a secretary and the donning of the red bathing suit returns Vera to her past, and paradoxically brings the past back to Vera by reuniting her with a long-buried self of female sexuality and desire.

The scene of Vera's death encapsulates the production's strategy of shifting significance away from the killer's identity and privileging character psychology. Audience engagement with the role of investigator concludes with the provision of a closing resolution. A final revelation that only Vera and the audience are privileged with presents Vera as a hybrid form that sees both Gothic heroine and Bluebeard fused into a single subjectivity. In *And Then There Were None*, Vera is a Gothic red herring, in that she is the secret behind the door. On the verge of hanging herself, Vera whispers the name 'Hugo' as she watches her bedroom door open. This utterance engages the spectator as investigator and returns the spectator to earlier incidences of clues 'hiding in plain sight' that confirm Vera's internal crisis was not guilt or remorse, but rather a self-reproach of a different kind. The audience was warned by Lombard that Vera was 'pretending', while the adaptation offered clues to puzzle together in order to reach the 'truth' of Vera. The initial train journey in episode one offers the sight of a pensive Vera gazing on the curtain handle, styled as a hanging rope. This initially implies a rumination on death, her culpability, regret, and remorse over her killing of Cyril. In a later flashback, Hugo tells Vera he would see her hang if he could prove her guilt of the murder, linking it back to the image of Vera on the train. Vera's eventual hanging reveals the regret she feels is not for killing Cyril, but rather for the absence of Hugo, which symbolises her failure in securing a husband. With this final clue, the length of the scene invites the spectator to be complicit in Vera's fate and sit in judgement as to whether Vera is deserving of being hanged. The scene dismisses a supernatural reading of events. Shots privileging Vera's feet struggling to remain on the chair as she hangs, while she listens to Justice Wargrave reveal his responsibility for the murderous events, provide a final scene of suspense and one fused with questions of morality and ethics of murder, justice, and retribution. If we are to condemn Vera, it is not for a child's murder, but rather for her indifference and rejection of liability.

Conclusion

But what does this generic vacillation mean? What can we make of the intervention of the BBC's *And Then There Were None*? As this chapter has argued, to approach the adaptation as a reimagining of the original novel enables deliberation over how this programme renews the television crime thriller by shifting the focus away from the revelation of the culprit's identity to meditate on the psychology of criminality and the morality and ethics of justice. Treating the novel to a Gothic rendering invigorates Agatha Christie on the small screen and draws out the philosophical enquiry and high concept of the structure of the murder mystery that underpins the novel. The application of the Gothic as a 'promiscuous and fertile aesthetic' (Hanson, 2007: 33) provides opportunity other than the usual motifs of a period drama, such as costume and *mise en scène*, to animate historical periods by endeavouring to bring the time to life through characterisation. While the Gothic, in terms of the ghost story, has a rich and seasonal lineage, not only on British television, but in wider national popular cultural forms, this adaptation of the novel as ghost-story-at-Christmas develops the form of staple British television crime drama, energising it away from the 'cosy' (Hannah, 2015) to a more contemporary resonance of an unflinching confrontation with a philosophical rumination on murder and death.

References

Botting, Fred (1996) *Gothic*. London: Routledge.
Conlan, Tara (2015) 'BBC's And Then There Were None Puts a Darker Spin on Agatha Christie'. *The Guardian*, 13 December. www.theguardian.com/media/2015/dec/13/bbc-and-then-there-were-none-agatha-christie [Accessed 31 January 2019]
Cowie, Elizabeth (1997) *Representing the Woman: Cinema and Psychoanalysis*. Basingstoke: Macmillan.
Curtis, Barry (2008) *Dark Places: The Haunted House in Film*. London: Reaktion Books.
Doane, Mary Ann (1987) *The Desire to Desire: The Woman's Film of the 1940s*. Bloomington, IN: Indiana University Press.
Flood, Alison (2015) 'And Then There Were None Declared World's Favourite Agatha Christie Novel'. *The Guardian*, 1 September. www.theguardian.com/books/2015/sep/01/and-then-there-were-none-declared-worlds-favourite-agatha-christie-novel [Accessed 31 January 2019]
Hannah, Sophie (2015) 'Agatha Christie: With Drugs, Violence and Swearing, Will the Queen of Crime Recapture Christmas?'. *The Guardian*, 24 December. www.theguardian.com/books/2015/dec/25/agatha-christie-bbc1-adaptation-and-then-there-were-none [Accessed 31 January 2019]
Hanson, Helen (2007) *Hollywood Heroines: Women in Film Noir and the Female Gothic Film*. London: I.B. Tauris.
Hastings, Chris (2015) 'What HAS the BBC Done to Agatha Christie?', *Mail on Sunday*, 13 December. www.dailymail.co.uk/tvshowbiz/article-3357749/What-BBC-Agatha-Christie.html [Accessed 31 January 2019]
Hollander, Anne (1993) *Seeing Through Clothes*. Berkeley, CA: University of California Press.
Jackson, Jasper (2015) 'And Then There Were None Helps BBC Dominate Christmas Ratings'. *The Guardian*, 29 December. www.theguardian.com/media/2015/dec/29/and-then-there-were-none-christmas-boxing-day-ratings-bbc-agatha-christie [Accessed 12 February 2019]
Modleski, Tania (1984) *Loving with a Vengeance: Mass-Produced Fantasies for Women*. London: Methuen.

Punter, David (1980/1996) *The Literature of Terror: A History of Gothic Fictions from 1765 to the Present Day*. Republished in two volumes, 1996. Harlow: Longman, Vol. 1: The Gothic Tradition.

Spooner, Catherine (2004) *Fashioning Gothic Bodies*. Manchester: Manchester University Press.

Tatar, Maria (2006) *Secrets Beyond the Door: The Story of Bluebeard and His Wives*. Princeton, NJ: Princeton University Press.

Todorov, Tzvetan (1975) *The Fantastic: A Structural Approach to a Literary Genre*. Ithaca, NY: Cornell University Press.

Waldman, Diane (1984) '"At Last I Can Tell It to Someone!" Feminine Point of View and Subjectivity in the Gothic Romance Film of the 1940s'. *Cinema Journal*, 23(2): 29–40.

Wheatley, Helen (2006) *Gothic Television*. Manchester: Manchester University Press.

PART IV

National cinema and the Gothic

11

EAST GERMAN GOTHIC

Kurt Maetzig's *The Rabbit Is Me* (1965)

A. Dana Weber

Arm in arm, a young and a middle-aged woman walk up a spiralling stone staircase in an ornate building. As they leave the frame, a high-angle shot reveals a whole system of crisscrossing stairways behind them. Later in the film, we see the young woman walking in and out of iron gates whose metal sheets are kept in place by heavy bolts. The staircases are in a courthouse. The gate is that of a prison. Imposing buildings, ominous staircases, and forbidding doors are standard elements in many British and American Gothic films. They are also characteristic of Bluebeard stories. The architectural elements that I am referring to, however, appear in the film *The Rabbit Is Me* (*Das Kaninchen bin ich*, 1965), an East German production based on a screenplay by Manfred Bieler and directed by Kurt Maetzig. Considered one of the 100 most important films in German cinema today, *The Rabbit Is Me* was also one of the most politically vilified films produced in socialist Germany. Banned just after it was made, it only premiered in 1990 after the fall of the Berlin Wall.

This chapter discusses *The Rabbit Is Me* as a production whose use of Gothic themes and aesthetics contributed to its prohibition. The analysis treats the Gothic style, especially the Female Gothic, and the Bluebeard theme as consubstantial. Although the East German censors and party functionaries did not reference either of them explicitly to denounce the film, my interpretation will identify *The Rabbit Is Me* as a political Bluebeard story that employed an aesthetic familiar from women's melodramas such as those made in Hollywood. The film's thematic and visual features 'confused' its censors and the political functionaries who criticised it publicly (Heiduschke, 2013: 79). As I argue, these critics disliked the film's dialogue and its Western cinematographic style, which, as we will see, included popular Anglo-American cinema and emerging Nouvelle Vague trends. The opponents of *The Rabbit Is Me* could not accept a film that was both critiquing the limitations of its society and attempting to escape the aesthetic endorsed by the ruling East German Socialist Party (SED)[1] as the most appropriate in representing this society: socialist realism. The latter did not equate to authenticity, but rather the depiction of a socialism without conflict; the state as democratic, progressive, and close to its citizens; and these people as 'ideological-moral' models (Hermann Axen, quoted in Kötzing, 2015: 41–42). The 'critical principle' that governed *The Rabbit Is Me*, however, ran contrary to the 'mobilizing, positive "socialist impulses"' expected from 'socialist-realist art' (Raddatz, 1972: 581).[2]

A brief history of *The Rabbit Is Me*

The Rabbit Is Me tells the story of young East Berliner Maria Morzeck (Angelika Waller) shortly after she finishes high school in the summer of 1961 when the Berlin Wall was built. Maria lives with her aunt Hete (Ilse Voigt) with whom we saw her on the stairs on the way to her brother Dieter's (Wolfgang Winkler) political trial (the siblings are orphans but have another sister who lives in West Berlin). Maria and Hete are excluded from the court proceedings, but Maria later visits Dieter in jail where he asks her to draft a request for pardon on his behalf. As a result of her brother's conviction, Maria must give up her aspirations of being accepted to the university. For most of the film, she therefore works as a waitress. Soon Maria starts an affair with Paul Deister (Alfred Müller), a married man and by chance the judge who had sentenced Dieter. He represents the GDR's penal system and, as Maria realises, its fickleness and opportunism. Paul exploits her brother's case twice: first, when he convicts Dieter too harshly for a trivial political offence to profile himself as a stern judge; and second, when he plans to criticise himself[3] for this harsh conviction later. It is relevant to note the historical progression of Paul's decisions: he had convicted Dieter before the Berlin Wall was built and tried to disavow the sentence later when that Stalinist severity was no longer in demand and such a self-critique could further his career. Maria breaks up with Paul because of this callousness. When Dieter is released soon afterwards and finds out about the affair, he beats Maria. The film ends with Maria's curious apotheosis: dressed in her Sunday best and pulling a little cart with her meagre belongings, she sets off to create a new life for herself on a bright summer day.

One could read this ending as positive affirmation of a socialist society that gives Maria a chance after all. In fact, many GDR films focused on strong female characters, and 'a woman alone (partly due to her confidence in the support of socialism) is the final image of numerous DEFA films' (Byg, 1999: 31).[4] In my view, however, this ending is ambiguous. Erich Honecker,[5] the future General Secretary of the SED (the first position in the GDR state), criticised the banned films of 1965 for representing 'our reality' as a difficult transitional state to an 'illusory beautiful future'.[6] The emphasis here is on 'illusory'. Although Honecker did not specify *The Rabbit Is Me* in this statement, it was still the 'flagship' film of all censored productions (Richter, 1994: 194). The critique therefore addresses it covertly and suggests that Honecker did not find the film's positive end convincing. Indeed, the novel Bieler wrote after the film was banned told the same story, but ends with Maria still a waitress, psychologically broken and socially marginalised.[7] In the film, Maria's buoyant final appearance, dressed in bright tones, bathed in sunlight, and walking on in glory, could also be read as an ironic, even cynical statement about her social-ist future. Male passers-by turn their heads and offer Maria friendly help, yet, only shortly before, most men wanted to sexually exploit her. Maria's voice-over now repeats a dialogue in which she is accepted to the university at long last, whereas previously spectators had heard the opposite message. Even the well-maintained, clean boulevard on which she walks is a far cry from the war-torn Berlin streets the film had shown so far. This sudden change in administrative flexibility, gender attitudes, and even Berlin's appearance seems too good to be true. Viewers would have realised only too well that Maria's character never stood a chance and recog-nised them as a sarcastic statement. After all, the whole premise of *The Rabbit Is Me* was to show how Maria's future is hampered (Rother, 2015: 179). This fairy-tale happy end highlights Maria's true situation by ironic inversion. It pays lip service to what the party liked to see, but shows what viewers would have recognised as a mockery of the official line's pretense. Worse, the film employed socialist realist aesthetic tenets – the representation of a bright socialist future soon to come and Maria as the ideal socialist character – after the entire film had run against the grain of these expectations, as my interpretation will show.

Yet *The Rabbit Is Me* was banned for more specific reasons than its ambiguous ending. For instance, the film 'showed a dysfunctional justice system, an economy of scarcity without access to food staples such as citrus fruit, and buildings that still bore the marks of the war that had ended 20 years before' (Heiduschke, 2013: 79). As Maetzig remarked, it was 'really surprising' that it 'could be made at all' (Brady, 1999: 85). Nevertheless, work on the film had started in the atmosphere of gen-eral optimism that ensued after the building of the Berlin Wall. Artists, writers, and film-makers truly believed that from then on, they could address social and political problems in order to improve life in the young republic. Most (Maetzig among them) were believers in the cause of socialism and did not wish to upturn the political system. Encouragingly, in other socialist countries, a new generation of film-makers was already exploring innovative aesthetic paths. General reforms (including economic ones)[8] and a more liberal youth politics promised to take seri-ously the problems and concerns of young people in the GDR (Kötzing, 2015: 13, 46). This era of political thaw turned out to be short-lived, however. Leonid Brezhnev's ascent to power in the Soviet Union in 1964 also meant a regression to conservative communist politics in the GDR (p. 79).

Films that had been made with faith in new opportunities, and therefore had started on new narrative and aesthetic paths, felt the brunt of the backlash. At the Eleventh Plenary of the SED in 1965, such works were castigated as 'philis-tine'. Functionaries used negative buzzwords such as 'decadence', 'skepticism' (p. 98), 'nihilism', 'anarchy' (p. 109), and 'critical realism' (p. 40) to reprimand them. *The Rabbit Is Me* was chastised as 'the thing' and accused of insulting the repub-lic's capital Berlin. Its aesthetic was described inaccurately as a 'primitive Italian social-critical trick [that made the speaker sick]' (pp. 104–105). Maria's gendered outspokenness, and the fact that she expressed her sexual needs frankly, conferred her character an undesirable 'psychologism' (p. 40) made worse by her dangerous lack of political partisanship (Berghahn, 2005: 149). It did not help that she was disrespectful about some aspects of life in the GDR, especially its secret police. Just as problematic was the film's depiction of a married man's affair with a younger woman, which alone would have garnered it an 'official rebuke' (Rother, 2015: 184). It became a downright 'scandal' since the affair was interwoven with a critique of law: Dieter's legal case highlighted the corruption of the judicial system (Rother, 2015: 182). These aspects identified *The Rabbit Is Me* as an especially 'harmful' film with 'subversive tendencies' aimed against 'socialism and its reality' (Kötzing, 2015: 96–99). Although the film-makers professed that, in Maria, they wanted to create a character that had the honesty and steadfastness of a true socialist (Rother, 2015: 187), the party did not see her as a model for the 'ideological guidance which the film was expected to provide' (Berghahn, 2005: 149).

   The Rabbit Is Me became the paradigm for all works that the Eleventh Plenary banned, books and theatre plays among them. In its aftermath, the film was even used to train Stasi[9] officials how to detect traces of ideological diversion (Berghahn, 2005: 146). All censored films were called 'rabbit films' afterwards and the careers of many of those who made them were destroyed (Kötzing, 2015: 122–124, 140).[10] In hindsight, this political 'clear cutting' (*Kahlschlag*), as it came to be known, constituted one of the most relevant caesuras in GDR cultural politics (Kötzing, 2015: 139), one from which East German cinema took decades to recover.

Bluebeard and the Gothic

Apart from these explicit reasons for which *The Rabbit Is Me* was banned, the film has implicit, underlying dimensions that might have aggravated the official retaliation against it. In my view, these elements – the purpose of which may not have even been clear or evident to the film's critics – caused a visceral, emotional response that accounted for the vicious attacks against *The Rabbit Is Me*. The two aspects behind this strong reaction are the film's Bluebeard plot and its feminine Gothic aesthetic. Both have predecessors in a popular German and international (especially Anglo-American) narrative tradition and manifest themselves in the film's thematic structure and cinematography.

   Recognisable to most individuals literate in Western culture, 'Bluebeard' is the story of a husband who kills his wives and hides their bodies in a secret chamber until his last wife discovers them and frees herself. 'Bluebeard' is not, however, only a type of story or simply a 'fairy tale' (Hanson, 2007: 69–70):[11] the conflicts that it narrates between individuals, genders, institutions, and even abstract powers, such as economy and law, constitute a specific model of thinking about power relations in society. In my view, 'Bluebeard' is a meditation about oppression and tyranny, and the risks of confronting them with curiosity and courage.[12]

   The Rabbit Is Me follows the Bluebeard model because it presents a specific view about gender and family relationships in spaces of power and violence that are both abstract and architectural. More specifically, in this film a younger woman reluctantly falls for an older, influential man about whom she knows little. A married man, he has not killed his wife but become estranged from her. As in Charles Perrault's classical version of the tale,[13] the female protagonist has a sister and a brother, although in Maria's hour of need they do not help her as they should: the sister is far away and the brother is violent towards her. Like 'Bluebeard', the film also juxtaposes public and private realms prominently. It abounds with inside shots of courts of law and a prison replete with bleak gates, staircases, courtrooms, and courthouse offices – the domains of Paul's authority. In contrast, Maria's and her aunt's apartment, a small vacation cottage where the lovers spend one summer together, and Maria's own room (where her brother beats her) are intimate, feminine spaces. The plot also includes the indispensable object that gives away the dangerous secret:[14] a golden watch given to Maria by Paul reveals her affair to Dieter, just as the key betrays Bluebeard's wives.[15] The film also addresses violence in three scenes that I discuss later.

Gothic film, especially the Female Gothic as defined by Helen Hanson (2007), incorporates the major features of the Bluebeard story. The Female Gothic always focuses on an independent heroine, a 'working-girl investigator' (p. 29) or 'investigative figure' (p. 53) whose exploits 'foreground questions of knowledge and interpretation' (p. 55). As she attempts to uncover potentially dangerous secrets, the mood is one of suspicion, uncertainty, and suspense (p. 57). The Female Gothic also pertains to stories about relationships, often marriages, in which the female protagonist transitions to adulthood (p. 82). The development of these relationships often exposes the dark side of romance (p. 131). Additionally, as Fred Botting (2008) notes, Gothic romance arises in conditions of restraint rather than freedom, and passion is grounded in misfortune and unhappiness (p. 20). Its heroine is oftentimes naïve and disoriented, yet susceptible to passion, and therefore curious and disobedient to patriarchal authority (p. 63).

These elements are overt in *The Rabbit Is Me*. Maria is not only intelligent and single-minded, but also a 'working girl' who explores both her budding sexuality and the GDR's penal system, as demonstrated when she visits Dieter in jail and attempts to formulate the letter of pardon for him. The formerly naïve schoolgirl matures to a woman at the same time as she begins to understand that the GDR's legal system is neither as fair and humane as the socialist state would like its citizens to believe, nor is it led by judicious moral principles. Romance and marriage are doubly under attack in the film: Paul's adulterous affair exposes the estrangement within his own marriage, while his affair with Maria – which slowly settles into the routine of a matrimonial relationship – is motivated by exploitation. Passions rise and fall under conditions of restraint – namely in Berlin, a city that had been literally walled in only months before Maria and Paul commence their sexual relationship. With its urban references, the film borrows one of the stock features of the Gothic: the ominous streets of the modern city and its intimidating public buildings (Hanson, 2007: 34).

Betrayed romance, passion, secrets, and lies are also characteristics of melodrama, a genre in which Maetzig had excelled as a director long before he made *The Rabbit Is Me*. One of the great traditions of Weimar film (apart from Expressionism), the melodrama acquired an ambivalent reputation in German cinema after the Second World War because it had been appropriated by the Nazis, yet it had also been used for early East German anti-fascist films (Byg, 1999: 29). The German melodramas' themes of heterosexual love affairs and of women being seduced by pleasure were 'consistent with melodramas from Hollywood' in the postwar period (Byg, 1999: 30). Of these, the productions that attempted to create heroic structures for the female voice count as Gothic women's films. They foreground the emotional and physical risks to the protagonist, and her thoughts and feelings in a culture of distrust (Hanson, 2007: 43). *The Rabbit Is Me* is a melodrama by these standards. Maria lets herself be seduced in an affair that causes her sexual and personal pleasure but also psychological and physical torment. For example, she is as apprehensive of telling Paul that she is Dieter's sister as she is about telling her brother about her affair. She is also under constant pressure to produce the pardon request, which is a complicated legal task. The fact that Dieter was condemned with excessive harshness makes Maria concerned that others might be treated like him in courts of law.[16] Additionally, Maria's voice-overs accompany the action, allowing her own subjective and feminine perspective to frame the events depicted; these words demonstrate the anxiety that Maria aims to conceal behind the chutzpah of a streetwise Berlin gal.

The tension in *The Rabbit Is Me* is not caused by a specific secret; all its main characters have personal secrets. What Maria discovers most painfully, however, is the fickleness and abusiveness of a penal system that hides its violent core. The relationships between the characters reflect this violence. As a judge, Paul did not mistreat Dieter directly when he condemned him, but he put him into the hands of a penal system that, as he knew only too well, would abuse a political inmate. While the judge never harms Maria physically either, he 'shoots' her symbolically (as explored later). Paul also facilitates Dieter's attack on Maria, as the brother uses the violence learned in prison against his sister. Even Gabriele (Irma Münch), Paul's wife, enacts Maria's symbolic execution, in a scene to which I will return. Together, these relationships reveal the concealed web of direct and indirect brutality that marked legal, social, and gender relations in the GDR.[17]

Another Gothic characteristic of *The Rabbit Is Me* is its non-linear narrative. Gothic plots are 'more typically retrogressive than progressive' and force characters and viewers 'to move backwards and forwards, and to reproduce their present conditions and knowledge in relation to events and secrets in the past' in the service of 'social critique' (Hanson, 2007: 35). Since Maria tells her own version of her story in voice-over, she remembers and anticipates, explains, and comments almost constantly. Although *The Rabbit Is Me* is only one among many East German films with a 'highly subjective narrative structure' and a female protagonist, its 'directness is rare' among them (Feinstein, 2002: 14, 131).

Gothic and film style

This cinema of non-continuity is typical of two directors whose films have come to be regarded as 'paradigmatic' for 'pure cinema': Fritz Lang and Alfred Hitchcock

(Elsaesser, 2009: 218), Maetzig's contemporaries. The final part of this chapter therefore discusses *The Rabbit Is Me* in light of the style and critical features that it shares with their works.[18] A brief biographical digression on Maetzig will contextualise his aesthetic affinities with Lang and Hitchcock, and through them, within an international and particularly Anglo-American cinema. Maetzig (1911–2012) was one of the most respected East German film directors. He made numerous landmark films in genres such as science fiction, biopic, and comedy. Born in the era when German cinema was founded, he lived through four German political regimes and two world wars. One of his earliest cinematographic recollections was seeing Charlie Chaplin's *The Kid* (1921),[19] and he later trained as a photochemist, studied at the Sorbonne, and worked in animation, documentary, and feature film. The Nazis persecuted him because he was a communist with a Jewish mother. After the Second World War, Maetzig co-founded the GDR's state-owned film company DEFA that continued the Nazis' former UFA studios, themselves an appropriation of interwar film companies.[20] In these studios, Lang had produced his Weimar-era masterpieces *Die Nibelungen* (1924) and *Metropolis* (1927), and Hitchcock had famously acquired a part of his 'German influence' there (Elsaesser, 2009: 211).

Given his biography, Maetzig had clearly formed his aesthetic conceptions well before the separation of the two German states and was keenly aware of international film trends.[21] He also surely knew that Lang and Hitchcock had worked for the film company that he had helped reinvent. He may even have attended Berlin's first international film festival in 1951 when travel was still possible between the Eastern and Western parts of the city. None other than Hitchcock's and David O. Selznick's *Rebecca*, one of the classics of the Female Gothic, opened this festival. Incidentally, Maetzig's first feature film was also a marriage melodrama: *Marriage in the Shadows* (1947), the most successful German film after the Second World War (Brady, 1999: 79). In it, a German-Jewish couple commits suicide because the Nazis' racial laws require the partners to divorce.[22] The film's popularity with the German post-war public was owed partly to its recognisable genre that made it easier to transmit its painful message (Brady, 1999: 81).

These details suggest the likelihood of Maetzig's affinity with Hitchcock's and Lang's cinema. By *The Rabbit Is Me*, Maetzig had even participated in the 'philosophical convergence' that Thomas Elsaesser (2009: 213) has identified between the aesthetics of the two great film-makers. Lang's and Hitchcock's melodramas have shaped film history, and Hitchcock is the recognised master of the woman's picture, one of Hollywood's most important genres (p. 217). As we have seen, Maetzig was versed in melodrama and *The Rabbit Is Me* is a women's film. Moreover, Lang and Hitchcock were committed to popular audiences and fond of using newspaper stories, dramatic clichés, and fairy-tale elements (p. 217). Both also favoured the theme of the wrong man. Not only was *The Rabbit Is Me* made as a popular film that referenced fairy tales even beyond 'Bluebeard',[23] but both Dieter and Paul are wrong men for Maria. Both betray her from two of the most trusted positions that men can inhabit in intimate relationships, those of the lover and the brother. (One could even argue that the state, which should have adopted the father function for the orphan girl, betrayed her first and foremost by hindering her development as a citizen and exposing her to multiple forms of abuse.)

Moreover, both Lang and Hitchcock promoted a cinema of non-continuity (Elsaesser, 2009: 214), which, as we have seen, is also a heritage of the literary and filmic Gothic. The two most conspicuous cinematographic methods by which Lang and Hitchcock implemented non-continuity are sound and the 'metaphysics of the close-up' (p. 231). Both treated sound as a 'physically separate element' and a non-synchronous counterpoint to the images (p. 214). Both also thematised seeing as a theme in their films and illustrated it by the specific actions of the camera. Lang, for instance, used close-ups, which showed viewers that they could never be certain of what they were seeing as a way of highlighting surveillance (p. 230). In contrast, Hitchcock's close-ups of faces initiated or concluded point-of-view shots, thus offering complicity with the audience (pp. 227–231).

The Rabbit Is Me uses similar effects. For instance, Maria's voice-overs create a distance between what one sees and her interpretation of it and separate the sound and the action. Another example of asynchronicity is the scene of the lovers' first meetings. We see Maria and Paul taking the same walk in different seasons but hear them having one continuous conversation (Blanchard, 2002). Sebastian Heiduschke (2013) has shown that *The Rabbit Is Me* 'fractures the time continuum' with numerous other cinematographic methods as well, such as the handheld camera, long uncut sequences that position viewers as observers in the same space, whip pans that suggest points of view, and 180-degree pans (pp. 81–82).

However, the most striking moments of dissonance between sound and image are the close-ups of Maria's face. In an already highly stylised film, such shots constitute a downright formal extravagance (Kötzing, 2015: 179). Through them, Maria enters a direct, urgent dialogue with the audience which suggests that the viewers see not only a story, but something that affects them directly (p. 180). This dialogue is highly ambivalent. On the one hand, it reminds spectators of their position as unseen observers in the story, a position they share with the camera's lens and the state's surveillance system. On the other, precisely this set-up is a warning against surveillance: in the close-ups, Maria communicates with the viewers candidly, unlike in her interactions with the representatives of the state. For example, she is bold yet reserved toward the secret agents who visit her at home after Dieter's arrest and she lies in a country court. The film's combination of direct address and close-ups creates moments of subjectivity and interpellation by which *The Rabbit Is Me* practically communicates with its audience behind the backs of censors. Subversive storytelling is not new in German culture and often relies on the suggestive power of fairy tales. For example, German writers often used such stories as means of political critique (Zipes, 1983: 141; Zipes, 1993: 192). East German films that alluded to fairy tales likewise allowed a 'conspiratorial understanding between the film-makers and their audience' (Rinke, 2000: 56). There is no question that viewers habituated to fairy tales and melodrama would have recognised the Bluebeard and Gothic allusions of *The Rabbit Is Me*; Maria's close-ups communicate the urgency of their insinuations all the more insistently.

Key close-ups

The analysis of relevant close-ups of the film gives an impression of how *The Rabbit Is Me* uses this technique to communicate with its viewers. They occur in three scenes in which Maria is subjected to symbolic and actual violence. In the first, Paul throws snowballs at a window behind which Maria is standing on the morning after they have consummated their relationship. It is 1 January 1962, the beginning of the GDR's first walled-in year. In the second scene, Gabriele visits the vacation cottage to show it to a potential buyer while Maria is there. She knows who the young woman is, but does not expose her. However, Gabriele engages in a target shooting contest, during which she mimics killing Maria. It is the summer of 1962, about a year after Maria and Paul met.

The scene with Paul consists of only two shots. A medium shot shows the judge bending down to pick up a snowball. A quick sweep traces the projectile to the window and cuts to Maria's close-up. The camera stays with her. She smiles slightly, but her expression quickly becomes grave. Each next snowball hit makes her wince as she faces the shots. The sound in the scene is free of any intradiegetic background noise. The clinical studio-recorded soundscape consists only of Paul's laughter, the dead thumps of the snowballs hitting the glass, and Maria's voice-over. At first, it is not clear to whom she speaks. She remarks that everything is untrue, incorrect. She asks whether that is Paul or Dieter? Then she addresses someone, saying, 'Shoot me. I love you', anticipating the words that she will speak later when her brother beats her. The fact that she also summons Paul, presumably to 'shoot' her, is an odd linguistic choice for snowballs, which one normally 'throws' in German. In this scene, the sound and visuals create an eerie, oblique mood that accompanies this ambiguous meaning. Only later, spectators would realise the event foreshadows Dieter's actual violence, thereby conflating it with Paul's symbolic act.

The scene with Gabriele is more complex in its interplay between camera movement, plot, character perspectives, dialogue, and sound. A medium shot of Gabriele and her visitor cuts to a close-up of her air rifle shot on the target, a sweep as Maria checks the score, and the camera settling on the young woman's face in close-up. This sequence complicates that of the snowball scene and is repeated four times. It equates the young woman with the target because it positions her face near the marking board and shows both in close-up. In the beginning, Maria's voice-over and the intradiegetic sound are in dialogue. Addressing the audience, she remarks on Gabriele's cold-bloodedness and determinacy that supposedly distanced her from Paul. Meanwhile, Gabriele relays the cottage's sale to her absent husband and explains a bad shot with standing on high-heel shoes. She then announces that the next two shots will be for Maria, leaving her meaning ambiguous as to whether this refers to the girl's turn to shoot or to Gabriele shooting her. At the last repetition, an inserted medium shot of Gabriele's, who cocks the gun with a sardonic grimace, cuts to Maria's close-up just as she is starting to move towards the camera. The young woman freezes, musing whether someone can be killed with an air rifle. Maria suspects that '*she* will shoot' her if Maria said anything. The camera cuts to a tableau of the three characters. Behind Gabriele, the buyer looks into the distance, his gaze averted. The two women face each other, erect, in stiff postures, as Gabriele hands the gun to Maria. The younger's voice-over delivers the line that gives the film its title: 'We're standing there like the snake and the rabbit. The rabbit is me' (see Figure 11.1). Notably, the intradiegetic sound is bracketed in this moment. We only hear Maria's voice in a space of silence. The scene immediately returns to reality, however, as the sound of a machine that we have heard earlier resumes at a distance and Gabriele asks her buyer jokingly about the punishment for shooting someone by accident. Upon hearing that it is prison, she teases Maria: 'Bang-bang, you are stone dead'. The two scenes announce and intensify the danger of direct violence that will materialise in the third scene: when Dieter hits Maria. Significantly, Maria covers her face with her arm after Dieter strikes her. It is the only time when her character actively prevents the audience from seeing her face's close-up and she is quiet both intradiegetically and in the voice-over. The implication is that Maria has been silenced. The film thus indicates that the feelings caused by the violence from loved ones are unspeakable and leaves the audience to imagine them.

These scenes use cinematographic techniques that also mark Lang's and Hitchcock's styles as I have described them earlier. They separate sounds from images either to anticipate or to communicate with the audience. They employ close-ups to show a victim from the perspective of the perpetrator or a character in communication with the viewers. If Lang's close-ups highlighted surveillance

FIGURE 11.1 Gabriele Deister (Irma Münch), Maria Morzeck (Angelika Waller), and an unidentified actor in the film's title scene
Das Kaninchen bin ich/ The Rabbit Is Me (Kurt Maetzig, 1965) – used with permission of the DEFA Foundation

and Hitchcock's communion, then Maetzig's vacillate between these two orders of seeing, showing them alternatively at work. In this manner, *The Rabbit Is Me* thematises a society of total control, one in which nobody can be trusted as all watch others and are under their surveillance.

One would expect that a Gothic women's film, especially one shot in black and white as is the *Rabbit Is Me*, would also employ light and visual contrast to convey this meaning. Maetzig's film does not: Paul's and Gabriele's symbolic violence is perpetrated in the broad daylight of bright winter and summer days. Dieter's physical aggression is in a room with regular daylight. Elsaesser (2009) notes, however, that in Lang's and Hitchcock's films, 'the powerful neither hide nor show themselves: they hide in the light' (p. 229). This also applies to *The Rabbit Is Me*. The film does not make a dramatic exhibition of the exposure to surveillance in a state whose observation mechanisms are at work in the open. It does not allude to this status quo with the help of Expressionist shadows or film noir contrasts, but locates it in the uniform natural light that the film's characters share with their audience. The film thus confirms that those who wield any type of 'power' in the GDR indeed 'hide in the light', and in doing so *The Rabbit Is Me* shares another critical drive of Lang's and Hitchcock's films: their suspicion against 'masks of decorum and rectitude put on by dictatorships' as raised via themes of falsehood and fakery (Elsaesser, 2009: 216). *The Rabbit Is Me* clearly has the same agenda. Not only are the discussed scenes driven by suspicion between the characters, but the entire film is about dishonesty, deception, and betrayal: the brother feels betrayed by his sister, the husband betrays his wife who colludes in her own betrayal, the lover betrays his partner, the state too harshly punishes what it regards as political betrayal, and overall betrays its own citizens. The only honesty one can assume in a thus structured social and political environment is that between the film medium and its audience, between the protagonist and her viewers.

Conclusion

The party's unforgiving treatment of *The Rabbit Is Me* confirmed the film's accurate diagnosis of the GDR state as 'both a patriarchal and a controlling system' (Heiduschke, 2013: 120). In the manner of a Bluebeard, the political system accused and tried the film and cast it into its censorship vaults. It did so because the production had uncovered inconvenient secrets, the corruption and violence of the state's penal system and its dysfunctional social and gender roles. Fittingly for a Female Gothic film, the Bluebeard narrative carried an easily understood warning of the establishment's dangerous power. The caveat was that in the GDR, Maria's courageous forages into this secret remained unsuccessful. The effectiveness of the film's warning about the system's punishment of such forbidden explorations, however, explains the critics' strong reactions to *The Rabbit Is Me*.

The chapter also discussed how the film employed a Western popular cinematographic and genre aesthetic that it shared with German pre-war and Hollywood post-war melodramas, particularly Lang's and Hitchcock's. Techniques that made these film-makers' oeuvres cornerstones of world cinema, especially the breaks of continuity resulting from the juxtaposition between sound and image and the close-up, also structure *The Rabbit Is Me*. Likewise, they informed New Wave cinemas across Europe when they rediscovered and reinterpreted Lang and Hitchcock in the 1960s. Heiduschke (2013) has noted the 'stylistic proximity' of Maetzig's film to these movements (p. 81) and interpreted its aesthetic ruptures as an encouragement for viewers to reconsider East German society with a 'critical eye, and to dare to take risky but necessary steps out of a socialism' whose structures had calcified (p. 82). While this did not sit well with East German potentates, as we have seen, this cinematographic style identified the film as a forerunner to an 'East German "New Wave"' (p. 77) that never materialised, owing to the 1965 banning. The Bluebeard model, the melodrama genre, the affinity with an international aesthetic tradition best represented by Lang's and Hitchcock's works, and its attempts to enter a stylistic dialogue with the emerging Nouvelle Vagues made *The Rabbit Is Me* not only politically unacceptable, but also far too cosmopolitan for a state that had walled itself in not long ago. These elements nevertheless highlight a specific and lost dimension of East German cinema's internationalism in the 1960s, one that referenced Anglo-American film, and especially its Female Gothic melodramas.

Notes

1 Its full name was the Socialist Unity Party of Germany (Sozialistische Einheitspartei Deutschlands, SED).
2 Here, Raddatz cites a polemic against *The Rabbit Is Me* that was published in 1966 in the party newspaper *Neues Deutschland*.
3 The self-critique was a humiliating public procedure by which those found guilty politically supposedly recognised their mistakes. In the hope to deflect the party's repressions from his colleagues when *The Rabbit Is Me* was banned, Maetzig did it too, unsuccessfully. His creative abilities never reached their full potential again after this fiasco (Richter, 1994: 200).
4 See also Feinstein (2002: 132).
5 At the time, he was still the Socialist Party's Central Committee's Secretary for Security Questions.
6 Quoted in Kötzing (2015: 99). All direct translations from German are mine.
7 Manfred Bieler, *Maria Morzeck or The Rabbit Is Me* (1969).
8 The introduction of the biweekly five-day-week in 1965 (Kötzing, 2015: 13).
9 The abbreviation of 'Staatssicherheit' (state security), the GDR's notorious secret police.
10 Bieler's is a case in point. The screenplay for *The Rabbit Is Me* was based on his eponymous novel that itself went through a censorship process prior to and during the production of the film. Michael Westdickenberg (2003) has chronicled its almost grotesque course. Eventually, the novel was banned. The film *The Rabbit Is Me* could only be made because the Culture Minister ruled that it could be considered a separate matter from the book (Feinstein, 2002: 165). After the Eleventh Plenary, Bieler was the only artist to draw radical consequences. He left the GDR and eventually settled in West Germany where he published his novel and became an acclaimed writer.
11 The Aarne-Thompson-Uther Classification of Folk Tales lists it as type 312 with several variants.
12 Puw-Davis (2001) calls it a 'theology' in which a curious woman causes man's downfall and is punished violently for it (p. 40).

13 Charles Perrault, 'La barbe bleue' from the collection *Histories ou contes du temps passé* (1697).
14 Besides Perrault's 'Bluebeard' ('La barbe bleue'), any of the German versions in the collections of Ludwig Bechstein ('The Fairy-Tale of Knight Bluebeard' ['Das Märchen vom Ritter Blaubart'], 1845) or the Brothers Grimm (KHM 40 'The Robber Bridegroom' ['Der Räuberbräutigam'], KHM 45 'Fitcher's Bird' ['Fitchers Vogel'], and Nr. 14 'The Murder Castle' ['Das Mordschloß']) – to name a few of the best-known examples – contain these elements in this specific structural arrangement. ('KHM' is the standard abbreviation of *Kinder- und Hausmärchen*, the German title of the Grimms' *Children- and Household Tales*. 'The Murder Castle', a Dutch story, was only published in the first of the many editions of the *Tales*, and is therefore not listed as KHM.)
15 The film contains numerous other instances that one could read as elements from the tale, although my analysis shall focus on the most pertinent.
16 A subplot of the film shows Maria spending a summer in Paul's vacation cottage in the village of Grambow. Here, she recovers from a back illness that she has contracted out of lack of access to vitamin C-rich foods. She is involved in the village trial of a fisherman who has insulted the state's army publicly because the soldiers had disturbed the village's fishing grounds. Afraid that, like Dieter, he will be given an excessively harsh sentence, she lies in court about what the fisherman had said. However, it turns out that communal law-giving is far more humane and only sentences the culprit to several hours of social work.
17 There is another dimension to this violence in Paul's self-aggression: he attempts to commit suicide twice, possibly to manipulate those close to him.
18 The directors' works are also integral to the Hollywood Female Gothic films of the 1940s. These films are referenced elsewhere in this collection.
19 Brady (1999: 86).
20 Founded in 1917, the Universum Film AG (UFA) was appropriated by the Nazis.
21 Already in 1949, one of Maetzig's films was selected as the first East German contribution to the Cannes Film Festival. After 1965, he became the president of the International Federation of Film Societies (IFFS) and served on the Berlinale jury.
22 Despite the director's left-wing political leanings and the film's clear anti-Semitism, this early work still stood in a stylistic continuity with Nazi melodrama (Byg, 1999: 30). Bertolt Brecht, East Germany's leading theatre maker and theorist, considered the film 'terrible kitsch' (Brady, 1999: 82).
23 The discussion of such references is beyond the scope of this present chapter, but these allusions include the Grimms' fairy tales *Snow White* and *Cinderella*.

References

Berghahn, Daniela (2005) *Hollywood Behind the Wall: The Cinema of East Germany*. Manchester: Manchester University Press.
Blanchard, Benoît (2002) *Das Kaninchen bin ich und die Ästhetik des Neuen Films*. www2.hu berlin.de/francopolis/films/Kaninchen.htm [Accessed 2 April 2018]
Botting, Fred (2008) *Gothic Romanced: Consumption, Gender, and Technology in Contemporary Fictions*. London: Routledge.
Brady, Martin (1999) 'Discussion with Kurt Maetzig'. In Seán Allan and John Sandford (eds), *DEFA: East German Cinema, 1946–1992*. New York: Berghahn Books, pp. 77–92.
Byg, Barton (1999) 'DEFA and the Traditions of International Cinema'. In Seán Allan and John Sandford (eds), *DEFA: East German Cinema 1946–1992*. London: Berghan Books, pp. 22–41.
Elsaesser, Thomas (2009) 'Too Big and Too Close: Alfred Hitchcock and Fritz Lang'. In Sidney Gottlieb and Richard Allen (eds), *The Hitchcock Annual Anthology: Selected*

Essays from Volumes 10–15. New York: Columbia University Press, pp. 211–235. www. thomas-elsaesser.com/images/full_texts/elsaesser-hitchcock%20%20lang.pdf [Accessed 2 April 2018]

Feinstein, Joshua (2002) *The Triumph of the Ordinary: Depictions of Daily Life in the East German Cinema, 1949–1989*. Chapel Hill, NC: University of North Carolina Press.

Hanson, Helen (2007) *Hollywood Heroines: Women in Film Noir and the Female Gothic Film*. London: I.B. Tauris.

Heiduschke, Sebastian (2013) *East German Cinema: DEFA and Film History*. New York: Palgrave Macmillan.

Kötzing, Andreas (2015) 'Sturm und Zwang. Das 11. Plenum des ZK der SED in historischer Perspektive'. In Andreas Kötzing and Ralf Schenk (eds), *Verbotene Utopie. Die SED, die DEFA und das 11. Plenum*. Berlin: Bertz und Fischer Verlag, pp. 11–146.

Raddatz, Fritz J. (1972) *Traditionen und Tendenzen. Materialien zur Literatur der DDR*. Frankfurt am Main: Suhrkamp.

Richter, Erika (1994) 'Zwischen Mauerbau und Kahlschlag 1961 bis 1965'. In Filmmuseum Potsdam (ed.), *Das zweite Leben der Filmstadt Babelsberg. DEFA Spielfilme 1946–1992*. Berlin: Henschel, pp. 158–211.

Rinke, Andrea (2000) 'Sex and Subversion in German Democratic Republic Cinema: "The Legend of Paul and Paula" (1973)'. In Diana Homes and Alison Smith (eds), *100 Years of European Cinema: Entertainment or Ideology?* Manchester: Manchester University Press, pp. 52–63.

Rother, Rainer (2015) 'Eine künstlerische Entwicklung – nicht ohne Kontraste. *Das Kaninchen bin ich*'. In Andreas Kötzing and Ralf Schenk (eds), *Verbotene Utopie. Die SED, die DEFA und das 11. Plenum*. Berlin: Bertz & Fischer Verlag, pp. 176–194.

Puw-Davis, Mererid (2001) *The Tale of Bluebeard in German Literature: From the Eighteenth Century to the Present*. Oxford: Clarendon Press.

Westdickenberg, Michael (2003) '. . . somit würde man die Darstellung abschwächen, daß dogmatisches Verhalten, Karrieristentum, Fehler im Justizapparat gesetzmäßig wären. Die Zensur von Prosaliteratur der DDR in den sechziger Jahren am Beispiel von Manfred Bielers Roman Das Kaninchen bin ich'. In Beate Müller (ed.), *Zensur im modernen deutschen Kulturraum*. Tübingen: Max Niemeyer Verlag, pp. 163–179.

Zipes, Jack (1983) *Fairytales and the Art of Subversion: The Classical Genre for Children and the Process of Civilization*. New York: Methuen.

Zipes, Jack (1993) 'The Struggle for the Grimms' Throne: The Legacy of the Grimms' Tales in the FRG and GDR since 1945'. In Donald Haase (ed.), *The Reception of Grimms' Fairy Tales: Responses, Reactions, Revisions*. Detroit, MI: Wayne State University Press, pp. 167–206.

12

'I SEE, I SEE . . .'

Goodnight Mommy (2014) as Austrian Gothic

Lies Lanckman

When attempting to define the Gothic in 'The Gothic on Screen', Misha Kavka (2002) notes that 'there is no established genre called *Gothic cinema* or *Gothic film*', and instead goes on to note that '[t]here are Gothic images and Gothic plots and Gothic characters and even Gothic styles within film, all useful to describe bits and pieces of films that usually fall into the broader category of *horror*' (p. 209, original emphasis). Nonetheless, in spite of this lack of a clear definition of Gothic cinema, loose from the horror genre, Kavka (2002) also notes that 'we perfectly well know the Gothic when we see it. There is, in fact, something peculiarly visual about the Gothic' (p. 209). It is this visual quality – or lack thereof – of the Gothic genre that this chapter will focus on.

The chapter will examine the Austrian film *Goodnight Mommy* (2014) in the context of the Gothic genre, and will, in doing so, interrogate this 'peculiarly visual' element as a necessary condition for a Gothic film, since the film does not, at first sight, appear to carry these specific visual markers frequently associated with the genre. Instead, the chapter will argue that this film – originally titled *Ich Seh, Ich Seh*, or *I See, I See* – is Gothic less because of any visual markers, and more because of what remains visually ambiguous, and indeed invisible, throughout the film. This very specific brand of Gothic is supported by the film's status as an Austrian, and thus non-Hollywood, film; I will argue that this Austrian-ness is expressed less through the film's specific geographic setting and more through references to Austria's sociocultural history, which are used to underline and steer the film's plot. It, too, is thus present more in the invisible and ambiguous allusions than in the directly and obviously visible elements.

These sociocultural markers, as I will explore, particularly serve to underline the importance of familial relationships and especially of parenthood/motherhood within the film's narrative; this chapter will therefore use the evolving status of the eponymous 'Mommy' as a guide to the film's Gothic quality. It will do so by noting especially the transformation of 'Mommy' throughout the film, from bad, even monstrous, mother at the beginning to classic Gothic victim-heroine at the end.

Goodnight Mommy focuses on a mother and her 10-year-old twin sons Elias and Lukas, who inhabit a large, modern house in the Austrian countryside. At the beginning of the film, the mother has just undergone a mysterious surgery and returns to the house with her face entirely swathed in bandages. Soon after, she begins to display strange behaviour: she expects the children to keep the blinds down, since she cannot handle sunlight, and generally treats her sons in a cold and dismissive way, particularly Lukas, whom she does not serve food to, talk to, or even acknowledge at all. Over the course of the film, then, the children gradually become convinced that the bandaged woman in their home is not, in fact, their beloved 'Mommy', but an impostor, an evil doppelgänger whom they must capture, interrogate, and ultimately kill. At this point, the viewer's perception of Mommy becomes destabilised, and we begin to wonder whether she might not, perhaps, have been telling the truth all along.

In spite of the centrality of the characters of mother and sons, however, the film does not open with an image of any of them; instead, it starts with an entirely black screen, accompanied by disembodied voices singing the first line – 'Good evening, good night' – of Brahms' Lullaby. Only upon the second line – 'bedecked with roses' – is the viewer allowed an image to go with the song; this image consists of a minute and a half of grainy, borrowed footage featuring a mother and seven children singing. The mother is classic German movie star Ruth Leuwerik, and the clip comes from the very end of the 1956 film *Die Trapp-Familie*, a film that would be turned into a Broadway musical in 1959 and into the much more famous Hollywood film *The Sound of Music* in 1965. The scene, filmed in bright Technicolor, is the very last one of the original film; the Von Trapps, all dressed in traditional dirndls or lederhosen, are performing in the United States and give a deliberately slow rendition of the lullaby in order to indicate the end of a concert.

I argue that this short clip effectively sets the scene for the remainder of the film in a number of specific ways. First, it establishes motherhood as a central theme of the film; much like *The Sound of Music*, *Die Trapp-Familie* is essentially a story about good and bad parenthood, and especially good and bad motherhood. As the novice Maria enters the dysfunctional Von Trapp home and sets about mending the relationship between father and children, she becomes an iconic figure – in the scene featured here, as indeed in the film in general – representing loving and traditional motherhood. In this way, within the film, the character of Maria is contrasted sharply with the 'unnatural' lack of motherly feelings displayed by the sophisticated, urban Baroness Schraeder/Princess Yvonne, the original love interest of Captain Von Trapp, who enjoys Viennese society life and believes children belong in boarding schools. In this way, the *Sound of Music* story, perhaps one of the most internationally famous narratives popularly associated with Austria, is used here to place the contrast between 'good' and 'bad' motherhood at the very heart of the narrative of the Austrian horror film that is *Goodnight Mommy*.

At the same time, however, the clip hints at more than this theme of good versus bad motherhood. While, in the context of the earlier film, the scene provides a gentle bookend to the narrative, it can be read entirely differently when placed at the beginning of this film. Here, the tiredness of the children is transformed into something more sinister than originally meant, and the slowness of the song takes on an almost dirge-like quality. Similarly, the lyrics, simple and innocent in the original film, are here transformed into something quite different, particularly the final, repeated lines, 'Tomorrow morning, if God wills it, you will wake up again'. The clip thus lends the beginning of the film an eerie and rather dark quality. This hints at a different and more unsettling side of Mommy's character, a monstrosity that may perhaps touch on the supernatural.

Initially, however, the film shows Mommy to be a bad mother to her sons on the most basic level; in contrast to the aforementioned Maria Von Trapp, Mommy fails to embody acceptable, self-sacrificing, and unconditionally loving motherhood. Instead, she is represented as a cold, selfish, emotionally abusive, and almost malevolent presence, indeed very much a 'non-nurturing, unyielding mother-figure, far from the idealised patriarchal feminine' (Kaplan, 1992: 112). Her behaviour towards the children, even at the film's very beginning, is odd at best, and at worst both psychologically and physically abusive. Favouring Elias over his brother Lukas, she seemingly ignores the existence of the second child altogether; she is seen preparing breakfast for Elias, but not for Lukas, and when offered two seashells, 'One from me and one from Lukas', she only takes the one from Elias. Later on, her utter dislike of one boy leads her to force Elias to promise not to talk to his brother anymore. While even her maternal feelings towards Elias are depicted as problematic – for example, when she physically wrestles with him and almost strangles him – she seemingly entirely loathes his brother's very existence, for reasons that remain unexplained. Her bad and uncaring motherhood also extends beyond the boys to her behaviour towards their pets; when they find their cat dying, they instantly suspect Mommy of having murdered her, and when they subsequently hide from her, she lures them out of hiding by pouring jars filled with their pet cockroaches into water, drowning them. Her nature is defined as essentially unfeeling and anti-maternal, even towards animals.

The condemning of Mommy for her anti-maternalism also ties into Austrian history on a further level, hinted at and underlined by, but not limited to, the narrative of *Die Trapp-Familie* or *The Sound of Music*. Both films are set within a particular Austrian time period, and while these respective narratives served primarily to react against events specific to this history, the approach to motherhood adopted by the stories is not so very different from the one that dominated the era portrayed in each film's setting. After the annexation of Austria in 1938, in fact, Austrian women – at least those considered Volksdeutsche or of ethnic German origin – qualified, like their German counterparts, for the state decoration of the Mother's Cross (Mutterkreuz). A parallel decoration to the highest military honour, the Iron Cross, the Mother's Cross could be awarded in different grades to ethnically German mothers with four or more children, who also demonstrated appropriate 'probity' – defined within Nazi Germany along extremely traditional lines (Stephenson, 2001: 31). This was but one of a number of symbolic gestures by the Nazi government in Germany and Austria to honour women primarily as good mothers. It was also part of a wider promotion of traditional womanhood, which included a rejection of women within the workplace, particularly in higher positions of authority; women on the lower rungs were tolerated primarily for the benefit of the war effort (pp. 64–65). While the status of working women, and especially working mothers, was a widely discussed topic in many places throughout the 20th century, therefore, it carries specific historical meaning within a German or Austrian setting, particularly a rural rather than urban one.

This film plays with these historically and geographically specific expectations and restrictions by subtly tying Mommy's bad motherhood to her blonde and visibly 'Aryan' sons, as well as to her status as a working mother. Indeed, Mommy's professional identity as a semi-famous television presenter is stressed throughout the film, from the guessing game mother and sons play at the beginning to the search results when the twins attempt to Google their Mommy. These search results then also hint at another element of Mommy's background, which is her divorce from the twins' father, further demonstrated by the removal of wedding pictures from the family photo album and the empty spaces among the family pictures on the wall. As such, Mommy is shown as not just a failure as a mother, but also as a wife – most likely, the film implies, because of her excessive focus on her career. The fact that her chosen profession is one in the public eye only exacerbates this transgression; much like *Imitation of Life*'s Lora, who is an actress:

> the career the narrative chooses . . . only supports the charges of narcissism, indulgence and promiscuity brought to bear on [her]. She is condemned for desiring to be desired in the public sphere, instead of confining this desire to the private marital sphere.
>
> *(Kaplan, 1992: 176)*

Her surgery, then, while never expressly defined as plastic and purely for cosmetic purposes, is automatically assumed to be so by the viewer; the skinny, blonde Mama, who has a dressmaker's dummy in her bedroom, is seen as a vain, cold figure, removing herself from her children for selfish and superficial reasons. She is thus singularly unfit to be a mother. Additionally, this alienation of 'Mommy' from the persona of mother is demonstrated through her own inability to see herself as such; during the guessing game at the beginning, when one player gets a Post-it note with a name attached to his or her forehead, she is unable to guess that she is, in fact, 'Mama' – even after the boys give her a number of hints, including the fact that she is a television presenter, and, more tellingly, that she has two children. If her primary role should be that of a traditionally 'good' mother, then Mommy has indeed failed. Her failure is strongly emphasised here through the contrasts the film offers. A first and explicit contrast is, of course, the image of the traditionally maternal Maria Von Trapp; indeed, Mommy could be identified more usefully with Maria's nemesis, the Princess Yvonne/Baroness

Schraeder figure, who, like Mommy appears to, thrives in public life and within an urban environment much more clearly than she does in a familial and rural one. This is not the only contrast drawn between Mommy and a 'better' mother; throughout the film, we also find traces of an earlier, more caring version of 'Mommy', particularly in the recording of her voice as she sings the lullaby 'Weißt du wieviel Sternlein stehen?' ('Do you know how many stars there are?') to her children. In this way, Mommy is doubled; she is the Mr Hyde to the Dr Jekyll of her own former self.

Indeed, the narrative of the film takes this doubling further, beyond the psychological doubling of Mommy's 'good' (i.e. caring) and 'bad' (i.e. selfish) natures. After all, as the twins open a photo album, they find an image of Mommy and another, almost identical woman, who is dressed in exactly the same clothes; at this point, children and viewer alike begin to wonder whether the Mommy who sang the recorded lullaby might not be a different person altogether from the sinister, bandaged figure who now haunts the house. This physical doubling is underlined by the image we see immediately after the discovery in the photo album; here, Mommy, who is crouching down to clean the windows, is reflected in the window and is, as such, shown physically doubled on the screen (see Figure 12.1). At this point in the narrative, the film's earlier incorporation of the *Trapp-Familie* clip, and the manner in which this reframing evokes a sinister tone, becomes meaningful again: after all, this alienation of the supposed 'Mommy' in the minds of her children is not just characterised by her attitude to both her sons, but goes beyond that and into the physical, potentially supernatural, realm. Mommy is first introduced to us – and re-presented to her sons – upon arriving home after the mysterious surgery she has undergone, with her face wrapped in bandages, leaving only her eyes and mouth visible. She is a physically ambiguous, almost repulsive presence, and becomes, within this first re-meeting, uncanny in perhaps the most primal way; she is a mother become unrecognisable to her own children, who soon start questioning why she is not 'like our Mommy', and later, after the discovery of the photograph, even whether she is their real Mommy at all.

FIGURE 12.1 Mommy is 'doubled' by the window
Goodnight Mommy/Ich Seh, Ich Seh (Veronika Franz, Severin Fiala, 2014)

The bandages remain in place for the first 50 minutes of the film, and they perform a number of different functions within the narrative. First, they mark Mommy as a barely human, physically monstrous figure, reminiscent of a living mummy or Frankenstein's monster. Milbank (2002) notes that 'the monstrous, the hybrid and the disgusting are central to the Gothic genre' (p. 75), and in this sense Mommy fulfils this role. Indeed, she embodies what Milbank (2002) terms the role of the 'bleeding nun', conjoining the opposite categories of 'death and life, physical and spiritual, natural and supernatural in a monstrous form' (p. 81), a convergence encapsulated for the author by Mary Shelley's *Frankenstein*, and particularly the quote 'a shroud enveloped her form and I saw the grave-worms crawling in the folds of the flannel' (Shelley, quoted in Millbank, 2002: 81). These descriptions illuminate the monstrousness of Mommy even further: on the one hand, her bandages serve as a shroud; on the other, when the boys slash open her belly in a dream, cockroaches crawl out. She is simultaneously and uncannily dead and alive. At the same time, the comparison between Shelley's words and the character of Mommy also highlights her position as a disgusting, abject figure. In considering the notion of the abject, Creed (1993) notes that the 'concept of a border is central to the construction of the monstrous in the horror film, [and] that which crosses or threatens to cross the border is abject' (p. 10). Examples of such boundaries include the border between human and inhuman, man and beast, normal and supernatural, as well as the line 'which separates those who take up their proper gender roles from those who do not' (p. 11). The career-obsessed, unmaternal, shrouded Mommy is an ideal candidate for each of these borders, and the fact that her body – presumably still capable of childbearing – produces cockroaches when cut open by her sons underlines the notion of her failed motherhood even further.

However, the bandages-as-bandages also serve to demonstrate the border between 'the clean and proper body and the abject body, or the body which has lost its form and integrity' (Creed, 1993: 11). As Mommy's wounded visage is hidden behind bandages, her face becomes a horrifying mystery, a hidden thing that the viewer simultaneously wants and does not want to see. This becomes apparent in the scene depicting the twins' dream whereby Mommy runs into the forest and strips off her clothes and bandages, permitting us to almost, but not quite, glimpse her bare face. A similar moment occurs earlier in the film, as one of the twins appears to catch a brief view of Mommy's unbandaged face in her bedroom mirror, but is confronted instead with an extreme close-up of her bloodshot eye; this edit underlines the physical horror of Mommy's body that the film – much like the bandages – hints towards but ultimately denies any further visual confirmation. This contrast between Mommy's monstrous, all-seeing eye and the boys' inability or unwillingness to see, which the viewer shares, also serves, throughout the first half of the film, to highlight the importance and yet ambiguity of visual perception in the context of this film, originally titled *Ich Seh, Ich Seh*. This emphasis on seeing and not seeing will become important, if in a crucially different manner, in the context of the film's second half, in which Mommy is transformed into a Gothic victim-heroine.

This second half is also heralded, indirectly, through the use of the bandages, since these serve to demonstrate one very particular way in which the border between man and beast, discussed by Creed (1993), applies to Mommy; after all, perhaps the bandages on her face are reminiscent most of all of the exoskeleton of an insect. This association is supported by Mommy's sudden and unexplained love of dark places, which even in the midst of summer causes her to remind the children to keep the blinds closed. The insect connection is also underlined by the presence of bugs within the narrative of the film, including the twin boys' collection of large pet cockroaches. These cockroaches themselves then become a part of the film's horror narrative, first as the boys experimentally put a cockroach on their sleeping mother and watch – in horror – as it crawls into her mouth and she eats it, which once more dehumanises her as a monster herself; and second as they cut open their mother with an X-ACTO knife and watch as bugs crawl out of her abdominal cavity.

Just as the *Trapp-Familie* clip set up the film's theme of motherhood at the very beginning, then, the bug comparison is another crucial element of the film's Austrian heritage, which works here again to adjust the direction of the film for its second half. After all, the presence of bugs, specifically cockroaches, echoes the famous Kafka novella *Die Verwandlung*, or *The Metamorphosis*, in which main character Gregor Samsa wakes up one morning, having been transformed into a monstrous, cockroach-like bug, physically repellent to everyone around him and described in the story as an 'ungeheures Ungeziefer', or 'monstrous vermin'. This echoes Mommy's transformation in this film, from the gentle, maternal figure singing lullabies on tape to the disgusting, bug-like monster we find upon her return from the hospital. What is most important here about the reference to Kafka's story, however, is not so much the apparent monstrosity of the central character, but the fact that it is not Samsa, but his relatives, who reveal their monstrous natures over the course of the novella, as his parents and sister insult and neglect him, ultimately injuring him and contributing to his death. Familial relationships break down, but not in the way the reader first expects. This twist, too, is a key element of the plot of *Goodnight Mommy*; about two-thirds into the film, it becomes gradually apparent that it is not Mommy who is a threat to her sons, but her sons who pose a threat to Mommy. In this way, *Goodnight Mommy* develops our sympathy for the character of Mommy as the film goes on.

The transfer of sympathy from the boys to Mommy happens gradually; at the film's beginning, the viewer is firmly allied with the boys and sees Mommy only as a threatening intruder; at this point, we are even allowed a subjective look into the boys' inner world as we see their dream of the monstrous mother almost – but not quite – revealing her unbandaged face in the woods. Over the course of the film, however, we are gradually allowed further glimpses into Mommy's private life; twice we see her crying by herself, and as her bandages are removed just past the halfway point of the film, her appearance suddenly becomes mundane rather than monstrous. At this point, our fears about her unbandaged face are proven to be unfounded, and this further encourages a shifting viewpoint on behalf of the viewer. The real moment of transformation happens approximately two-thirds into the film, after Mommy has removed her bandages and the boys have been returned to their home by the priest they asked for help. Elias and Lukas run inside the house and hide there; only in the middle of the night, as Mommy has cried herself to sleep, do we see them reappear, as shadows, from their hiding place under her bed. When Mommy awakens, she is tied to her bed by her hands and feet and finds herself faced with her sons. Just like her face was obscured by bandages throughout the film's first half, their faces are now obscured using a set of identical, diabolical green masks. Soon it becomes apparent that Mommy is not simply an abusive or disappointing mother, nor is she a bug-like monster: instead, she transforms, I argue, into an incarnation of the Gothic victim-heroine, underlining the film's status as a Gothic film.

At this point, we must return to definitions of the Gothic genre. One particularly useful definition for the purpose of analysis is that cited by Waldman (1984), which summarises the Gothic as 'the image of woman-plus-habitation and the plot of mysterious sexual and supernatural threats in an atmosphere of dynastic mysteries within the habitation' (p. 29). All this takes place, according to Kavka (2002), in an atmosphere characterised by darkness and a sense of the distant past; the habitation is often a 'ruined castle or abandoned house on a hill made hazy by fog', with 'high, arched or leaded windows that cast imprisoning shadows', while outside a 'black cloud' passes 'across a full moon' (p. 210). As highlighted at the beginning of this chapter – with Kavka's (2002) statement that 'we perfectly well know the Gothic when we see it' (p. 209) – these definitions do indeed focus strongly on the visual. As such, they do not, at first sight, support this chapter's suggestion that *Goodnight Mommy* is a Gothic film, and in fact rather underline the different ways in which, visually, the film almost deliberately steers clear from any Gothic tropes. Its setting is not, by and large, characterised by darkness; instead, the greater part of the film is set in broad daylight, in a summery, Austrian countryside landscape perfect for *Die Trapp-Familie*, but not so much for a Gothic horror film. There is no fog, and all is bright and easily visible. In fact, the film even seems aware of the contradiction between its setting and the viewer's expectations of a horror film, and often plays with these expectations by visiting and then rejecting particular spaces more typical to its genre.

At the film's beginning, for example, the twins visit both a graveyard and a subterranean crypt, both prime settings for the beginning of a classic horror (or Gothic) story, but these expectations are soon thwarted. The graveyard is sunny and unthreatening, and the crypt – which does feature bones and skulls – is only visited once, and therefore inconsequential for the main narrative action. Similarly, the house does have a cellar – another space potentially associated with the Gothic – however the space turns out to be simply home to a large freezer filled with pepperoni pizza, and not, as we might expect, a location associated with terror. Again and again, the film evokes these easily recognisable Gothic settings only to counter the conventional use of these generic tropes. The house itself echoes this sense of thwarted expectations. Rather than an 'antiquated or seemingly antiquated space'

(Hogle, 2002: 2), a ruined castle, or a named, ancient mansion or estate, the house is ultra-modern, impersonal, and sterile in its appearance, with huge windows, blinds rather than curtains, and sparse, light, and neutrally coloured furniture. It has no dark corners, no hiding places, and, as opposed to houses such as Manderley in *Rebecca* (1940), it has no historical ties or ancestral connections to any of the characters involved. The 'habitation' featured in this supposedly classic woman-plus-habitation set-up appears here disappointingly devoid of meaning.

However, the 'woman', too, is an unlikely Gothic heroine in several ways. First, the Gothic heroine typically tends to be in some sense a prisoner within the house; Milbank (2002) notes that 'almost all nineteenth-century women were in some sense imprisoned in men's houses' (p. 155), without the freedom of movement or the financial independence afforded their male counterparts. More modern heroines, such as *Rebecca*'s second Mrs de Winter, are, if not trapped physically or by moral convention, still the newcomer in the Gothic house and certainly financially or emotionally dependent. Mommy is not in this position; she is the only adult in the house, which she has presumably chosen; she controls the family's finances and, since she can drive, their comings and goings. Her dominant persona in the earlier half of the film, as well, is a far cry from the traditional Gothic victim-heroine. Furthermore, the only example of 'closeups of mad, staring eyes' (Kavka, 2002: 210) we see in this film is the mirrored image of Mommy's gigantic, bloodshot eye; ostensibly, she is the dominant, sinister figure within the house, rather than its victim.

Nonetheless, both habitation and woman do conform to certain traits associated with the Gothic in certain ways. In terms of the house, for all its clean and blandly modern aesthetic, the bizarre paintings adorning its walls are particularly interesting. Unlike in older films, such as *Rebecca, Gaslight* (1944), or *The Two Mrs Carrolls* (1947), however, these are not straightforward portraits of a specific character, of a predecessor within the family or an ancestor within the house; instead, they include a set of rather amorphous images of women, reminiscent in some sense of

FIGURE 12.2 Mommy echoes the mysterious figure in the paintings
Goodnight Mommy/Ich Seh, Ich Seh (Veronika Franz, Severin Fiala, 2014)

the looks of the main character, but never shown in enough focus or detail to be positively identified as such. Two paintings especially are interesting in this regard: one shows a woman with her face averted from the viewer, whereas another shows a woman in frontal view with her face blurred. I argue that these paintings carry a number of different meanings within the narrative, and in a sense provide a clue to the secret running through the film (see Figure 12.2).

First, of course, the fact that the figure on the paintings resembles but is not clearly identifiable as Mommy appears to echo the question about Mommy's identity; we are not allowed to see the face of the women pictured, just like we are not allowed to glimpse Mommy's face for the greater part of the film. Mommy's true self remains a conundrum even as she becomes the victim-heroine near the film's end. This is the most immediate interpretation of these paintings: they look like Mommy, but they cannot be clearly identified as Mommy. Second, the paintings differ from those in other Gothic films in another key way, because they are at no point interacted with or commented upon, nor do they play a particular role within the film's narrative. Jacobs and Colpaert (2013) note that in films of this kind:

> the painting itself is usually presented as a character in its own right. Other characters treat the portrait as a real person, looking, talking, shouting, or even throwing things at it. In films, painted portraits invite the same reactions as human beings do.
>
> *(p. 17)*

This is not the case in this particular film, where the paintings are simply a part of the backdrop and are never even noticeably looked at by the characters; as such, the supposed invisibility of the portraits ties into the wider theme of the unreliability of the senses that permeates this film, on a number of levels. The portraits are unseen yet in plain sight; in this way, they echo the mystery at the heart of the film – the fact that Lukas, one of Mommy's twins, is dead and invisible to her, yet in plain sight to the viewers. Having concluded that the paintings depict a Mommy-like figure with an unidentifiable face, and that they are never interacted with by any character in the film, we can thus arrive at the third and, I believe, most pertinent interpretation of these paintings. After all, while it is true that the paintings' blurred or invisible faces might signify the horrific unknown of Mommy's face, this also means that Mommy herself cannot see. Her obscured face in both images also means she is unable to see what happens inside her own home, and this ultimately lies at the crux of the film's denouement.

This also highlights the way in which the woman within this habitation might fit into the paradigm of the Gothic victim-heroine after all, particularly when we consider the ways in which this unlikely victim becomes entrapped just like her other Gothic sisters before her. The entrapment exists on multiple levels, with the most obvious one being the physical one: for the last third of the film, Mommy is restrained to the house and isolated 'within the nuclear family' (Waldman, 1984: 35); in films such as *Rebecca* or *Gaslight*, this restraint was emotional, financial, or psychological, whereas here the restraint is physical. As she wakes up, Mommy finds herself strapped to the bed and cannot release herself, even as her sons torture her by burning her face with a magnifying glass in order to make her confess that she is not their real mother. Her suffering as a trapped victim is physical as well as psychological and utterly complete; she cannot leave the house, and even when she eventually escapes, a trap set by the boys trips her up, and she is once more dragged inside and tied up, this time in the living room. However, the sense of entrapment goes further than Mommy's physical whereabouts: it is also connected to the way her sensory perception and her ability to physically express herself are curtailed. Her entrapment is directly enacted upon her body: this is apparent when, as Mommy manages to remove the tape on her mouth, her twin sons decide to glue her mouth shut to keep her from screaming for help, and by the film's end at least one of her eyes has been similarly glued shut. This distorts her vision, as we can tell when, for the very first time within the film, we are firmly and literally aligned with Mommy's point of view and we see a set of blurred images as she is dragged across the floor by her children.

The relationship between the senses and Mommy's status as a trapped Gothic heroine – both figuratively and literally – also connects with one of the central features of the genre: the female protagonist's search for the solution of a central mystery. Waldman (1984) describes this trope as follows:

> The central feature of the Gothics is ambiguity, the hesitation between two possible interpretations of events by the protagonist and often, in these filmic presentations, by the spectator as well. This it shares with other filmic and literary genres, for example, the horror film and the fantastic. Yet in the Gothic, this hesitation is experienced by a character (and presumably a spectator) who is female. Within a patriarchal culture, then, the resolution of the hesitation carries with it the ideological function of validation or invalidation of feminine experience.
>
> (p. 31)

In this film, the ambiguity experienced by Gothic heroine Mommy is connected to the status of her deceased son Lukas – does he, as his brother Elias claims, still exist as a living, ghostly figure within the house, or is he simply a figment of Elias' guilt-ridden imagination? The answer to this question is not revealed in a conventionally Gothic manner: the house is not a dark, ancient Gothic mansion, and because Mommy is not psychologically or financially dependent on her male family members (i.e. her children), she does not wander through darkened hallways with a candelabra. Instead, the solution to the mystery – the figure of Lukas – is hidden in plain sight, visible to the spectator but ultimately inaccessible to Mommy's 'feminine experience', to her eyes. Just like the paintings in her house are unable to see or interact, so too is Mommy's inability to interact with or see Lukas an example of the 'problematic nature of the heroine's perception' (Waldman, 1984: 32) typical to many Gothic narratives. The film's original title,

Ich Seh, Ich Seh – I See, I See – echoes this, since it is a play on the German version of 'I spy with my little eye': 'I see, I see what you don't see'.

This becomes particularly apparent at the very end of the film, when the problematic limitation of Mommy's senses becomes fully clear to the spectators and culminates into a threat to Mommy's life. At this point, when Mommy is tied up on the living room floor and her son prepares to set the house alight, Elias poses his mother the ultimate test as a chance to save her life: she must tell him what Lukas is doing since, as their real Mommy, she should be able to see and hear her son. Mommy cannot, however, and thus the house burns down, killing both Mommy and Elias, who are next seen outside the house, alongside Lukas, singing a lullaby. The film's final depiction of the characters shows a Mommy with an unbandaged face, wearing an old-fashioned dress; this image of a mother and children singing echoes the film's very first images, the borrowed footage from *Die Trapp-Familie*, reference to which effectively bookends the narrative. The film is thus constructed around two ambiguities, or hesitations 'between two possible interpretations of events by the protagonist and often, in these filmic presentations, by the spectator as well' (Waldman, 1984: 31). First, the viewer is faced with an ambiguity around the identity of Mommy: is she the twins' real mother, or is she a malicious doppelgänger, either physically or in a supernatural sense? Towards the second half of the film, however, another and more crucial ambiguity surfaces: as the viewer identifies more with Mommy, we begin to share her own concerns and join her in questioning not her own, but her son's, identity or even existence. It is this second ambiguity, connected to the ability or lack thereof of Mommy's senses, that ultimately leads to her death at the hands of her – ghostly and living – sons. In this sense, Mommy has been transformed from a potentially monstrous figure to a Gothic victim-heroine, who ultimately dies when the limitations of her perception will not allow her to discover the truth about the film's central mystery.

This sense of perception, of the unreliability or ambiguity of the visual, also applies more broadly to the film's Gothic setting, and is in fact key to the film's very Gothicness. Unlike other Gothic films, whether older films such as *Rebecca* or more recent films such as *Crimson Peak* (2015), this film deliberately steers clear from obvious Gothic visual markers, and even deliberately plays with the viewer's expectations in this regard. Indeed, Mommy's entrapment long predates her physical restriction by her sons, and the true nature of the film's narrative has been under our very eyes, seen but unseen, from the film's very beginning. In terms of physical setting, too, the film plays with our expectations, and it is not the spatial specificity of the Austrian countryside setting that ultimately adds to the film's Gothicness. Instead, the series of 'dynastic mysteries', the sense of history that runs through so many Gothic narratives, is present here within the invisible elements of this setting, the sociocultural markers conveyed throughout this film. It is therefore not the presence of a large ancestral house, bedecked with portraits of ominous ancestors, but the regionally specific historical references that underlie and steer the plot, which make this film an Austrian Gothic film.

References

Creed, Barbara (1993) *The Monstrous-Feminine*. London: Routledge.

Hogle, Jerrold. E. (2002) 'Introduction'. In Jerrold E. Hogle (ed.), *The Cambridge Companion to Gothic Fiction*. Cambridge: Cambridge University Press, pp. 1–20.

Jacobs, Stephen and Lisa Colpaert (2013) *The Dark Galleries: A Museum Guide to Painted Portraits in Film Noir, Gothic Melodramas and Ghost Stories of the 1940s and 1950s*. Gent: MER Paper Kunsthalle.

Kaplan, E. Ann (1992) *Motherhood and Representation*. London: Routledge.

Kavka, Misha (2002) 'The Gothic on Screen'. In Jerrold E. Hogle (ed.), *The Cambridge Companion to Gothic Fiction*. Cambridge: Cambridge University Press, pp. 209–228.

Milbank, Alison (2002) 'The Victorian Gothic in English Novels and Stories, 1830–1880'. In Jerrold E. Hogle (ed.), *The Cambridge Companion to Gothic Fiction*. Cambridge: Cambridge University Press, pp. 145–166.

Stephenson, Jill (2001) *Women in Nazi Germany*. London: Routledge.

Waldman, Diane (1984) '"At Last I Can Tell It to Someone!"' Feminine Point of View and Subjectivity in the Gothic Romance Film of the 1940s'. *Cinema Journal*, 23(2): 29–40.

13

THE BABADOOK (2014), MATERNAL GOTHIC, AND THE 'WOMAN'S HORROR FILM'

Paula Quigley[1]

Like many Australian films, *The Babadook* (2014) initially fared far better overseas than it did at home. Arguably, this can be attributed to several factors that apply to Australian cinema as a whole: risk-averse programming that favours US productions backed by big marketing budgets, the associated tendency for Australian films to be limited to short runs in independent cinemas, along with escalating cinema ticket prices and increasing competition from television in terms of the availability of 'quality' drama (see Dow, 2014). Certainly, as Monica Tan (2014) points out, the film's positioning as art house in Australia and its modest marketing campaign mitigated against its exhibition in multiplexes and more mainstream outlets, unlike the more extensive campaign that supported its relatively widespread release in the UK, for example. That said, it seems that 'Australians still want to see Australian stories' (Dow, 2014), even if those stories must succeed internationally before being embraced locally.

Identifying the film as an 'Australian [success] story' is not without irony however, given the director's emphasis on creating a non-specific sense of place. In interview, director Jennifer Kent states, 'I didn't want it to be particularly Australian. I wanted to create a myth in a domestic setting. And even though it happened to be in some strange suburb in Australia somewhere, it could have been anywhere' (quoted in Lambie, 2014). As Aoife M. Dempsey (2015) argues, the idea of creating a myth in a domestic setting undermines 'the assertion that the film is placeless, given that myths are typically deeply culturally inscribed and inherited' (p. 131). Considered in this light, the film, and the figure of the Babadook in particular, is clearly available to being read in terms of a racialised schema of representation. Anthony Lane (2014), for instance, notes that the Babadook's name 'has a nice Australian tang; Aboriginal legend tells of a frog called the Tiddalik, with an insatiable thirst'. Christopher Sharrett (2015) focuses on the Babadook's appearance, observing that as well as looking like the hypnotist Caligari from *The Cabinet of*

Dr. Caligari (1920) or Lon Chaney from Tod Browning's *London After Midnight* (1927), the Babadook 'also looks like a black-faced minstrel'. As such, Sharrett suggests that 'further study of the film might explore its racial dimension, and Australian white culture's alternating valorization/demonization of the Aboriginal culture and population'. Dempsey's (2015) review of the film develops this line of thought, highlighting both the striking juxtaposition of an all-white cast of Australian middle-class characters with the sinister black Babadook, as well as the Aboriginal associations of the Babadook's name. 'The word Babadook itself', she writes, 'is evocative of Aboriginal etymology, similarly constructed using a combination of elongated vowels and hard g/k sounds' (p. 131). For Dempsey (2015), then, the Babadook and its possession of Amelia can be read as representing 'the Aboriginal, the Australian Other, the shadowy figure that haunts the white Australian consciousness as a result of collective cultural trauma, a legacy of colonialism' (p. 132).

Nevertheless, the fact that Kent considers the film to be first and foremost 'a myth in a domestic setting' speaks both to its inflection by culturally specific discourses around race and ethnicity, and to the ways in which its 'horror' is informed by generic paradigms that foreground the domestic context and the woman's – and particularly the mother's – place in it. For the editors of a recent dossier by *Senses of Cinema* (Horner and Zlosnik, 2016a), entitled 'Beyond *The Babadook*: Australian Women's Filmmaking and the Dark Fantastic', the film's international success offers a way of understanding the history of Australian women's film-making within the domain of the 'dark fantastic' (understood as encompassing, but not limited to, the horror genre), as a kind of enclave, simultaneously working within and against a male-dominated industry and a traditionally male-oriented genre. Careful not to elide the differences between artists and film-makers as diverse as Tracey Moffat, Anne Turner, Rosemary Myers, and Ursula Dabrowsky, nor to essentialise some notion of Australian women's film-making, the editors suggest that 'The dark fantastic has afforded a number of these film-makers with a space to think through feminist and other ideological issues in ways both creative and urgent, in a range of different ways'. In this context, the national provides a way of highlighting 'the sense of community that underscores women's film-making as potentially a kind of activism in and of itself'.

The Babadook's depiction of a mother and son trapped in a nightmarish domestic setting, via a reimagining of the Female Gothic and its relationship to the horror genre and the woman's film, both submits to and exceeds a specifically national interpretation. While Dempsey et al. make a convincing case for reading the film's racial politics in terms that recall the Gothic scenario itself (that is, as haunted by the traumatic legacy of a colonial past on the collective psyche), the Gothic as a mode or sensibility could also be said to offer a 'sense of community' that transcends a single region or historical period, insofar as it is available for reconceptualisation across a range of sociocultural contexts, while retaining an emphasis on the telling of women's stories.

Ellen Moers (1977) coined the term 'Female Gothic' to refer to a kind of literary fiction written by women for women, since the late 18th century.

Subsequent scholarship has undermined any automatic correspondence between the author's gender and a focus on 'female' issues (see Smith and Wallace, 2004: 2), but this category continues to be understood as preoccupied with women's experiences within patriarchal power structures. As the editors of the recent collection *Women and the Gothic* put it:

> Gothic texts still frequently convey anxiety and anger about the lot of women . . . While these vary in expression and representation across the centuries and across cultures, they are depressingly constant and suggest that women have been and still feel disadvantaged and disempowered.
>
> *(Horner and Zlosnik, 2016b: 1)*

In other words, the Gothic is best understood as an extensive category that traverses temporal and geographical conditions; its elasticity offers opportunities for reflecting and/or resisting 'women's lot' across a diverse range of media and sociocultural contexts. This collection alone, for instance, considers Gothic films ranging from the 1940s to the present day, from various countries, including international co-productions. Indeed, some of the earliest films were based on Gothic fiction, and Gothic tropes are visible in a variety of genres, spanning science fiction, noir, thrillers, and comedy (see Kaye, 2012). Within film studies, feminist critics have explored the often contradictory fascinations offered to female spectators in particular by a kind of film that emerged in Hollywood cinema in the 1940s, variously labelled 'the Freudian feminist melodrama' (Elsaesser, 1972) or 'the paranoid woman's film' (Doane, 1987). Films such as Hitchcock's *Rebecca* (1940) and *Suspicion* (1941), and George Cukor's *Gaslight* (1944), enact familiar Gothic scenarios whereby a young female protagonist's marriage to an apparently ambivalent older man is played out in an unsettling domestic environment, steeped in a mood of anxiety and uncertainty. As Helen Hanson (2007) argues, 'neo-Gothic' films such as *Jagged Edge* (1985), *Pacific Heights* (1990), and *What Lies Beneath* (2000) rework elements of these earlier films, in dialogue with feminist and post-feminist concerns (p. 183), and Gothic themes and motifs continue to inform popular fiction, television, and cinema. As Hanson (2007) puts it, '[the Gothic] has repeatedly found new outlets, while its dominant mood is an anxious and fraught relationship to the past' (p. 174).

Arguably, *The Babadook*'s international success is due in no small part to the ways in which it recalibrates Gothic and horror conventions, which have become part of a common cultural vocabulary. In the process, the film reflects on the repositioning of the mother figure in recent iterations of horror and the Female Gothic in film. In particular, the Gothic reworking of the 'horror' of the protagonist's conflicted experience of motherhood explores what Molly Haskell (1987) identifies as the great unspoken of the 'woman's film', namely women's guilt for their 'inadmissible feelings' about motherhood (p. 170). Considering the film in this light draws on Sue Thornham's (2013) reading of *We Need To Talk About Kevin* (2011) in relation to both feminist counter-cinema and maternal melodrama, as a critique of the post-feminist model of over-invested motherhood currently idealised in popular culture, as discussed below. Similarly, I argue that the ways in which *The Babadook* restages existing generic conventions challenges deeply embedded social and cinematic expectations around the maternal relationship. In this, *The Babadook* engages with contemporary currents across a range of national and generic contexts; for example, what Sarah Arnold (2013) calls 'Bad Mother gothic ghost stories', such as *The Others* (2001), *The Dark* (2005), *Silent Hill* (2006), and *The Orphanage* (2007) (p. 92), or what Tammy Oler (2014) calls 'the new crop of female-driven horror films', including Kimberly Peirce's *Carrie* (2013), Marina de Van's *Dark Touch* (2013), and Stewart Thorndike's *Lyle* (2014), which revisit and/or revise the role of the mother in the Gothic and horror traditions.

The film tells the story of Amelia (Essie Davis), a widow who is still grief-stricken seven years after the death of her husband, and her troubled young son Samuel (Noah Wiseman). After reading a storybook called *Mister Babadook* together, strange things start to happen in their house. Events escalate, and the Babadook, the monster of the storybook, appears and begins to terrorise Amelia, who in turn becomes increasingly violent towards Samuel. Finally, Amelia is able to confront the Babadook, and a kind of peace is restored. The film invites an association between the emergence of the Babadook and Amelia's grief at the death of her husband and rage towards her son. As such, virtually all of the critics and reviewers of the film have read the Babadook as embodying the 'return of the repressed' – that is, as the uncanny manifestation of Amelia's repressed emotions.

The film's mingling of the psychological and the supernatural complicates any easy classification. Kent considers it a 'crossover film' (quoted in Lambie, 2014), and it has been variously described as 'a chilling Freudian thriller' (Bradshaw, 2014), 'a maternal horror film' (Elfassy Bitoun, 2016), and an example of 'Australian Gothic' (Krake, 2015). Trying to identify the film solely with one of these categories is not particularly productive, however, as their delineation is more often based on popular perception and/or critical bias than on any clearly defined generic boundaries. For instance, through an analysis of film reviews published during the 1930s and 1940s, Mark Jancovich (2013) argues that the psychological thrillers he calls 'Gothic (or paranoid) woman's films' were clearly understood as 'women's horror films' at the time of their release. If Jancovich identifies the horror in women's films, David Greven (2011) finds the woman's film hidden in the horror genre. With Hitchcock's *Psycho* (1960) and the concomitant transition from the clearly identifiable monster of classical horror to a focus on 'the family and its attendant terrors' (p. 88), Greven (2011) argues that many modern horror films, such as *Carrie* (1976) and the *Alien* films (1979–1997), can be read as 'concealed women's films', insofar as they place 'female desire at the center of the narrative' (p. 36). Arnold (2013), for her part, more precisely identifies the key point of intersection between horror and melodrama in representations of the mother. Since *Psycho* and the focus on family horror in Western cinema, she argues, the mother has become a prominent feature of horror cinema (p. 37). The 'Good Mother' is defined by 'self-sacrifice, selflessness and nurturance' (p. 37). The 'Bad Mother' is 'a multifaceted and contradictory construct', manifesting as either a rejection of the traditional expectation of self-sacrifice and devotion to her children, or its inverse, 'the mother's fanatical conformity to the institution of motherhood' (p. 68). According to Arnold (2013), both models of motherhood are evident throughout the horror genre and the melodrama, although the level of complicity and/or resistance to these models within individual texts is a complex field of interrogation (p. 26).

Thus, the boundaries between the melodrama, the 'Gothic (or paranoid) woman's film', and the horror film are especially permeable, more like membranes if you will, permitting certain elements to pass through while restricting others, depending on the particular permutation of the film's articulation, production, and reception. *The Babadook* reframes the maternal melodrama's investment in 'the spectacle of a mother owned by her children' (Haskell, 1987: 169) in terms of the Female Gothic, and in so doing foregrounds the issue of maternal subjectivity that inheres in both categories.

Although the cycle of Hollywood films from the 1940s frequently referred to as Female Gothic is quite diverse, most 'involve a woman who feels threatened or tortured by a seemingly sadistic male authority figure, who is usually her husband' (Jancovich, 2013: 21). As discussed below, *The Babadook* retains core elements of the Female Gothic, such as the heroine's relationship to a stifling domestic space, and the weight of the past on the present. Its significant revision is to replace the young female protagonist's suspicion of her husband with a mother's suspicion of her son. This recasts the Oedipal scenario from the mother's point of view and resists the idealised image of motherhood that sustains the melodrama in its maternal mode. In addition, altering the perspective from that of a childless bride to that of a mother reconfigures the maternal function within the Gothic framework. No longer the 'spectral presence' of Gothic fiction (Kahane, 1985: 336) with and against whom the young protagonist (i.e. the daughter) must identify in order to individuate, the mother becomes an active agent whose subjectivity is privileged within the diegesis. Privileging the mother's perspective in this way permits what is typically concealed in both the maternal melodrama and the Female Gothic – namely, ambivalence around the maternal relationship and the Oedipal model in which it participates – to erupt violently in all its 'horror'.

If self-sacrifice is the privileged theme of the woman's film, in the maternal variant, the woman must sacrifice her own welfare for that of her children. When we first meet Amelia, just before Samuel's seventh birthday, she is in precisely this position, having to sacrifice her own needs for those of her son. Samuel is troubled, suffering from nightmares and seeing monsters. He is demanding, seeking constant attention and reassurance, and, apart from working in a care home for elderly people, Amelia's life revolves around looking after him. While the maternal melodrama typically struggles with reconciling the woman's maternal and sexual identities – the good mother, such as Stella of King Vidor's paradigmatic *Stella Dallas* (1937), will reject romantic relationships for the sake of her child – it seems that Amelia has had to literally sacrifice her husband Oskar (Benjamin Winspear) for her son, as Oskar was killed in a car accident while driving Amelia to the hospital to give birth to Samuel. Despite her loneliness, Amelia is so exhausted caring for others, and for Samuel in particular, that she seems oblivious to her colleague's (Daniel Henshall) gentle overtures. Thus, Samuel seems to have supplanted the father's place in his mother's life, with all the Oedipal associations that implies, as discussed below. Rather than surrender herself to this situation, however, Amelia's repressed grief and anger at the loss of her husband is the source of her 'monstrous' rage and resentment towards Samuel. Here, the tradition of female self-abnegation within the maternal melodrama is undercut by the 'horror' it conceals from the outset, signalled via an intensification and inversion of Gothic conventions.

As Margaret Anne Doody (1977) argues:

> the 'real world' for characters in a gothic novel is one of nightmare. There is no longer a common sense order against which the dream briefly flickers; rather, the world of rational order briefly flickers in and out of the dreamlike.
>
> *(p. 529)*

The Babadook begins by bringing us straight into Amelia's nightmare, and the distinction between what is 'real' and what is a (very) bad dream becomes difficult to discern. The first shot is of Amelia's face in close-up, breathing as if in labour, illuminated by the intermittent flash of a bright, white light. Suddenly, broken glass sprays across her cheek and she is thrown from side to side in slow motion. A child's voice calling 'Mum! Mum!' is barely audible over discordant sounds such as muffled roars and metal scraping. A point-of-view shot from Amelia's perspective shows us a man slumped in what we now realise is a driving seat. What sounds like the rush of an oncoming car in slow motion gets louder as the child's voice grows more insistent. Amelia turns her head sharply and a bright, white light explodes on the screen. Samuel's voice, increasing in volume, brings Amelia (and us) back to her current context: lonely, widowed, grieving, and caring for an emotionally damaged little boy in the dark, foreboding house typical of the Gothic scenario. Soon after, a series of close shots shows parts of a sleeping Samuel, his leg flung over his mother, his hand kneading her neck, the abrasive sound of his grinding teeth heightened on the soundtrack. Amelia's sense of physical and emotional entrapment is palpable. She disentangles herself from him and a symmetrically composed overhead shot shows them lying on opposite sides of the bed, Amelia's back to her son, the distance she has put between them foreshadowing her increasingly violent desire to escape her child as the film progresses.

It is clear that Amelia is struggling not only with other people's reactions to Samuel, but also with her own ambivalence towards her son. She suspects him of persecuting her (by defacing a photograph of herself and Oskar, or putting shards of glass in her soup), and the Gothic suspicion at the heart of the maternal melodrama shatters its veneer of maternal devotion. As events escalate and her suspicion shifts from Samuel to the possibility of an unknown stalker, Amelia's ambivalence towards Samuel remains and gains force, transforming from suspicion to a 'monstrous' rage towards her child. The film goes on to embrace the full 'horror' of this taboo, which, as Haskell (1987) argues, is repressed in mainstream maternal melodrama.

Kent is explicit in her desire to foreground this issue, which she believes is under-represented, both cinematically and socioculturally. She states:

> Apart from *We Need to Talk About Kevin*, I can't easily think of other examples [that address maternal ambivalence] and it's the great unspoken thing. We're all, as women, educated and conditioned to think that motherhood is an easy thing that just happens. But it's not always the case.
>
> *(quoted in MacInnes, 2014)*

Referencing *We Need to Talk About Kevin* (2011) links *The Babadook* to the maternal melodrama and to its inverse – films that unpick the pervasive idealisation of maternal self-sacrifice in popular culture – interrogating the mother's role in Female Gothic and horror films in the process.

Thornham (2013) situates Lynne Ramsay's film within the twin histories of feminist counter-cinema and maternal melodrama, and reads it as a critique of 'new momism', the idealisation of motherhood that gathered momentum in the 1990s as part of a backlash against the gains of second-wave feminism. The key difference between 'new momism' and the representations of domesticated femininity that dominated 1950s American culture is that the woman's subservience to her husband now is replaced by subservience to her child. Importantly, however, this emphasis on intensive mothering is framed as the woman's liberated choice (p. 3). As such, Thornham (2013) argues that 'new momism' is the post-feminist version of overinvested mothering that Haskell (1987) maintains conceals the hatred lurking beneath the surface of classical women's films:

> Children are an obsession in American movies . . . The sacrifice of and for children – two sides of the same coin – is a disease passing for a national virtue . . . Both of these transactions represent beautifully masked wish fulfillments, suggesting that the myth of obsession – the love lavished, the attention paid to children . . . – is compensation for women's guilt, for the deep inadmissible feelings of not wanting children, or not wanting them unreservedly, in the first place.
>
> *(Haskell, 1987: 168–170, quoted in Thornham,*
> *2013: 3, with ellipses)*

According to Thornham (2013), 'such hatred is also the subject of . . . *We Need to Talk about Kevin*' (p. 3). Eva (Tilda Swinton) struggles to love her son Kevin (Rocky Duer, Jasper Newell, Ezra Miller) and to relinquish control of her body and her life in the ways that are expected of her, first as a pregnant woman and then as a mother. Her relationship with her son is fraught from infancy, and as he grows older his disturbing behaviour becomes increasingly violent, culminating in his murder of his father and sister, and massacre of his fellow high-school students.

Thornham (2013) identifies Kevin, 'with his violence, mockery of parental authority and unreadable self-possession', as the obvious 'successor to both the monstrous children of 1970s horror and, in an ironic gesture, to the wise innocents that succeeded them' (p. 7). She traces Vivian Sobchack's (2015) history of the male child in horror and family melodrama since the 1970s in terms of his role in shoring up patriarchal power structures against the pressures exerted by second-wave feminism. According to Sobchack, the political and sociocultural upheavals of the 1970s produced in popular horror films such as *The Exorcist* (1973) and *The Omen* (1976) portrayals of children as 'uncivilized, hostile, and powerful Others' who threatened the family and social institutions (Thornham, 2013: 6; Sobchack, 2015: 178). By the end of the decade, the impact of feminism is such that the role of the child within this scenario has shifted significantly. The previously destructive power of the horror-film child transforms into a kind of special insight, and the child of the family melodrama becomes both markedly precocious and particularly vulnerable to the threat posed by the cold, selfish (i.e. feminist) mother, as illustrated by the 1979 hit *Kramer vs. Kramer*. As Thornham emphasises, it is now 'the (male) child who has the power to authorize the family . . . who denies or legitimates the particular family's existence as a viable structure' (Thornham, 2013: 6; Sobchack, 2015: 183).

Thornham (2013) argues that the shift from second-wave feminism to post-feminism has altered the terms of reference once again. While motherhood is now framed as a choice, the woman must choose to devote herself to the child entirely if the child is to thrive. An essential aspect of *We Need to Talk About Kevin*'s critique of this model, therefore, is its emphasis on the mother's, rather than the child's, subjectivity (p. 6). Similarly, Arnold (2013) suggests that 'the [horror] genre is increasingly being used to explore maternal desires and conflicts rather than infantile ones' (p. 70). 'Gothic melodramas' such as *The Others* increase our access to the 'Bad Mother's' perspective and question her subordination within patriarchal power structures, articulated within an oppressive domestic space (p. 107).

Notably, an emphasis on the mother's, rather than the child's, perspective is central to the reimagining of the Female Gothic with which *We Need to Talk About Kevin* and *The Babadook* can be aligned. Mothers, albeit in disguised or displaced form, have haunted the Gothic tradition since its inception. Claire Kahane (1985) identifies the young female protagonist's problematic identification with 'the spectral presence of a dead-undead mother' – 'the ongoing battle with a mirror image that is both self and other' – as central to the Gothic scenario as initiated by Ann Radcliffe in the 1790s (pp. 336, 337). Similarly, 'Modern Gothics', according to Tania Modleski (1982), 'help women to deal with their ambivalent attitudes towards their mothers as well as their "masochistic identification" with them' (p. 69). For Moers (1977), on the other hand, Mary Shelley's *Frankenstein* (1818) is a 'distinctly . . . woman's mythmaking on the subject of birth', insofar as it displaces 'the [maternal] drama of guilt, dread, and flight surrounding birth and its consequences' onto the figure of the male scientist (p. 93).

Scholars have identified analogous impulses in Female Gothic films. Modleski (1988/2005), for instance, argues that Hitchcock's *Rebecca*, at least on one level, enacts 'the long discredited "Electra complex"' (i.e. the daughter's rivalry with an oppressive mother figure) (p. 44). Andrew Scahill (2015) identifies an alternate strand of 'maternal gothic', typified by Polanski's *Rosemary's Baby* (1968), which 'centers on the prenatal stage and the horror of an independent alien organism growing inside of the female body' (p. 9). Arguably, recent iterations of the Female Gothic in film such as *We Need to Talk About Kevin* and *The Babadook* move beyond limiting the maternal function to a metaphorical space, or a horror of the pregnant female body as a site of monstrous invasion. Instead, the figure of the mother and her ambivalent experience of motherhood becomes the focal point of the narrative and the vehicle for an exploration of questions of female identity and agency.

As discussed, Thornham (2013) argues that *We Need to Talk About Kevin* confronts difficult issues around motherhood and maternal ambivalence within the context of a popular culture that is, arguably, over-invested in images of idealised mothering. While Thornham reads the film refracted through the maternal melodrama and feminist counter-cinema, Ginette Carpenter (2016) suggests that the film's interrogation of 21st-century gender roles and the cultural surveillance of maternity is 'channelled through the conventions of the Gothic'. She states that '[its] generic instabilities, use of excess, overlapping of past and present and depictions of uncanny and abject monstrosity combine with the visual tropes of the horror film to create unsettling depictions of feminine embodiment, pregnancy, birth and mothering' (p. 47). As Carpenter (2016) points out, the source novel's unreliable narration is restricted to Eva's point of view in the film; 'this is', she notes, 'very deliberately the mother's tale' (p. 53). Similarly, for Kent, aligning the spectator with Amelia's perspective was vital to *The Babadook*'s organisation. She says:

> Even when she goes to some really dark places, I still tried to keep it within her point of view as much as possible, so that people would not sit back with their arms folded and judge her, but they'd actually travel through that experience with her.
>
> *(quoted in Sélavy, 2014)*

In other words, to borrow Thornham's (2013) description of Eva in *We Need to Talk About Kevin*, in *The Babadook* 'it is [Amelia's] fractured subjectivity, hate, and sense of guilt that we inhabit' (p. 27). Privileging Amelia's 'fractured subjectivity' allows us to witness the 'horror' of a mother's hatred of her own (male) child break through the mask of maternal self-sacrifice, while avoiding her vilification.

From the close-ups of Amelia's shocked and frightened face during what is revealed to be the car crash that killed her husband, through close-ups revealing her increasing panic as the Babadook makes its presence felt in her home, to close-ups of her radically transformed face as she tries to strangle her son, tight framings of Amelia's face chart her psychic dissolution. These tight framings are alternated with long shots of Amelia that create a sense of her being cut adrift from her surroundings and from 'normal life'. For example, when Amelia visits a shopping mall instead of rushing home to care for Samuel, we see her sitting alone on a sofa eating ice cream, surrounded by empty space, as people pass in front of her. The lack of ambient noise on the soundtrack, replaced by non-diegetic music, increases our sense of her isolation. As Amelia unravels, the sense of time, too, becomes more disordered, drawn out or compressed around Amelia's intensified experience. As discussed, time is extended in slow motion in the opening nightmare scene. Later in the film, by contrast, when Amelia finds the *Mister Babadook* storybook on her doorstep after she had torn it up and burnt it, accelerated footage speeds up her walk back into the house, as if the horror of its return concentrates her experience of time.

Like *We Need to Talk About Kevin*, which, in Thornham's (2013) words, 'replays the Oedipal story – the son's usurpation and murder of the father, the disturbingly sexual overtones in the relationship between son and mother . . . from the mother's perspective' (p. 23), *The Babadook* stages the Oedipal overtones of Samuel's relationship with his mother from Amelia's point of view. According to Bradshaw (2014):

> Kent shows that as Samuel gets older, he starts to intuit ever more clearly his father's absence and his own quasi-conjugal relationship with his mother. He is always clambering over her and heedlessly touching her in ways he doesn't understand.

From Amelia's perspective, however, their physical intimacy is shown to be deeply intrusive. These Oedipal overtones are unmissable in the scene where Samuel disturbs his mother masturbating, a scene that ironically recalls the maternal melodrama's insistence that the good mother surrender her sexual identity for the sake of her child.

Thus, the son replaces the husband in this Gothic retelling of the maternal melodrama, where 'the woman's place is in the home' is not a refuge, but a prison. The heroine's relationship to the dark, oppressive house is of course a defining aspect of the Gothic scenario. The house maps the female protagonist's fears and anxieties; her relationship to its forbidden spaces arguably literalises her own relationship to those aspects of herself that are similarly hidden from consciousness. As Steven Jacobs (2007) puts it:

> In Gothic romance films, the forbidden room is a metaphor for the repressed experience. The heroine attempts to disclose and visualize the secrets and mysteries, just like the psychoanalyst opens up the mysterious depths of the soul. Opening up the forbidden room is . . . the cathartic moment in the story.
>
> *(p. 39)*

Amelia's relationship to the house, and particularly (as is the convention if not the cliché) to the basement, dramatises her relationship to those aspects of herself and her history that she cannot articulate. Her most violent confrontations – with Samuel, with her dead husband, and with the Babadook – take place there, and ultimately the basement becomes 'home' to the uncanny manifestation of those fears and anxieties that she must confront in order to save herself and Samuel.

If the house, and particularly the basement, constitutes a spatialisation of Amelia's fears and anxieties in particular, as in the Gothic tradition, it also has a specific relationship to time. The basement is where Amelia stores her memories of Oskar, in the form of his clothes and belongings, and thus it speaks to what John Fletcher (1995) calls 'the Gothic realm of a past preserved and suspended and awaiting reanimation' (p. 355). When the Babadook emerges from the basement, he does so, as many critics have noted, as an uncanny embodiment of the arrangement of Oskar's clothes that Amelia keeps there (see Barker, 2014). Thus, the basement is a place where time is suspended in space, a frozen past that Amelia must incorporate into her personal narrative if she is to 'move on'.

As such, the psychic mapping of the house in *The Babadook* corresponds closely to that of its Gothic predecessors. Privileging Amelia's 'fractured subjectivity' within this oppressive space aligns us with her as she transitions from what we might call the Gothic victim of a maternal nightmare to what Arnold (2013) describes as the 'Bad Mother' in her guise as the 'monster or the villain' (p. 68). As Amelia's mask of maternal self-sacrifice begins to slip, she becomes wildly abusive and violent, and the conventions of the horror genre provide a vocabulary capable of articulating the 'real' feelings beneath Amelia's façade. Like Sobchack's (2015) model, outlined above, Amelia's ambivalence towards her son seems to turn her into a 'monster', while Samuel plays a pivotal role in the family's survival, preparing weapons to defend himself and his mother well in advance of the Babadook's first appearance to Amelia. It is Samuel who assures Amelia, 'I just want you to be happy' when she articulates her murderous feelings towards him, and Samuel who intuits her possession as repression and tells her, '[y]ou have to get it out'. Thus, while Samuel begins the film suggesting the possibility of the monstrous or possessed child of 1970s horror cinema (screaming fits, seeing things, an apparent propensity for violence, and so on – see Wood, 2012), he corresponds more closely to the subsequent iteration of the child as 'wise innocent' the more Amelia turns into a 'monster'.

In spite of this, the film privileges Amelia's, rather than Samuel's, perspective and does not resolve by aligning Samuel with a viable father figure and eliminating or punishing Amelia. As such, the film refuses to condemn the mother and endorse the son, as is the case in the films Sobchack (2015) discusses. Instead, the film focuses on Amelia's ultimate acknowledgement and integration of her own 'monstrous' feelings about motherhood, allowing us to sympathise with her as an exhausted, grieving widow struggling with the demands of motherhood, as well as with Samuel as a vulnerable little boy. This process is facilitated by having Amelia inhabit in turn the role of mother-as-Gothic-victim, mother-as-monster, and finally mother-as-saviour. In this, Amelia complicates the typical Gothic protagonist, described by Moers (1977) as 'simultaneously persecuted victim and courageous heroine' (p. 124). Allowing the 'monstrous' aspect of her maternal ambivalence to manifest itself, via the hyperbolic conventions of the horror film, means that Amelia is not limited to the role of essentially 'good' victim and/or heroine; her 'badness' is an intrinsic, if hitherto unacknowledged, aspect of herself. In so doing, the film subverts the dichotomous representation of the mother as either good or bad that, as Arnold (2013) argues, has tended to sustain earlier iterations of both the maternal melodrama and the horror genre.

Hazel Cills (2014) notes that usually when a child is in danger in a horror film, it is incumbent upon the child's family, and specifically the mother, to save the child. Whether it is against a supernatural force – such as Diane Freeling in *Poltergeist* (1982) – or against a demonic husband – such as Wendy Torrance in *The Shining* (1980) – the mother's role is as protector. As Cills (2014) puts it, '[j]ust as slashers have their sainted final girls, home invasion and possession films have their final mothers'. The key difference, as Cills (2014) sees it, between a film like *The Exorcist* and *The Babadook*, both films featuring hard-working single mothers with children threatened by evil forces, 'is that in the latter film, Amelia is the one who becomes possessed'. Thus, Amelia's possession seems to turn her into the 'Bad Mother', who must be eliminated in order for the child to survive. However, as Cills (2014) argues, while the horror genre is heavily populated by evil mothers – Mrs Bates in *Psycho*, Margaret White in *Carrie*, Mrs Voorhees in *Friday the 13th* (1980), and so on – 'what makes Amelia compelling is how she literally embodies both roles – the unstable villain and the resilient child-saver'.

In fact, Amelia could be said to assume three roles over the course of the film: Gothic victim, 'Bad Mother', and 'final mother', in Cills' (2014) terms. Ultimately, Amelia's fury is turned upon its proper object – the Babadook – and she confronts it, screaming, '*[i]f you touch my son again I'll fucking kill you!*' The Babadook falls to the ground, light and insubstantial. When she touches it, it roars at her, but she withstands its rage, her terrified face in tight close-up, lit once again by a bright, white light. Visually, this recalls the opening nightmare scene; as Amelia can now confront this horror, the Babadook retreats to its generic home – the basement. Amelia reconciles with her son and with herself as a mother by recognising the 'horror' of her unexpressed grief and rage towards her child. In this sense, the Babadook practically begs to be read as 'the return of the repressed', the Freudian scenario – which Wood (2012) argues is central to the horror genre – whereby material that has been 'sunk into' the id manifests in conscious formations, often in greatly distorted or disguised form.

The possibility that Amelia may be the author of the *Mister Babadook* storybook – and thus the origin of the Babadook itself – is suggested by the fact that Amelia says she used to write 'kids' stuff' in a conversation with her sister and her sister's friends. Jeffrey Jerome Cohen (1996) elaborates on the idea of the monster as originating in the self in his thesis that 'the fear of the monster is also a kind of desire' (p. 16). In other words, the figure of the monster permits forbidden fantasies of aggression and domination to be safely expressed in a clearly defined, liminal space. As Cohen (1996) argues, '[w]hen contained by geographic, generic, or epistemic marginalization, the monster can function as an alter ego, as an alluring projection of (an Other) self' (p. 17). In this case, shifting generic registers from Gothic terror – where, as Moers (1997) puts it, 'fantasy dominates over reality' (p. 123) – to the conventions of classical horror – whereby the threat posed emanates from an externalised, recognisable monster – allows the Babadook, understood as the projection of Amelia's 'Other' self, to take shape, as it were, and become an acknowledged part of Amelia's and Samuel's shared reality.

Cohen (1996) suggests that the answer to the question '[d]o monsters really exist?' can only be '[s]urely they must, for if they did not, how could we?' (p. 20). In other words, monsters exist insofar as their creation constitutes a vital component of how we map our social and psychic universe, and, however much we might try to exclude them, their inevitable return brings with it a fuller knowledge of our selves. Similarly, the return of the Babadook as the 'monstrous' manifestation of Amelia's repressed feelings about motherhood brings with it the opportunity to reconsider the maternal role in ways that can accommodate ambivalence.

According to Thornham (2013), the ending of *We Need to Talk About Kevin* 'points us beyond the twin fantasies of post-feminist maternal masochism and unproblematic feminist agency' (p. 27). *The Babadook* similarly avoids a simple reversal or straightforward endorsement of maternal sacrifice. In finally resisting the Babadook and saving her son, Amelia appears to conform to the 'Good Mother' model of both horror film and maternal melodrama, but this is undermined by the *mise en scène*. The bare tree outside their house has flowered, but its green leaves and pink flowers seem hyperreal, saturated. While the final scene takes place in the garden, we arrive there by coming up through the earth, accompanied by a distant, roaring sound. Spatially and temporally disorientating, it feels like we have returned to the earlier horror, until we emerge in the garden, in daylight, to witness a happier scene between mother and son. This scene is nonetheless infused with an uncanny quality that undermines any easy reading of the mother–child relationship as fully resolved in terms of the reconciliation of the 'Good Mother' with her 'wise, innocent' son.

The Babadook has not been eliminated, but is still with them, if somewhat subdued. According to Cohen (1996), '[m]onsters are our children' (p. 20). Amelia's recovery implies a recognition of this as, ultimately, she assumes a quasi-maternal role towards the Babadook itself, giving it a home (in the basement), soothing it during its (epic) tantrums, and feeding it (worms). At one level, then, the Babadook can be read as the monstrous progeny of the 'Bad Mother', as convention would have it. Yet, unlike the 'gothic melodramas' discussed by Arnold (2013), all of which 'either exclude or are about the exclusion of the Bad Mother' (p. 112), the resolution of *The Babadook* does not depend upon the exclusion of the mother or of the monster. Instead, the impulse is towards integration; Amelia's acknowledgement and acceptance of the Babadook is integral to her revised relationship not only to her son, but also to herself as a mother. This is facilitated by a process of generic assimilation, whereby the victimised protagonist of the Female Gothic (whose male child assumes the role of persecutor hitherto occupied by her husband) transforms into the horror mother in both her 'Good' and 'Bad' modes, and finally reconciles with those aspects of herself that are more typically concealed and/or reviled in mainstream cinema. *The Babadook*'s international success may thus, at least in part, be accounted for by the ways in which it revisits and revises the representation of the mother figure in the closely related categories of Female Gothic, maternal melodrama, and the horror film, and in so doing reflects on current cinematic and sociocultural expectations of the maternal role.

Note

1 An earlier version of this chapter was published as 'When Good Mothers Go Bad: Genre and Gender in *The Babadook*'. *Irish Journal of Gothic and Horror Studies*, 15 (Autumn 2016): 57–75.

References

Arnold, Sarah (2013) *Maternal Horror Film: Melodrama and Motherhood*. London: Palgrave Macmillan.

Barker, James B. (2014) '*The Babadook*: When Allegory Meets Expressionism in a Therapeutic Horror Classic'. *The Bark Bites Back*. https://thebarkbitesback.wordpress.com/?s=babadook [Accessed 2 April 2018]

Bradshaw, Peter (2014) '*The Babadook* Review – A Superbly Acted, Chilling, Freudian Thriller'. *The Guardian*. www.theguardian.com/film/2014/oct/23/the-babadook-review-chilling-freudian-thriller [Accessed 2 April 2018]

Carpenter, Ginette (2016) 'Mothers and Others'. In Avril Horner and Sue Zlosnik (eds), *Women and the Gothic: An Edinburgh Companion*. Edinburgh: Edinburgh University Press, pp. 46–59.

Cills, Hazel (2014) 'Mother Dearest: How *The Babadook* Inverts the Horror Movie Mom'. *Grantland*. http://grantland.com/hollywood-prospectus/mother-dearest-how-the-babadook-inverts-the-horror-movie-mom/ [Accessed 2 April 2018]

Cohen, Jeffrey Jerome (1996) 'Monster Culture (Seven Theses)'. In Jeffrey Jerome Cohen (ed.), *Monster Theory: Reading Culture*. Minneapolis, MN: University of Minnesota Press, pp. 3–25.

Dempsey, Aoife M. (2015) '*The Babadook*'. *Irish Journal of Gothic and Horror Studies*, 14: 130–131.

Doane, Mary Ann (1987) *The Desire to Desire: The Woman's Film of the 1940s*. Bloomington, IN: Indiana University Press.

Doody, Margaret Anne (1977) 'Deserts, Ruins, and Troubled Waters: Female Dreams in Fiction and the Development of the Gothic Novel'. *Genre*, 10: 529–573.

Dow, Steve (2014) 'What's Wrong with Australian Cinema?' *The Guardian*. www.theguardian.com/film/2014/oct/26/australian-film-australian-audiences [Accessed 2 April 2018]

Elfassy Bitoun, Rachel (2016) 'Maternal Horror Films: Understanding the "Dysfunctional" Mother'. *The Artifice*. http://the-artifice.com/maternal-horror-films-dysfunctional-mother/ [Accessed 2 April 2018]

Elsaesser, Thomas (1972) 'Tales of Sound and Fury: Observations on the Family Melodrama'. *Monogram*, 4: 4–15.

Fletcher, John (1995) 'Primal Scenes and the Female Gothic: *Rebecca* and *Gaslight*'. *Screen*, 36(4): 341–370.

Greven, David (2011) *Representations of Femininity in American Genre Cinema: The Woman's Film, Film Noir, and Modern Horror*. New York: Palgrave Macmillan.

Hanson, Helen (2007) *Hollywood Heroines: Women in Film Noir and the Female Gothic Film*. London: I.B. Tauris.

Haskell, Molly (1987) *From Reverence to Rape: The Treatment of Women in the Movies* (2nd edition). Chicago, IL: University of Chicago Press.

Horner, Avril, and Sue Zlosnik (2016a) 'Beyond *The Babadook*: Australian Women's Filmmaking and the Dark Fantastic'. *Senses of Cinema*. http://sensesofcinema.com/2016/beyond-the-babadook/beyond-the-babadook-introduction/ [Accessed 3 January 2017]

Horner, Avril and Sue Zlosnik (eds) (2016b) *Women and the Gothic: An Edinburgh Companion*. Edinburgh: Edinburgh University Press.

Jacobs, Steven (2007) *The Wrong House: The Architecture of Alfred Hitchcock*. Netherlands: 010 Publishers.

Jancovich, Marc (2013) 'Bluebeard's Wives: Horror, Quality and the Gothic (or Paranoid) Woman's Film in the 1940s'. *Irish Journal of Gothic and Horror Studies*, 12: 20–43.

Kahane, Claire (1985) 'The Gothic Mirror'. In Shirley Nelson Garner, Claire Kahane, and Madelon Sprengnether (eds), *The (M)other Tongue: Essays in Feminist Psychoanalytic Interpretation*. Ithaca, NY: Cornell University Press, pp. 334–351.

Kaye, Heidi (2012) 'Gothic Film'. In David Punter (ed.), *A New Companion to the Gothic*. London: Blackwell, pp. 239–251.

Krake, Kate (2015) '*The Babadook* (2014) – Movie Review'. *Pop Cultured*. www.pop-cultured.net/the-babadook-2014-movie-review [Accessed 3 January 2017]

Lambie, Ryan (2014) 'Jennifer Kent Interview: Directing *The Babadook*'. *Den of Geek*. www.denofgeek.com/movies/the-babadook/32451/jennifer-kent-interview-directing-the-babadook [Accessed 2 April 2018]

Lane, Anthony (2014) '*The Babadook*'. *The New Yorker*. www.newyorker.com/goings-on-about-town/movies/babadook-2 [Accessed 2 April 2018]

MacInnes, Paul (2014) '*The Babadook*: "I Wanted to Talk About the Need to Face Darkness in Ourselves"'. *The Guardian*. www.theguardian.com/film/2014/oct/18/the-babadook-jennifer-kent [Accessed 2 April 2018]

Modleski, Tania (1982) *Loving with a Vengence: Mass Produced Fantasies for Women*. Hamden, CT: Archon Books.

Modleski, Tania (1988/2005) *The Women Who Knew Too Much: Hitchcock and Feminist Film Theory*. New York: Routledge.

Moers, Ellen (1977) *Literary Women: The Great Writers*. Oxford: Oxford University Press.

Oler, Tammy (2014) 'The Mommy Trap'. *Slate*. https://slate.com/culture/2014/11/horror-movies-about-mothers-and-children-the-babadook-lyle-and-other-films-by-women.html [Accessed 2 April 2018]

Scahill, Andrew (2015) *The Revolting Child in Horror Cinema: Youth Rebellion and Queer Spectatorship*. New York: Palgrave Macmillan.

Sélavy, Virginie (2014) '*The Babadook*: Interview with Jennifer Kent'. www.electricsheepmagazine.co.uk/features/2014/10/24/the-babadook-interview-with-jennifer-kent/ [Accessed 2 April 2018]

Sharrett, Christopher (2015) '*The Babadook*: Ghosts in the Bedroom'. *Film International*. http://filmint.nu/?p=14436 [Accessed 3 January 2017]

Shelley, Mary (1818) *Frankenstein; or, The Modern Prometheus*. London: Lackington, Hughes, Harding, Mavor & Jones.

Smith, Andrew, and Diana Wallace (2004) 'The Female Gothic: Then and Now'. *Gothic Studies*, 6(1): 1–7.

Sobchack, Vivian (2015) 'Bringing It All Back Home: Family Economy and Generic Exchange'. In Barry Keith Grant (ed.), *The Dread of Difference* (2nd edition). Austin, TX: University of Texas Press, pp. 171–191.

Tan, Monica (2014) '*The Babadook*'s Monster UK Box Office Success Highlights Problems at Home'. *The Guardian*. www.theguardian.com/film/australia-culture-blog/2014/oct/29/the-babadooks-monster-uk-box-office-success-highlights-problems-at-home [Accessed 28 December 2016]

Thornham, Sue (2013) '"A Hatred So Intense . . .": *We Need to Talk About Kevin*, Postfeminism and Women's Cinema'. *Sequence: Serial Studies in Media, Film, and Music*, 2(1): 3–36.

Wood, Robin (2012) *Hollywood From Vietnam to Reagan . . . and Beyond*. New York: Columbia University Press.

FILMOGRAPHY

Alien (Ridley Scott, UK/USA, 1979)

Alien³ (David Fincher, USA, 1992)

Alien Resurrection (Jean-Pierre Jeunet, USA, 1997)

Aliens (James Cameron, USA, 1986)

American Honey (Andrea Arnold, UK/USA, 2016)

And God Said to Cain . . ./E Dio disse a Caino . . . (Anthony Dawson, Italy/ West Germany, 1970)

The Babadook (Jennifer Kent, Australia, 2014)

Before I Go to Sleep (Rowan Joffé, UK/USA/France/Sweden, 2014)

Billy the Kid versus Dracula (William Beaudine USA, 1966)

The Black Cat (Edgar G. Ulmer, USA, 1934)

Blow-Up (Michelangelo Antonioni, UK/USA/Italy, 1966)

Blue Velvet (David Lynch, USA, 1986)

Bluebeard/Barbe Bleu (Catherine Breillat, France, 2010)

The Cabinet of Dr. Caligari/Das Cabinet des Dr. Caligari (Robert Wiene, Weimar Republic, 1920)

Calamity Jane (David Butler, USA, 1953)

Carrie (Brian De Palma, USA, 1976)

Carrie (Kimberly Peirce, USA, 2013)

Caught (Max Ophüls, USA, 1948)

Citizen Kane (Orson Welles, USA, 1941)

Crimson Peak (Guillermo Del Toro, USA, 2015)

Curse of the Undead (Edward Dein, USA, 1959)

D.O.A. (Rudolph Maté, USA, 1950)

The Dark (John Fawcett, Germany/UK, 2005)

Dark Touch (Marina de Van, France/Ireland/Sweden, 2013)

Destry Rides Again (George Marshall, USA, 1939)

Die Nibelungen (Fritz Lang, Weimar Republic, 1924)

Die Trapp-Familie (Wolfgang Liebeneiner, West Germany, 1956)

Django (Sergio Corbucci, Italy/Spain, 1966)

Django Kill/ Se sei vivo spara (Giulio Questi, Italy/Spain, 1967)

Django the Bastard/ Django il bastardo (Sergio Garrone, Italy, 1969)

Dr Jekyll & Sister Hyde (George Roy Baker, UK, 1971)

Dragonwyck (Joseph L. Mankiewicz, USA, 1946)

Duel in the Sun (King Vidor, USA, 1946)

The Duke of Burgundy (Peter Strickland, UK, 2014)

Ex Machina (Alex Garland, UK/USA, 2015)

The Exorcist (William Friedkin, USA, 1973)

Experiment Perilous (Jacques Tourneur, USA, 1944)

Fish Tank (Andrea Arnold, UK, 2009)

Forty Guns (Samuel Fuller, USA, 1957)

Friday the 13th (Sean S. Cunningham, USA, 1980)

Gaslight (George Cukor, USA, 1944)

The Ghost Train (Walter Forde, UK, 1941)

Gone with the Wind (Victor Fleming, USA, 1939)

Goodnight, Mommy/ Ich Seh, Ich Seh (Veronika Franz & Severin Fiala, Austria, 2014)

The Haunting (Robert Wise, USA, 1963)

High Plains Drifter (Clint Eastwood, USA, 1973)

The Hunter (Daniel Nettheim, Australia, 2011)

Imitation of Life (Douglas Sirk, USA, 1959)

In the Cut (Jane Campion, USA/UK/Australia, 2003)

Inception (Christopher Nolan, USA/UK, 2010)

The Innocents (Jack Clayton, UK, 1961)

Intermezzo (Gregory Ratoff, USA, 1939)

Jagged Edge (Richard Marquand, USA, 1985)

Jane Eyre (Robert Stevenson, USA, 1944)

Jesse James Meets Frankenstein's Daughter (William Beaudine, USA, 1966)

Johnny Guitar (Nicholas Ray, USA, 1954)

Keoma (Enzo G. Castellari, Italy, 1976)

The Kid (Charlie Chaplin, USA, 1921)

Kramer vs. Kramer (Robert Benton, USA, 1979)

Little Lamb (Heidi Lee Douglas, Australia, 2012)

London After Midnight (Tod Browning, USA, 1927)

London to Brighton (Paul Andrew Williams, UK, 2006)

Lyle (Stewart Thorndike, USA, 2014)

A Man Called Blade/Mannaja (Sergio Martino, Italy, 1977)

Marriage in the Shadows/Ehe im Schatten (Kurt Maetzig, Soviet Occupation Zone, 1947)

Mary Reilly (Stephen Frears, USA, 1996)

Metropolis (Fritz Lang, Germany, 1927)

My Name Is Julia Ross (Joseph H. Lewis, USA, 1945)

Notorious (Alfred Hitchcock, USA, 1946)

The Omen (Richard Donner, UK/USA, 1976)

On the Buses (Harry Booth, UK, 1971)

The Orphanage (J.A. Bayona, Spain, 2007)

The Others (Alejandro Amenábar, Spain/USA/France/Italy, 2001)

Pacific Heights (John Schlesinger, USA, 1990)

Pale Rider (Clint Eastwood, USA, 1985)

The Piano (Jane Campion, New Zealand/Australia/France, 1993)

Poltergeist (Tobe Hooper, USA, 1982)

Psycho (Alfred Hitchcock, USA, 1960)

The Rabbit Is Me/Das Kaninchen bin ich (Kurt Maetzig, East Germany, 1965)

Rebecca (Alfred Hitchcock, USA, 1940)

Red Road (Andrea Arnold, UK, 2006)

Rosemary's Baby (Roman Polanski, USA, 1968)

The Second Woman (James Kern, USA, 1950)

Secret Beyond the Door (Fritz Lang, USA, 1947)

The Shining (Stanley Kubrick, USA/UK, 1980)

Shutter Island (Martin Scorsese, USA, 2010)

Silent Hill (Christophe Gans, Canada/France, 2006)

Sleep, My Love (Douglas Sirk, USA, 1948)

The Sound of Music (Robert Wise, USA, 1965)

Spellbound (Alfred Hitchcock, USA, 1945)

The Spiral Staircase (Robert Siodmak, USA, 1946)

Stella Dallas (King Vidor, USA, 1937)

Suspicion (Alfred Hitchcock, USA, 1941)

Tale of a Vampire (Shimako Sato, UK, 1992)

The Tale of Ruby Rose (Roger Scholes, Australia, 1987)

A Taste of Honey (Tony Richardson, UK, 1961)

A Town Called Bastard (Robert Parrish, UK/Spain, 1971)

The Two Mrs Carrolls (Peter Godfrey, USA, 1947)

Undercurrent (Vincent Minelli, USA, 1946)

Underworld (Len Wiseman, UK/Germany/Hungary/USA, 2003)

The Vampire Lovers (Roy Ward Baker, UK, 1970)

Van Diemen's Land (Jonathan auf der Heide, Australia, 2009)

Vengeance/Joko invoca Dio . . . e muori (Antonio Margheriti, Italy/West Germany, 1968)

Vertigo (Alfred Hitchcock, USA, 1958)

We Need to Talk About Kevin (Lynne Ramsay, UK/USA, 2011)

What Lies Beneath (Robert Zemeckis, USA, 2000)

When Strangers Marry (William Castle, USA, 1944)

Opera

Duke Bluebeard's Castle/A kékszakállú herceg vára (Bela Bartok, 1911)

Television series

And Then There Were None (2015)

The Avengers (1961–1969)

Marple (2009–2014)

Midsomer Murders (1997–)

Poirot (1989–2013)

Star Trek (1966–1969) Episode: 'Requiem for Methusaleh' (1969)

Top of the Lake: China Girl (2017)

INDEX

For Product Safety Concerns and Information please contact our EU
representative GPSR@taylorandfrancis.com
Taylor & Francis Verlag GmbH, Kaufingerstraße 24, 80331 München, Germany

www.ingramcontent.com/pod-product-compliance
Lightning Source LLC
Chambersburg PA
CBHW071357100726
47908CB00004B/1025